CHAPTER 1

Friday June, 16th
Glendale, California

I went across the street to the Celtic Cross for a mid-afternoon meal. The lunch crowd had already disbursed and the happy hour revelers were still a few hours away. I had the place to myself and I was working my way through a plate of fish and chips accompanied by a pint of Guinness. I was half-watching the Dodger game on the muted TV above the bar while helping Brigid with the Time's daily crossword puzzle. The Dodgers were on a hot streak and were looking for their eleventh win in a row. Brigid was showing off, using a pen to work the puzzle. She had this cute habit of chewing on the end of the pen when she was deep in thought. A simple thing but I thought it was sexy as hell.

We actually gave it a go awhile back but things, as they always seem to, got complicated and we agreed to put the physical thing on the back burner. That's where it remains, simmering at a low heat. Brigid checks off a lot of boxes for me. She has the smarts, the wit and the looks plus she's managed to keep that sing-songy Irish accent that never fails to make my boat ride a little higher in the water. Also in my favor is the fact that she's been with enough bad men to appreciate a mediocre one when he comes along.

"Okay," she said, "ten down, an eight letter word for a Polynesian surf spot. Fourth letter is an h."

I considered it. "Teahupoo," I said while dragging a chip through a pool of ketchup.

"Spell it."

"T-E-A-H-U-P-O-O, I think." She bounced the pen down the column to make sure it worked then filled it in.

"Idiot Savant," she muttered under her breath.

"Rainman," I replied.

"Are you enjoying yourself?" she asked giving me the evil eye.

"Yeah, I guess I am. Or at least I was."

She slapped my wrist but let her hand linger. I broke the tension by glancing away just in time to see the Dodgers take a 5-3 lead. Things were looking good. The front door swung open and we both turned towards the sunlight.

"Well look what the cat dragged in." I said. "How'd you know where to find me?"

"I'm a detective remember? Plus your mail carrier said you'd probably be over here."

That would be Rubio. The guy's nosier than a gossip columnist.

I got off my barstool and gave him a big hug. "How you doing Harvey? It's been way too long."

"I'm doing well OT," Harvey said not taking his eyes off of Brigid. "And who's this lovely lady?"

I made the quick introductions.

"Harvey this is Brigid. She owns the place. Brigid this is an old friend, Harvey Dwyer. He's a detective with the LAPD, Robbery and Homicide."

"I think you meant to say chief of detectives didn't you?" Harvey asked with a big grin on his face.

"Sorry, chief of detectives. Better be careful Harvey. If you keep swinging that thing around someone's gonna get hurt."

I think Brigid was impressed. Not so much that Harvey held such an impressive position but the fact that one, I had a friend, and two, he wasn't a complete derelict.

"Able," she proclaimed in a rather dramatic fashion, "you never told me you had such handsome friends. I need to hang out with you more often."

Oh brother. Brigid had her charm-mobile fully gassed up now and was ready to take it down the highway.

"What are you drinking detective?" she asked coquettishly.

"That Guiness looks pretty good and how about one more for my friend here."

She looked over to me. Brigid knew I wasn't much for day drinking. Having one during the day was unusual but two was an extraordinary event. There was definitely going to be a nap in my near future.

"Oh my," she said deepening her brogue, "I better unplug the karaoke equipment before this whole business gets out of hand." She gave us a conspiratorial wink, pulled the beers and then politely busied herself at the other end of the bar.

Harvey's detective radar was pinging on full alert now. "Wait a minute, are you two an item?" This would be big news to Harvey.

"No," I said way too quickly. "Well yes, kind of but we haven't for....." The truth is I have no idea what we are at this point so I decided on discretion being the better part of valor. "Brigid, can you handle this one for me please?"

She was more than happy to oblige. "He's nice enough I guess," she said, "but the whole snoring thing was just a little too much to handle. It was becoming a problem with my neighbors. Plus, sadly, he has the ugliest feet on the planet."

It's true, I do have ugly feet.

"And we all know what they say about ugly feet," Harvey said, chiming in.

"Exactly. I'll leave you lads to it then," Brigid said. She brushed by me on her way to the kitchen and whispered in my ear. "What's he mean by OT?"

"It's a long story. I'll tell you later."

Harvey watched her round the corner and disappear from sight.

"Damn OT, you just might be the only guy that can make lemons out of a perfectly good batch of lemonade."

We fell into chit-chat mode and got caught up. He said he didn't work cases much anymore, only shuffled the pieces of paper and people that did. Full retirement was available in just three years and the timing seemed right. His marriage was strong and his kids were doing well. He still surfed when he could which was practically never. His free time was mostly spent with his five grandchildren now. 'They are the payoff at the end of the road' was the way I think he put it.

I caught him up also and told him about a couple of the interesting cases I'd work on recently including the Bobby Lee Hooker fiasco. Harvey's department had referred the case to me and he had a good chuckle when I gave him the sordid details.

"Have you been paid yet?" he asked me.

"Anytime now. Maybe even today. Once again Harvey, I owe you."

"Well," he said reaching into his coat pocket and handing over a single sheet of paper, "I was hoping you'd say that."

I took a look. It was a copy of a missing persons report with the County Sheriff's logo emblazoned in the top left corner. I quickly scanned the particulars. The name on the report was a Reina Montes, twenty one years old. It had been filed two weeks ago. I looked at Harvey and shook my head. I didn't recognize the name.

"Do you remember Marta?" he asked.

"You mean your Marta? Tia?"

He nodded.

Marta Ramirez had come into the Dwyer's life when they were trying to balance nascent careers while raising three young boys. Harvey had just passed his detective's exam and Jennifer was about to begin her fellowship at Children's Hospital. The juggling act had been a real struggle. Marta was initially hired to help out three days a week but within a month's time she had moved into the family guesthouse where for the next fifteen years she would play the role of the Dwyer's indispensable Girl Friday. The kids, who are bilingual to this day, simply called her Tia. She was and still is a part of the family.

"Reina is Marta's niece," Harvey explained.

I nodded. It was clear why he needed my help. She went missing on the Sheriff's turf which meant this wasn't the LAPD's case to work.

"I'm not sure what the Sheriff's Department's done other then put her into the system. I do know there's been zero forward movement on the case. Marta is beside herself and my wife and kids are upset. Jennifer asked me, actually told me, to come see you. Can you look into it?"

How could I not. For one thing, Harvey has referred a lot of paying customers to me over the years. Runners, missing persons, private security work, white collar crime, you name it. Cases that either presented him with jurisdictional issues or were simply out of the purview of the LAPD. We also share a rather remarkable past but I'll get into that later. He handed me a photo of Reina. It was a headshot, most likely a high school graduation picture. She was undeniably a beautiful young woman with olive colored skin, raven-black hair and big brown eyes. I told him I'd see what I could do. The relief on his face was palpable.

"Thanks OT. It means the world to me."

Harvey shared Marta's contact info with me and I promised I'd call her in the morning.

"Great," he said, "Jennifer will call Marta and tell her to expect a call from you."

His phone started blowing up and it was time for him to go. I walked him to the door and he paused at the threshold.

"I almost forgot. How's Hassam doing?"

"Great. He's super busy with work but when I need him he's always there for me."

"Sounds like Hassam," Harvey said. "Please tell him I said hello. The three of us need to get together soon. It's been way too long."

He put his hand on the door to leave then turned to me one more time.

"You know OT, I still think about Beirut almost every day."

"Me too Harvey," I replied. "As you said when we first met it was a like showing up uninvited to the Mad Hatter's Tea Party."

He smiled at the memory then opened the door and followed the sunlight out.

At that moment we never could have imagined what we had set into motion that day. The events that would soon unfold were so surreal they defied reason. They were very real however, as were the consequences that would inevitably follow. Like Harvey also said so long ago, the past is the present and the present is the past. Now thirty five years later the three of us would reunite to finish what we started.

I took one last look at the television before I left. The Braves scored three runs in the bottom of the ninth ending the Dodgers ten game winning streak.

CHAPTER 2

Before I took my post-Guiness nap I went online and checked my bank account. There it was, a direct deposit for $25,000. Thank you Harvey, thank you Beau, and most of all thank you Bobby Lee Hooker.

About two months ago I received a phone call from an irate bail bondsman out of Biloxi, Mississippi by the name of Beau Grummond. He had contacted the LAPD who eventually sent him my way at Harvey's recommendation. Beau was a real swamp water Cajun and I understood about a third of what he was trying to tell me. He had a skip he thought was heading my way and wanted me to work the case. I prefer not to do bounty work but business was slow and quite frankly, I could use the money. He emailed the file which included the bond application, police report and Beau's own editorial.

The runner was a guy by the name of Bobby Lee Hooker. As you will soon see, it is a name that is dripping with irony. He was born at a crossroads officially known as Escaptawpa, Alabama which in Choctaw Indian means the 'creek where the cane is cut.' I looked it up. In 2007 he moved to the bright lights of Biloxi in search of a little work and a lot of fun. In boom times he got roustabout work on the offshore rigs then valeted cars at Harrah's when oil prices tanked. In 2014 he married a local girl by the name of Lorraine. She was sweet, naïve and if her choice in men was any indicator, probably not the sharpest tool in the shed.

According to Beau, Bobby Lee loved two things more than anything else in the world, bowling and Asian call girls. Wednesday nights were league nights and Bobby Lee had long ago established a routine of not coming home until the next morning. He told Lorraine he stayed at a friend's house to avoid getting another DUI. On the night of the incident Bobby bowled a very respectable 213, 188 and 203 for a league high average of just over 201. He gathered his winnings and said his goodbyes. He stopped at the Gas 'n Go and purchased a twelve pack of Budweiser, a Red Bull and a three-pack of condoms. This was confirmed by a time stamped receipt later found in his front, right pocket. He then drove over to the Sand Dollar Motel where he paid $73.00 in cash for an upstairs room.

Using a burner phone Bobby Lee called his sometimes boss, John Pixton, who managed the valet service at Harrahs as well as one of the more popular escort services on the Redneck Riviera. Pixton was eventually interviewed by the police and he told them Bobby Lee wanted one of his regulars but due to the heavy convention traffic in town that night none of them were currently available. 'Send me a round eye then,' is what Bobby Lee told him.

At 10:42 the girl pulled into the motel parking lot and texted Bobby Lee asking for the room number. Bobby Lee texted back 'Room 208' and told her to come on up and have a beer. He was going to jump into the shower.

At 10:59 the police responded to a 911 call from the motel's night manager. They arrived on the scene at 11:15 pm and had Bobby Lee cuffed, mirandized and placed in the back of a cruiser before the clock struck midnight.

Beau filled in the blanks. The woman let herself in and quickly downed a beer to calm the nerves. She was new to the escort game but discovered she actually enjoyed the work. It helped make ends meet and besides, she was getting here what she wasn't getting at home. You can imagine the surprise on both their faces when Bobby Lee emerged from the bathroom wearing nothing but his birthday suit while sweet, naive Lorraine stood there in her push up bra, black mini-skirt and 6" stiletto heels. I pictured them both momentarily speechless as they processed the enormity of the situation. In the end, Bobby Lee suffered some decent scratch marks on his face but he managed to beat the living hell out of Lorraine. He broke her jaw, fractured her left orbital rim and knocked out three of her teeth before the police officers could pull him away.

Hooker was booked and charged for gross domestic assault and battery. To make bail he sold his two jet skis and his beloved Harley Davidson then walked out of the Harrison County jail forty eight hours later on a $250,000 bond posted by Beau. Bobby Lee had one meeting with a public defender who told him the best he could hope for was a five year sentence with a possible walk after three. He told his attorney he'd consider it but after spending two days in the county lockup Bobby Lee knew there was no way he could do the time. So the next day he walked into his bank and closed out the Hooker's joint checking and savings accounts then drove his 2009 Dodge Caravan far away from the distracted eye of the Mississippi judicial system.

On the bond application Beau had circled the name of Arthur Hooker in the next of kin section. He was apparently Bobby Lee's brother and showed a home address up in Bakersfield, an agricultural town about one hundred miles north of Los Angeles. I had nothing else to occupy my time so the next morning I headed over the Grapevine to see what Arthur had to say.

Traffic was light and I made the trip in less than ninety minutes. Even with the help of GPS I passed the address twice before I realized the dirt road that cut across an almond orchard was in fact the driveway. It was a decent piece of land maybe four or five acres in size with a ranch style home in the front of the property and a sizeable workshop set in the back.

My pulse quickened as I exited my truck. Stepping onto

another man's land, especially as a fugitive recovery agent, is always a potentially volatile situation. I've been swung at, shot at and gotten my ass kicked more times than I wish to admit. I was once invited into a home by the mother of a runner who served me up some freshly baked chocolate chip cookies and then as soon as I let my guard down she buried a fire poker into my right thigh.

With those lovely memories fresh in my mind I walked up a short flight of stairs to a wrap-around porch, knocked on the door then stepped to one side. There was no answer. The sounds of grinding metal started up in the back building so that's where I headed.

A chorus of guttural growls stopped me dead in my tracks. Two huge rottweilers exited the building and bounded up to the edge of the concrete pad. They were up on their haunches ready to attack. I slowly popped the latch on my shoulder holster and gave it a quick pat just to make sure my Sig was where it was supposed to be. I did some quick calculations. I figured I could probably take one out but there was no way could I get them both. Then a short, stocky man stepped outside wiping the sweat off his face with a greasy rag.

"Stand down, play nice," he said and just like that the tongues came out and the tails began wagging. Theirs, not mine. I walked over and gave them both a quick pat.

"Well you don't look like a Jehovah Witness," he said, "and I'm too damn old to buy any life insurance, so you want to tell me what you're doing on my land."

"I'm sorry to bother you. Are you Arthur Hooker?"

"Depends on whose asking. What's your business?"

"I'm here about your brother."

"You mean my half-brother." It wasn't a question.

"Okay, well that's why I'm here."

"Which one? I've got several and they're all good for nothing sons of bitches. Got a couple of half-sisters too if you're looking to get hitched." A playful grin appeared in that space between his beard and mustache. "My old man was a long haul trucker," he explained, "had a real bad case of stickitinitis."

"OK, I'll bite. Stickitinitis?"

"Yeah, on the road if he could find a woman willing and able, he'd stick it in."

Good one. "I'm here about Bobby Lee," I said.

He sighed and his shoulders sagged. "Figured as much." He held out his hand. "Call me Artie. Let's go inside and get the hell out of this heat."

There was a line of motorcycles in various stages of being converted into custom choppers. The finished product was very impressive. "That's some beautiful work," I said.

"Thanks. Do you ride?"

"Used to until I laid one down. That was enough for me."

We talked for about a half an hour. I touched on a few details of the case but Artie told me he hadn't seen his half-brother in over five years and he hoped it was another twenty before he saw him again. The conversation played itself out and he walked me back to my truck.

"That looks like a military patch," I said pointing to a faded tattoo on his right arm. I was unfamiliar with the design. A fleur-de-lis on the right and angel's wings on the left. "Did you serve?"

"I did. '70 to '76. 160th infantry regiment, California National Guard. Never had to go to 'Nam though, thank God." He gave me the once over then said, "You've got the look of ex-military yourself."

I nodded. "Marines, 24th MAU. I was in Beirut in '83."

I think that impressed him.

We got to my truck and I played the last card in my deck. I grabbed Bobby Lee's file and handed over several pictures of a beaten Lorraine. They were not easy viewing.

"Listen Artie, I know he's your blood but this guy's got to pay for what he did. Here's my card. If the situation changes give me a call." I had a gut feeling he was holding out on me.

"Abel Kane huh," he said giving my card the once over, "must be quite a story there."

"Artie, you have no idea." And on that note I got in my truck and headed for home.

I wasn't even to Valencia when a 661 area code number flashed on the truck's monitor. It was Artie.

"Did he really do all of that to that poor girl?"

"I wish I could tell you differently Artie, but yeah, it was all him."

"I didn't even know the little pissant was married." I could hear him sigh over the phone. "OK, I'll tell you what I know. It ain't much but I guessing it's something."

"Thanks," I said. "Hold on one second. I'm pulling over."

I took the Rye Canyon Road off ramp and parked. He had in fact received a call from Bobby Lee ten days ago and met him at a Denny's Restaurant near Disneyland. Bobby Lee hadn't been very forthcoming about what he was doing in California other than the fact he was on the run from the law and needed some cash. Artie gave him $2500 and told him it was a one-time deal. No problem Bobby Lee assured him. He had a line on some work and was off to Mexico in two weeks never to return.

"That's about it," Artie said, "as soon as I gave him the cash he asked me if I wanted to go hit a strip club. Not a thank you, just 'let's go hit a strip club.' I'm afraid the poor kid just isn't wired right."

"And?" I asked.

"I didn't go. That's not my thing."

"Was he still driving the blue Caravan?"

"I don't know. He was in the restaurant when I got there and was still sitting in the booth when I took off. He hasn't contacted me since and that's the God's honest truth."

This time I believed him. He was right though, it wasn't much to go on. Bobby Lee had stopped using his cell phone and credit cards the day before his no-show court date and the truth is, even in today's world, you can still hide in plain sight if you're using cash and burner phones. I thanked Artie and hung up. I figured I had four days, five tops, to find Bobby Lee. I headed home to come up with some kind of a plan.

The next morning, under a cloudless sky, I drove to Anaheim. I was working under two assumptions. One, he was living somewhere near where he met his brother for lunch and two, he was a stranger in town and didn't have someone's couch to crash on. So I made my way over to the homeless encampments which have sprouted up around here like backyard weeds, both unwanted and unabated. Lining the edges of our freeways and flood control channels and only twenty minutes from some of the most desirable enclaves in the world live our addicted, confused and broken pieces of society. I was on a quixotic journey in search of a 2009 blue Dodge Caravan with Mississippi plates and a confederate flag decal on the right rear bumper. My journey ended as I expected it would, in failure.

I stopped at an In-N-OUT for lunch before going to Plan B. Artie's comment about his brother's desire to go to a strip joint seemed to have some merit so last night I googled gentlemen's clubs within a ten mile radius of the Denny's. There were an even dozen. I spent the next few hours driving from one to the next. Nobody admitted to recognizing his mug shot. I gave each doorman my card and a hundred dollar bill both paper clipped to Bobby Lee's photo. I also left them with a promise of an additional $1000 dollars if I got a call the minute he walked through their door. By 5'oclock I was heading home disappointed and $1200 poorer.

Three days later I got the call. It came from a young man by the name of Danny Cho, a daytime bouncer at Saigon Sally's in Santa Ana. I fired staccato questions at him as I raced out the door of my office.

"Sure it was him?"

"Yes I'm sure."

"How long has he been there?"

"Just got here. You said a grand right?"

"I did, what's he driving?"

"Don't know, it's self-park here."

"Check if there's a Dodge Caravan in the lot?"

"A what?"

"A blue van. Can you check?"

"Really Dude?"

"Yes, really."

A minute later he got back on the line. "Yep, looking at it right now."

"Mississippi Plates?"

"Nope, Texas." Bobby Lee must have switched them out. Maybe he wasn't as dumb as I thought.

"What about a confederate flag on the bumper?"

"Yep it's there. What's this racist asshole done anyways?"

I take it back, Bobby Lee is an idiot. "Ok, I'm on my way."

A normal forty five minute drive took a frustrating ninety minutes including several inappropriate forays into the carpool lane. Luck was on my side however. The Caravan was still in the lot. I parked across the street and headed over to Danny Cho who was outside waiting for me.

"Still in there?" I asked holding a wad of hundred dollar bills in my hand.

"Yeah he's there. A cheap bastard too. Just sits next to the stage sipping on Budweisers. He's creeping the girls out and they want him gone."

"Let's see what I can do about that."

I asked him to do one more thing for me as I made a big production of pulling five more Benjamin's out of my wallet and wrapping them around the stack.

"No problem," he said, "it's your show. This job sucks ass anyways."

I told him to give me five minutes and then I went back to the truck to get suited up. I put on a bullet-proof vest and covered it with my official F.R.A (Fugitive Recovery Agent) jacket. I then called the Santa Ana Police Department and explained the situation to the duty sergeant. I gave him the address, the case number and my F.R.A. ID. He said he's send a unit over as soon as possible.

The fire alarm went off just as I drove my KA-BAR knife through the van's rear passenger tire. Less than a minute later the few patrons who were spending the early afternoon at Sally's began filtering out of the club. There he was. He looked thinner than his picture and he'd grown a bushy salt and pepper beard. That was a solid ID by young Mr. Cho. There was a chance Bobby Lee would smell a rat and take off on foot but my instincts told me the van was his lifeline to freedom and there was no way in hell he'd leave it behind. I was right. When he saw the flat tire he cursed out loud but then got to work changing it. I waited until the car was on a jack before I introduced myself.

"Hey there Bobby Lee, you're a tough guy to find. Lorraine says to go screw yourself by the way."

The Caravan was parked up against a twelve foot retaining

wall and there were buildings to his left and right. It was an urban box canyon. The only way out was through me and we both knew it. He grabbed the tire iron, sprang to his feet and charged me. I was eight feet away and he didn't cover half that distance before the taser sent him to the ground. By the time he came around he found himself propped up against the van with his hands and ankles zip tied. I asked him to smile before I snapped his picture but he wouldn't oblige.

Three minutes later he was in the back of a police car crying his little heart out. I got the officer's name and badge number and had him sign the fugitive transfer document which was already filled out and ready to go. I forwarded the documentation and Bobby Lee's picture to Beau then made it home in time for a great meal at my favorite steakhouse. Thus ended the sad, pathetic tale of Bobby Lee Hooker.

CHAPTER 3

Saturday, June 17th

The next morning I called Marta and she suggested I come over for lunch. The traffic was light as I made my way over to Pico Rivera. June gloom had arrived in earnest and at 12:30 when I pulled up curbside to her house the marine layer was just beginning to dissipate. Her home was a charming bungalow size craftsman that had recently been painted. The yard was immaculate and the rose garden that fronted the property had announced the arrival of summer with an explosion of whites, reds and yellows.

She greeted me at the door with a hug. "Abel, thank you so much for doing this. I'm going crazy with worry." Marta had refined her English since I had last seen her. It was now impeccable.

"Well I haven't done anything yet." My fear of failure began to settle in. I'd let a lot of good people down if I couldn't get to the bottom of this.

"You will, I know you will. Come in, lunch is ready."

I neglected to eat breakfast and now I was glad I didn't. I'd forgotten Marta was such a phenomenal cook. She was born and raised on the Yucatan Peninsula which has its own unique culinary style. She made all of my favorites starting with a lime infused tortilla soup. We then moved on to a Cochinita Pibil then finally Marquesitas for dessert. She cleared the table and poured us some coffee. I started in with the missing person's report.

"Marta," I said, "I see that it was seven days between your last contact with Reina and the day you filed the report. That seems like a long time to me."

She explained to me that Reina had moved out of the house about ten weeks earlier and they'd only seen each other twice since then. They would talk on the phone quite a bit but Reina was always in a hurry to end the call.

"Did the two of you have some kind of fight?"

She shook her head. "No, nothing like that. I got the feeling something good was happening for her and she was enjoying her independence."

"So she wasn't depressed as far as you were concerned?"

"No, not at all. In fact just the opposite."

"So why did you file the report at all then?"

"The last time we talked was on a Thursday. She was going to come over for dinner on Sunday but she never showed up. I called dozens of times over the next few days but it always went straight to voicemail. That's when I filed the missing persons report."

"Where was she living?"

"I don't know. She wrote an address down for me but after she skipped dinner and didn't return my calls I drove over there."

"And?"

"And it ended up being a business, not any kind of place a person would live."

"What kind of business?" I interjected.

"A self-storage place, I think."

"I'll need that address Marta."

"Of course, I'll get it for you."

And so it went as I extracted as much information from Marta as possible. She confirmed Reina was going to Cal State LA taking courses in business administration and driving Marta's Toyota Camry. She thought Reina had a part time job at the Verizon store inside the Citadel but wasn't absolutely sure about that. They had reached a point in their relationship where Reina no longer asked for money and Marta didn't want to pry. There were no visible scars or tattoos but she did wear a silver ring which was a present from her mother. Marta didn't know of a personal doctor but they did share the same dentist. As far as Facebook, Twitter, Snapchat, Pinterest etc. were concerned, Marta was of no help. She didn't do social media. There was an email address but Reina had been unresponsive there also.

"Boyfriend?" I asked.

"No.....maybe...I'm not sure. Something had changed in her life, maybe it's that simple."

"Friends?"

"Julie Herrera is the only friend I know. "

"I'll need her contact info also."

"Of course."

I asked to use the bathroom and Marta led me down a hallway framed with family pictures. One photograph stood out.

"This is Reina and her parents I'm assuming?"

"Yes," she said tearing up, "in happier times."

"May I ask what happened?"

"Car accident. They were involved in a head on collision with a drunk driver on their way home from a dinner out."

"How old was Reina at the time?"

"She was thirteen. She wasn't feeling well that day so she stayed home thank goodness. I was the only family she had left and she's been with me ever since."

I pointed to another picture. It was Marta standing in front of a white, commercial van with a business logo that said 'Top 2 Bottom Cleaning Service.' Kneeling in front of her were a couple dozen Latina women in navy blue golf shirts and white uniformed pants. I looked at Marta quizzically.

"This was my business until I sold it. After Harvey and Jennifer lent me the money for the down payment on this house I realized I now had a mortgage to pay and no job. So I started cleaning houses again. One led to two which led to some commercial work and before I knew it I had a workspace, vans, cleaning equipment and two dozen employees. Julie came to work for me right after high school and she still works for the new owners."

"When did you sell it?"

"About a year ago. I didn't even know it was a possibility until an attorney walked into my office and told me he had a client that would like to buy my business."

"Who was the buyer?"

"A company by the name of EZX Enterprises. I got the impression they were a big outfit. It was an all-cash transaction so I didn't ask a lot of questions. My only stipulation was they keep all the employees on for at least two years."

"And have they?"

"The last time I checked in with some of the girls, yes. So far they've kept their word."

"Do you have the paperwork?"

"Paperwork?"

"On the sale. I'd like to take a look."

"I do. Do you think it's important?" she asked.

"Most likely not," I said honestly. "I just like to look under all of the rocks if you know what I mean."

It was 2:15 by the time I left Marta's house. I didn't need to be anywhere until 5:30 so I thought I'd get started. I located the nearest Kinko's and with the help of one of their associates I printed up 200 missing person posters with Reina's image front and center along with the promise of a $2500 reward for any information leading to her recovery. I thanked the young man for his help then headed off to check on Reina's employment.

It took less than a hundred years for the Citadel to go from the largest tire factory west of the Mississippi to an outlet mall selling t-shirts, shoes and other sundry items. It's an old, iconic building architecturally inspired by the ancient Assyrian culture. Spread out across the top of the ornate frontage sit five winged guardians with cloven hooves and human faces. I've been told they are replicas of a mythological creature named Lamassu who the Assyrians believed could help fight off evil spirits. I hoped they still had a little mojo left in the tank for Reina Montes.

The Verizon store sat in a smallish space sandwiched between an Ann Taylors and Ecco. Walking into the phone store was yet another affirmation of how little I had in common with my younger, fellow citizens of Planet Earth. First there was the young man sporting a rather impressive rainbow colored Mohawk. He had full tattoo sleeves on both arms and wore those lovely tunnel earrings that I bet I could poke my pointer finger through. Then there was the 'Goth' girl with her chemically enhanced black hair which complemented her eye shadow, lipstick and fingernail polish. The nose ring was a nice touch also. And those were just the employees. The customers with all their tattoos, piercings, torn jeans and colored hair weren't much better.

I bypassed all of that and headed straight for the door marked 'Manager' and let myself in. It was a very small office with just enough space for a desk and a path in and out of the room. The unmistakable smell of Fritos hung heavy in the air. The man behind the desk, according to his name tag, was Chuck the store manager. He was about my age, a little rounder and maybe a little bit more the worse for wear. He had a surprised look on his face, the kind you get when you're caught looking at something naughty on the internet. I felt an immediate surge of empathy for Chuck.

I flashed my LAPD detective's badge. It's obsolete but it's the real deal. I got it the same way any law abiding citizen procures one, on EBAY. I normally just play the role of Abel Kane, private detective, but there is no doubt the badge gets you where you want to go a lot quicker. Rule number one though is never use your real name.

"Jack Johnson," I said quickly returning the badge to my jacket pocket.

"Like the singer?"

Oops. "I'm sorry, who?"

"Jack Johnson. He's a singer. Beach and surf stuff. How can I help you Detective?"

"Sorry about barging in on you but Megadeath and Elvira out there told me to come on back." That got me a laugh and hopefully I was on my way.

I slide Reina's poster across the desk. "Do you recognize her?"

His face showed no nothing. "I don't, should I?"

"I have reason to believe she's employed here."

"Not since I came on board but I've only been here a month."

"How about those two out there? Could they possibly know her?"

He shook his head. "They're both new hires and between you and me I don't think they're going to make the cut. Thank God the phones sell themselves."

Chuck was flashing a sense of humor. Now let's see if he had a soul. "Chuck, I'm going to need you to go on that computer and tell me what it knows."

He hesitated.

"Listen," I said, "this poor girl's been missing for over two weeks. You can force me to go get a search warrant but that's going to take at least 48 hours. Every second is precious here Chuck. She could be in a lot of trouble."

As it turned out Chuck did have a soul. With a few keyboard taps he got us to where I needed him to go. I walked around to his side of the desk to take a look. There she was, Reina Montes.

"OK," he said, "looks like she started in February of 2016, always part-time. The employment was terminated on April 16th of this year."

Interesting. Just around the time she moved out of Marta's home. I pointed to a code next to her termination date.

"What's IBA mean Chuck?"

"Initiated by Associate."

"Meaning she wasn't fired, she quit?"

"Exactly."

I took a picture of the screen and let Chuck get back to whatever the hell he was doing before I barged in on him. I did ask him to put a copy of Reina's poster in the storefront window but he demurred. We compromised and he hung one on the wall next to the employee bathroom. Chuck was a good guy. Everybody, be like Chuck.

I spent the next thirty minutes in the adjacent food court showing the counter people her picture. I got one hit but it wasn't much help. The cashier at Panda Express recognized Reina but hadn't seen her in months. I clandestinely hung a few of the peel and stick posters on the support columns around the tables. Mall security would eventually take them down but it was worth a shot. As a wise fisherman once said, you can't catch any fish unless your line's in the water.

On the walk back to my truck I put in my ear buds and started listening to one of my Spotify playlists. The first song was 'Home' by Jack Johnson. Just a small tribute to my new friend Chuck.

CHAPTER 4

(THE PAST)

In late May of 1981, my identical twin brother Jonah and I graduated from Clay High School in South Bend, Indiana. It was our third school in four years and it felt like I had matriculated with a group of total strangers. Even though we both graduated cum-laude and were members of the National Honor Society none of our family members were present at the ceremony. A month earlier my grandparents and my father informed us they were on to something big and disappeared. We still hadn't heard from them.

Two days after graduation I boarded a bus in Chicago bound for Parris Island, South Carolina. I had joined the U.S. Marine Corps six weeks earlier without telling a soul, not even Jonah. Even though he arrived on this planet just minutes before me we've never really been equals. Jonah's smarter, a lot more athletic and he has always moved through life with an ease and self-assurance I was never able to achieve. He would have tried his best to talk me out of it and with his uncanny powers of persuasion he most likely would have succeeded. I had decided a long time ago that the Kane Family business was not for me. It was time to untangle myself from its web. I called my brother at the first stop along the way and he was predictably furious. I had rehearsed what I was going to say a thousand times but the words came out all jumbled and distorted.

Jonah stopped me mid-stream. "Abel," he said, "I hope you catch a bullet." That was it. He hung up the phone. It would be twenty years before I would talk to him again. The day he was released from prison.

While I was at Parris Island I summoned the courage to call home. The phone had been disconnected with no offer of a forwarding number. I tried again two weeks later with the same result. After completing basic training I was given a two week furlough before I reported to my new unit at Lejeune. I caught a flight to Chicago, rented a car and made the ninety minute drive to South Bend. There were new renters living in our house. They seemed like a nice family consisting of a husband, wife and three young children. I was hoping my family had left behind a note letting me know how to get in contact with them. They did not.

"The only thing they left behind was a pile of past due bills on the kitchen floor," the man sadly informed me.

My next stop was across town to our landlord, Mr. Walters. He owned five rentals around town including ours. He ran a contracting business and I had worked quite a bit for him after school and on weekends. He taught me a lot of the trades including plumbing, electrical and finish carpentry.

"What happened to your hair Abel?" he said with a mischievous grin.

I told him what I was up to and he nodded his approval. He also didn't know where they went off to only that they departed in the middle of the night owing two months back rent. I sheepishly offered to pay the arrears but Mr. Walters wouldn't hear of it. My final stop was to Jonah's girlfriend's house. She hadn't heard from him either. Not even a goodbye. My family had once again vanished into thin air. The only difference was, this time, I wasn't with them. I had been disowned.

CHAPTER 5

Named after the 13th Commandant of the Marines, Camp Lejeune is a sprawling 246 square mile facility with fourteen miles of uninterrupted beachhead all dedicated to the art of killing efficiency. Nearby Wilmington and Morehead City both maintain deep water ports allowing easy access to and from the missions that send Marines all over the world. I was assigned to the 2nd Reconnaissance Battalion, Intelligence Division and attached to the 24th Marine Assault Unit (MAU). I spent the next thirteen months there learning and honing my tradecraft. I could jump out of a perfectly sound airplane and dive one hundred feet below the earth's surface. Theoretically at least I could tail, protect or interrogate you. I could analyze you, assess you as a potential threat or just kill you. If I got my hands on you I knew a dozen different ways to terminate your existence or I could simply take you out from three hundred feet away with a single shot. I was itching to give at least some of my new founded skills some real world experience. Finally in April, 1983, the 24th MAU received its marching orders. We were going to a place called Beirut. I had to look it up on a map.

My first three weeks 'in-country' were spent riding a desk and the only combat experience I encountered was an unruly photocopier that constantly paper jammed. There were thirty of us in an open air tent outside the Battalion Landing Team building (BLT). The job was to read, analyze and interpret NSA and CIA intercepts as they came through our department. Most of the intercepts were conversational in nature and seemed both harmless and irrelevant. I couldn't sleep at night worrying if the next, seemingly innocuous dispatch was hidden code for 'We attack tomorrow, Tora,Tora,Tora.' One day I was sifting through a seemingly unending stack when my CO told me to change into civvies and report to a Lt. Harvey Dwyer asap. Thirty minutes later I was riding shotgun in a 1978 mustard-yellow Ford Pinto with a serious halitosis problem.

"What's that smell?" I asked my new CO.

"Don't know," he said, "but you do kind of get used to it."

I couldn't imagine that ever happening. "Where are we headed?" I asked.

"We are on our way to East Beirut to meet a local informant. A guy the CIA said might be beneficial to our mission. So how much do you know about Lebanon and its history Private Kane?"

I told him next to nothing and explained the anxiety I was having at my previous assignment. Just then an MP stepped onto the road and gave us the halt sign. A large military convoy was just starting to cross the intersection directly in front of us. Lt. Dwyer took this opportunity to pull out a hard box of Marlboro Reds and tilted the pack towards me. I shook my head.

"Good for you," he said, "nasty habit. Going to have to quit myself someday before it kills me." He then lit up and proceeded to blow the most perfect smoke ring I'd ever seen. It gently floated across the front seat until it hit my side window and disintegrated. "Ok then," he said, "a quick history lesson. Why are we here? It begins with the end of World War One and the fall of the Ottoman Empire. Do you know who the Ottomans were Kane?"

"The Turks sir?"

"Correct. So at the Treaty of Versailles the British and the French claimed the Middle East for themselves and started carving it up. They drew arbitrary boundaries for new nations that served no one's needs but their own. The French controlled this area and made up two new countries, Lebanon and Syria. They then tried to impose their own style of western democracy on a disparate group of people who wanted nothing to do with it or each other. Then thirty years later the French basically said 'We're bored, we're leaving and the best of luck to all of you.'"

The convoy finally cleared and Lt. Dwyer threw the Pinto back into gear and took off.

"Anyways, the political and religious differences here are extreme, complex and as old as time itself. I'll try to give you the cliff notes." He paused just long enough to blow another perfect smoke ring that rose slowly to the car's roof spreading out to three times its size before dissipating.

He continued. "First you have the Maronites who are the Christians. They are the ruling elite but are also very much in the minority. They still control the government but for how much longer is anybody's guess. Then you have the Sunni and Shia Muslims. They've been arguing with each other since the death of Mohammed. Same religion but totally different views about how they go about their business. Lastly you have the Druse, who are kind of Muslims and kind of not. It's all very complicated stuff."

We came to a roadblock manned by Marines. We slowed down as we approached the blockade but we were waved through when they recognized the lieutenant.

"They all hate each other with a passion that runs so deep we can't begin to plumb its depths. They've been going at each for thousands of years and will continue to do so long after we're back home watching I Love Lucy reruns. They can, however, all come together and unite on one subject."

He looked over at me but I could only shrug my shoulders. "The Jews, Kane. As much as they despise each other it pales in comparison to the contempt they feel for the State of Israel."

I asked the next logical question. "So how does the PLO fit into all of this?"

Lt. Dwyer banged his hand against the steering wheel. "Great question. Are you a baseball fan Kane?"

"Yes Sir, the Cubs."

He looked at me and smirked. "Oh! Well how unfortunate for you. I'm a Dodger fan myself. Anyways to use a baseball analogy, consider Arafat and his band of thugs as the bat that all the Arab countries use to take swings at Israel. They publicly denounce him when it suits their needs but always privately support him. He's a hero one day and a scapegoat the next. Quite a brilliant strategy if you ask me."

Israel had invaded Lebanon the previous year in an attempt to eradicate the PLO once and for all. Guess they got tired of being hit by the bat. They bombed West Beirut for eight weeks straight before the Lebanese finally relented and agreed to send Arafat and his band of thugs packing. That's why we're here. To keep the peace and provide safe passage to 15,000 Palestinians and Syrians as they are escorted out of the country. Lt. Dwyer abruptly pulled the car over to the side of the road and looked me straight in the eye.

"You're a smart guy Private Kane. I've seen your G-2's and that along with your cool name is why I handpicked you for this assignment. So listen closely. We have not been thrown into the middle of some noble crusade. The line between good and bad here is anything but clearly delineated. In Lebanon and the entire Middle East for that matter, the past is the present and the present is the past and the future is just more of the same."

He paused for a second to throw the last third of his cigarette out the window. "Private Kane, we have shown up uninvited, to the Mad Hatter's Tea Party. So do as I say and I'll try to get both us out of here in one piece. Capiche?"

Capiche. One piece is always good.

CHAPTER 6

Unfortunately to get to East Beirut one must travel through West Beirut. I witnessed firsthand what eight years of civil war had done to this once beautiful city. The rubble of what used to be architecturally proud buildings had spilled out into the streets like so much concrete lava. Yet in perfect juxtaposition I observed youths laughing and playing soccer using the husks of burned out vehicles as goals while men playing chess were using a fallen retaining wall as a table. Life, it appears, always marches on.

We pulled up in front of something called a patisserie. Lt. Dwyer informed me from this point on we were dropping all military protocol. I was Abel and he was Harvey. We were officially undercover. This was East Beirut now and the majority of the area had side-stepped the ravages of war. The French influence could be seen throughout with the ornate balconies and fanciful ironworks. Fully operational Mercedes and BMW's moved about while people walked the streets as if they didn't have a care in the world. Through the open doors of the patisserie drifted the redolent aromas of freshly baked bread and brewing coffee. The place was busy with the sounds of neighborhood gossip and commerce. I recognized French and Spanish being spoken as well as what I thought was German proving wherever there's a war on there's business to be had. Lebanon was no exception. An anxious, elderly man behind the counter caught our attention and motioned to a table in the far back corner where a young man sat waiting for us.

He stood as we approached holding out his hand. He was

extremely handsome with a disarming smile. "Gentlemen," he said with a perfect English boarding school accent, "I am Hassam Ali and I sincerely wish we could have met under more optimal circumstances."

Have you ever met someone and knew instantly that you were going to like them? That's how I felt about Hassam. He was both affable and sincere and yet there was a sadness behind his eyes that could not be fabricated. As we sat down the man from behind the counter set a crescent shaped treat in front of me. Hassam eyed me looking at the plate. "Able, that is a croissant au beurre. My uncle makes the finest in all of Lebanon. He will be offended if you don't at least give it a try."

Try it? From the way it smelled I wanted to swallow it whole. I bit into the light, flaky crust tasting toasted caramel and a hint of almond.

"Well?" Hassam asked.

"It's the best thing I've ever tasted. Thank you." I meant it.

Harvey and I ate while Hassam told us about himself and some of the events which led him down the path to today's meeting. He was twenty three and a devout Sunni Muslim. He was sent to England for his education, first Harrow in London and then Oxford, before returning here to join his family's multi-generational construction business.

"We were the second largest contracting firm in the entire country," he said with unmasked pride. "My great grandfather started the firm back in the 1850's. Half the high rise buildings you see in Beirut were built by us. For that matter, the same can be said for half the buildings you don't see anymore."

"What happened Hassam?" Harvey asked.

"What happened? The civil war happened. Money was fleeing Lebanon faster than rats deserting a ship. We probably could have done the same but our wealth was tied up in projects and equipment. We were owed a fortune by people who could not, or would not pay us."

The elderly man returned this time with cups of a mahogany colored liquid. I was informed this was called espresso. It was nothing like the coffee that was served at home. The aroma was deep, rich and complicated in the sense I wasn't sure what olfactory memories were being evoked. I will tell you one thing though, it was fantastic.

"Gentlemen," Hassam said, "This is my Uncle Farhoud. A great chef and even a better man." Farhoud bowed ever so slightly then quickly retreated.

"So," Hassam continued, "we sold everything we could. The beach house in Batroun, the chalet up in the Shouf and all of our equipment for cents on the dollar. My father and my uncle were able to settle all of their obligations and have just enough left over to start this business."

"Is your father here Hassam?" Harvey inquired.

Hassam shook his head and his eyes welled up. "About a year ago, an IDF (Israeli Defense Forces) patrol was ambushed right outside of our apartment building by a PLO militia group. The street fight lasted for several hours. When the PLO's position began to weaken they rode the elevators up to the higher floors of our building and broke into the apartments that were facing the street. We owned the penthouse suite where my entire extended family lived together. They were all at home watching television before the battle began. The elevated position proved to be a huge advantage and the PLO began tearing up the IDF. Retreating wasn't an option since the PLO had blocked all avenues of escape."

Hassam took a sip from his espresso allowing himself a moment to regain some composure. "So the commander of the patrol, a young Lieutenant, had a decision to make. Watch as he and his men got slaughtered or call in an air strike. He chose the latter. Twenty minutes later our building was reduced to rubble. Over three hundred people died that day including my parents, my siblings and all of my cousins. My uncle was thankfully out of the country on business and was spared."

"And where were you Hassam?" It was a logical question.

"Where was I?" he said with a hint of self- loathing, "I was with a girl at the beach working on my bloody tan. That's where I was."

Hassam suggested we take a drive. There were a few things he wanted to show us that might provide some more clarity regarding the situation in Beirut. He offered to drive.

"No way, you're riding shotgun," Harvey said pointing to the front, passenger seat. "Abel," he said handing me his service revolver, "you sit in the backseat behind me. If he pulls any bullshit put a bullet in the back of his head. " He was kidding, I think.

Hassam led us down the Corniche and up through Martyr Square so named to honor the many Lebanese that were executed under Ottoman Rule. This was the city center which served as the demarcation line between East and West Beirut, between Christian and Muslim. It was a virtual no man's land. He deftly led us around ad-hoc roadblocks which were illegally set up by loosely formed militia groups. Shake down stops Hassam called them.

"What do you notice about the trees Abel?" he asked.

It took me a moment. "No leaves."

Hassan nodded. "Car bombs. When a car bomb goes off, the compression blast knocks all the leaves off of the trees. Around here we call it perennial autumn."

We drove another five minutes then Hassam asked Harvey to pull over. We walked across the street to another bombed out building. This one however was frantically being rebuilt.

"This," Hassam said, "was the building where President Gemayel was assassinated. He had been the leader of our country for all of two weeks. This was his party headquarters and he was scheduled to give his first speech to the nation. A man by the name of Habib Shartouni planted a bomb in the apartment directly above the first floor. Gemayel died instantly."

We caught the attention of a couple of serious looking men who were heading our way. Hassam waived them off. "Let's go," he said.

We headed north out of the city proper. The neighborhoods started looking shabbier, poorer. We continued onto a dirt road that led us to an uninhabited hilltop overlooking the city. Hassam continued with his narrative.

"The Christian Militia was furious because Gemayel was their guy. Everyone was sure the assassination was going to circle back to the PLO but ultimately it didn't. Yes, Shartouni was Syrian but he also ended up being a Maronite Christian. He simply disagreed with the president's politics. The facts, as they often do here, refused to get in the way. In the end Shartouni didn't just kill the man, he ended up destroying an entire country."

We parked the car where the dirt road ended and walked the last fifty yards up to a narrow ridge with a commanding view of Beirut. He pointed left towards a shanty town made up of dilapidated homes, makeshift shelters and exposed sewer trenches.

"That's Shatila," he said, "and over there, just to the right, is Sabra."

"The refugee camps," Harvey said, understanding.

"Someone want to fill me in?" I asked.

Hassam continued. "Two days after the assassination, the IDF came rolling down that highway." He pointed off into the distance at a four lane road that skirted the edges of the two camps. "They encircled the camps cutting off all avenues of escape which paved the way for the Christian militia."

Hassam picked up a rock and casually tossed it into the ravine below. "After the IDF gave the 'all secure' signal the militia entered the camps. It was their intent to eradicate, once and for all, any PLO members who were using the camps as a protective shield. That was the official reason for the campaign. What they really wanted was revenge and they went in there with bloodlust on their minds."

Harvey picked up the dialogue at that point. "Thirty six hours later over one thousand innocent people, many of them women and children, were murdered. The killing went on unabated, day and night, with the help of IDF illumination flares. The atrocities were as numerous as they were unfathomable."

A red-tailed hawk flew directly overhead. It banked left into the sun and we all shielded our eyes to watch. It settled over the ravine where Hassam had thrown his stone and made several passes before it dove out of sight. Seconds later it reappeared with a small snake in its beak. The hawk banked right and effortlessly disappeared from our lives as quickly as it had entered.

"That's probably the only living creature in this country that doesn't have a natural enemy." I said.

"Yes Abel, I think you're right," Hassam said agreeing. "You catch on very quickly. Wouldn't it be a wonderful thing, to be a hawk?"

We headed back to the patisserie while Harvey finished up my history lesson. "One of the militiamen when asked why he was killing pregnant women simply replied 'because they will soon be giving birth to more terrorists.'"

When we pulled up to the curb Hassam added a final consideration. "In the end the Christians and the Israelis said they were only doing God's work which is the same excuse that's been used in this region since the time of Abraham. We've been descending down the steps of hell ever since."

As he stepped out of the car, I proclaimed, "And they cried out with a loud voice saying, how long O Lord, holy and true, will you refrain from judging and avenging our blood on those who dwell the earth."

Hassam looked at me the way an anthropologist might look at a newly discovered species. "Revelations?" he asked.

"6:10" I nodded.

"Interesting," he said then added with finality, "by the way Gents, your car, it smells like shit"

After we dropped Hassam off Harvey and I pulled into the long, horseshoe driveway of the Viceroy Hotel. A respected foreign correspondent once mused that all great wars have a hotel and during the Lebanon Civil War that hotel was the Viceroy. As you walk into the ornate hotel lobby complete with gold leaf ceilings and terra cotta sculptures, you are greeted by two jocular cockatoos, one white and one pink, residing in two separate cages. They both talk non-stop and say the craziest things. The pink one named Victor does a stirring rendition of Le Marseillaise as well as a great imitation of Jimmy Walker yelling "Dyno-mite." The white one's name is Hugo and his greatest claim to fame is the mimicking of an incoming artillery shell complete with the sounds of the explosion at impact. When Hugo is done detonating the device, Victor, without fail, says 'Bombs away' and then they both break out in unabashed laughter.

The hotel bar, located at the other end of the lobby, is called the Darwin. It was 'the place' to acquire intelligence and exchange information under the conviviality of a drink. It is aptly named for two reasons. First of all, the characters you'd encounter here were as unique and colorful as anything Sir Charles discovered while visiting the Galapagos. At cocktail hour the hammered tin circular bar would be leaned on by politicians, journalists, drug dealers and international financiers as the money launderers preferred to be called. Secondly, no one has done a more admirable job of adapting and surviving in a harsh environment than the management of the Viceroy. The owner, a rather mysterious chap known to the patrons only as Harry, acquired the hotel under nebulous circumstances back in the late 1970's. When the war started he installed a 50,000 gallon fresh water storage tank and a gas powered generating system so his guests would never have to be inconvenienced by such troubling things as an incoming rocket attack or a terrorist siege. The Viceroy even employed its own platoon strength militia that protected the hotel grounds with fully armed RPG's and automatic weapons. When you booked a room at the Viceroy the concierge would ask you, without being sardonic, if you prefer the sea side or the siege side of the hotel.

Harvey tossed his car keys to a parking attendant who was fully decked out in a Grenadier Guards outfit complete with bearskin hat and knee high riding boots.

"I come here for two reasons," Harvey explained. "First, it's a great place to gather intelligence, and second, they make the best martini this side of London."

It was only 4:00 pm and we had the bar pretty much to ourselves. I didn't want to remind him I was still underage. My cumulative drinking experiences to date consisted of a six pack of beer before a high school football game and a bottle of apple laced Boone's Farm wine just before a Sadie Hawkins dance my senior year. Neither foray went well.

The bartender tossed a bar towel over his shoulder and ambled on over. "What can I get you fellas?"

"Tootsie, this is Abel, Abel, Tootsie." I offered my hand and Tootsie gave it a firm shake.

"Two of your gin martinis kind sir," Harvey said. "Let's put some hair on the kid's chest." Tootsie nodded and went to work. Apparently proof of age isn't required in the middle of a civil war.

"You are now going to get life lesson number two Abel," Harvey proclaimed.

"What was number one again?"

"Get out of Lebanon alive and in one piece."

"Oh yeah, right."

"Lesson number two. Watch and learn," he said as Tootsie began making the martinis. "First off, martinis are made with gin, not vodka. A vodka martini is just cold vodka. A proper martini is the blessed marriage of the gin's juniper berries and the herbal quality of dry vermouth. Start with a quality gin like a Hendricks or a Blackwood. The gin must be stored in a freezer for maximum coldness. The ice then goes in the shaker followed by a coating of vermouth. Just a capful please Tootsie."

Tootsie turned around and gave him a dirty look then poured in the capful.

"Thank you," Harvey said laughing. "Now just three ounces of gin. There's no need to overwhelm it. Abel the next part is very important. The martini needs to be shaken firmly but not violently so. You don't want to bruise the gin."

Tootsie grabbed two stemmed glasses out of the refrigerator and poured in the contents. He then pared away two, inch long strips of lemon peel including the white pith. He gave them a twist above the martinis and then dragged them around the rim of the glasses. He finally dropped the peels into the martinis and served them up.

Harvey finished his dissertation. "Just like the gin, the glasses should also be frozen. A martini can never be too cold. Finally it's important to know there are only two legitimate garnish choices. The lemon peel or the olive. People who put onions in their martinis are monsters."

I took a sip. It was clean and dry with just the right amount of tang. It warmed my entire body as it headed south. It would be the beginning of a long, wonderful love affair.

Harvey gave me a knowing smile. "Not bad, huh? By the way never more than two. I don't want to be picking you up off of the floor."

As we sat and sipped our drinks we mutually agreed Hassam Ali was a guy we could work with and trust.

"My only question is why?" I asked.

"Why what?"

"Why would a guy like Hassam help us betray some of his own people?"

Harvey pondered the question as he ordered another martini. Tootsie put two fingers up but I shook my head. One was plenty.

"Well," Harvey said, "the short answer is opportunity. The CIA made a deal with Hassam that if he helped us save some lives we'd bring him back to America as a U.S. Citizen. The longer answer is a bit more complex. You have to ask exactly who are his people? It's obviously not the Maronites who swooped down into the refugee camps and it's certainly not the Israelis who invaded his country. Is it his fellow Muslims? The ones who invaded his apartment building which led to the killing of his entire family or the ones that plant car bombs all over town? I don't think Hassam's betraying anyone because, quite frankly, Hassam has no people left. He's simply trying to do some good before he gets the hell out of Dodge."

For the next hour Harvey and I came up with a simple but effective dead drop system and then implemented it with Hassam the next day. We identified five telephone poles in a relatively safe part of the city. Every morning we would drive by the patisserie and if there was a fifth outdoor table set up (normally there were only four) we knew Hassam was scheduling a meet. At that point Hassam would have already stuck a thumbtack, either red, green or white on the street side of one of the poles. Five poles and three colors gave us fifteen combinations which would tell us the time, location and risk factor of the meet. Three thumbtacks side by side told us Hassam was in trouble and we needed to send in the cavalry.

Over the next few months Hassam's intel began flowing in. A lot of it was no good of course but some of it was spot on which led to some highly successful missions. We took down a huge heroin for arms operation up in the Bakaa Valley and thwarted an assassination attempt to kill the Deputy Prime Minister just to name a few. The three of us were spending countless hours together and we were becoming very close friends. Closer than I had ever felt to anybody.

One night we were hiding out in an ancient olive grove overlooking a small harbor just north of the town of Byblos. Above us a full moon sat in a cloudless sky illuminating this ancient Phoenician town as it had for the last 5000 years. We were waiting for a Russian trawler that was expected to dock sometime before morning with a cargo of RPG's. Our plan was to let them offload, follow the cargo to its final destination and then call it in. For whatever reason, the trawler was a no-show.

The night was brilliant with stars. It was the kind of sky that made you feel small and inconsequential. As was my lifelong habit, I began identifying the constellations of the northern sky. First there were the circumpolars. Cassiopeia, the vain queen and Cepheus her king. Off to the left was Ursa Major, the Great Bear, whose brightest stars formed the Big Dipper. Next to him was his smaller sibling Ursa Minor whose tail formed the Little Dipper. The summer constellations were also presenting themselves. There was Hercules of course and Cygnus the swan. Off to the right was Aquilla, the eagle that carried Zeus' arrows into battle. Hassam was watching me with amusement.

"Do you know the stars Able?"

"I do. A gift from the old man."

"Old man?"

"Sorry, my father." Hassam's English was so good I tended to forget he wouldn't understand certain American colloquialisms. "He owns a Hermes Traveller."

"We had several of those when I was at Oxford. That's a lot of telescope for a hobbyist."

Hassam was right about that. My father had paid $12,000 for it back in the mid- 1970's. That was real money back then. My grandfather was furious with him and I couldn't understand why until I found out my father had stolen the money from the church rebuilding fund. I think he loved that telescope more than any other person or thing in his life. He would spend countless hours, sometimes days, making elaborate charts of the stars which he kept in an old Burberry briefcase. They were his sacred text.

"I played around with it a bit but it was my brother who had a real talent for the stars."

"You have a brother?" Hassam asked.

"Yes a twin. His name is Jonah."

Harvey chuckled. "Able and Jonah Kane. That's about as Old Testament as you can get. I'm going to start calling you OT." He did and the nickname stuck.

For reasons I can't quite explain I started telling them about my life, about my father and grandfather, the preaching, the fraud and the constant running from the law. I told them about my mother who died mysteriously when Jonah and I were only five years old. As my story poured out I could feel a yoke's weight lifting from me.

Hassam then picked up the thread and told us about his early years growing up in a peaceful Lebanon that seemed a lot more idyllic than the dystopian society that existed today. How in Beirut, if the weather was just right, you could snow ski in the morning and be playing in the ocean's waves by the afternoon. He prayed for the Lebanon of his youth to return but he now also dreamed of a new start in America. Perhaps meet a strong, beautiful American woman, have lots of children and start his own construction business to honor his father.

Harvey joined in also. He was a third generation Marine officer following in the wake of his dad and paternal grandfather. He grew up in a quintessential California beach town by the name of San Clemente. Heaven on earth was how he described it. He went to college up the coast at a place called California Polytechnic State University in San Luis Obispo. There he joined the ROTC and graduated with a degree in criminology. Half way through Officer Candidates School he realized a career in the Marines was not going to be for him but he'd serve his six years with honor and dignity. What he really loved to do was surf and it was something he'd been doing since he was a grommet which he explained, in surf talk, was a young boy. He married his high school sweet heart who would soon be starting medical school and he was counting the days until he could go home.

As the sun came up we realized the mission was a scratch and it was time to head back to Beirut. Harvey threw Hassam the keys and said, "You drive." Hassam winked at me as we piled into the Pinto.

"Just remember Able," Hassam said, "if he tries to pull a fast one, put a bullet in the back of his head." We all shared a good laugh over that one.

Hassam was building a reputation amongst his fellow Lebanese as a man who could help put an end to some of the madness that tormented the country. We were awash in success but blinded to the simple reality of Isaac Newton's third law of motion. That is for every action there is a reaction of equal force. Yes, we were making friends in high places but we were also making enemies in the lower ones. We were pissing in the soup of some very serious people and the fact we didn't see it coming proved to be our downfall.

CHAPTER 7

On October 20th, we picked Hassam up in front of the venerable American University. I specifically remember the fragrant smell of honeysuckle as we pulled up alongside him.

"Today, a surprise for both of you," Hassam proudly announced. His broad grin was infectious and I found myself chuckling as I asked for details.

"Well that would wreck the surprise now wouldn't it?" he added.

Hassam took the wheel and we headed south out of the city along the Sidon Highway for about a half an hour until we reached the charming seaside village of Jiyeh. He pulled up in front of a tidy, gabled restaurant which backed up to a deserted beach studded by cacti and fruit bearing palm trees. Hassam excused himself and entered the restaurant. Harvey and I walked down towards the crystal clear waters.

"Jesus," Harvey said, "look at that left." He pointed to a finger of land about 150 yards out where a beautiful wave was breaking in domino like fashion from south to north.

"That wave is perfect OT. Double overhead and pure glass. It rivals anything I've surfed back home."

As if on cue, Hassam emerged from the restaurant holding a surfboard in one hand and a pair of swim trunks in the other. The look on Harvey's face was one of pure, unmitigated joy.

"All right LT," I said, "let's see what you got."

Ten minutes later Harvey had paddled through the wash

and was sitting up straddling the board. A good sized breaker began to crest and with a few quick paddles he caught the wave, jumped to his feet and steered the board down its face. He rode it until it ceased to exist then headed back out to do it again. Hassam and I watched him surf for another fifteen minutes until he paddled around the point disappearing from sight.

"Come on," Hassam said, "I want to show you something." He talked while we strolled along the strand. "Like all things and places in my country this beach town has a remarkable history. Alexander the Great, St. Peter, St. Paul, they have all spent time walking this beach which has been fought over and conquered since the dawn of time."

Jiyeh would soon be fought over again. It was a strategic seaport which made it vulnerable to attack and counterattack and would ultimately receive some of the harshest blows from the Civil War. But not today. As we walked along the strand the onshore breeze freshened making a perfect day that much better.

"Okay, here we are," Hassam said as we stopped in front of a large excavation site. There were architectural stakes tossed haphazardly around the hole and large mounds of earth and rock had been pushed to the sides but never transported away. It was an archaeological dig. The walls, made of degradated stone, were supported by thick, timber poles maybe fifty feet in length. They ran from the top of the tell down to the floor. The wood was beginning to show the early stages of dry rot due to the constant exposure to the elements.

"This was discovered accidentally about five years ago when a developer was trenching lines for a condominium project. Sadly, the government had to stop the dig due to the war. What you're looking at Abel is the vestigial remains of an 8th century Byzantine church, specifically the nave." The floor below was a perfectly preserved mosaic and I now realized why

Hassam had brought me here. He glanced over at me and noticed the tears welling up in my eyes. "Do you recognize the images Abel?"

Indeed I did. There was a man holding an oval shaped, red shield in one hand and a sword in the other trying to fight off a great fish that was just about to swallow him. "Jonah," I said.

Hassam turned towards the water. "According to the Bible it is right here, on this beach, where the whale spit Jonah back on to dry land. Do you remember the story?"

Only like the back of my hand. Good old Jonah, my brother's namesake. An obstinate, vindictive prophet of the Old Testament who was asked to warn a Gentile people to repent or be smited by God and then became disappointed when they did just that. A strange character that Jonah.

"I'm worried about them Hassam. My family. I know I did the right thing for myself by leaving but I should have handled it better."

He put his hand on my shoulder. "You're a good man Able. That much is plain to see. I know you'll make it right with them. My father used to say that time acts like the wind and water on our grievances, slowly eroding them away until they are nothing but distant memories."

We stood there for a moment without saying a word. "I'm hungry," Hassam said breaking the silence, "let's eat."

We entered the restaurant and I was immediately hit with the aromatic smells of garlic and mint. The LT was still somewhere out on the water so we decided to start without him. Hassam introduced me to the proprietor, a short, lugubrious gentleman by the name of Azeed. He shook my hand without making eye contact. There was an uneasiness about him I chalked up to the fact that an American in his place of business could spell nothing but trouble. He then led us to a discreet table in the back corner of the room under the watchful eyes of the other patrons. A young waiter brought us waters, a piping hot loaf of olive bread and a whitish looking dip. Hassam tore off a piece of bread and dragged it across the dip. I did the same and plucked it into my mouth. I tasted something akin to yogurt and what I thought was cucumber. It was very good.

"What is this?" I asked Hassam.

"It's called Labneh and it's about as Lebanese as you can get."

We dined family style on lamb kebabs, fresh fish and fava beans. Half way through the meal Azeed brought over a bottle of unlabeled wine. He opened it and departed without a word.

"He's not happy we're here Hassam."

Hassam waved his hand in a dismissive fashion. "Azeed's an asshole but he's harmless. He's a Druse and the Druse are never happy."

He poured a glass of wine, held it up to the light and gave it a quick swirl. Finally he placed his nose directly over the glass and took in a deep breath.

"Perfect," he proclaimed and handed me the glass.

I took a sip. I was no expert on the subject of wine, but this, a burgundy, was very good. Smooth and complex would be how I would have described it later in life.

"What you are drinking Able is biblical history," Hassam pointed out. "The vines that produced this are the direct descendants of the wine of Kings. Abraham, Solomon, David, and even Jesus drank from the same source as you do today. I figured it was something you could appreciate."

My hand was actually shaking a bit at the solemnity of the moment. "Amazing Hassam. Thank you."

After two glasses of wine I got up to relieve myself. I glanced out the plate glass window facing the sea and saw Harvey furiously paddling back into shore. We made eye contact and I waved to him. He bolted upright on his board waving his hands frantically. I looked around the restaurant and realized we were the only ones still here. The staff and the other customers had disappeared. That was when I saw the glint of the sun reflecting off the barrel of a rifle. We were in trouble.

"Hassam," I yelled turning around but he was already on the move. My pack was hanging off the back of a chair and he was unzipping it to get at our guns. Just as he tossed me my Sig there was a deafening explosion followed by a searing hot, white light and then, total darkness.

A flash grenade. We had trained against these at Lejeune and the more you are subjected to them the quicker you can react. My eyesight was returning so I knew only five to ten seconds had elapsed since the detonation. Hassam was unconscious and bleeding profusely from a gash on the back of his head. I counted four men entering the restaurant from the far side but the smoke from the explosion bought me a few precious seconds. Grabbing Hassam under his armpits and around his chest I headed down the hallway to the bathrooms and hopefully a way out. The passage was L-shaped and just as I got to the elbow two men appeared at the other end. I let go of Hassam and fired off several rounds, dropping one of the men as the other ducked back behind the wall. I picked Hassam up again and headed down the remaining hallway towards the door. It was chained shut but two rounds into the lock broke it free. As I stepped out into the sunlight the last thing I remember was the butt of an AK-47 descending onto the bridge of my nose. Again, darkness.

When I came to I found myself in a small, spartan room. I was completely naked and my feet and hands were zip-tied to an exposed sewer pipe. Hassam was nowhere in sight but the muffled screams on the other side of the wall sounded a lot like him. I was cold, disoriented and scared to death.

Twenty minutes later the door opened and two hairy knuckle types tossed the unconscious body of Hassam Ali into the room. His face had been battered beyond recognition and there was quite a bit of blood dripping down the back of his thighs. I assumed he was dead. They then turned to me. I was cut loose and dragged from the room. It was my turn.

I was bound again, this time to a plain, metal chair that had been bolted to the hardwood floor. Ironically, under normal circumstances I probably would have admired the view that lay in front of me. I was looking out through a huge circular window at a set of craggy, mountain peaks dotted with majestic cedar trees. Off to the left I could see the idle chairlifts of a ski resort. It really was quite beautiful.

A cold wind was blowing in from my right and I looked towards the source. The entire façade of the house was gone and the electrical conduit and HVAC ducting hung down from the ceiling like the tentacles of an army of Portuguese Man-of-Wars. My skin was turning blue and I recognized the early onset of hypothermia. Yet as miserable as I was the fear of what might be coming next made me wish I could remain in that moment forever.

Finally, another door opened and the same two men, Thing One and Thing Two, returned with a friend. He was younger than his compatriots but I instinctively knew he would be the one calling the shots.

"So you are the infamous Abel Kane," he said positioning himself in a chair behind the desk facing me. "Funny, you don't look like much but you and your buddies sure have been causing a lot of trouble around here haven't you? Unique name by the way."

He spoke perfect English without a trace of an accent and his knowledge of American slang was disconcerting. He was clearly an Arab and I put his age range in the late twenties, early thirties. He wore his hair tightly cropped to his head and had a tidy beard without a hint of gray. He noticed my shivering which at that point I could no longer control.

"My apologies for the cold Abel but you can thank your

Navy's flying volkswagons for that. "

He was referring to the oversized bombs the U.S.S. New Jersey had fired from offshore up into the Shouf. They weighed the same amount as a VW Beetle, hence the nickname. The bombs proved to be tragically inaccurate and the Navy eventually ceased the operation.

"So," he said, "you and I have a problem. I need to know what you know and you somehow have to convince me you're telling the truth. Can you do that Able?"

I nodded my head emphatically. At that point I would have given him the combination to the safe at Fort Knox if I knew it.

"You see your Lt. Dwyer is dead and I'm afraid we were a little over zealous with your friend Hassam. That leaves just you so we might as well get started."

He pulled a thick telephone book out of the desk drawer and handed it to Thing One who reared back and with two hands swung the book into my jaw as hard as he could. I groaned as I heard bone crack. Two of my teeth dislodged and I reflexively swallowed them along with the blood that was pooling in my mouth. The pain was intense.

"That was just to get your full attention Able. I hope I have it now." He returned the phone book to the drawer then said, "Oh, I'm sorry, I'm being quite rude. I haven't properly introduced myself. My name is Mubari and I belong to an organization called Hezbollah. Have you heard of us?"

I said no which was true. There were so many terrorist organizations running amok in this country that they all eventually blended together.

"Well you will my friend, trust me, you will." He stared right through me and flashed one of the most malevolent smiles I had ever seen. I knew right then and there I was peering into the eyes of pure evil.

He went on to ask me questions about my background, service record and the missions we had completed over the last few months. He seemed particularly interested in the Marine barracks and the BLT building asking questions about sentry allocations, troop movements and command structure. I'd answer when I could, always truthfully, and told him when I had no idea. He seemed to take all my answers in stride writing my responses into a small notebook.

Finally he placed it down on the desktop and pulled a screwdriver out of the top, center drawer. He began tapping it on the desk's surface and that was when I noticed he was missing the ring finger on his left hand.

"OK then Able, what do you know about our operation scheduled for October 23rd?"

I sensed a glacial shift in the interrogation process. Everything before this was strictly foreplay leading up to the main event. October 23rd? I had no idea and the fact I didn't scared the living hell out of me. Today was the 21st so we were talking about something that would happen two days from now.

"The 23rd?" I asked. There was a depth in the fear in my voice now. "I know nothing about you, Hezbollah, or the 23rd." I prayed I sounded convincing.

Mubari nodded and handed the screwdriver over to Thing Two who grabbed my left hand and plunged the blade down under my thumbnail all the way to its base. When it was adequately separated from the skin he pulled a pair of pliers from his back pocket and ripped it off.

The pain was so excruciating it blinded me momentarily. Two minutes would go by before I could stop hyperventilating. Mubari offered me a glass of water which I greedily drank down and then asked me the same question. I gave the same answer. This continued until all ten of my fingernails were gone.

When this task was completed they moved on to a device called a 'picana.' The picana is a close relative to the cattle prod and what makes it so unique is it operates at high voltages and low current. This translates to a lot of pain but never death. They worked my body's most sensitive areas, namely the mouth and genitals. As Mubari increased the voltage I could feel my body burning from the inside out until I would mercifully lose consciousness. We did this time and time again and I prayed to God for a death that refused to arrive. After an hour they gave up, unbound me and tossed me back into the room with a still lifeless Hassam.

I remember nothing after that until Thing One and Thing Two dragged me back out to the study and forcibly sat me down in the same chair. Mubari was there, waiting for me. The sun was rising over the peaks announcing a new day, October 22nd.

Then he shocked me. "Well Able, I believe you. Nobody could have endured what you went through without telling us the truth. You have my humblest of apologies. If you would follow these two gentlemen they'll lead you to a nice warm shower, a fresh set of clothes and a hot meal."

I couldn't believe what I was hearing and I took him for his word. I thanked him effusively and broke down and cried. He didn't lie to me. I showered, put on the fresh set of clothes and sat down to a meal that included vegetable soup and French bread. They then led me to a room with a king-size bed and a thick, down comforter. Just as I was about to lie down the Thing brothers violently grabbed me and I was dragged back to the chair in the study. Mubari was there waiting for me. I would find out later in life that this was an old KGB trick. Interrogate the suspect, let him think he's believed, assure him of his pending release and then yank him back in. Trust me, it is extremely effective.

I was once again bound to the chair. Without saying a

word, Mubari grabbed a power drill and made a dramatic motion of screwing a bit into its port. My heart was leaping out of my chest.

"Now once and for all, tell me what you know about tomorrow," he demanded.

I told him the truth. I knew nothing. He shrugged his shoulders and then I watched him drill all the way through my left foot. I involuntarily cleared my bowels and violently retched up the meal I'd just enjoyed less than a half hour earlier.

"Again, tell me what you know."

I was unresponsive until one of his thugs pressed a thumb into one of my open wounds. The pain shot through my entire body.

"I don't know anything," I said but it was barely whispered and I wondered if he had even heard me. He drilled through the other foot but this time I didn't feel a thing.

When he finished, he hovered the spinning drill just outside my right eye. If I was going to die I was going to do it with as much dignity as I could muster.

I leaned into him until the drill was less than an inch away. "It's all fun and games until someone loses an eye isn't it asshole?"

He laughed. Of all the bizarre reactions in the world he started laughing. Thing One and Thing Two joined in also like the whole thing was just a misunderstanding amongst friends. He laid the drill down on the desk and the other two men began cutting away the zip ties that had bound me to the chair. As they were doing that Mubari picked up the desk phone and spoke to someone on the other end. "All is good," he said, "the operation is a go."

As the men dragged me from the room Mubari yelled out, "I believe you Abel. This time I really do and if you happen to survive tell the world that Hezbollah has arrived!"

They tossed me back into the room and I fell on top of Hassam. Just before I drifted into unconsciousness and what I assumed was impending death, I felt him grab my hand and give it the faintest of squeezes.

At dawn the next day, October 23rd, 1983, a man by the name of Ismail Ascari drove a Mercedes Benz stake bed truck across the south end of the BLT parking lot. He ran over the concertina wire, through an open security gate and into the building itself detonating 21,000 pounds of TNT. The guards at their sentry posts were not allowed to carry loaded weapons per the bizarre rules of engagement mandated by the ironically named 'peace keeping mission.' By the time they were able to arm their weapons it was too late.

The blast lifted the building up in an inward 'V' position before it collapsed upon itself like a house of cards. The crater at the bomb's epicenter was thirty feet wide by fifteen feet deep. It killed 241 people, almost all active U.S. Marines. A previously unknown terrorist group by the name of Hezbollah (The Party of God) proudly claimed responsibility for the attack. As Hassam and I were hovering somewhere between life and death in an abandoned mountain chalet high above the city of Beirut, the war on terrorism had begun.

CHAPTER 8

(BACK TO THE PRESENT)

Saturday, June 17th

It was going to be a slog on the way home so I texted Hassam to tell him I was running a little late. After a few years of unsuccessfully chasing Mubari around the Middle East he decided to take the U.S. Government up on its original offer and entered the United States as a full-fledged American citizen. He first headed to Chicago where there is a strong Lebanese community. He got on as a forklift driver at a Home Depot distribution center but the work was uninspiring and Chicago's weather was too capricious. After that it was Dallas, then New Orleans and finally Tucson before he showed up at my door with nothing but a suitcase full of clothes. That was twenty years ago. We lived together for a few years and I introduced him to a friend who owned a home remodeling business. Hassam ended up running projects for him until he passed the contractor's exam. He then set out on his own and has never looked back. All of his dreams ended up coming true. He married a strong, beautiful American woman who has given him five wonderful children and he owns a successful construction company that he dedicated to his father. He is my closest friend.

We were meeting at our gym, Tommy Z's, which was established in 1949 by its eponymous founder, Tommy Zabowski, or TZ-1 as he is affectionately and posthumously known. It's now in the very capable hands of his grandson who we of course call TZ-3. Tommy Z's is a fighter's gym and on any given day you can find yourself training shoulder to shoulder with world class boxers and MMA professionals. But tonight TZ-3 closed early for us and we had the place to ourselves.

I pulled into the parking lot twenty minutes late and let myself in through the back door. Hassam was off to the side skipping the speed bag and TZ-3 was still there, wiping the day's sweat off the equipment.

"Hey TZ-3, how's it hanging?"

"Low and to the left Abel." He then lowered his voice and said, "be careful tonight. Hassam seems a little more focused than usual."

I laughed. Hassam is always the most focused human being I've ever met. "That's ok. Tonight I've got a thing or two up my own sleeve. We'll lock up if you need to take off."

TZ-3 smiled. "There's no way I'm missing this."

Hassam had begun boxing in the English public school leagues. He was very good and I witnessed him dismantle many a bigger, stronger Marine in the all-comers ring the Corps had built in the BLT parking lot. He is what is known in boxing circles as a counter puncher. The counter puncher's strategy is to frustrate their opponent into making a mistake and then make them pay dearly for it. To do so successfully, you must be very patient and near flawless in your craft. It is, in my opinion, the most artful of strategies.

I am more of a slugger. Hassam, years ago at my request, taught me the basic techniques and how to train but I could never elevate myself to anything close to his mastery. I'm bigger and stronger than Hassam so I try my best to get inside and trade punches. When I'm successful against him, which isn't very often, I'll try to cut off the ring by driving him against the ropes and into a corner.

We have been sparring on and off at Tommy Z's for over

twenty years. We've had to make some concessions to age like wearing the headgear and moving up to the 16 oz. gloves but none of that has lessened our competitive spirit. Our rules are pretty straight forward. Eight three minute rounds with sixty second breaks in between. If you kiss the canvas more than once the fight is over or you can simply tap out if you've had enough.

The first two rounds that evening were fairly uneventful. There is always a certain sizing up of your opponent regardless of how familiar you are with his techniques. I did get a real nice combination in on Hassam during the second round while he was more than content to countering with body blows whenever the opportunity availed itself. I'm a pretty straight forward boxer. I try to pressure my opponent and I rely on the simplest of combinations, either the jab-cross or the jab-cross-left hook. Hassam on the other hand has the entire portfolio at his disposal. He's put me down more than once with a five way combination that is a thing of beauty. Late in the third round I made my move. I came at him aggressively trying to cut off the ring. I pumped back with my left hand as if to throw a jab and he ducked right in anticipation. It was a fake and it worked perfectly. He was momentarily exposed and I came with a sharp cross that caught him square on the button. He was staggered. I charged in trying to finish the job but the bell rang and he was still standing.

Between rounds he was leaning against the ropes taking in some water and smiling.

"Well that was interesting Able," he said, "Where did you learn that one?"

"The internet of course. Isn't that where you learn everything these days?" It was time for the fourth round. "Haven't you had enough Hassam?"

"Not yet Able, maybe one more round."

He was tired and hurting so he clinched me every chance

he could. I drove him into the corner and scored a couple of nice 1-2 combinations before he could maneuver away. He retaliated with a few uppercuts but they had nothing on them. I was very much the aggressor now and I pushed him towards the ropes. Then, somehow, he slipped under my cross and now forced me into the corner reversing the advantage. He suddenly had all the energy in the world and I realized too late his fatigue had been nothing but a ruse. A jab-jab combo was followed by a jab-cross and then finally he delivered that five way combo and I was down for the count. He was right, maybe one more round.

Afterwards we walked across the street to a Mexican restaurant for a quick meal. I nursed a margarita along with my pride and Hassam drank his usual club soda. I told him about seeing Harvey and the Reina Montes case. He also knew Marta and ensured me he was there to help in anyway. We ate our meals and I picked up the check. Loser pays. I headed back to my bachelor apartment and Hassam returned to his five children and his beautiful, strong American wife.

CHAPTER 9

Sunday, June 18th

I woke up the next day sore and bleary eyed. Last night I had every intention of getting a good night's sleep and hitting the ground running today. At around 9:00pm I was sitting in my EZ chair reading a Pat Conroy novel with a wee dram of single malt by my side. I was rapidly approaching The Land of Nod when my cell phone rang. It was Brigid.

"Abel Kane, private detective to the stars, how can I help you?"

"Good one. What are you doing right now?"

Well that piqued my interest but I decided to play it cool. "Stuff. Vital, important stuff."

"Yeah, what kind of vital stuff?"

"I promised the president I wouldn't talk about it."

"Oh brother," she said. I could almost see her rolling her eyes. She explained her bar back Alex just went home sick and they were swamped. Would you? Could you help out?

"What's it paying?"

"Free drinks."

"Ok I'll do it. But just remember I chose you over protecting our great country."

"Excellent choice," she said hanging up.

Brigid had hired a new chef about two months ago and he was really turning out some great fare. The place was slammed and the dinner crowd stuck around to listen to an acoustic guitarist who played great covers until midnight. Her publican ancestors would have been proud. I helped her clean up after closing and it was 1:30 by the time I slid, alone I may add, underneath the sheets.

I whipped up some scrambled eggs and bacon, made a pot of coffee and pulled out the paperwork pertaining to the sale of Marta's cleaning business. I have never bought or sold a company but I'm familiar with the documentation involved. I've worked several cases of fraud that have arisen from transactions similar to this one. The disputes almost always involve misrepresentation, usually by the seller, over the true financial condition of the business. Revenues overstated, costs understated, fraudulent tax returns, the possibilities are endless. With that in mind I went through the documents pertaining to the sale of Top 2 Bottom Cleaning Services looking for something out of the ordinary. The buyer was a corporation by the name of EZX Enterprises. I looked them up online and they had similar operations in both Las Vegas and Phoenix. The purchase agreement was signed by a Rahid Gamal, President and Jose Pacheco, Secretary. The whole thing looked pretty straight forward to me. A UCC search was completed showing no judgements or liens against Marta's business and there were letters from the State Board of Equalization and the EDD evidencing a company in good standing. Since this was an all-cash transaction there was no promissory note and the only requirement on Marta's end was the signing of a seven year covenant not to compete. I reviewed the financials and it appeared the buyers had paid a sizeable premium for the business relative to its actual worth. There can be a myriad of legitimate reasons for doing this especially if a firm like EZX is looking to gain access into a new market. It wasn't much but it was a thread to pull on and see if anything unraveled.

I then sent a text to one of my renters, Nate Isaacson, to see if he had a minute. He replied immediately telling me to come on up. Nate's an interesting guy. He's a bit of a capricious personality who can go from ebullient to morose and back again before you can reheat last night's leftovers. He's a computer geek who makes a living writing code for companies and individuals who are creating app's for smartphones. If he thinks the application shows promise he'll do it for a piece of the action. If not, he'll charge an hourly fee. I don't know how well he does and to be honest, I don't really care. What I do know is the rent check is slid under my door on the first of the month with a reliability that would make the German train system envious.

"You were out late last night," Nate said without taking his eyes off one of his three monitors. His work desk faced out the window which looked down upon the street scene below. He's constantly watching the comings and goings of people living their everyday lives even though he wants no part of it. I explained what I had going on and then ran some questions by him.

"Can you access someone's email without having possession of any of their devices?" I asked.

"Maybe. Probably not though. Do you have any information on her?" I handed him a copy of the missing person's report.

He spun his chair around to grab it. "I've got a program that will run millions of permutations based on this data. It's a real longshot though. I'll let you know."

"How about text messages off of her cell phone?"

"I assume you don't have her phone either?" Nate asked.

"Correct."

"Forget it, no chance."

"Ok, well any suggestions?"

"Is she on Facebook?" He didn't wait for an answer. He started feverishly typing away. I'm always amazed by the speed at which the younger generation can attack a keyboard. Being a two finger hunt and peck guy I find the whole thing rather impressive. "There she is, Reina Montes. She hasn't posted in months but she has fifty six friends."

I'm not on Facebook. Perhaps I'm just a product of my dinosaur generation but I really don't want the world to know everything that's going on in my life and I sure as hell don't want to know what's going on in theirs.

"What I can do," Nate continued, "is send all her friends a private message."

"You can do that?"

"Sure. EZ Peezy."

I thought about it. Of course there would be some risk involved if one of those fifty six people had been involved in her disappearance. It would tip them off and possibly give them a chance to cover their tracks. But I think Reina was running out of time and I didn't have a lot of options at this point.

"OK, let's do it," I decided.

"Do you want to be contacted on your cell or the landline?"

"Landline." I didn't want a bunch of crazies harassing me all day. Nate typed while I dictated a short message that hopefully conveyed the seriousness of the situation.

CHAPTER 10

When I'm out driving on Sundays I like to set my satellite radio to the Christian stations and listen to the Gospel preachers. I'm not looking for any epiphanies. I'm simply curious as to what scam they're running on that particular day. Remember, this was my family's business and as my grandfather Ezekiel used to say, 'religion is the greatest long con in the world and God is its greatest shill.'

My grandfather was born in late 1915 just outside the town of Texarkana, Arkansas. He would eventually be the oldest of six siblings. There was a seventh but he lost a sister and his mother during a tragic childbirth. My great grandfather Jacob was the towns Baptist minister. He was revered by his congregation but at the same time loathed by his own family who he forced both the Bible and the switch upon with equal measure. After school, Saturdays and for most of the summer months Jacob would pile his brood onto the family wagon and deliver them either to the farms, picking fields or timber stands depending on who was paying the highest wages at the time. While my grandfather and his younger siblings were toiling away Jacob would sit atop the wagon reading his bible and making handwritten notes in the margins. Those thoughts would inevitably appear in a Sunday sermon somewhere down the line. All the money the Kane children generated from their labors went directly into his pocket. They never saw a dime of it. This was okay for my grandfather who never minded a hard day's work and the money he earned for his father paled in comparison to the side cons he had going. He ran them all,

three card monte, pig-in-a poke, the badger game, you name it. Ezekiel Kane had perfected each and every one of them. He worked his craft at school, in town and out in the fields. He even ran a loaded dice game in the small copse of trees directly behind his father's church after Sunday services. Disagreements were settled with his fists and it was the rare time when he came out on the short end of the stick. By the time he turned sixteen he had amassed a small fortune of over $800 which he kept in an old biscuit tray buried in the crawl space underneath the house.

Sundays of course were the Lord's Day and Jacob would shine his family up and march them to the front pew of his church for all the parishioners to admire. There were three services every Sunday and the Kanes had to sit with their hands politely folded from 9:00 in the morning until 1:00 in the afternoon. His younger siblings grew bored quickly, but not my grandfather. He was getting an invaluable education from a master craftsman. Jacob Kane was a strong orator who stood tall in the pulpit and recited biblical verse verbatim. He would hold the closed bible in his hand and reach both arms towards the heavens as if he were communicating with the Man himself. His sermons were eloquent and fiery and he never missed the chance to remind his flock that what you pay here on Earth will be repaid seven fold in the afterlife. The congregants sat in rapture, hanging on every word. At just the right time he'd pass the basket and my grandfather would shake his head in disbelief as the churchgoers willingly separated themselves from a half days wages each and every week.

After the services were concluded my grandfather would help his father with the day's count. With his practiced dexterity he easily could have skimmed the rake but this was his father's con and he had to respect that.

Then one day, in the gloam of a humid summer evening, he walked up the driveway to the house after a long day of hewing timber and noticed a saddled up bay tied to a fencing post. He walked through the front door and froze. There was his father sitting at the kitchen table with the biscuit tray opened. He was arranging the lucre into conforming denominations.

"That's mine," my grandfather said to him. There was a hard edge to his voice.

Jacob Kane looked up and smiled. "No it's not. You lied, cheated and stole this money from God fearing people. This is the Devil's money."

He'd been turned in by one of his brothers or sisters. He looked around the room trying to identify the Judas. Not one of them would look him in the eye. They were all guilty.

"Out, now," my grandfather said to his siblings and they scurried out the door but only as far as the front room window.

My grandfather wasn't in any mood to back down. "Tell me Jacob, how much of Satan's cash did you spend on that Morgan out there?" He had never called his father by his given name. It was openly derisive and a direct challenge.

Jacob rose from his chair with the air of authority that had served him well his entire life. "I exorcised the evil from this currency and it's now mine to serve God's will."

My grandfather started laughing. "I've got to tell you old man that's quite a reach. Even for a charlatan like you."

"Pull your britches down boy," his father said screaming at the top of his lungs as he removed the metal studded belt from his pants.

Now Jacob Kane was not a small man but at sixteen years old my grandfather stood six feet, two inches tall and carried 215 pounds of corded muscle. "No," he simply said.

His father was going sideways with fury now. "Bend over Ezekiel Kane or I will pray to God for your eternal damnation."

"Enough of this," my grandfather said walking over to his father. He punched Jacob in the stomach with everything he had. Jacob Kane doubled over and dropped to his knees gasping for air. My grandfather then, with his size 12 boot, kicked him in the ribs and Jacob crashed to the floor stomach first. My grandfather then grabbed the belt out of his father's hand and gave him five vicious lashes of his own medicine. He then counted his money and put the roll back into the biscuit tray.

"You stupid son of a bitch," he said, "you paid $300 for a horse that's not worth $250. I figure you owe me at least $50 so I'm taking that bible of yours and we'll call the account settled. And by the way, if you kick up a fuss about this I'll make sure Sheriff Conway finds out about those special spiritual meetings you and his wife have been having. I'm sure he'd love to hear all the unsavory details."

My grandfather then stuffed some clothes and the biscuit tray into a saddle bag and rode away on a $300 Morgan that was probably worth $250. He would never see his father or his siblings ever again.

Ezekiel Kane would eventually become a circuit rider for the Methodists. He travelled the western slopes of the Appalachian Mountains as he headed north and skirted the eastern foothills on his way back south again. He preached the word of God to anyone who'd listen and separated fools from their money whenever the opportunity arose. He claimed, and my grandmother swore it was true, that he won her in a game of Faro one evening in Morgantown, West Virginia. She was fourteen years old at the time.

"Things were just different back then Able." he once explained to me. "No one even batted an eyelash when your father was born eighteen months later.

CHAPTER 11

Marta was right. The address Reina had given her was in fact a business called Otto's Warehousing and Self-Storage. There were two L-shaped buildings both four stories high and painted in a bright lime-green color. It seemed like a nice place to go and visit all your old crap. I wanted to get a closer look so I pulled into the driveway, found a parking spot and made my way over to the manager's office. I was immediately taken aback but not because the man sitting behind the counter was clipping his toenails into a wastebasket. I've been guilty of that myself. I was taken aback because the offender was the spitting image of Jeff Spicoli, Ridgemont High's most illustrious alum. The resemblance was uncanny.

"Be right with you," the man said.

Gotta get that last toe. He clipped it and I watched the nail fly over the basket and hit the wall behind the desk. He then slid into his flip flops and made his way over to the counter. "Hi, I'm Joe, but you can call me Bump like everyone else."

"But I don't call anyone else Bump." I said not being able to resist.

"Huh?"

"Never mind. Hi, I'm Pete Best. I'd……"

"Whoa, like the fifth Beetle, awesome," Bump said interrupting me.

"Yeah I get that a lot." I needed to start diving deeper into my musical rolodex. "Anyways Bump, I'm interested in renting a couple of spaces. Do you have any available?"

"Yeah, we have a few. How much square footage do you need?"

"Bump," I was having fun just saying his name, "I'm kind of spatially challenged. Can we go take a look at what's available?"

"Sure, everyone's like that. I'll grab my keys."

We hopped into his golf cart and he gave me the tour. I peppered him with questions to validate my interest in renting a space. How long have you been open? Have you had any security problems? Who's Otto? Have you talked to Mr. Hand since graduation? Is Phoebe Cates as cool as she appears in the movie? I actually didn't ask the last two but it wasn't necessary. Bump was a real talker. He's worked at Otto's for almost ten years and had been promoted to the weekend and night manager about a year ago. He'd been married twice but was very emphatic about there never being a third Mrs. Bump. He played left field on a softball team, thought Kurt Cobain was the truth and was seriously threatening a move to Idaho if California didn't get its 'shit together.' He did a lot of gesticulating with his hands while he chatted away and I couldn't help notice a few scabs on his left arm that hovered directly over his veins. I think Bump chased the dragon on occasion. All in all, he showed me a half-dozen spaces in both buildings and not once did Reina Montes jump out of a unit and yell surprise.

After the tour we headed back to the manager's office. I told him I wasn't quite ready to commit but if he could print me out a copy of the rental agreement I'd run it by my attorney for review. He ducked into the office while I grabbed something from my truck. He was waiting for me at the counter with their standard form. I grabbed it and one of his business cards. Joseph Gunter, Manager.

I thanked him, we shook hands and then I slid Reina's poster across the counter to him.

"Hey Bump, a friend of mine's daughter has gone missing

nearby. Don't suppose you've seen her around?"

He looked down at the poster and there it was. It was subtle but there was a flash of recognition. I was sure of it. In a split second it was gone and his composure had returned. He slid the poster back over to me. "Sorry, I don't know her."

"Are you sure Bump? It kinda looked like you might have recognized her."

"Nope, I've never seen her before," he said defiantly. "She's just real pretty that's all. I hope she's OK."

I pushed the poster back towards him. "Could you hold on to it just in case you see her around?" You never know, right?"

I decided to stick around a bit and see if Bump did something out of the ordinary. There was a Starbucks across the street, two storefronts up. It wasn't the best vantage point but it would do. I found a seat at the window, opened my laptop and pretended to write a screenplay like everyone else in here. Ninety minutes went by and a few customers hauled stuff in and out of Otto's. I was just about to call it quits when a black town car pulled into the driveway and parked next to the office. I could hear the faint sound of a car horn and a few seconds later out came Bump with a sheet of paper in his hand. He came alongside the car's back door and passed it through the window. That was when I realized I had left my camera in the truck. Stupid, stupid, stupid. Bump walked back to the office but only to lock the door. He was going with them. I ran out to my truck which was parked about twenty yards away cursing myself the entire time. I grabbed my camera and popped in the telescopic lens just as the town car turned around. I caught a break. They were making a left turn onto a very busy street and had to wait until the traffic cleared. I still had to hurry however and I ran as fast as my arthritic joints would allow. As it made the turn I dropped to one knee and started clicking away. After it disappeared from sight I scrolled through the photos. I got the license plate, clear as day, but what I was looking at made absolutely no sense to me at all. It read S-KV2378. The unusual letter-number configuration along with the red, white and blue tri-color design told me it could be nothing else but a diplomatic license plate. What it was doing at Otto's Self Storage is anyone's guess. There was some good news however. A diplomatic license plate can provide you with a wealth of information if you know how to read it. Let me provide a little background. These plates will always lead with the letter C, D or S. The D, which stands for Diplomat, is an embassy designation and if you ever find yourself wandering the streets of our nation's capital you will undoubtedly see a few. The C is a consulate designation and these can be found anywhere a foreign government maintains a consulate presence. In the United States this includes most major cities including Los Angeles. Consulate activities are very similar to those of an embassy. Their mission is to promote trade and support its citizens who are living or visiting here on foreign soil. Finally, the S designation is for Staff. These plates can be found attached to cars at both consulates and embassies and may be driven by anyone who has some level of diplomatic status. The second two letters are country designations. The Office of Foreign Missions which issues the plates does not make the coding obvious by design. It is a protective measure for our guests. I googled the KV designation. It is the code for Saudi Arabia.

I highly doubted Bump was playing left field for the Saudis so it begged the question, 'What in the world was a consulate staff car doing picking him up less than two hours after I showed him a picture of Reina Montes?' This was starting to get interesting. I packed up my belongings and headed for home. I had some phone calls to make along the way.

Marta picked up on the first ring. "Hi Able, any news?"

"Not really," I said lying, "I do have a couple of questions though."

"OK," she sounded hesitant. I don't think she believed the

not really part.

"Did Reina say anything about that address she gave you?"

"No. I found it on my kitchen counter after she left. Maybe it was never intended for me. Why did something happen?"

"Possibly. I showed a guy who works there Reina's picture and I think he may have recognized her. He denied it so I could be wrong."

"You're scaring me Able."

"I know and I'm sorry but I do have one more question. Have you or Reina had any contact with a Saudi or a group of Saudi's?"

"Sowdee's? Marta asked, "What's that?"

Well that answered that question. I explained it to her and she said no.

"Now you're really scaring me Able. Maybe this wasn't such a good idea."

"Marta, there's no reason to panic at this point. I truly don't know anything more than I did yesterday. I'm just...."

"Pulling on a thread?"

"You remember that do you?"

"Sure, that's your line. Harvey used to borrow it all the time."

I scolded myself for not being able to get the answers I needed without scaring her but the time for subtlety had passed. I had a sinking feeling the sands in Reina's hourglass were running out.

My next call was to Harvey and it went direct to voicemail. This wasn't a surprise. He is monumentally difficult to reach. I left a message giving him the entire rundown of what I had to date and asked him to call me as soon as possible.

What exactly did I have? I knew Reina quit her job, moved out of Marta's house and stopped asking for money all about the same time. Then there was the connection to Otto's. But what was that connection, drugs? Maybe, but she just didn't seem the type even though it would certainly explain why she stopped asking Marta for financial support. Were the Saudis involved somehow? That seemed like too big of a reach. There were dots out there to be connected but I wasn't there yet.

I pulled into my driveway and headed towards my office. Nate stuck his head out the window and let me know the computer program to find Reina's password was a bust. He also mentioned his garbage disposal was jammed and I needed to call the plumber.

I had six new messages on my machine so I hit play and let my greeting run its course. 'Hi, this is the Abel Kane Detective Agency. Sorry I missed your call. Please leave your name, call back number and a detailed message. I will respond as soon as possible.' The first message was a telemarketer as were calls two and four. The third call was from a young woman who had responded to the Facebook message Nate had privately sent to all Reina's online friends. She worked at the Verizon store and she and Reina had been friends. She was genuinely concerned about Reina but didn't have any information about her disappearance. I saved the message but she probably wouldn't be getting a call back. The fifth call was a real hit and I cursed myself for not being around to pick up. I played it over a second time.

'Hello. My name's Frank Garcia and my son Frank Jr., is dating Reina. After receiving your message I texted my son and he responded right away. He and Reina are on an extended vacation in Mexico so I don't think you have anything to worry about.' He went on to explain he was an Alaskan fishing guide and was never home from May through September. He and two clients were just about to board a bush plane and there was no way to reach him until he returned to Anchorage late Tuesday afternoon.

Well this was really big news indeed. I had no reason not to believe Frank Sr. but if I had been around to take the call I would have asked him if he had actually talked to Junior. Let's face it, a text is just a text. It could be sent by anyone with access to his phone. I decided it didn't change anything and I certainly wasn't going to give Harvey and Marta any false hope. I would keep working the case.

I called Nate.

"Did you call the plumber yet?"

"Of course," I said lying. "Question, how do I transfer landline calls to a cell phone?"

"Jesus Abel," he said with as much exasperation as he could conjure up, "someday you're going to have to climb out of the tar pits and join us in the modern world." He walked me through it and I'll be damned if it didn't work.

I was just about to head upstairs to my apartment when I remembered I hadn't played the last message. I hit play again. 'I was wondering if that was you.' That was the entire message. You get a lot of crank phone calls when you offer reward money but this one felt different. There was something about that voice that sounded eerily familiar. I played the message again and felt a chill crawl up the back of my neck. I hovered my finger over the delete button but I couldn't get myself to press it.

CHAPTER 12

(BACK TO THE PAST)

I was brought back to consciousness by the distinctive thumping sound of a helicopter landing. There were muffled voices outside and seconds later the door to our room flew off its hinges. The cavalry had arrived.

Hassam and I were airlifted to a hospital ship about five miles out at sea. Because there were so many injured and dying Marines being treated the only place they could put us was in a corridor across from the nurse's station. The medical staff stabilized us as well as they could with intravenous fluids and painkillers. Two days later we were again airlifted to the Naval Air Station at Catania, Sicily where we were kept under 24 hour monitoring. We were both in terrible shape and were told later the whole thing was very touch and go. Once we made it off the extremely critical list we underwent one final transfer to the Ramstein Air Base in Germany where we were hand delivered to the nearby Landstuhl Regional Medical Center, one of the finest in all the world. The Marines take care of their own.

I was pleased to hear that my fingernails would grow back. My broken teeth and jaw were a problem but not an insurmountable one according to my oral surgeon. Now for the bad news. The electrical shocks had done a number on my internal organs. I was going to lose my spleen and most likely one kidney. The massive internal bleeding I had experienced damaged my heart and only time would tell how well it would rehabilitate itself. My feet were the most problematic. They suffered horrific damage. Specialist after specialist was brought in to consult. The general consensus: There was a strong chance I would never walk again.

About a month into our stay at Landstuhl we received a visit from a young CIA agent by the name of Victor Ortiz. He arrived with information and it was the old good news and bad news deal except in this case it was fantastic and horrific. Harvey was alive, albeit in critical condition himself. He had been shot twice as he tried to make it to shore and then paddled out to sea once he realized it was futile. He floated along in the currents for two days until he was picked up by an Israeli fishing boat ten miles out at sea.

Ortiz then lowered his voice. "Hassam, I'm sorry to tell you this, but your Uncle Farhoud is dead."

Apparently on the same day of the BLT building attack a suicide bomber walked into the patisserie, shouted Insha Allah and then detonated a device. His uncle, all his employees and several customers were instantly killed. The anonymous caller who took credit for both attacks on behalf of Hezbollah also notified the authorities that there were two Marines in critical condition who could be found in a certain mountain chalet up in the Shouf. Why Mubari decided to keep us alive was a mystery I have never been able to solve.

Ortiz would return a few times each month and question us about our missions. He sought any information, regardless of how trivial, about Mubari and his two cohorts. He brought in a sketch artist and Hassam and I agreed we came up with an excellent composite of all three of them.

Weeks turned into months as the operations and treatments began to pile up. When we were in that hospital room at the same time Hassam and I would watch TV and talk. There was one particular discussion I'll never forget. We were watching some dreadful German soap opera when Hassam grabbed the remote and turned off the television.

"Hey, I was watching that," I said.

He ignored my complaint. "I'm going to share something with you Able and I want you to tell me if you think I'm insane."

"Yes. Oh sorry, you haven't shared yet."

"Clever Able, very clever. Anyways, when we were lying in that room up in the mountains I knew I was slipping away and I'd made my peace with dying."

Hassam paused but I couldn't think of anything to say so I waited for him to continue. "Then it was just how people described it. I saw the lit tunnel and knew exactly what it meant. I then felt a force assist me in leaving my body. Does that sound crazy to you?"

"Hassam," I said, "you're the most uncrazy person I've ever met so no it doesn't. I just don't know if what you experienced was real or just a hallucination."

"Fair enough," he nodded, "but that's not all. As I approached the end of tunnel my pathway was blocked."

"By what?"

"Not by what," he replied, "by whom. My entire family. There was such a feeling of love at that moment I cannot even describe it to you. They were telling me it wasn't my time and I needed to go back. That made me very sad but I guess you could say I acquiesced and then I felt that same force guiding me back to my body which now seemed like nothing more than an empty carapace."

"And you think that force was God don't you Hassam?"

"I know it was Able. I never expected him to come but he did anyways. So what do you think?"

"What I think doesn't really matter Hassam but I'll tell you something ironic. The whole time I was there I prayed to my God and fully expected him to come. But my God, he was a no show."

Hassam was recovering at a much quicker pace than myself

and one day as I was being wheeled back into our hospital room he was standing by his bed fully clothed and packing up his possessions. Victor Ortiz was by his side. "It's time for me to go Able. Victor has a lead on Mubari and I'm going to help track him down."

I didn't argue with him because I knew this was something he had to do. "Just be careful Hassam, please."

"I will Able. If you need me you can track me down through the American Embassy."

"OK," I said. It was all I could get out without getting emotional. As he headed out the door I said to him, "You are my brother and my friend. I will never forget you."

He stepped back into the room and wiped a tear from his cheek. "We have a saying in Arabic," he said. " a zamu hadiyyah fi alhayah hiya al-sadaqah, we laqad istalamtuha. It means...."

"Don't let the door hit you in the ass on the way out?" I said interrupting him. Humor, my old standby defense mechanism.

"No Able, it means the greatest gift of life is friendship and I have received it from you." He came over to my wheelchair to shake my hand. "I also will never forget you. I love you Able."

As he was leaving for good I yelled out one more time. "When you find him Hassam put a bullet in his head for me."

"Mine then yours Able. Mine then yours." Then he was gone and I cried like a baby.

CHAPTER 13

A lot of me was healing but my feet remained a serious problem. It wasn't just the feet however. My legs had atrophied to the point I could barely move them. Finally, after operation number four my orthopedic surgeon informed me they finally got it right.

"Now it is up to you to learn how to walk again," he announced then promptly turned tail out of the room.

I was introduced to a physical therapist by the name of Billy Connors. He was from Atlanta and had attended Georgia Tech University on a full football scholarship. He blew his knee out his sophomore year but stayed in school and graduated with a pre-med degree in three and one half years. He joined the Navy and signed on for an eight year hitch in exchange for a free medical school education. I would go on to call him my 'Black Angel.' He would call me a pussy, quitter and his absolute favorite, 'my little bitch.' Whatever it took to keep me motivated. For the first six days, using the support bars, I wasn't able to take one step. We would try and we would fail ten times a day. Between attempts he would rub my legs and take me into the gym pushing my lower body against the leg press.

"How's the pain level on a scale of one ten?" he would ask.

"A twelve Billy, damn that hurts."

"Good," he'd say, "if it was a two or three you'd be in serious trouble."

The whole thing started to feel like a Sisyphean task. Not only could I not get the rock up the hill, I couldn't get it to even budge. Finally on day seven the rock moved. I took one step and it felt like I had scaled Mt. Everest.

"Let's go celebrate Billy," I said, "beers are on me."

He scowled. "You want to celebrate after taking one damn step? Go celebrate by yourself," and he stomped out of the room. He would tell me much later that he was grinning from ear to ear.

One step on the bars became two, which became four. We eventually replaced the bars with a walker which would take me down the corridor of my hospital floor and back again. That was then exchanged for a cane and the corridor was replaced by the grounds around the hospital. I was beginning to move the rock up the hill. The first day I circumnavigated the entire property Billy was waiting for me at the elevator.

"Now it's time to celebrate Able. Beers are on me."

"Celebrate?" I said smiling, "over a walk around the hospital using a cane. Go celebrate yourself." I walked right by him and headed up to my room.

One day Harvey called. He was back at Pendleton recovering from his bullet wounds. His prognosis was a full recovery.

"Able," he said, "I've been trying to track you down for a month. How are you guys doing?"

I filled him in, leaving nothing out.

"Jesus, Able, I don't know what to say." He began to apologize but I stopped him short.

"Nothing you could have done LT. I know you tried." He gave me his contact information and we promised to keep in touch. He extended an open invitation to come to California anytime I wanted.

In another month the cane was gone. I was soon doing five mile walks two to three times a day. I was a man possessed. By my eighth month of rehab I started to jog. The day I stretched it out to ten miles I stopped at a Schnapsladen and bought a case of champagne. I invited Billy, my surgeons, the nurses, orderlies and all the people that were instrumental in bringing me back from the brink. I gave a toast of thanks then hugged each and every one of them. It was time to go. It had been nine months, one week and three days since I was gurneyed into this place teetering on death.

On the day of my release from Landstuhl I was told to report to the Marine personnel office 'at my convenience.' I found that interesting since nothing in Marine protocol was ever at anyone's convenience. As I was about to leave the entire medical staff surprised me with a chocolate cake and a going away present. A new pair of running shoes. There were a lot of tears and then I walked through the hospital doors a scarred but healthy man.The Marine personnel office at the giant Ramstein AFB is located in a Quonset hut at the northwest corner of the facility. I was greeted by a Captain Barker who escorted me into his office. "I've read about your experience Private Kane. That was a true FUBAR."

"Thank you sir," I think.

I was shocked by what came next. He, on behalf of the United States Marine Corps, offered me two options. I could transfer back to Lejeune where a desk job was waiting for me or I could take a compensatory honorable discharge 'with distinction.'

"Either way," Captain Barker said, "I'm proud to present you with this." He walked around his desk and pinned the Purple Heart on my uniform. I was speechless. He said I could take my time to decide but it wasn't necessary. It took about two hours to process the paperwork and when it was completed the captain handed me a check. He shook my hand and thanked me for my service. I walked out of his office with some money in one pocket and my discharge papers in the other. At the ripe old age of twenty-one I was a retired U.S. Marine.

CHAPTER 14

So what was next? That was the big question. Since I had nowhere to go I decided I'd go anywhere. I met Billy that night at a tavern in town and he brought along a buddy, an Air Force captain, who flew transports and cargo runs. Over a few beers I told him my story and my less than exact plan.

"Able, I'm making a run to Istanbul the day after tomorrow. I've got plenty of room if you want to hitch a ride."

"Instanbul?" I pondered, "sure, why not." And that was that.

I splurged and stayed at the Pera Palace where Agatha Christie had written Murder on the Orient Express. I spent my days sightseeing and walking the vast Grand Bazaar. I was planning my next move when I started up a conversation at the hotel bar with two retired Navy men. They were half way through sailing around the world and invited me along for as long as I wanted. Get on a boat with a couple of guys I've never met before? Sure why not.

The next day I climbed aboard their 52 foot ketch and we set off under the Galatin Bridge. From there it was across the Marmara Sea and through the Dardanelle Strait. I was following in the footsteps of Alexander the Great, Marco Polo and the millions of sailors that have set this course ever since man had learned to harness the wind.

We sailed around the Cyclades Islands in the Aegean, stopping occasionally and drinking frequently. I impressed them with my knowledge of the stars and they taught me how to celestial navigate using the sextant. They loved what they called sailor music and introduced me to the likes of Crosby, Stills & Nash, Loggins and Messina and Jimmy Buffett all the while drinking longnecks at a breakneck pace.

By the time we reached the top of the Aegean I had them drop me off in Venice. It was a lot of fun but my liver needed a break. I travelled the breadth of Italy by train and then headed to Paris where I spent over a month wandering its 'rues et ponts,' absolutely captivated by every nuance the City of Light had to offer. I took a side trip to Normandy and walked the beaches and the hedgerows where so much killing had occurred. As I awaited the train back to Paris I stood on the platform at Colleville-sur-Mer and stared out at the sea of white crosses that so dominate the landscape there. How many of these lives cut so short would have gone on to be the next Twain, Einstein or Churchill. We would never know. War truly is the greatest folly of them all.

When I returned to my hostel it had been invaded by a group of rambunctious Australians. We hit it off immediately and they hired me, pro bono, as their unofficial tour director. For seventy two hours I guided them through the city Ernest Hemingway had once described as a moveable feast and we did Paris in a way I'm sure even the sybaritic author would have applauded. When it was time for them to go, one of their group, a very pretty girl by the name of Rachel, asked me if I wanted to join them on the walk to Santiago de Compostela.

"What is that?" I asked.

She explained it was a centuries old pilgrimage from the French Pyrennes across the north of Spain to where the body of the apostle St. James is entombed. It covered 780 kilometers. A 500 mile walk to go see a famous dead guy? Sure why not. We hopped on a train to Bayonne and then bussed our way up to Saint Jean Pied de Port and off we went.

I was hoping the 'Camino de los Peregrino's' would reignite

my spiritual pilot light but it never happened. God and I were still on non-speaking terms. There was a seminal moment on the journey however. On day 20 in an alburgues just outside of the city of Leon I finally lost my virginity. I was asleep in a bottom bunk when Rachel slid under the covers next to me. When we were done I whispered to her that she was my first.

"I know," she said with a giggle. "I was your first but I can assure you, Abel Kane, I won't be your last."

"I hope your right and guess what?"

"What?"

"You are going to be my second." We rolled over and changed positions. She giggled again.

On our last night together I splurged for a suite at Santiago's finest hotel. We bathed together and dined like Galician royalty. The next morning Rachel and her friends were taking a train to Madrid to board a flight back to Sydney. I was headed for Barcelona and a flight to Dublin. We walked hand in hand to the station.

"Rachel," I said, "I think I'm in love with you."

She looked at me and smiled. "No you're not. All good boys think they're in love with their first. You're not in love with me Able. You're in love with the idea of love." We all have a lot to learn from the Australians.

We said our goodbyes and promised to keep in touch but of course we didn't. I still think of her though when anything 'down under' crosses my mind. She will always be my first. And my second for that matter.

CHAPTER 15

My next stop was Ireland because my mother had been an O'Rourke by birth and her family was from a town called Ballina in County Mayo. I vaguely remembered meeting a man by the name of Kevin when I was very young. Whether he was a brother, a cousin or just a friend I really didn't know but I intended to find out.

I never made it to Ballina. I experienced Dublin for several days and enjoyed it immensely. The people, the music and the Guiness all combined to create, as the Irish say, great craic. I did have one bad experience though. I took the tour of Kilmainham Gaol, the famous jail where the British imprisoned and executed the Irish revolutionaries of the 1916 Easter Uprising. As our guide led us through the claustrophobic hallways and cramped prison cells I had a horrific flashback to that chalet up in the Shouf. I recused myself from the rest of the tour and rushed outside to get some fresh air. I sat on a park bench for quite some time until I could compose myself enough to walk back to my hotel. It was a not so subtle reminder that although my body had healed my mind and spirit still had a long way to go.

I decided to hitchhike across the country and just outside a town called Tullamore a girl in an emerald green Renault pulled up beside me.

"Where you headed?" She had flaming red hair and she was cute. Real cute.

"Ballina."

"I can get you more than half way there. Hop in."

She stuck her hand out and we shook. "I'm Maggie."

"I'm Able"

"Like Cain and Able?"

"Actually, believe it or not, my name is Abel Kane."

"Oh Jesus, Mary and Joseph," she said laughing, "your parents must have had quite a sense of humor."

"Yeah, they were real comedians alright. You should hear what they called my twin brother."

"I'm dying to hear it. What?"

"Nova."

"Nova?"

"Yeah, you know, Nova Kane."

Maggie started really laughing this time and she honked her horn twice. I soon discovered this was her go to move whenever she found something was hilarious. She was in her final year of law school at the prestigious Trinity University in Dublin. Her family owned a pub in the market town of Tralee. She was on her way home to help prepare for the big St. Patrick's Day celebration. 'All hands on deck,' is what Maggie said her mother liked to say. She had a brother, Liam, who was heir to the family business and a father, Peter, who in addition to helping out in the pub was the caddy master at a golf links called Ballybunion.

I told Maggie about my recent adventures, omitting the bad stuff, and the reason I was headed to Ballina. We talked, we laughed and I got her to honk the horn a few times. She was wonderful and I was smitten.

"You don't have a cigarette do you Abel?"

"No, sorry, I don' smoke."

"Well then what good are you?"

"I did hear a funny joke the other day."

"Let's hear it then."

"Ok, there's this pub in Ireland....."

"Hold on," Maggie said interrupting me. "What's the name of the pub and what city is it in."

"Does it really matter?" I asked.

"Of course it does. I'm going to be an attorney. Details are everything."

"Fine then. There's a pub in Dublin City by the name of Flanagan's....... Happy?"

"Much better thank you. Please continue."

"Your welcome and I will. Well Flanagan's is famous for owning the longest bar in all of Ireland. You can enter from one street, walk down to the end of the bar and exit out on to another street. Are you with me?"

"Yes, brilliant so far."

"There's this patron," Maggie was just about to interrupt me but I beat her to the punch, "his name is Seamus and he asks the bartender for another pint of the good stuff. Well Seamus was a bit in his cups you might say so the bartender, Mr. Flanagan himself, says 'Seamus, you're cutoff. No more.' Seamus politely nods his head and gets up and leaves. He makes a left, another left and still another left and walks into the first pub he encounters."

"Flanagans!" Maggie shouts.

"Correct. A pint of Guiness Seamus says as he sits down. Well there's old Mr. Flanagan again and he tells him the same thing. 'I said you're cutoff Seamus.' So Seamus gets up and leaves. He makes a right, another right and still another right and walks into the first pub he sees. Mr. Flanagan's now waiting for him and says 'Really Seamus, are you daft?'
Seamus looks him in the eye and in a very somber tone says 'Ok, I'm leaving but first I have to ask you a question. Do you own every pub in Dublin?"

Honk, honk.

When we hit Galway City Maggie suggested we stop for a pint. She took me to a 400 year old establishment, The Quays Pub, located in the Latin Quarter of this wonderful, musical city.

"I have an incredible idea," Maggie said.

"I'm listening."

"Why don't you come down to Tralee for the St. Patrick's Day weekend? It'll be great craic and I'll drive you up to Ballina myself on my way back to Dublin."

Well the reasoning to go to Ballina in the first place was nothing more than a lark. A few more days delay in trying to find a long, lost relative seemed rather trivial. Plus the fact that Maggie had put her hand on my knee as she made the suggestion certainly streamlined the decision process.

"On behalf of my three split personalities, I accept your invitation."

"Split personalities?"

"Yeah. Ready, Willing and Able."

You guessed it. Honk, honk.

Just before we turned into her family's driveway Maggie pulled over to the side of the road and kissed me. "Well we got that out of the way now didn't we?"

I kissed her back. "Yes we did."

The Vales lived in a nice Georgian style home directly adjacent to the family pub. Behind the house was a small guesthouse that had seen better days.

"It's got a working shower and a proper loo," she announced when she saw the look on my face.

I was introduced to her family who looked at Maggie like she'd brought home a feral cat. Really Maggie, now? I threw my duffel into the guesthouse and asked her father Peter how I could help. He put me to work painting, landscaping and hauling trash. On the day before the big celebration they overloaded the electrical circuits and blew out the panel. There was a great panic because their electrician was away on holiday. I took a look at it and told Peter I could repair it. We drove together to the trade supply and I told him exactly what I needed. Three hours later I had them up and running again and I felt like a stray cat no longer.

St. Patrick's Day was one for the ages. I had no idea of the population of Tralee at the time but it seemed like every man, woman and child participated in the celebration at Vales that day. For the kids there were clowns, balloon makers and a petting zoo right on the front lawn of the house. A band of local renown called the Celtic Lords played all day under an unusually warm, cloudless sky while the empty barrels of Guiness, Harp's and Smithwick's began piling up pyramid style behind the pub. The traditional meal of corned beef and cabbage was served buffet style and we couldn't replace the food trays fast enough. I spent my day frantically bussing tables and washing dishes but I never seemed to get ahead of the curve. It was exhausting but a lot of fun. Nobody parties like the Irish.

When the sun went down the music moved inside. Local musicians would come and go and I marveled at their ability to show up in the middle of a set and seamlessly join in. Near the end of the evening the musicians gave way to the Vale family. With Margaret on piano, Liam on the uileann pipes, Maggie on the fiddle and Peter on vocals and guitar they played a broad set of music that ranged from traditional Irish to the likes of Van Morrison and Bob Dylan. They were an extremely tight quartet and Peter's sonorous voice floated across the room quieting the raucous crowd. Their set ended just before midnight with the singing of The Fields of Athenry, an Irish song about social injustice at the hands of the British. A song yes but it was really more of an anthem to these people. As Peter belted out the opening stanza, 'By a lonely prison wall,' the entire crowd linked arms and sang together in melodious harmony. It made me so proud that I was tied to such a magical land through the blood of my mother, may God rest her soul. That would have been the highlight of my night except for the fact Maggie snuck into the guesthouse and played with my instrument. Everything was second fiddle after that.

The next morning after a full Irish breakfast Peter offered me two jobs. He was eager to renovate the guesthouse and had neither the time nor the inclination to do it himself. Additionally, the busy season at the golf links was rapidly approaching and he was desperately short of caddies. With Maggie beaming across the table from me I impetuously accepted. We agreed that I would work Monday through Wednesday on the guesthouse and Thursday through Sunday up at golf course where the golfing tourists would soon be arriving en masse.

The guesthouse needed a lot of work. A new slate roof, completely new plumbing and electrical and a total renovation of the kitchen and bath. For this work we agreed on a wage, free room and board and the keys to a 1972 VW van that ran most of the time.

The men in the caddy shack accepted me as one of their own and taught me the basics along with the three tenants of the job. Show up, keep up and shut up. I really enjoyed my time looping and found out I was pretty good at it. I ended up having an uncanny ability to read the breaks and speeds of the greens which made me a favorite amongst many of the low handicappers.

While I was at Ballybunion I befriended a promising, young golfer by the name of Sean Maher. He hit it long and straight off the tee and complemented that strength with an excellent short game. He played the game without fear and never bridled in the face of pressure. I was learning the game and we played many late evening rounds together on the old course talking about futures and pasts. I caddied for him in amateur events all over Ireland and we had our share of successes. He earned his European Tour Card late that summer and he asked me if I'd consider taking his bag on a permanent basis. I was honored and thanked him effusively. I declined.

Maggie had met another third year law student months ago and had fallen in love. The guesthouse was finished and as one of my wise, aged fellow caddies said, 'I'm tired of living in an impecunious state.' The quick visit to Tralee for a St.

Patrick's Day weekend had now lasted over six months. It was time to go to Ballina and see if I could find a man by the name of Kevin O'Rourke. So as Sean headed off to his golf career I headed back to the Vales to pack up my things.

But first, a side story. Years later I was reading the sports page and noticed Sean was going to play in the Los Angeles Open at Riviera that week. It would be his first ever appearance at the tournament and by then he was a world top twenty player with sixteen victories including two major championships. His tee time on Thursday was mid-morning so I decided I'd go see him play. Riviera is a fantastic golf course. An absolutely brilliant design and it possessed the best opening shot in golf. When he arrived to the first tee the gallery was four deep but I was still able to catch a glimpse of him blistering the ball down the middle of the fairway and off he went.

As he and his fellow playing partners headed out into the heart of the golf course the crowds began to thin. On the 11th hole, a long par 5, I headed down the right side of the fairway ahead of the players teeing off. He hit his ball high with too much fade and it came to rest not five feet away from me. As he walked down the fairway I could see him slapping his golf glove against his thigh. I smiled. He did that as a young player when he was upset at himself. His caddy arrived first, set the bag down near the ball and walked off to check yardages.

"Still having trouble with that high block are you Sean?"

He looked over at me, thought about saying something but wisely decided against it.

"I remember that was your miss back when we played Ballybunion together. Stay down through it kid." I said smiling.

Sean looked at me again and the light clicked on.

"I'll be damned. Abel Kane."

He walked over to the ropes and gave me a bear hug literally lifting me off the ground.

"Guess I should have taken you up on that offer huh Sean."

He laughed.

"I'm so proud of you," I said sincerely, "but I'm not surprised. Not one bit."

"How are you Able?" Sean knew of my past. The question was heartfelt.

"I'm great Sean, thanks for asking." It dawned on me as I answered him that I actually meant it, maybe for the first time in my life.

His caddy was curious about what was going on and ambled on over.

"Paddy," Sean said, "this is the guy I was telling you about. Meet Able Kane."

We shook hands and Sean and I tentatively agreed to meet for a drink at the barrel shaped Holiday Inn at Sunset and the 405. He showed up. We sat at the bar and ordered pints of Guinness. The bartender filled the glasses on one pull and we shook our heads. To make a pour like that in Ireland would be considered a crime against humanity.

"Guinness just tastes different over here Able," he said taking a swallow.

It's true," I said. "I actually looked that up and it's a proven fact. The good stuff just doesn't travel well."

He caught me up on his life and showed me a picture of

his beautiful wife and three young daughters all of whom wore the map of Ireland on their faces. "Leaving them to go play golf gets harder and harder every year Able. In my wildest of imaginations I never would have dreamed I'd have this kind of money. I'm considering cutting way back."

He went on to regale me with hysterical stories about life on tour and he had me doubled over in laughter. We had a second pint but not a third.

"This game is hard enough to play with a clear head much less hungover," he opined.

We headed out to the parking lot and I walked him over to his courtesy car. We said our goodbyes and as Sean climbed into the driver's seat he said, "Abel, I have worked with a lot of people in my career but you were hands down the best caddy I've ever had. I really mean it. Nobody could read greens like you. How'd you do it?"

"You know Sean, I always felt the break in my feet," and I showed him how I used to flex my knees twice to anchor them to the ground. "The eyes could deceive but my feet never lied."

His face scrunched up as he considered this new revelation. He nodded, smiled and then was gone.

That Sunday I got home from working a case just in time to catch the end of the tournament on television. Sean and another player were tied after 72 holes and involved in a playoff. After his opponent tapped in for par, Sean rolled in a fifteen foot downhiller for a birdie and the win. After shaking the other player's hand he found the active TV camera, pointed to it and then flexed his knees twice. Thanks, Sean, you are the best.

CHAPTER 16

The next day as the Vales were heading to Dublin for Maggie's graduation I handed them a present for her. It was a brown, leather briefcase embossed with her initials. I followed them out of the driveway and when we hit the Galway roundabout I gave them a final wave as they headed east towards Dublin and I continued north to the town of Ballina. I drove through a lashing rainstorm that had barreled down from the North Sea. Luckily the van kept chugging along and I made it to Ballina by early afternoon.

At the time I really had no idea how to go about locating someone. This was before the days of the internet and Google when a click of a button tells you everything about everybody. My first stop was to the local garda station, a three story affair painted the color of egg yoke. I walked through the front door soaking wet.

"Whoa there laddy," the officer at the front desk said, "don't be getting my floor all wet now."

If you were looking to cast an aging Irish cop character in a movie then look no further. Silver haired and ruddy faced, he was right out of central casting. I took off my coat, hung it on the rack and wiped my feet off on the mat.

"Much better. Now what can I do for you?"

I briefly explained my situation.

"Aw, Christ on a bike. Another Yankee coming home to dig up his Irish roots."

He made me laugh. "Something like that."

"Well I don't personally know a Kevin O' Rourke but that doesn't mean he doesn't exist. Let's take a look shall we?" He punched a few keys on a Commodore 64 computer. "Well good news and bad news. Which would you like first?"

"Let's go with the good."

"Alright then. Your Mr. O'Rourke is neither missing nor wanted by the Garda. The bad news is I can't help you."

"Any suggestions?"

Between bites of a pastry he gave me a couple of ideas.

"Thank you Sargent…..?"

"Kelly, my name is Kelly."

Sargent Kelly, coming to a theatre near you.

My next stop was to the local post office. Officer Kelly suggested my long, lost relative just might have a post office box.

"Ask for Sylvia," he said, "and tell her I sent you meself."

The rain was finally beginning to yield so I decided to walk. It was a beautiful town with the River Moy flowing right though it's center. The fishermen had their poles in the water now trying to nab a salmon or two as the fish raced upstream. I crossed over an arched, stone bridge and found the post office right where it was supposed to be. It was deserted except for Sylvia and myself. She was a kind, genteel woman who wore thick lensed glasses and a yellow sweater buttoned only at the top.

"So the old goat sent you down here did he?"

"I'm afraid so Sylvia," I said, "can you help me?"

"You seem like a nice enough boy. Let's see what we can find out."

She pulled out a dusty, six inch thick file of box receipts that were in amazingly precise chronological order. I got the idea things didn't change much in Ballina. It took her twenty minutes to go through each and every receipt dating back ten years. Nothing. No Kevin O'Rourke. I thanked her for her time and checked into the cheapest hotel I could find. My wallet was getting thin.

After coaxing a hot shower out of the hotel's antiquated plumbing I opened up the local phone book to the O's. There were five O'Rourke's including a K. O'Rourke which piqued my interest. I dialed that number first. He wasn't my guy. His name was Kiernan and he was thirty three years old. He also informed me that two of the other O'Rourke's in the book were his mother and sister. He had never heard of a Kevin. I thanked him and crossed the three names off my list. One of the other two numbers was disconnected. I left a message on the last phone number leaving my name and the number of the hotel. The voice on the recorder sounded elderly. Her name was Anne.

What next? If there's one thing I've learned during my time in Ireland is that if you're looking for free flowing information head down to the local pub. There were fifteen in town and I visited them all. On a Thursday night, my third night in Ballina, I talked to a couple of old salts in a pub named Raffertys. They vaguely remembered a Kevin O'Rourke who lived out beyond the Belleek Castle but it was many years ago. They weren't really sure. That priceless bit of information had cost me two rounds of whiskey. It was getting late so I headed back to my hotel. The night clerk handed me a note as I climbed the stairs to my room. It was from Anne. She did not know a Kevin O'Rourke but wished me all the best in my search.

I went to bed despondent. The unsuccessful search for the mystical Kevin O'Rourke didn't really bother me. It had always been a longshot at best. It was the 'what next' question that was hanging over my head now like Damocle's sword. The travelling had been fun but I was quickly growing tired of my nomadic existence. My money was about gone and I wanted to head for a home that no longer existed. I could sell the van and travel for another month or so but then I'd be having the same conversation with myself in another hotel room in another country. At this moment I was living proof of the old adage that there are no atheists in foxholes. I prayed to my ambivalent and baffling God hoping to reopen the lines of communication. I continued to do so until I fell into a fitful, dreamless sleep.

The next morning I woke up to the sounds of commercial activity on the streets of Ballina. I looked out my window and saw moving vans delivering office equipment to the bank building across the street. Time to get up I guess.

I wandered down to the lobby to get something to eat. The breakfast buffet looked extremely uninspiring but I cobbled together a meal of cereal, white toast and fruit cocktail out of the can. I sat at a small table next to the window and watched the men work. There was a ramp connected to the back of the truck and they were walking furniture dollies up and down it retrieving boxes of new computers and printers. My attention finally drifted to the side of the van and I couldn't believe my eyes.

KEVIN O'ROURKE TRUCKICOMPANY

You're Logistics partner for today, tomorrow and into the future

SLIGO, COUNTY MAYO

There was a phone number on the very bottom. I committed it to memory and hurried upstairs to make the call.

"Good morning, O'Rourke Trucking, how can I help you?"

I took a deep breath. "Is Kevin O'Rourke available?"

"Yes he is. Can I ask who is calling?"

My heart raced. "Well believe it or not, I think I'm his nephew from the United States."

"Aah, lovely then," she said, "please hold."

I was put on hold for no more than a minute but it felt like an eternity.

"He's in a meeting right now but wants to know if you're Able or Jonah."

I was speechless and sat down on the bed to catch my breath.

"Well, which is it?" she asked.

"It's Able. I'm Able."

"I'm sure you are boyo," she said laughing at her own joke. "Well, where are you calling from?"

I told her and she put me on hold again. This time it was very quick.

"Kevin says, and I quote, get your ass over here ASAP."

"On my way," I said and I packed up my meager belongings and headed to Sligo and family.

CHAPTER 17

The Kevin O'Rourke Trucking Company was a pretty big operation. I counted 15 loading docks and they all had trucks backed up against them. I parked in a 'visitors only' spot and walked into the office. There were a dozen or more women working in the large, open room. The phones were ringing and the faxes were coming in. It was a bustling affair. All activity stopped when they noticed me standing at the counter. An attractive woman in her mid-forties got up from a desk and came over to me.

"Hello," I said, "I'm......"

She leaned over the counter and gave me a hug. "I know who you are Able Kane. The family resemblance is uncanny. I'm Shannon. We talked on the phone earlier." She linked her arm in mine and said aloud to the entire office, "Girls, looks like Kevin's been holding out on us. This hunk of a man is his nephew from America, Able Kane."

Most of them said hello. There were a few giggles also. I shyly raised my hand and said hello back.

"Come now," Shannon said, "someone is very excited to see you."

We walked down a long corridor to a door that said 'Boss Man' and Shannon pushed through without knocking. "Kevin," she said, "look what the cat dragged in."

My uncle came around from his desk and gave me a hug. "Able, I can't believe it's you. I thought I'd never see you or your brother again."

Shannon was right. There was a strong family resemblance. I had obviously inherited my mother's genes.

"Able," Shannon asked, "can I get you some tea?"

"I don't want to impose. I'm fine thanks."

"Nonsense, tea it is then."

"I'll have some too babe," Kevin said to her.

"You'll get your own you smarmy bastard," but she said it with a wink. "I'll be back. I need to throw some water over the girls out there. You're bad for business Able."

My uncle and I stood there looking at each other and then we both broke out laughing.

"Like looking in an old mirror," he said. "Come over and sit, I want to show you something."

He grabbed a pewter framed picture off the corner of his desk and handed it to me. "Do you remember this?"

I did, well kind of. It was a picture of Jonah and myself when we were very young. Identical twins in matching St. Louis Cardinal hats and t-shirts. The photo had been taken inside of Busch Stadium with our backs to the field. I was surprised and mildly confused how a copy of the photo had landed on my uncle's desk.

"How in the world do you have a copy of this picture?"

"Because I was the one who took it."

"You were there with my dad and us?"

"Your dad?" Uncle Kevin said and then I noticed him do a quick recalculation. "Yes, I was."

I nodded, letting it go. "I really don't remember ever meeting you."

"Well," he sighed, "you guys were very young and it was shortly after your mom died. There was a lot going on."

"Wait! You were at my mother's funeral?"

"I was. I gave one of the eulogies at the graveside. Your mother and I were extremely close until circumstances took us away from each other."

At that point Shannon came in with a tray of tea and biscuits. She steered the conversation towards me. I told them about my unsettled, peripatetic life growing up and my subsequent escape into the Marines. I told them about Beirut but only skimming over the days up in the Shouf. From there I continued on about my rehabilitation, my travels through Europe and finally my time with the Vales. When I finished talking Shannon and Kevin looked at each other not saying a word. She dabbed her eyes with a tissue.

"I'm sorry," I said, "I didn't mean to upset you."

She got up from her chair, came over and gave me a big hug. "Come on, let's get you home and put some meat on those bones."

They lived on a horse farm outside of Sligo on the shores of Lough Gill. This was the land of William Butler Yeats my uncle explained to me. The poet laureate drew much of his inspiration from the lough and the beautiful rolling hills that encircled the crystal clear waters.

Shannon made a dinner fit for kings and then Kevin walked me down to the barn and stables area.

"Impressive," I remarked as we walked down the gravel road to the facilities.

"Thanks," he said, "I call it my passion. Shannon calls it my addiction."

We entered the stables through the tack room and the combined odors of hay and manure were heavy in the air. Kevin explained there were thirty stalls, fifteen on each side which led out to a paddock, track and indoor jumping facility. We ambled over to one of the stalls and he started to stroke the mane of a beautiful, light gray stallion. He slipped him an apple that he had stashed in his coat pocket.

"This big fella is a draughter," Kevin said. "The draught horse is Ireland's national horse. They were originally bred for farm use and some are still used for that to this day. These guys are real workers. We cross them with thoroughbreds and produce what is now known as the Irish sports horse. We've been lucky enough to have great champions all over the world."

"This doesn't come cheap does it Uncle Kevin?"

He laughed. "No it doesn't Able. In fact there's an old joke amongst breeders that goes like this. How do you become a millionaire in the horse business?"

"I don't know?" I replied.

"You start with two million." Funny.

As we walked back up to the house I asked him how he'd become so successful. He told me his story and it was a good one. After he completed his secondary education it became obvious the university level was not in the cards. He moved to Dublin, slept on a mate's couch and went about looking for a job. There weren't a lot of options but he got on as a lorry driver for a food distribution company. The hourly rate was low but the work was steady. He was given the route none of the other drivers wanted; namely the northwest counties which included Donegal, Mayo, Leitrim and Fermanagh. The customer base was often difficult to reach and the drive back and forth from Dublin was long and time consuming. He drove that route for eight years and was the sole lifeline of product to the pubs, restaurants and food stores that carried his company's wares. The customers constantly groused to him about the infrequent deliveries and the lack of choices that were made available. The vendors also complained about a market that wasn't properly being exploited. He sensed an opportunity. By concentrating on this overlooked region there just might be the possibility for success. He cashed out his entire life savings, purchased a lorry and decided to set out on his own. His instincts were correct.

"I almost went bankrupt four times," he said. "Cash flow was a problem for years but between my customers and my vendors, we made it. We built the warehouse ten years ago and it was at that time I met Shannon. Besides falling head over heels for her she squared away the business end of things. Bank financing, receivables collection, payables, all the things I was terrible at. Not to say things are ever easy but we're proud of what we've built."

Later that evening we sat in his study next to a fire Shannon had started for us before saying good night. My uncle pulled out what he called the 'special occasion' bottle, a thirty year old Middleton whiskey. He poured three fingers each into crystal glasses.

"Slainte," he said and we raised our glasses. The whiskey had a smooth, smoky taste and it warmed my entire body after one sip.

"I'm so glad this happened Uncle Kevin," I said.

"Me too, laddy, me too."

We stared into the fire for a few moments watching the flames rise and fall then I asked him about my mother. It wasn't a casual question. My memories of her were opaque at best and my father and grandparents made it succinctly clear they didn't want to talk about her, ever. Our questions about her would be rebuffed by generic answers such as 'she loved you very much,' or 'the past is the past and is best left alone.' We didn't even have a pictures of her around the house. She had been successfully erased from our family history. As Jonah and I grew older we stopped asking but the mystery surrounding her remained unsolved. I've felt like a bastard child for as long as I can remember.

Uncle Kevin rose from his chair and grabbed a picture from the mantle above the fireplace. "This is your mother," he said, "this is our Mary."

It was a photo of a pretty, young girl with brown, curly hair tumbling away from her church veil. She was standing ramrod straight with her hands pressed firmly together. There was a rosary hooked around her pointer fingers that dangled down between her palms. She had the look of someone who took her sacraments very seriously.

"Your mother was my one and only sibling," he explained. "Even though she was three years older than me we were very close. I was a shy child and I had a heck of a time making friends. For years she was all I had."

He briefly described his early years. Born and raised in Cork City to a vagarious alcoholic father and an indifferent mother who's alleged, promising singing career was cut short by children she never wanted.

Kevin refilled our glasses. Just a finger this time. He leaned his head back and sighed before continuing. "When I was twelve years old my mother told me she and Mary were moving away. I asked to where and she said Philadelphia. I was informed I'd be staying in Ireland with my father. That was the end of the discussion. As she headed upstairs to pack Mary and I went down to the creek behind our house. There was a small cave there and it was our secret hiding place. I cried on her shoulder for hours. She tried to reassure me that everything would be alright but I was inconsolable. They left the next day. Ultimately it probably ended up being a good thing for me. It forced me to grow up quickly and I had to learn to take care of myself. At the time, however, the whole thing felt like a death sentence."

"So my mother's parents got divorced?"

"No. Back then, hell even today, you don't get divorced in Ireland. You either stay together in a miserable fashion or you emigrate and pretend the whole thing never happened."

I started peppering him more questions but he stopped me short. He walked over to his desk and pulled an old shoebox out of the lower, right drawer.

"I know you want to know everything about your mother and God knows Able you've more than earned the right. So I think it's best we let her tell you herself."

He handed me the opened shoebox and it was crammed full of letters in a multitude of colors and sizes. They were secured and separated by rubber bands that I'd soon find out represented individual years of correspondence.

"These are all the letters your mother wrote to me over the years. You'll find a lot of your answers in there." He paused for a moment trying to choose his words carefully. "Able, I'm a big believer in letting a sleeping dog lie but if you want to wake him up that's your choice."

Kevin gave my shoulder a reassuring squeeze and said he'd see me in the morning. He headed upstairs to be with his wife leaving me alone with a box that felt like it belonged more to Pandora than it did to me. I stared at it for a few moments thinking about dogs that can't bite if they're not awake. Then I sat down at the desk and took off the first rubber band and started reading.

CHAPTER 18

My mother wrote to Uncle Kevin quite frequently in the beginning. Her first person narrative described a lonely, homesick teenage girl who missed her brother and friends. She described Philadelphia as hot, humid, and dirty with a metallic odor in the air that never went away. She was now sharing a room with a distant cousin who did not appreciate the intrusion. 'Our mother's attitude,' she informed Kevin, 'had not changed with the change of scenery.' I noticed as I read along that my mother had impeccable cursive form and a very strong, economic writing style.

The letters slowly started sounding more optimistic. School had begun and she met some 'wonderful' friends who collectively called themselves the Four Musketeers. She was accepted on to the school newspaper and the yearbook committee which ignited her passion for the written word. There were football games and fifth quarter dances as well as infatuations and the heartbreaks that inevitably followed. My mother would normally include a photograph of herself and I enjoyed watching her grow up from the desk in my uncle's study.

She became the editor of the school newspaper her senior year and earned a full scholarship to the journalism school at Villanova. She was thrilled to move out of her cousin's room and into the campus dormitories where she met a whole new group of friends from all over the country. Her horizons were broadening and she relished the opportunities that now presented themselves. She wrote for the Villanovan and often included story clippings along with the letters. Gone were the reports of homecoming courts and science fairs. The stories were bigger now and there was true gravitas beneath her by-line. She was writing about matters of social consciousness and even weightier subjects such as the Bay of Pigs, the Cold War and even a little known place called Vietnam. The furnace of my memories was being stoked as I began to remember this smiling woman with brown hair and long legs looking up at me from her photographs.

In her third year of college she was covering an anti-nuke protest on the steps of Independence Hall under the shadow of the Liberty Bell. 'I've met someone Kevin,' she said. As she described the man to her brother I realized my father, Isaac Kane, had now entered the picture. He was manning a booth, handing out anti-war literature and was willing to debate anyone that was up to the task. He was of course collecting money for the cause and my mother dropped a few dollars into the can and asked him for an interview. That was it. It was obvious from her letter that she had fallen hard for my ridiculously charismatic father. She never stood a chance. A few letters later included a photograph of the two of them arm in arm. I was surprised to see my father with shoulder length hair and mutton chop sideburns. It made no difference. They were such a handsome couple. The bundles of letters began to thin out now as time, space and circumstance separated her from her Irish past. Then, months later, came the lightning bolt. She didn't mince words. 'I'm pregnant Kevin. Everything with Isaac has changed along with the news. He says it's all my fault, that I tricked him and he expects me to terminate the pregnancy. I will not hear of it. We argue about it constantly. I haven't told Mother by the way, not that she would give a damn. I miss you terribly.'

It's not an easy thing to find out your father didn't want you. It saddened me of course, but even more so, it pissed me off and I relished the day I could tell him how I felt. Putting my emotions aside I picked up the next letter and kept plowing through.

Eight months would go by before the next letter arrived. I of course knew what happened next but it was so interesting to hear my mother's point of view. 'Kevin, I'm so sorry I haven't written you until now. A lot has transpired since I wrote you last. I am married. Isaac finally came to terms with being a father and he's made an honest woman out of me. (Ha-hah!). Congratulations, you are now the proud uncle of twin boys. We have named them Jonah and Able and they are the sum total of my life. I am so happy.' There was a photo of the two of us on our mother's lap. Our names were on our T-shirts. Jonah had his hand on the side of my face trying to push me away. Of course, I thought to myself grinning.

The good times were short lived. What few letters she wrote now evidenced a despondency about the life and the man she had chosen. She described their time together as a rootless existence with in-laws that were both demanding and unbending. Isaac and his father were pastors and spiritual leaders but they seemed more concerned about making money than they did saving souls. They looked down on her Catholicism and grew incensed when she questioned the moral implications of their actions. Isaac didn't make any time for his sons and the child rearing fell squarely on her shoulders. She was now hinting at finding a way out of the marriage.

The next letter wasn't written until our second birthday. There was a photograph enclosed showing Jonah and I blowing out two candles on a birthday cake. In the body of the letter she made an interesting observation. 'Kevin, I don't know how identical twins can be such different people. Jonah is so strong and self-assured and he takes whatever he wants as his own. He learned to walk and talk much earlier than his brother and seems to win stranger's affections with the ease of just a smile. He is really something. Able, on the other hand is such a quiet and gentle boy. I worry about him sometimes but then I see the intelligence behind those eyes of his and I know he'll be fine.

He will sit and observe for hours on end and I get the sense he is passing judgement on everything and everybody. It's like the two of them had agreed upon their individual roles in the womb and are now acting them out accordingly.'

The frequency of the letters picked up again as my mother's situation grew more dire. She had asked for a divorce and sole custody of my brother and myself but was denied both by a St. Louis court of law. She admittedly had moved into a serious state of depression. I picked out the last letter in the shoebox and my body convulsed with tears as I read the final paragraph. 'Kevin, I have lost on all fronts in my war with the Kanes. I have just received a letter from Isaac's attorney notifying me of his intention to have me declared clinically insane and sent away. They have high powered friends through our church and I don't doubt for a minute they will succeed. I am nothing without my two boys. I miss you and need you.'

The next morning my Uncle Kevin found me sitting in the same chair fast asleep. He gently shook me awake and informed me that breakfast was on the table. "Let's eat," he said, "and then I'm going to take you fishing and we'll talk."

We hitched his skiff up to the truck and headed for Lough Gill. The road to the lake was canopied by old growth rowan and oak trees while ivy broomrape and lady's mantle skirted its edges. The sun was ducking in and out of the cloud cover which made the water change colors from cobalt blue to metallic gray and back again. It was quite a breathtaking scene. As we passed a turnout called Dooney Rock Kevin told me what happened next.

"As soon as I read that last letter I picked up the phone. I always called after hearing from her and she normally had calmed down by then. Your mother was a bit mercurial that way. This time was different though and I knew we had to do something. He paused just long enough to point out a romp of otters playfully floating on their backs in a small cove near the road. "We hatched a rather desperate plan," he said. "I would fly to St. Louis and, for lack of a better term, we were going to kidnap you and your brother and bring you back to Ireland. There were a few problems to overcome however. First off, I didn't own a passport and your mother had let hers expire years earlier. Money was another issue. Neither one of us had any. The little I had was tied up in the new business and your father had complete control of your family's finances. A month would go by before my passport came through and I was able to borrow enough money to purchase all the plane tickets."

We turned right off of the main highway and headed down a serpentine road towards the boat ramp. He continued the story. "To avoid arousing suspicions, we both agreed it would be better to cease all communications from that point on. The plan was for me to show up at your school at 3:00 and park across the street. If your mother was wearing a green scarf I would pull up beside her and the three of you would hop into my rent-a-car and we'd head straight for the airport. A red scarf meant there was a problem and we would try the next day."

I was shocked to hear all of this but nothing about it sounded unbelievable. My father and grandparents had presented such an edited version of my youth I knew deep down they were always protecting themselves from something more insidious.

"What we didn't have a plan for was her not showing up at all," he explained. "Just after 3:00 o'clock I saw the two of you walk out of your classroom and up to the sidewalk. A few minutes later a white Cadillac pulled up and your father and grandparents got out of the car. Your mother had told me she always picked you up after school so I knew something had gone terribly wrong. As the two of you climbed into the back seat your father started scanning the street and then he pointed in my direction. Your grandparents drove you away and he crossed the street heading in my direction. I'm sure I don't have to tell you Able, your father has a presence about him you cannot easily forget."

My Uncle Kevin was right about that. About the time I became a teenager I began noticing it also. Whenever he'd walk into a room or make the short climb up into a pulpit the crowd, large or small, would be transfixed on my father. They were his for him to do whatever he pleased. It would prove to be both a blessing and a curse.

"Anyways, he came around to the passenger side of the car and without asking permission climbed into the front seat. 'You must be Kevin' he said and offered me his hand. 'I'm sorry to tell you our Mary is dead.' He then gave me directions to your house and we made the short drive in total silence."

We took a break to get the boat in the water. We filled it with poles, creels and a lunch that Shannon had made for us. Kevin started the engine and we headed out into the lake.

"If it helps at all," Kevin told me, "I really do believe your father was shaken by your mother's death. When we made it back to your house he told me his version. I'm sure you've learned by now Able that there are always three sides to any story. Her side, his side and somewhere in between, the truth. Mary, he said, had suffered deep bouts of depression to the point where she couldn't get out of bed sometimes for days on end. She took up drinking at an alarming pace and was, on occasion, abusive with you and your brother. Yes, he admitted, there was a divorce proceeding but it never went as far as the courts. He thought they had worked out their issues. He also confirmed he did have her committed to a facility but it was always meant to be temporary. I sensed real emotion as he defended his position. When he was done I didn't know what the hell to think."

"So did she or didn't she die accidentally?" I asked.

"She was found at the bottom of the sanitarium's pool early

in the morning by the groundskeeper just five days before I arrived in St. Louis. She was in bed at 'lights out' the night before which was at 10:30. Sometime between then and the next morning she must have snuck out of her room to go for a swim. The authorities had already eliminated any foul play. Your father must have sensed my doubts so he handed me a copy of the coroner's report. Cause of death, accidental drowning."

According to Kevin my grandparents wanted to have him arrested for attempted kidnapping but he countered with the threat of exposing all the alleged criminal activity that Mary had documented in her letters over the years. Both parties backed off.

"I guess you could say we reached a kind of détente," he said. "The rest I already told you about. I stayed for the funeral and then spent about a week with you and your brother. We went to the zoo, the aquarium and to the Cardinals game where I snapped that picture of the two of you. Your father wasn't there. He hated baseball."

He reached into his coat pocket and pulled out another letter. "When I got home this was waiting for me."

It was from my mother to Kevin and it was short and brief. She was saying goodbye.

'Dear Kevin.

I am afraid our plan has been discovered. Isaac intercepted the mail and found my passport. He pressured me into an explanation and I admitted everything. I was dragged into court again and this time the judge ordered me into a facility immediately. I wasn't even allowed to say goodbye to Able and Jonah. I've been here three days and it's terrible. My first electroshock therapy was yesterday and the pain was unbearable. I'm already starting to forget the simplest things and I'm scheduled for sessions every other day. I see no hope for myself. I was able to steal a bottle of sleeping pills from the dispensary and that seems like a nice, painless way to go. Please be there for my boys and tell them how much I loved them. Goodbye my sweet, kind brother.'

We trolled for fish around the many islands that dotted the lough. Somewhere down below us were salmon and sea trout that had made their way upriver from the Atlantic. They shared the depths with massive pike and bream but none of them seemed interested in what we had to offer. We returned to shore without a nibble.

"I'm afraid the waters were a bit cold and unsettled today," Kevin admitted.

That seemed appropriate since that was exactly how I was feeling.

"A penny for your thoughts?" Kevin asked me as we hitched the skiff back up.

"I'm ok I guess. It's terrible but you've given me the answers I've been searching for and to be honest, it was a long time ago."

As we headed back up the road to the main highway I realized that whatever grieving I did over my missing mother was behind me now. The grief had now been replaced with something even more powerful, anger.

"I cannot thank you enough," I said to my uncle, "and I'll tell you this, if I ever track my family down we're going to have a very serious conversation."

"Well, I might be able to help you out with that too Able," he said pulling another letter out of his coat pocket. "When I finally settled my emotions down I wrote your father a letter and included a copy of your mother's last correspondence. I knew I had him over a barrel and I warned him if he ever harmed you or your brother I'd blow his world up. I also demanded that he keep me updated about your lives and to his credit he did, over the years, send me the occasional note. I was astonished by how much you guys moved around but now I know why. Once my business started to take off I began sending money on your birthday with the explicit request to put it towards your college funds."

"Jonah and I never saw a dime of that," I informed him.

"I'm not surprised. Your father assured me that's exactly where it was going but as we both know, Isaac could sell ice to an Eskimo. Happy belated birthdays by the way."

I nodded and began reading. It was a simple thank you letter and he explained how well Jonah and I were doing. The generous check was going to come in handy as the boys college tuitions were becoming more than he could handle. It was just another lie from a master prevaricator. The letter was dated only nine months earlier and the return address was a city in California by the name of El Cajon. The addressor was Isaac Kane, Eureka Christian Community Church.

"I also got this for you," he said pulling something out of another pocket.

"Wow, Uncle Kevin, how many pockets do you have?"

We both laughed. "Keep that sense of humor Able. It will serve you well in life."

It was a first class ticket to San Diego. "Uncle Kevin, I can't afford this."

"I'm not asking for money."

"I promise I'll pay you back. I don't know when but I will."

"Tell you what," he said, "I've talked to Shannon about this and for some reason that girl just loves that old van of yours. I think maybe it puts her back in touch with her hippie youth. We'll take that old dog off your hands and call it even."

I mean how many times can you say thank you to someone.

The next morning was cold and rainy when Kevin drove me to the airport. The weather seemed to match our collective moods. To find him after so long and to leave so abruptly felt off kilter. He had reassured me last night that he understood but it didn't stop me from feeling terribly guilty. We got to my gate and he pulled over to the curb.

"Here, I want you to have these," he said. They were all the pictures of my mother including the framed photograph that had rested on the mantle.

"Uncle Kevin," I said, "I can't possibly take these." I tried handing them back but he wouldn't hear of it.

"You're searching for your place in life Able and I think these will help you get there. I'm fine now. My journey has ended and I'm exactly where I'm supposed to be."

"I really don't know what to say other than once again, thank you."

"That's more than plenty. I am so very proud of you Mr. Able Kane."

We hugged and he drove away. I realized he was the first person in my life that had ever uttered those words to me. The rain was coming in sideways now pelting me in the face. That was a good thing. Nobody would notice the tears rolling down my cheeks.

On the way to the airport I assured him I'd be back next summer with my brother in tow. I was so adamant about it that we got a bit excited and started making plans. The trip would never happen. In six months my Uncle Kevin would be gone. He suffered a massive heart attack sitting at his desk behind the door that said 'Boss Man.' He'd been signing payroll checks and when Shannon found him his head was resting on the desk, pen still in hand.

CHAPTER 19

Less than a year later Shannon sold both the business and the farm and walked away with enough money to live comfortably for the rest of her life. She explained to me over the phone that although she deeply loved them both, they were 'together things,' not 'alone things.' I understood completely.

The one thing she did not sell was the old VW van. "You've got to be kidding me. You held on to that piece of junk?" I asked.

"Don't talk ill of it Able Kane, it's very sensitive. We even gave it a name," she replied.

"Oh yeah, what did you call it?"

"The Barely-Drive-Able."

"That's hysterical," I said laughing, "does it still run?"

"Sometimes, when it feels like it."

She moved back to Kenmare, the village where she was born and raised until my uncle had swept her away. She eventually opened up a charming bed and breakfast. Over the years I had recommended it to friends that were heading her way and they, to a person, came back with nothing but rave reviews.

"It keeps me busy," she told me, "and stops me from thinking about things." I think she loved every minute of it.

We kept in contact and sent birthday and Christmas presents back and forth. Finally, on my fortieth birthday, I swept my life to the side and went to Ireland for a visit. I grabbed my luggage from the baggage claim and walked out to the curbside. I heard a horn honk and there she was, Shannon, behind the wheel of the Barely-Drive-Able.

"Want to take it for a spin?" she asked.

"Move over," I said and off we went.

She had taken up golf about five years earlier and had gotten proficient to the point of winning the woman's club championship at her home course in Kenmare. We headed out on a three week road trip traveling the edges of Ireland and played all the great links courses the island has to offer. We would play a different course every day and then gorge on extravagantly expensive meals in the evening. After dinner we'd walk the villages and follow the sounds of music until we located the source. It was all great craic. I had planned on saving Ballybunion for last and three days prior I had called Peter Vale to see if he could squeeze us in. He told us they were booked solid but to come on by and he'd see what he could do. As we pulled into the parking lot I was flooded with memories of my days here which of course opened the gates to everything else that had happened way back when.

Shannon noticed my far off stare and understood. "Are you ok Able?"

I gave her my best smile. "Yes. Let's go play some golf."

Two attendants grabbed our bags and notified us the only available time was in ten minutes. Shannon and I hurriedly put on our golf shoes and headed to the first tee. Waiting there for us were none other than Peter and Sean Maher. Peter, besides a bit of salt in the hair, hadn't changed a bit. He was ageless. Sean, true to his word, had cut way back on his appearances but not before adding another five victories to his total since the last time I'd seen him. He played in only about a dozen events a year now and was more than happy to ferry his children around to all of their activities.

I hit last and I sliced the ball out of bounds into the graveyard just to the right of the first fairway. It rattled around three hundred year old tombstones until it too came to its final resting place.

"You still having trouble with that high block Able?" Sean said with a huge grin. "That used to be your miss when we played together."

I stopped laughing just long enough to call 'mulligan' and then ripped the next one right down the middle of the fairway. It was such a magical day.

After saying goodbye to Sean we followed Peter back to Tralee for a great meal at the Vales. Shannon and I were exhausted but we stayed for the lively sing along that followed. We closed the place and then dragged our tired bodies to bed. Shannon stayed in Maggie's old room. Maggie, Peter said, was now a highly sought after defense attorney in London. She did marry that third year law student but it didn't last very long. He passed along her information and said she'd love to hear from me. I never called.

I slept, you guessed it, in the guesthouse where I can proudly say the lights worked, the water ran hot and the roof didn't leak.

The next morning Shannon drove me back to the airport and about one hundred feet from my gate the Barely-Drive-Able decided to take a break and coasted itself to the curb. We looked at each other and started laughing.

"Go," Shannon said, "You've got a flight to catch."

"You'll be ok?"

"Of course. He's just a little tired and maybe a little sad you're leaving."

We hugged and said our goodbyes. Sadly that would be the last time I saw Shannon. Two years later she would contract leukemia, the bad kind, and would slowly lose the battle of the blood cells. When we would talk on the phone she reassured me she was up to for fight but I really didn't believe her. The great thing about believing in God is the certainty of an after-life and Shannon's faith was stronger than most.

"There's a smarmy bastard waiting for me over there," she'd say, "and I've got a lot on my mind he's going to hear about."

One month before she passed I called her but hospice was on the job now and she couldn't get to the phone. They asked me if I wanted to leave a message. Yes, I did. Tell her to tell Kevin I said hello. A week after her death there was a knock on my apartment door. I opened it to a man holding a clipboard.

"Delivery for an Abel Kane."

"That's me," I said, looking past him for the package.

"Follow me please," he said.

We headed out to the street and there on a flatbed truck was the Barely-Drive-Able. He offloaded it and handed me the keys.

There was a note taped to the steering wheel. 'Dearest Able, he's all yours now. Be nice. Love, Shannon.'

I still have that damn thing. It lives in my garage and I take it out only when I don't know where I'm going and don't care when I get there. The back of the Barely-Drive-Able is full of ghosts but they're friendly and loving. There are moments when I play just the right music at just the right time, they'll join me for a bit of a sing along as we head on down the road.

CHAPTER 20

(BACK TO THE PRESENT)

Monday, June 19th

I just cannot buy a good night's sleep. But first let me digress. When I received my first sizeable bounty commission I was living in a studio apartment in North Hollywood. Everyday I'd go to bed and wake up to the steady drone of traffic on the 170 Freeway. There was a homeless guy that lived under the awning of our apartment building. His name was Larry and he smelled like a restaurant trash bin. On his few lucid days he would remind me he was once a chiropractor by trade and could help me with my bad back. On all the other less coherent days he'd scream, yell and hurl F-Bombs as you came and went from your ridiculously overpriced flat. He would occasionally have some of his peers drop by and on those days the sidewalk would be so cluttered with bodies and shopping carts that you'd have to use the emergency exit at the back of the building. At the same time I was growing weary of my 'trying to make it in Hollywood' neighborhood which I found to be full of self-absorbed, insecure egomaniacs. It was time to move.

I contacted a realtor and she showed me over a dozen homes all of which I ultimately rejected. She fired me as a client and accused me of being a 'tire-kicker.' Shortly after, an attorney who I'd done some P.I. work for told me about a small rental property he was putting up for sale in north Glendale. It had two office spaces on the ground floor and two one bed/one bath apartments above. There was a breezeway on the south side of the building that led to a small courtyard. Behind that was a garage which backs up to an alleyway and there is another two bedroom unit above that. It was more than I could afford but I figured the incoming rents would help cover the higher mortgage. I borrowed some money from Harvey for the additional down payment and the seller and I closed the deal with the property never hitting the market. I had found my home. The larger, street side office is currently rented to a young C.P.A. and I use the smaller space in the back for my business. Nate, the computer guy, rents one of the one bedroom apartments and I live in the unit above the garage. The other apartment is currently vacant. I've learned to be extremely patient and picky about who I bring in as a renter. As my wise attorney friend cautiously advised me, no tenant is better than a bad one.

So back to last night. My motion lights down in the courtyard went on and off three times. This happens fairly routinely on weekend nights when a few of the locals, on their way home from a night at the Cross, use my breezeway to gain access to the alley and the neighborhood beyond. But this was a Sunday and Brigid's place was closed. I do get some dogs and even the occasional coyote that wander through but I was pretty sure I set the sensors at a level where an animal that size wouldn't trigger the lights. Someone had definitely been in the courtyard but by the time I made it downstairs I was alone. It was well past 2:00 a.m. before I finally fell back asleep and now I'd have to fight through the tiredness because today was a big day for the Reina Montes case. It was Monday, a business day and I could investigate all the meager leads I had before heading back to Otto's this evening to put the sweat on Bump.

My first stop was going to be Cal State L.A. where, according to Marta, Reina was chasing a degree in business and pre-law. As I headed down the 2 freeway Harvey finally called me back.

"Hey OT, sorry about getting back to you so late. It's been a rough couple of days."

"How so?" I asked as I drifted over to the right lane to merge on to the Golden State freeway.

"People weren't very nice to each other the weekend."

"How many?"

"Fourteen by last count."

Harvey was referring to the homicide numbers. The City of Los Angeles averages about 275 murders a year so fourteen over a forty eight hour period was unusually high.

"Did you listen to my voicemail?" I asked him.

"I did. What are you thinking, drugs?"

I was off the 2 freeway now and joined the commuter traffic on its crawl into downtown.

"That seems to be the most obvious explanation but she just doesn't seem the type to me. Then the whole Saudi thing is strange."

"Yeah, I can't figure that one out either," Harvey replied.

I went on to tell him about my plan for the day and he couldn't think of anything else to add. He did say he was going to contact the State Department and request them to make a formal inquiry to the Saudi Arabian Consulate for some clarification on what was going on at Otto's yesterday. He'd call me as soon as he heard something. Before we hung up I asked him to patch me through to Victoria. He told me to be nice and then transferred the call. Victoria is Harvey's gate-keeper. She makes sure his busy days are handled as efficiently as possible and protects him from any unnecessary and time consuming contact which I think includes me. I do get access to her on occasion to acquire information through the LAPD's data banks but only if Harvey has given her the green light. If he hasn't that gate she guards becomes an impenetrable wall. Victoria has somehow through the years successfully resisted my charming personality. I know, I can't believe it either. She picked up on the first ring.

"Good morning sunshine," I said with my most cheerful voice.

"Save it Able. Harvey's informed me that I am here at your beck and call for whatever you need."

"My garage needs painting." It was worth a shot.

"Ugh. Do we have to do this today?"

I guess not.

I gave her the license plate and V.I.N. number off the Toyota Camry. It was missing and I wanted to see if it had been ticketed or towed into a police impound lot over the last couple of weeks. I also asked her for a list of all missing person cases for the last three months. I was looking for trends.

"That's going to be a big list Able and it's going to be filled with lots of columns, numbers and dashes. Are you sure you can handle it?" That was Victoria trying to make a joke. She was right though, the LAPD investigates about four thousand missing person's cases annually. That parcels out to about 350 a month.

"Good one Vicky." She hates it when I call her that. "Can you help me?"

"Yes. I'll email you the list and call you about the car after I've done a little research."

"Thank you."

"You're welcome."

Time for a little levity. If you can make the girl laugh she's yours.

"Hey Vicky what's the difference between a female track team and a.........................."

She hung up. I think she's coming around though.

The morning traffic was brutal and I put the onus on Cal Trans. I counted six half finished projects just between Glendale and Monterey Park alone. Why they don't finish one job before they start another is one of God's great mysteries. I finally made it over to the campus and found a spot next to the Biological Sciences department. From there I made the short walk up a hill to the seven story glass and concrete administration building. Admissions was on the first floor, Room 101.

There were three women sitting at desks behind the counter. Two of them were young and attractive and I assumed they were students working part-time. The third woman was elderly, a bit on the corpulent side of life and had, as they say, a face better suited for radio. She was wearing a scowl and I got the impression it had set up shop on her forehead permanently. With great effort she rose from her chair and ambled over to me trying to catch her breath.

"Hi there," I said pulling out my badge, "I'm Detective Donald Fagan. LAPD."

"What can I do for you detective?"

I told her about the case then gave her a copy of Reina's poster. She pulled out a registry from beneath the counter and asked to see my badge again. I held it out and she grabbed it out of my hand. That's never good. She wrote down the serial number in the first column then set it aside, just out of my reach.

"How do you spell Fagan?"

Great question. I gave it my best shot.

"I'll need to see some I.D. too please."

I made a dramatic search of my pockets and then put my hand on my forehead. "I must have left it in the car."

The scowl had returned and her radar was starting to ping.

"Listen....?"

"Becky."

"Pretty name," I said. "Becky, please don't make me go all the way back to the car and get it. I'm parked all the way at the other end of campus."

"Sorry detective, but we have to properly identify any law enforcement officer that is requesting information about one of our students."

What to do, what to do.

"Ok, I'll tell you what. Why don't I give you the number of my boss. His name is Captain Harvey Dwyer and he's the chief of detectives for the entire Robbery and Homicide division."

At this point the other two girls had made their way over to the counter and took turns looking at Reina's picture while Becky deliberated on my fate.

"OK, what's the number?" she asked.

I knew Harvey wouldn't pick up the call but his personal greeting would include his name, title and occupation. I figured that would be enough for Ms. Nosey Pants.

"His cell phone number is…"

"Sorry detective," she said cutting me off, "no cell phone. I need an office number and the person on the other line better greet me with the words Los Angeles Police Department or you're in big trouble."

This was deteriorating quickly. I had no choice but to give her Harvey's private office number which meant Victoria would be picking up the call. She was going to feed me to the lions.

Becky flashed a sinister grin. She had now put my badge below the counter where there was no chance I could grab it and run. She dialed the number and someone picked immediately. Of course I could only hear Becky's end of the conversation.

"Yes. Good morning to you too. Hello, my name is Becky Johnson and I'm with the admissions office at Cal State, LA. We have someone here claiming to be one of your detectives. He has a badge but no identification and he wants some information about one of our students who has apparently gone missing. He says his name is Donald Fagan."

Now a security guard rolled up in a golf cart as Becky listened to the person on the other end of the line. This wasn't good at all.

"Okay, one second," Becky answered. "She wants you to tell me her name."

"Whose name?"

"Captain Dwyer's, and I repeat verbatim, incredible office manager." She said unable to suppress a grin.

"Victoria Andersen." I said.

"Good answer," Becky said to me. "Victoria, would you describe him to me please?"

As Victoria was describing me Becky would nod her head and say 'right, right,' then all of a sudden she burst out laughing.

She leaned over the counter to get a closer look at me. "Oh my God, you're right. That's hysterical."

Wait, what's hysterical?

"Ok, thanks Victoria. Sure, he's right here." She handed me the phone.

"Hello Victoria," I said.

"Really, you went with the Steely Dan reference?" This woman was full of surprises.

"Yeah," I said, "I guess I did."

Becky, at this point had waived the security guard away and whispered something in the younger girls' ears. They started laughing also.

"This is the greatest day ever," Victoria said to me before she hung up. "You owe me big time." I don't think she'll be painting my garage anytime soon.

Becky and the girls invited me back into their inner sanctum and they fired up the computer. Seconds later I was looking at Reina Montes' academic history. Becky walked me through it as the scowl returned home again.

"Looks like she had enough credits to be considered a junior but look at this," Becky said pointing to a series of capital I's for the recently completed spring term. I took a look. Reina had a history of being a solid A and B student but had received nothing but incompletes on her last transcript. It was disconcerting but it jived with everything else I was finding out about her. She had done a complete 180 degree turn on her life prior to disappearing.

Becky printed out the records and helped me with directions to where I wanted to go next. As I headed out the door with my newly acquired self-consciousness I couldn't help but notice the three of them were still giggling.

I was heading for the School of Business and Economics where the bulk of Reina's incomplete classes had been held. Two of those classes, Business Law and an elective called The History of U.S. Financial Crises were taught by the same professor, a Dr. Peter Evans. I figured he'd be a good starting point. What probably would have been about a ten minute walk took me almost twenty as I stopped to stick her poster on any support column or kiosk that crossed my path.

The building itself was one of the newer ones on campus with lots of stamped concrete and shiny stainless steel. Inside the main foyer, directly to my left, was a glass enclosed directory in alphabetical order. I quickly scanned it and rode the elevator up to the third floor. I caught a break. The door to Room 307 was ajar and a tall, willowy gentleman with silver hair was staring earnestly at his computer.

"Do you have a minute?" I asked as I stuck my head in the door.

He looked up and smiled. "Sure come on in. Take a load off."

There was the faint but undeniable smell of stale cigarette

smoke hanging in the air. The window behind him was open, the screen had been removed and a pack of American Spirit cigarettes lay front and center on his desk. He made no attempt to squirrel it away as I sat down in front of him. Tenure is a wonderful thing. I already had a stressful day playing the role of Detective Donald Fagan so I decided to go with the direct and honest approach. I handed him a copy of Reina's poster and explained my role in the investigation.

"Do you remember her?" I asked. "She had two classes with you last term."

"Ms. Montes? Of course I do. A wonderful young lady," he said without taking his eyes off of her picture. "I've been worried about her."

"Why do you say that?"

"Because she was a good, hard working student who just stopped coming to classes. I had no choice but to give her incompletes in both. Let me check something." He tapped away on his keyboard then continued. "Yes, just what I thought. She had solid A's in both subjects before quitting. I find that type of behavior quite disconcerting so I called her about it. I tried three or four times but she never picked up."

"Calling your students, is that a normal thing for a professor to do?" I asked.

"It is for me," he said without taking any visible offense to my question. "I give my cell phone out to all my students and I encourage them to reciprocate. It keeps the lines of communication going and helps limit any misunderstandings about what is expected."

"Did you convey your concerns to the authorities?"

"It didn't get that far. I finally received a text from her letting me know she was fine. She wrote that she'd decided to take time off from school and would be back in the fall. I wished her the best and she replied back with a thumbs up and a happy face. I felt she was making a big mistake but I didn't pursue it any further. She's an adult and it was her decision to make."

"When was that?"

"It would have been after she skipped mid-terms so I'd say late April, early May."

"Do you still have the text?"

"No, sorry. I generally delete them as I go."

I was about to ask another question but I noticed him staring at the pack of cigarettes with a bit of tobacco lust in his eyes.

"Go ahead. You won't be bothering me."

"You sure?" he asked and I nodded. "Thanks, I'm trying to keep it to four a day but I'm failing miserably."

He pulled a cheap, disposable lighter out of his desk drawer and lit up. He took a deep, protracted inhale and blew the smoke out the open window. He then placed the cigarette on the sill and I watched the smoke float up towards the fourth floor.

"What else can you tell me about her?"

"Not much unfortunately. I make it a point not to cross that social line with my students. Like I said earlier, she was smart and worked hard. She wasn't what I would call a naturally gifted student which made her performance all the more impressive. In my opinion, Reina, like the majority of my students that pass through my classes, was here to punch her ticket and move on to the next thing in life. What that would be is anybody's guess."

"Is there anyone who comes to mind that might be able to help me?"

He turned around in his chair, grabbed the cigarette and took another deep pull. He closed his eyes briefly in something akin to orgasmic relief. "I think I do. Her name's Helen Woodruff. She and Ms. Montes have partnered up on group projects for several years now. If anyone can provide you with some insight it will probably be Helen."

"How can I get a hold of her?"

"Like this." He pulled out his cell phone and scrolled through his contacts list. He dialed a number and put the phone on speaker.

She picked up on the third ring. "Hey Dr. Evans, what's up?"

He explained the reason for the call. She was currently on campus and had about thirty minutes before her next class. She said she'd meet me at Confucius.

"Confucius?" I asked.

The professor laughed. "Just head back towards the admin building and you'll figure it out." I thanked him, we shook hands and I headed for the door.

"Thanks," he said holding the cigarette up in the air, "for this."

I exited the building and thanked any and all higher authorities that I didn't smoke.

There was a young woman standing in front of the statue scrolling through her phone as I approached from behind. I stopped by her side and took a moment to admire it. The old Chinese philosopher towered at least twenty feet above me. Standing there in his loose fitting robe and his hair pulled back in a tight man bun, I'd have to say he looked pretty damn good for a guy who's been dead for over 2500 years. He had a knowledgeable grin on his face, the same kind you see on Jeopardy contestants when they know they've nailed the final answer.

She glanced over at me and put her phone in her back pocket. "Are you Mr. Kane?"

"Confucius say you are correct." She smiled but I recognize a charitable gift when I see one.

I apologized for the bad joke and thanked her for meeting with me. With a student population that was chiefly made up by Latinos and Asians, Helen Woodruff stuck out like a teutonic sore thumb. She had long blonde hair, blue eyes and was tall, as in volleyball player tall. She would quickly confirm my suspicions. She was, in fact, the starting middle blocker for the Golden Eagles.

We made the short walk over to the student union where I grabbed a coffee for myself and a bottled water for Helen. We sat under one of the yellow, metal umbrellas that seem to be everywhere on campus.

"I'm really worried about her Mr. Kane. I don't think she's the kind of person to disappear on her own like this."

"Unfortunately I have to agree with you. I think some-things happened to her." I hadn't forgotten about the phone message Frank Sr. had left on my machine but I had, at this point, discounted the possibility that she simply ran off with her boyfriend without telling a soul. "How did the two of you meet?" I asked.

"We had a freshman level economics class together and the professor told us to find a partner for a group project. We were sitting next to each other and I looked her way. She gave me a thumbs up and that was that. We were partners from that point on."

"Did the two of you get together socially?"

Helen shook her head. "We really didn't. Both of us were so busy. Volleyball pretty much consumes all of my free time outside of school and Reina was a commuter student. When her classes were finished for the day she always had to run off to work. Even when we were collaborated on assignments together it was basically done remotely through texts and emails."

"Helen," I said, "I'm kind of at my wits end here. In a period of one month Reina leaves school, quits her job and moves out of her aunt's house where she was living rent free. She did all of this on her own free will and apparently with a smile on her face. Unless she found a new, rich boyfriend or hit the Power-ball numbers none of this makes any sense. Quite frankly, I'm running out of ideas so if you can shed any light on the situation, now's the time."

Helen opened the bottle of water and took a sip. "Well I can't remark on the lottery or the boyfriend situation but I do know she had another job. All least back in March she did."

"And how do you know that?"

"Because the company hired me for a day." She went on to explain that Reina had called her because she knew Helen was fluent in Spanish. As it turns out, Helen is Mormon and she did a two year religious mission in Nicaragua. She could speak the language 'como una verdadera nativa.' Reina's employer held job fairs the first Saturday of every month and they needed help processing the applicants who were almost all Spanish speaking.

"What kind of business was it?" I asked the question but I think I already knew the answer. The first tumbler to the lock might have just clicked.

"It was a commercial cleaning service. I forgot the name of it but Reina mentioned it was once owned by her aunt."

"Was it called Top 2 Bottom?"

"Yes, that's it. I was surprised by how many people showed up to apply for what were basically maid positions but Reina explained that the company paid quite a bit above minimum wage and even offered health insurance for its employees. Jobs like that, she said, are rare in the immigrant community and apparently good news travels very quickly there."

I wondered why Marta hadn't mentioned this. My guess was because she had no idea. I'd give her a call when I got back to my truck. "So tell me how this job fair worked?"

"Reina called it a fair but it was really just an open job interview. We set up a canopy tent and folding chairs out in the parking lot where the applicants could sit and fill out the employment application. The interviews were scheduled to start at 8:00 a.m. and the applicants began arriving around 7:15. A few men showed up but it was mostly women and teenage girls. By 8:00 o'clock there must have been fifty people waiting to be interviewed. Reina and her friend....."

"Sorry to interrupt, but the friend, was her name Julie?

"Yes, Julie Herrera. A very nice girl. I think she and Reina were high school friends."

"You're right, they were. Anyways, so you were saying?"

"The women, at least those that could fill out the application, then sat down with either Reina or Julie for the interview."

I took a sip of coffee. It was already lukewarm. "What do you mean by those who could?"

"The majority of the applicants were undocumented workers and several of them couldn't read or write. In those cases Reina or Julie would ask the questions and complete the application for them."

The term undocumented worker is of course synonymous with illegal alien. We in California have what I would call a complicated relationship with the undocumented. We spend billions upon billions of dollars on border security trying to prevent their illegal entry into the state but at the same time we offer financial aid, health benefits and even educational scholarships to those who successfully slip through the dragnet. Arguments are made that they are a drain on social services and spike the crime rate but on the other hand they provide our economy with a low cost labor force and, let's face it, do the kind of work that most generational Californians have no interest in doing. For the most part these people are simply human beings looking for a better life than the one they left behind. They are inextricably woven into the fabric of our state and for better or worse, are here to stay. Like I said, it's complicated.

"And what was your role that day?" I asked her.

"When the interview ended they were sent to me and I'd take a Polaroid picture of the applicant and paper clip it to the application. I would then walk the forms into the office and hand them over to the big bosses."

"Big bosses? I thought this was a pretty small operation?"

"It is but I think Reina told me they owned two or three more cleaning businesses somewhere else."

"Got it." That was in line with what Marta told me as well as the information on the company's website. "Taking a Polaroid picture. That seems a bit unusual."

"I thought so too but Reina said it helped them remember the applicants they felt would be a good fit. It wasn't any of my business and besides I only worked for about two hours before they sent me home."

"Why was that?"

"She tried to make light of it, but Reina basically said my whiteness was scaring away some of the women. I'm pretty sure the decision came from the men inside."

That actually made sense to me. These are scared, desperate people who live in constant fear about being swept up by I.C.E. Seeing a blond hair, blued eyed gringo speaking fluent Spanish could have definitely made them feel skittish. Helen continued on. "I wasn't offended and they paid me the full three hundred dollars that Reina had promised. "

"And you said these job fairs happened every month?"

"That's what Reina said but I didn't get asked back so I don't really know."

"The two men, the bosses, what were their names?"

"I have no idea. They seemed nice enough but we were never properly introduced."

"Can you describe them for me?"

"They were both really old, maybe about your age." Helen caught herself and sucked in a deep breath. "I'm so sorry. I didn't mean it that way."

I laughed. It was an innocent observation and of course she meant no insult by it. Hey, I'm old, I get it. "Don't worry about it," I said, "please continue."

"The Hispanic man was short, overweight and almost completely bald. He was the one that came outside quite a bit and kind of supervised the process. Not to be mean but he wasn't very memorable."

"And the other guy?"

"He was a bit taller and in much better shape. He still had a full head of hair which was turning gray. I remember thinking he was a pretty good looking guy for someone his age. I'm not sure of his ethnicity though. He wasn't white and he wasn't Latino but he did have one distinguishing feature."

"What was that?"

"He was missing a finger on his left hand. I noticed it when I handed him a batch of completed applications. I'm afraid I might have stared at it momentarily and it became a bit awkward. I was asked to leave shortly after."

I started feeling numb while trying to process what she just told me.

Helen brought me back to the present. "Mr. Kane?..... Able, are you alright?"

"Sorry, yes I'm fine. Can you tell me what finger was missing?" I was afraid I already knew the answer.

"Yes. I forgot what they call it but it's the one next to the pinkie," she said pointing at her ring finger. She then glanced down at her phone. "Oh my goodness, I'm already late for class. I have to go. Is there anything else?"

"No, thank you Helen. That should do it."

"I'm sorry I couldn't be much help." She gave me her phone number and asked me to keep her updated about Reina then headed off for class leaving me wondering if the impossible wasn't not only possible but actually really happening.

CHAPTER 21

I've only known one person in my entire life that was missing the ring finger on his left hand. The last time I saw him he was drilling through my feet in an abandoned mountain chalet high above the city of Beirut so you can probably understand why I would jump to certain conclusions. By the time I made it back to my truck I realized there were a couple of fatal flaws in my logic. First and foremost is the fact that Mubari is dead and he has been for over twenty years.

When Bill Clinton was POTUS his foreign policy approach to terrorism was one of measured responses. It was more of an eye for an eye approach as opposed to the scorched earth doctrine that both Bush's adopted before and after his presidency.

On August 20th, 1998, in retaliation for the terrorist attacks against the American embassies in Kenya and Tanzania, President Clinton green lighted Operation Infinite Reach. An estimated 70 cruise missiles were launched from U.S. Navy ships directed at terrorist camps located in the mountains of Afghanistan. The strikes would go on to kill over fifty high ranking bad guys including a top Hezbollah operative by the name of Sahid Mubari. Our Mubari. Victor Ortiz, the CIA agent that had visited Hassam and myself in that German hospital so long ago tracked us down by phone that day to deliver the good news personally. This would be confirmed later in the evening at a press conference jointly held by the CIA and the White House notifying the American public of the operation. In hindsight Infinite Reach would ultimately be deemed a failure because the primary target, a relatively unknown terrorist by the name of Osama bin Laden, survived the missile strikes. He of course would go on to future fame and glory in three years time and imprint the date of 9/11 on the psyches of not just Americans but the entire world. At the same time the ICBM's were flying through the air, William Jefferson Clinton could be found standing chest high in extremely hot water. It was now coming to light that he had launched a guided missile of his own targeted at an unsuspecting female intern with absolutely zero terrorist connections. The rocket would prove to be extremely accurate as it would hit its mark again and again while never leaving the confines of the Oval Office.

So I called the same person I always call when I need to be talked off a ledge. Unlike Harvey who rarely picks up a dialing phone, the times Hassam has not picked up my call can probably be counted on one hand. Today was no exception. "Able, How are you?"

"I'm okay. Do you have a minute?" I knew he probably didn't but that never seems to matter. In the background I could hear the sound of pneumatic nail guns firing away.

"Of course. You sound a bit off kilter. What's going on?"

I caught him up on the Reina Montes case. Hassam has such a keen, analytical mind he can normally provide me with the insight I need to get my head around something I can't figure out on my own.

There was dead air when I finished talking as Hassam was working things through his mind. "That's interesting except for the fact that Mubari is dead Able."

"I understand that does put a bit of a crimp into my theory but just say for a minute that he isn't. That for some reason the government lied about his death."

"Why would they do that?"

"What, the government lie? Hell Hassam, the CIA has duplicity written into their operating manual."

"That's true. OK," he said, "for argument's sake let's say they did. Let's say they turned him and he started working for the good guys."

"Exactly," I said jumping in, "like a confidential informant."

"Yes, something along those lines. So he does whatever he's been doing for twenty years without being detected and then suddenly shows up in Los Angeles to buy Marta's cleaning business?"

"Well when you put it that way it does seem a bit ridiculous. But you have the finger, the Saudi connection......"

"But Mubari was Lebanese. We know that now."

"Yes he was Hassam but you know from personal experience these guys intermingle like they're at a freshman mixer. Then finally you have Helen's description of the guy that puts him at about the right age and the physical features that wouldn't rule him out."

The shrieking sounds of a circular saw started up. "Able, one minute, let me find somewhere a bit quieter."

While I was waiting for him to come back on line Victoria called in. I put Hassam on hold and took her call.

"Hi Victoria. Listen I really appreciate you pulling me out of that jam. I owe you one."

"My garage needs painting," she said. I waited for the hah-hah chuckle but it didn't arrive. "I ran the Toyota Camry through the system. It hasn't been towed but it did receive a parking ticket on Wednesday, May 24th. The stated reason was failure to move the vehicle prior to a scheduled street cleaning."

"Thank you. I have Hassam on the other line, can you text me the address?"

"Will do Detective Fagan." She hung up. That woman always has to get in the last word.

"OK, that's better," Hassam said, coming back to the conversation.

"So what do you think buddy? I'm barking up the wrong tree right?"

Instead of telling me straight away that was the case he asked me this. "You said there was a second man there that day correct?"

"Yes, a Latino guy. He pretty much supervised the morning."

"Do you have a description of him?"

"Not much. She described him as short, overweight and almost completely bald."

"Interesting," Hassam said. I could practically hear the gears grinding away in his brain.

"Why do you say that?"

"An old friend came to see me about ten years ago. He had recently retired and was interested in setting up an import/export business throughout the Middle East. He wanted to know if I was interested in joining him in the new venture. He had developed a lot of connections in the region over the years but he didn't have much of a business plan and by that time, my life was here. I declined his offer. Anyways, what I'm getting at is the fact that I hadn't seen him for a long time and I was quite surprised how much he had changed physically."

"Well, you have successfully piqued my interest. Who was it?"

"It was Victor Ortiz. He was always short but when I saw him he had put on a lot of weight and had lost the majority of his hair."

We hashed it out back and forth over the next ten minutes and we ultimately agreed the whole thing seemed just too implausible. Besides, Hassam reminded me, I had a job to do which was not to embark on an international manhunt but to find Reina Montes. He was right of course and I needed to focus all of my energy on just that.

As I drove to my next stop I had a few phone calls to make. I wasn't looking forward to the first one. She picked up immediately.

"Hi Marta, it's Able."

"Hi Able," she replied. She was breathing hard.

"Are you alright? You sound short of breath."

"Sorry, I'm fine. I've been working out in the yard. One second, I'm going to go inside. It's starting to get too hot out here anyways."

When she returned I updated her on all of the recent changes Reina had made in her life. I made her cry and I asked her if I should call back later.

"No, no, I'm ok," she said, "I just don't understand what is happening."

"Marta, did you know Reina had been working for Top 2 Bottom recently?" I went on to explain what I had heard from Helen.

"I had no idea. Why in the world wouldn't she tell me about that?"

I couldn't help her. "Can you tell me about these job fairs? Reina seemed to be involved with them."

"Well we never had such a thing. We were a small business. When we had a position available one of my girls always knew someone that would fill it. Maybe the new owners were growing the business."

"Maybe," I replied, "unfortunately I have a lot more questions for you than I do answers. When's the last time you talked to Julie? I've called her twice and she hasn't gotten back to me yet."

"I don't think I've talked to her since just before I filed the missing persons report. Do you want me to touch base with her?"

"Would you? I need to talk to her."

"Of course, I'll do it right away."

I then asked her about the nine fingered man and his partner.

"I don't know them. We actually never met. The entire transaction on their side was handled by an attorney."

"That's strange," I said. I was actually just thinking out loud more than I was responding to Marta.

"Is it?" she asked me. There was no reason for her to think it was.

"I think so. To buy a company sight unseen like that seems a bit unorthodox to me. Do you have the lawyers contact info?"

"I have his business card. I can take a picture of it and text it to you."

"That would be great. And Marta?"

"Yes?"

"Keep your chin up. I'll get to the bottom of this."

"I know you will Able. God bless."

My next call was to Nate, my renter.

"Able, what's wrong? Did you get a VHS tape stuck in the recorder again?"

Good one. "No, it's my 8-track player this time."

"Your what?"

"Nate, did you see anyone moving around the property last night. The motion lights in the courtyard kept going off."

"You probably have them set too low. I didn't see anyone or anything and I haven't been to bed yet. Do you want me to recalibrate them?"

"That would be great." So if there was an intruder last night he must have entered through the alleyway. Mr. All Nighter would have noticed someone coming through the breeze way from the street side. Perhaps one of my neighbors has alley cameras that picked something up. I'd ask Nate to make some inquiries but talking to people isn't exactly his strength. I'd check that out when I got home. "What's that noise in the background?" Someone was banging away on metal.

"That's Bob."

"Who's Bob?" I asked.

"Your plumber. I gave up on you and called him myself."

My next and final call was to the CPA that rents my street side office. He didn't pick up so I left him a voicemail. "Hey Mark, this is your landlord Able. You're late on your rent. Just kidding. Listen, I left a package in your mail drop this morning. It contains some copies of a bulk asset transaction relative to one of my cases. Can you take a look at it and let me know if you notice anything off kilter? Bill me for your time and deduct it from next month's rent. Sooner than later would be great by the way. Thanks."

CHAPTER 22

I needed to get over to Top 2 Bottom as soon as possible but first there was a dental appointment I needed to keep. Have I mentioned how much I hate the dentist? No? Well I do. I never received proper dental care as a child and I've been paying for it ever since. And it's not just the dentist. He just gets the ball rolling. It's the periodontist, the orthodontist and a guy they call an endodontist. I bet you didn't even know he existed. I know way too much about root canals, crowns, bleeding gums, bone loss and bone grafting. These guys, as a group, are the greatest purveyors of fear marketing in the world. They could have partnered up and bought a beachfront time-share together with all the money I've shelled out over the years. I wouldn't be at all surprised if they were there right now, lounging on some balcony sipping margaritas and toasting the current state of my teeth. When I get an email from one of them reminding me of an upcoming appointment I can feel the air leak out of my happy balloon. I hate them. Ok, I feel better now. As I pulled into the parking lot of a two story medical plaza in Arcadia I realized I got all worked up for nothing. It wasn't even my appointment. I was going to see Marta and Reina's shared dentist who graciously agreed to meet with me when I explained the situation. The office was closed for lunch but he said he'd eat in today. The door was locked but after a few knocks it was opened by an attractive, voluptuous young woman dressed in her uniform whites. Her name tag read Amanda so that's what I went with.

"Hello Amanda," I said sucking in my gut, "my name is Abel

Kane. I'm here to see Dr. Matthews."

"He's expecting you." She flashed a blinding white smile that said you too can have teeth like this for just sixty monthly payments at a ridiculously low $59.99. She led me past the receptionist desk and a series of open doors that led to various chambers of torture. Dr. Matthews' office was at the end of the hallway and true to his word he was working his way through a deli sandwich.

"What's for lunch?" I asked. I caught him in mid-bite. I love when that happens.

"Turkey and bacon," he managed to say. There was a second chair on his side of the desk with a half-eaten salad in front of it. A cozy lunch for two.

While he was still chewing I quickly scanned the glory wall behind him. Dr. Matthews catching a sailfish. Dr. Matthews posing with Kareem Abdul Jabbar. Dr. Matthews taking a selfie on the summit of Zermatt with the Matterhorn perfectly centered behind him. Off to the side, not in a position of prominence was a picture of the Matthews family complete with the doctor, his wife and two young daughters posing in front of a Christmas tree. It was ugly sweater day I think.

"Thank you for seeing me." I decided to go with the full, blunt approach. "What can you tell me about Reina Montes that will help me find her?"

"Amanda," he said with the stern voice of authority, "can you get me the Reina Montes' file please?"

I turned her way just in time to see her give him the full relationship glare. I knew that look. It's one thing to ask your hygienist to retrieve a patient's file. It's a whole other thing to ask her to do it when the two of you have been dancing the horizontal tango together. It's none of my business but I think Dr. Matthews has been dipping his pen in the company inkwell.

"Right away Dr. Matthews," she said. I wouldn't exactly say

she stormed out of the office but let's just say the dark clouds were gathering. While we were waiting he asked me questions about my profession and I gave him a couple of fun highlights. He was a dentist so of course my job must have sounded extremely interesting. I mean how many times can you ask someone to open their mouth and say aah before the shooting begins. Amanda returned and literally dropped the file on his desk then grabbed her half eaten salad and left in what I think the three of us could agree upon was a huff.

Dr. Matthews rolled his eyes, opened up the file and asked "What exactly would you like to know?"

Well," I said, "in a case like this when I'm not sure what I'm looking for, I guess everything that's in that file and of course anything that isn't."

As he explained his way through the file I realized Reina was my comrade in arms. She had started with Dr. Matthews at the age of sixteen and there was a pattern of cavities, crooked teeth that required braces and two root canals. He summed it up for me like this. "To put it succinctly, Reina is a beautiful young woman with bad teeth. Two of her incisors were badly chipped and there was some general discoloration that normal cleaning wouldn't remove. She was extremely aware of this and had perfected a smile that didn't require the opening of her mouth." He then got to the good part. "On April 17th she came in for the initial consultation to do a smile makeover."

"I'm sorry, a what?"

"A smile makeover. Veneers."

Got it. That's one of the products my orthodontist unsuccessfully tried to sell me. The veneers themselves are made out of porcelain and cover the front portion of the tooth. It is an extremely expensive cosmetic enhancement which will provide the recipient with a smile that would rival the one owned by the brooding Amanda.

"That's a lot of money isn't it doctor?"

"It is. I was surprised when she went ahead with the procedure. I didn't think she could possibly afford it. We completed it on May 12th."

At this point I wasn't the least bit surprised. Reina had planted a money tree somewhere and it was producing the forbidden fruit by the bushel.

"May I ask how much it was?"

"In for a penny, in for a pound I guess," he said. Once you've violated the doctor-patient privilege you might as well go all the way. "It was over ten thousand dollars."

That's kind of what I figured. "Now, the big question. How did she pay for it? Cash?"

"No, it was a credit card. It didn't belong to Reina though. It was a third party card."

That tingling feeling on the back of my neck returned. I felt like the tumbler was about to click again.

"Please tell me you have that info on file."

He flipped the turned pages in Reina's file back to their original position and slid it over to me. A photocopy of the card, a corporate American Express, was page one. I pulled my phone out and took a picture. The cardholder's name was Rahid Gamal, EZX Enterprises. The same Mr. Gamal who happened to be the president of the holding company that purchased Marta's business.

I thanked him and reiterated my promise to keep the whole thing confidential. He did the right thing by sticking his neck out to help Reina and I was truly appreciative. On the way out of the office I said goodbye to the pouting Amanda who was still able to manage one of her trademark smiles. She had a huge piece of lettuce stuck to her right canine covering the entire tooth. I decided to let it remain there.

Before my next stop I needed some fuel in the old system. I was hungry. There was a coffee shop across the street from the dental office so I headed over there for a quick lunch. There was a sign that said 'Please Seat Yourself' so I did just that. I grabbed a booth near the counter.

"Can't take that one honey," a voice shouted out from the kitchen, "it's reserved."

I looked around. I was the only customer in the place. "Okay," I said pointing at the next one over, "how about this one?"

"That's fine." The voice came around the corner. It belonged to a septuagenarian by the name of Rose. She didn't seem overly excited to see me.

"What's good?" I asked.

"The burger's safe."

Well that's encouraging. "Okay, I'll have that with some fries."

While awaiting the arrival of my safety meal I tried to make sense of what I just learned from Dr. Matthews. Reina's money source had been identified. That was something at least. Did that mean Reina and the mysterious Mr. Gamal were an item? That's one heck of an age split even for a guy with unlimited funds. If they weren't a couple, why in the world would he cover a $10,000 dental bill? Again, more questions than answers. My thought process was interrupted by the vibration of an incoming phone call. I didn't recognize the number.

"Able Kane here."

"Mr. Kane, my name is Miranda Claros. I'm a student at Cal State LA. I was just heading up to the library when I saw Reina's poster."

"Thanks for calling. Do you know where I can find her? She's worrying a lot of people."

"I don't know where she is now but I saw her at a party in

Las Vegas over Memorial Day weekend."

"What day exactly?"

"Saturday."

I checked my calendar. That would have been May 27th which makes Miranda my newest last person to have seen Reina. It was also just one day before she was supposed to have dinner with her aunt. "Miranda," I said, "this could be important. Tell me every detail you can remember."

Just as she began her story Rose set the plate of food right on top of my phone. A not so subtle message about having it on speaker mode. Yeah I get it, her turf, her rules, but I didn't have time to play games today plus I needed my hands free to take notes. I lifted up the plate, grabbed the phone and left it on speaker.

"Sorry Miranda, can you repeat that? I got interrupted there for a second."

Rose tossed daggers at me then skulked away like I had just kicked one of her eight cats. Miranda started over. She didn't know Reina well but they had a mutual friend, Natalie, who was celebrating her 21st birthday at the Aria that weekend.

"Did you talk to Reina?" I asked.

"Just for a moment," she replied, "she was with her boyfriend and they were pretty much in their own little world. I think they were having a fight."

"Any idea of what is was about?"

"No. They shut it down when I approached Reina to say hello."

"Miranda, can you describe the boyfriend to me?"

"Yeah, he was really cute. Tall, black hair and very muscular. He was wearing a wife beater to show off his arms. Lots of tattoos also, which I dig."

"I'm sorry, he was wearing a what?"

"A wife beater. You know, a tank top."

"Got it. How old was he Miranda?"

"I don't know. I didn't ask him."

Lord give me strength. "I mean approximately."

"Oh, sorry. He was my age, maybe a few years older."

"Was his name Frank by any chance?"

"Yeah, I think so."

"So you said you and Reina talked for a bit. What did you guys talk about?"

"Mostly about our friend Natalie who was getting totally wasted and hitting on every guy at the party. Besides that, just small talk. School mostly. I mentioned I was at Cal State and she laughed saying she used to go there but was now working full time. I asked about her job and she said she was in human resources. That seemed to amuse her boyfriend for some reason and Reina elbowed him right in the ribs. Like I said, I don't think they were getting along very well."

I questioned her a little bit longer but there was nothing else of importance. Reina and Frank left the party shortly after and Miranda ended up holding the birthday girls' head over the toilet all night long. She gave me Natalie's contact information before hanging up. I scarfed down my meal and signaled Rose for the check. She was filling up salt and pepper shakers and refusing to look my way. I was getting slow played. Normally I enjoy this kind of thing and I would retaliate by doing something like opening up all of the sweet and low packs and making an artificial sweetener mountain then sneezing as hard as I can. But like I said earlier there was no time for frivolity today. I grabbed forty dollars out of my wallet and tossed it on the table. That would surely cover the meal and any treble damages I owed Rose for the emotional trauma I inflicted. As I got up to leave she abandoned the condiments and swooped towards my table like a raptor half her age. Her attitude improved when she saw the Jackson's lying there.

"Change?" she asked smiling.

"Yes," I replied, "I think you should give that some serious consideration. It's never too late." Every once in a while it's my turn to get in the last word.

I headed down Rosemead Blvd. towards Monterey Park where Marta's old business was located. Traffic was terrible but it gave me the chance to make a few phone calls. The first one was to Natalie, the party girl. She didn't pick up. I wished her a happy birthday, left her a message about Reina and then asked her to call me back. My next call was to Julie Herrera and once again it went directly to voice mail. I left her a very stern message about friendship, responsibility and doing the right thing. I had better luck on the third call.

"Hello Able," Victoria said, "I'm thinking Alpine white with a Kelly green for the trim. I assume that's why you're calling."

The garage. "You sure you don't want to jazz it up a bit? I was thinking maybe something in the chartreuse family."

"No Able, my choice will be fine."

I'm starting to think she's serious about this. "Victoria, I need you to run the activity on a credit card. It pertains to the case Harvey green lighted. Can you do it?"

She hesitated. "Able, we need a warrant to do that and Reina's case as you know is not LAPD."

"Listen, it's important. I think it might break the case open." There was another pause on the line. "And I'll apply two coats of primer. You'll be the talk of the neighborhood."

"Fine. None of that cheap paint though. Text me the card information."

"There's one more thing."

"Shocking," she said, "what is it this time?"

"Can you check a Julie Herrera on that missing person's report? I know you sent it to me but it has so many columns, dashes and numbers on it I can't seem to make heads or tails out of it."

"I hate to say I told you so, but...."

"Thanks Victoria, got to go."

When I was sure the call had been disconnected I said out loud and to myself, "Vicky, hell will be frozen over before I paint your garage."

CHAPTER 23

The moment I pulled into the driveway of Top 2 Bottom I knew something was very much off kilter. There were no cars in the lot and the blinds to the front window had been drawn. There was a large octagonal sign stickered to the window warning me the premises were protected by the Goliath Security Company and any response to an alarm would be an armed one. There was also a wired-in security camera just above the entrance. I tried the door but it was locked so I rang the bell several times but no one came a calling. I decided to take a look around. It was an old, industrial building that lent itself more to utility than it did to aesthetics. On the north wall there was a large roll-up with a sign on it that said shipping and receiving. I gave it a quick tug but it was locked also. At the back of the property there was nothing but a dented, split top trash bin. I took a quick peek inside. Empty. The door on this side of the building was also being monitored by an active security camera. The lock was a classic pin/tumbler design and I made the decision then and there to go inside. I pulled out my kit which is nothing more than a tension wrench along with a three ridge pick and I had the key and driver pins aligned in a matter of seconds. The lock turned and the deadbolt slid free. Before going inside I tucked my left ring finger against my palm and waived the other nine at the camera before flipping it the bird. If the nine fingered man was involved in Reina's disappearance I wanted him to know I was coming for him. Upon entering I was greeted by nothing but total quiet. If there was an active alarm it was running silent.

The back part of the building was filled with racks of cleaning supplies and the tools of the trade. Mops, buckets, vacuum cleaners, floor polishers, you name it. Pretty much what you'd expect to see except for the fact they were all sitting here, idle, on a Monday afternoon. There was another opened door that led into the main office. The desk tops were completely cleared except for the dust free imprints of the computers that had recently resided there. The filing cabinets had all been emptied, the phone lines severed and the equipment tossed into a heap on the floor. There was a postal slot cut into the front door and no more than a day's worth of mail sat on the floor below it. There were two checks, a couple of bills and some junk mail all postmarked the previous Friday. Whoever cleared this place out had done it in a hurry and only quite recently. The not so good people of Top 2 Bottom were running scared. Just as I stuffed the mail into my coat pocket two Monterey Park Police cars raced into the parking lot blocking my exit. They were followed in by a brown Crown Vic, the vehicle of choice for the detective set. I unlocked the front door and sat down on the steps with my hands interlocked on top of my head. The uniforms were young which meant inexperienced which meant I needed to take control of the situation to ensure nobody, namely me, got hurt.

"My name is Able Kane," I said in my best air traffic controller's voice. "I'm a private detective working a missing person's case. I want you to know I'm carrying a gun in a shoulder holster and my concealed weapons permit is in my wallet in that truck right behind you. The back door to this building was open and I simply walked in. Oh, and I'm a Sagittarius and I love moonlit walks on the beach." The last part of my speech wasn't exactly true. I was born in June but telling them I was a Cancer or even worse, a Moon Child, might have gotten me arrested immediately. I do like those moonlit walks on the beach however.

The detective chose this moment to exit his vehicle. He

rested his arms across the hood of the car and then, in what I have to admit was a pretty damn good imitation of Humphrey Bogart, said, "Of all the gin joints in all the towns of the world he had to walk into mine."

I looked up at the guy and smiled. "Hey Joe."

"Able, how in the hell are you?"

Despite their protestations Detective Lewis assured the uniforms he had the situation under control and sent them back to the station house. The two of us went back inside to catch up. Joe had worked under Harvey for years at Hollenbeck before getting transferred to the Foothill Division where he finished out his career. He took an early retirement package at the ripe old age of fifty. Harvey threw him a big going away party at the house. That was just over ten years ago which we figured out was the last time we had seen each other. According to Harvey, Joe was always a solid detective. Not a superstar per se but a persistent grinder that closed a high percentage of his cases. He was a good cop. Joe went on to tell me he stayed retired for two years until he realized he actually hated to fish and discovered that his wife had numerous outside interests that didn't require his presence. He got on with the Monterey Police Department seven years ago and his plan was to remain there as long as they would have him. I gave him the brief overview of why I was tripping alarms on his turf. He remembered Marta fondly which made him a sympathetic listener.

"So Joe," I asked, "what's a detective doing rolling up on an alarm call?"

"Before we get into that Able, I want to know if you and I are going to play sharezeeys."

"Absolutely Joe, you first."

That made him laugh. "Considering the fact I can see your lock kit sticking out of your back pocket I think it's definitely your turn."

Fair enough. I laid it all out for him. Reina the college drop-out, the job fairs, the nine fingered man and I even threw in my philandering dentist just to spice it up a little bit.

Joe nodded, satisfied I wasn't pulling the wool over his eyes. He pulled out a pack of gum and withdrew two sticks, offering me one. As much as my time share owning group of dentists would have approved, I declined his generous offer. Juicy Fruit though, solid choice. Joe shrugged his shoulders and popped both pieces in his mouth.

"When I heard the address on the call out," he said, "it got my curiosity up. I've been here twice since the beginning of the year."

"Let me guess," I said, "missing person cases."

"Correct but nothing really concrete. Both visits were more of just filling in the subject's timeline prior to the disappearance. But if I recall correctly you like coincidences about as much as I do."

"Women?"

"Yes, and young."

"And they both worked here at Top 2 Bottom?"

"No," Joe said shaking his head, "but according to the people that filed the missing person reports they had both applied for jobs here. The first was in January and the second was in April I think. I'd have to check my notes to make sure though."

The job fairs. "So nothing became of it?"

"No. I mean obviously my suspicions had been aroused when the second woman went missing and the common link was established. I reinterviewed everyone in the office but their stories were all consistent. Yes, it was certainly possible that both women had interviewed for a job but no one on the staff had recognized either one of them."

"Did their answers feel rehearsed?"

"Maybe, I'm trying to remember. It certainly didn't seem that way at the time."

I thought back to how Helen had photographed each and every applicant and knew what the staff at Top 2 Bottom had told Joe probably wasn't true. I explained that to him and in hindsight he agreed. I also asked him about the nine fingered man but he hadn't been around at either one of Joe's visits.

"They were both undocumented by the way," Joe informed me, "so it's a miracle they were reported missing in the first place. You know how fearful that community is of the law."

I sure do. When I used to walk a beat down in the Boyle Heights area I'd watch people scurry for cover every time I tried to say hello. Most of these people worked multiple jobs and have families south of the border that rely on them to survive. Job number one is not to get deported.

"The last thing I want to bring up in my defense," he explained, "was the fact these two women weren't reported missing until about two weeks after they had interviewed at Top 2 Bottom. That put my antenna down but considering what I learned today it looks like I dropped the ball."

I assured him that wasn't the case and I meant it. We agreed to keep each other in the loop as we moved forward. We exited through the back and I used my kit to relock the door from the outside. It was time to head back to Otto's and find out exactly what Bump knew. I hoped for his sake he wasn't going to make this a difficult process.

CHAPTER 24

I had several phone calls to return and a few to make as I turned on to Monterey Pass Road heading for the 710 Freeway.

I called Harvey back first and miracle of all miracles he picked up on the first ring. I gave him the newest updates and just as I expected he found these developments quite disconcerting.

"Do you want me to call Marta?" he asked.

"No," I said, "I need to talk to her anyways."

"OT, I've hit a wall with the State Department. My guy says the U.S. Government is in the middle of renegotiating new leases on our air bases in Saudi Arabia. Apparently the political situation between the two countries is a bit tense right now. They aren't going to do anything that might upset the apple cart."

"Ok, I'll figure something out. But Harvey, just so you know, things are heating up now so I'm going to need you to….."

"Answer my phone?" He asked interrupting me.

"Ding, Ding, Ding. Correct answer." He chuckled then promised me he would do just that before hanging up the call.

Politics. Add that to the list of things I hate. It's why I dread election years and why I won't join the local Kiwanis chapter. It's the same reason why I stay away from friends that travel in packs and it had a lot to do with why I left the LAPD.

Harvey and I joined the department at just about the same time and we were in the same graduating class at the academy. We were patrol partners for years and took the detective's exam together. I had spent the previous five years going to night school to earn my college degree in criminology with the sole intention of giving me the necessary leverage to take this next step. Harvey and I talked immediately after taking the test. He was nervous about his performance but I knew for a fact that I had aced it. He made it into the bureau and I was told to retest in two years time. I should have read the tea leaves better than I did. Harvey is a great cop, probably the best I've ever known but he is also brilliant when it comes to playing the game. Politics is a lot like chess and the great ones can always see three or four moves ahead. Part of that is accepting the fact that sometimes compromises are necessary to achieve future goals. It's the old 'a good end justifies the means' philosophy and I've just never been wired that way. When I see a wrong I challenge it regardless of the consequences. In an organization like the LAPD that can sometimes equate to career suicide.

About six months after taking the detective's exam my new partner and I responded Code 3 on a possible home invasion call. The address was a two story apartment complex down in Frog Town. We arrived just as the perp was exiting one of the first floor units. I chased him up the stairwell and on to the roof. We fought and the two of us slipped off the ledge together. I landed in a construction dumpster that was three quarters full of demoed dry wall and insulation. That combination probably saved my life. The perp wasn't as lucky. The fall shattered my left hip however and I was put on immediate disability. I underwent replacement surgery which went well but here I was again with another long recovery ahead of me. During the time I was going through rehab a close friend referred me to a law firm that was looking for someone to do some private investigating. I found that I really loved the work especially having the autonomy of answering to no one but myself. Word of mouth advertising led me to other clients and by the time I was cleared to go back to the LAPD I decided I was going to give this new career a full time shot. I surrendered my badge and the rest is, as they say, history.

My next call was to Natalie, the Aria's favorite birthday girl. It was a dead end. She hadn't seen or talked to Reina since the party and had no new information for me.

I then spoke to my tenant, Mark, the CPA.

"Did you get a chance to take a look at that package I dropped off?" I asked him.

"I did," he replied. "I don't suppose they want to buy me out too?"

"That's what I thought. An over pay right?"

"Absolutely. They must have really wanted this business."

"Did you notice anything else unusual?"

"Nope. The paper work is all copacetic. Looks like it was all handled correctly."

"OK, thanks Mark."

"Oh Able, one more thing before you go."

Ugh. Please don't tell me the central air is on the fritz. "What is it?"

"Out of curiosity, I checked EZX's public records and they've never filed a tax return."

"Serious?"

"As a heart attack. I think they could use my services. Would you put in a good word for me?"

"Mark, you don't want any piece of these guys."

"That was sarcasm Able. It is a form of comedy you know."

A funny accountant. What's next? A herd of unicorns crossing the street?

My last callback was to my favorite antagonist, Victoria. As usual, she picked up immediately.

"Hello Sir," she said.

"Hello Ma'am."

There was a moment of silence. "What can I do for you Able?"

"Victoria darling, you called me."

"I did? Oh yes, you're right. Julie Herrera is a no-show on the missing persons report."

"Ok, thanks. How about the activity on that credit card?"

"I'm working on it."

Did I detect a bit of attitude in her voice? "Well you'll have to work faster."

"Excuse me? What did you say?"

"I said we'll have to rework the plaster. You know, the garage."

"That's what I thought you said."

The phone went dead. That little vixen beat me to the punch again.

As I made the transition on to the 10 Freeway East I called the San Gabriel Valley Inn. They had written one of the checks I found on the floor of the office at Top 2 Bottom. The check stub had referenced an invoice number and a vendor code so I made the easy assumption they were a customer.

"Hello," the voice said. It belonged to an Asian woman. My guess would be Chinese. "San Gabriel Inn, how can I help you?" She drew out the last word 'you' like it was the end of a line in a song.

"Hi, this is Alan Jardine from Top 2 Bottom, I'm doing a survey...................."

That's as far as I got. She really started yelling at me. When she got super revved up she switched over to Mandarin and hit me with both barrels blazing. She'd then calm down a bit and revert back to the King's English. The cycle repeated itself a few times and I was able to catch the gist of my dressing down. Boy did I deserve it. The cleaning service that Top 2 Bottom provided the San Gabriel Valley Inn was a no-show today which had left them high and dry with neither maid service nor clean sheets. If we didn't show up tomorrow morning they were going to terminate our contract. I shouldn't have done it but I did. I promised her we would try harder in the future and I'd knock 10% off her next invoice. She seemed to like that which made me feel terrible as soon as I hung up the phone.

It was official, Top 2 Bottom Cleaning Services had closed its doors. One more call to make. For some reason I always save the toughest for last.

"Hello Able."

"Hey kiddo, how you doing?" I'm sure my voice was as somber as the news I was going to deliver.

"Not well. I've been getting calls all day from my girls at Top 2 Bottom. They came to work this morning and the place was shut down. They're all panicked and I didn't know what to tell them. What's happening Able?"

I told her everything I'd found out since the last time we'd talked. The nine fingered man, the smile makeover and how it had been paid for. How Reina had been spotted in Las Vegas the night before she was supposed to have dinner with Marta and my fortuitous encounter with Detective Lewis where I had found out about the other two missing girls.

Marta was doing her best to fight back the tears. Unfortunately I was just getting started. "Marta, Reina's boyfriend is a guy by the name of Frank Garcia. Do you know him?"

"Yes. He worked for me as a driver. He drove the girls who couldn't drive themselves from job to job. He also helped out in the office with things like inside sales and ordering supplies. He and Reina are an item?"

"You sound surprised?"

"Well it's the first time I've heard of it so yes I am. He certainly wouldn't be my first choice for Reina."

"Why is that?"

"He's had a few run-ins with the law. Frank's parents went through a nasty divorce when he was a teenager and he acted out quite a bit."

"Can you be more specific? What kind of trouble did he get himself in?"

"I know he stole a neighbor's car a few years back. He claimed he was only taking it out for a joy ride but he got pulled over for speeding and was arrested. I think he got probation and community service for that one. There was some petty theft in there also."

I'd have Victoria pull up his sheet. "Did you have any luck getting a hold of Julie Herrera?"

"No. she hasn't called me back. I've tried twice and it's gone straight to voicemail both times."

That certainly didn't surprise me. "Ok now for the tough part Marta."

"You mean it gets worse?"

"Possibly. I'm going to ask you a very blunt question and I hope you don't take any offense."

"Ok," Marta said rather tentatively.

"At this point I'm absolutely certain Reina's disappearance is connected to your old business and the new owners."

"That wasn't a question Able."

I sighed. "No I guess it wasn't. What I was getting around to is the fact that I can't rule out the possibility that Reina might be involved in some kind of criminal activity. She's gotten her hands on a lot of money recently and that's never a good sign."

There was dead silence on the phone. We were both waiting for the other to say something. I finally did. "I thought you'd be screaming and yelling at me right about now."

"No, I would never do that to you Able. I do know my niece though and the Reina Montes I know would never get involved in such a thing."

"Marta, I'm going to follow this through to the end unless you want me to call off the dogs."

"No, I want you to continue. I'm beginning to prepare myself for the worst but even that will be better than never knowing what happened to her."

I asked her if she would call a couple of her ex-employees back to see if they knew anything about the nine fingered man or his sidekick. She said she'd get right on it. We said our goodbyes just as I pulled into the parking lot of Otto's Warehousing and Self-Storage.

CHAPTER 25

I parked in the same spot as yesterday which made me reflect on how much had transpired since Harvey walked into the Celtic Cross and asked me to look into the disappearance of Reina Montes. That thread I started pulling on a few days ago felt more like the Gordian Knot now. With that in mind I walked into the office for my showdown with Bump. He wasn't there. Sitting at his desk was an elderly gentlemen with a pasty, squared off face and a body to match. It was obvious the computer, whose keyboard he was flailing away at, was not behaving properly. He didn't seem particularly enthralled by my intrusion either.

"Can I help you?" he asked in an exasperated tone.

"Yes, I'm looking for Joseph Gunter."

"He's not here."

"Do you know when to expect him?"

"My guess is probably never. He quit yesterday."

"Did he say why he quit?"

The man rose from his chair and came over to the counter. "How about you telling me what this is all about first."

He was obviously having a bad day and needed a good old fashion confrontation to let off a little steam. I was more than happy to oblige.

"Okay," I said, "and may I ask who you are?"

"My name's Otto and I own the place. Who are you?"

Aah, Otto, the man himself. I pulled out my badge. "I'm

detective Bob Hannah, LAPD." Otto I will see your palindrome and I'll raise you one. "I'm here investigating the criminal activity I believe is occurring on this property. So why don't you stick that attitude of yours back into your civic, level kayak and start answering my questions. And remember Otto, 'Sums are not set as a test on Erasmus.'" I don't think he enjoyed my little palindromic adventure but I sure did.

As it turned out, under the rough and tumble veneer, there was a sweet, compliant ex-Bavarian who was more than willing to talk. He went on to tell me he received an email from Bump yesterday afternoon informing him he was quitting immediately. Otto lived in Big Bear now, fully retired from a career in cabinet making. This self-storage facility was the sum total of his nest egg. He had to come down from the mountain this morning to work Bump's shifts until he could find a suitable replacement. He adamantly denied involvement in any and all nefarious activities and I believed him. I showed him Reina's picture which drew a sincere blank. I then described what had occurred here yesterday morning and asked to see the security footage from the cameras positioned both inside and outside of the office.

Otto turned a little more pasty than usual. "I can't do that," he said. "Joe logged us out through my security company's website and I can't figure out how to get us back online. I'll lose my insurance if we're caught without the coverage. You don't know anything about computers do you?"

"Only that I wish they were never invented. But I do know someone who does. Would you like some help?"

I got Nate on the phone. He asked Otto a few questions and then sat him down in front of the computer. Nate barked out a few commands and less than a minute later he was operating Otto's computer from the apartment in Glendale. The fact that this was even possible is a very scary development for me. It served its purpose however because Nate had the security cameras up and running before you could say big brother is everywhere. I had a couple of questions for Nate before he disappeared into the ether.

"Nate, can you tell me exactly when the cameras were shut off?"

"EZ Peezy." Click, click. "11:17 a.m."

That was just minutes before the consulate car had shown up. "One more question. Can you tell me if this ever had happened in the past?"

"How far do you want to go back?"

"How about to the beginning of the year?"

Nate didn't verbally respond but the arrow on Otto's computer started flying around. We both watched in awe. Now I know how the cavemen felt when they saw fire for the first time. Thirty seconds later the printer in the office spit out a report. Nate loves to show off like that. I took a look at the data. There was quite a history of logging off and back on again during Bump's shifts, normally late at night. On the average it occurred five to six times a month with the intervals for each episode ranging from 45-90 minutes.

After Otto regained control of his computer I asked him to print out a current customers list. He was so grateful I had brought Nate into his life he didn't think twice about doing it. Otto had 200 units and all but 14 of them were currently rented out. It was a long alphabetized list but I had a good idea where to look.

I was correct in assuming that Gamal and Pacheco were both too clever to rent the units under their own names. I also didn't expect to find EZX Enterprises or Top 2 Bottom on Otto's customer list. My first, best guess was correct. Four units had been rented out to Frank Garcia back in September of the previous year. They had all been prepaid for a period of twelve months. I think I found my fall guy.

Otto had a sickly look about him when I explained what I thought was happening behind Frank's closed doors. I had a decision to make. I could continue to play the role of Bob Hannah, the dashing, palindromic detective who would certainly coerce Otto into opening up those units but that was a dangerous game. It's one thing to impersonate an officer to extract a bit of information. It's a completely different matter to convince someone to perform a crime while flashing the badge. Not only would it be an evidentiary nightmare for law enforcement down the road but I could lose my license and quite possibly go to jail if the blow back reached all the way to my front doorstep. Not to mention the fact that Harvey would be super pissed at me. So I compromised with myself. I told Otto to stay away from those units for the time being and I got him to give me Bump's cell phone number and home address.

I called Harvey and told him about the newest revelation. I asked him to obtain a warrant to search the premises. As expected he told me there wasn't a judge on the planet that would sign it given the scintilla of justifiable cause. He told me to get him something more substantial so I headed over to Eagle Rock in hopes of doing just that.

I decided not to call Bump to let him know I was coming. As well as we hit it off yesterday I had a feeling he didn't want a second date. This was going to be a surprise visit. He lived in a large apartment complex just south of Colorado Boulevard near Occidental College. The two story structure was rectangular in shape and it surrounded a common area dominated by a pool that was desperately in need of some chlorine and a good cleaning. That didn't seem to bother the tenants however. It was night time now and the pool lights were on. The barbeques around the square were fired up, the music was pulsing and the college age crowd was celebrating probably nothing more than just another day of being young. Reason enough if you ask me.

All of this activity provided a solid cover as I knocked on the door of Apartment 214. Bump didn't answer and the curtains were drawn. His lock was even more rudimentary than the one I picked at Top 2 Bottom. Apparently today was my day for breaking and entering. I donned a pair of latex gloves and with the slide of a credit card I was inside before the pool revelers could yell Marco Polo.

Bump was a slob. The living room was cluttered with fast food wrappers, empty beer cans and clothes that appeared to have been laundered but never folded and put away. The coffee table was covered with cigarette butts and marijuana shake. The large pipe that stood front and center had obviously been tipped over recently because the incomparable smell of spilt bong water permeated throughout the room. The kitchen sink was full of dirty dishes and the refrigerator was woefully stocked. A trail of ants had come through the wall via an electrical outlet and were lining up, buffet style, to feast on the smorgasbord of delights the kitchen counter was currently offering. The bathroom actually wasn't too bad if you discounted the mold that was spreading across the floor of the shower. I didn't lift up the toilet seat. I decided to give Bump the benefit of the doubt on that one.

I finally made my way into the bedroom. Under a poster of Nirvana he was sleeping so peacefully I almost didn't have the heart to disturb him. That is until I noticed the surgical tubing tied off just above his elbow and the needle and syringe resting in his open hand. Bump's eyes were still open and he was as white as the sheet he was laying on. I went in for a closer look and discovered the circular cut marks around his wrists. It was a long time ago but I knew from personal experience exactly what caused them. Bump had been tied up and struggled mightily to free himself. He didn't die from an accidental overdose. Someone had bound him to the chair and injected him with a hot shot. Bump had been murdered.

I called Harvey.

"What's going on OT?"

"Well you know that fourteen count on the homicides this weekend?"

"Yeah, what about it?"

"You can add another one."

Eagle Rock was LAPD turf so Harvey explained exactly what he wanted me to do. I went to a local pharmacy, purchased a burner phone and anonymously called it in to 911. When the call made its way through to police dispatch Harvey assigned himself as the investigating officer. Thirty minutes later Bump's apartment was swarming with uniforms, crime scene techs and a representative from the coroner's office. While they were all working the scene Harvey and I went to go look at the security footage.

The property manager's name was Dorothy. She was 27 years old and originally from Wichita. I swear I didn't make that up. These are the moments when I literally cannot help myself. I was about to dive in but Harvey, knowing me all too well, squeezed my shoulder and gave me the 'don't even think about it glare.' All I really wanted to know was if Toto is her favorite rock band of all-time. What would have been the harm in that? She was here at Oxy, as the locals call it, pursuing her doctorate in the field of economics. In exchange for managing the complex she lived rent free and received a small stipend for her troubles. Bump, she said, was a nice man and a good tenant who pretty much kept to himself. She couldn't recall him ever entertaining friends nor did he try to ingratiate himself with the other, mostly younger renters. There were times when he'd forget to put away his drug paraphernalia and on occasion the smell of marijuana would drift from his unit out into the commons. But, as Dorothy pointed out, the same could be said for half of the tenants in the building. She seemed a bit shell shocked from the unfolding situation here. I guess having someone murdered one floor above you can do that to a person. I'm sorry Dorothy but in case you haven't noticed, you're not in Kansas anymore. She popped Sunday's tape into the VCR, handed me the remote and then excused herself. I think she retreated to her bedroom to click her heels twice and then call Auntie Em who would tell her that everything was going to be okay.

I fast forwarded the tape to the 11:45 mark. If they had driven directly here from Otto's it would have taken at least that long to make it across town. I ran the video at 3x's actual speed until a longish, dark vehicle pulled up curbside in front of the building. The consulate car. The time was 12:12 p.m. The security system was antiquated and the quality of the black and white video wasn't very good. It had a grainy, jumpy quality to it that made even the most mundane occurrences look rather sinister. The lone camera was mounted high above the entrance to the building and was positioned in such a way that it covered the front door, about fifteen feet of sidewalk and no more than two feet out into the street. It was far less than ideal.

At 12:14 the rear passenger door opened and Bump stepped out onto the sidewalk then quickly passed under the security camera disappearing from sight. The town car didn't leave. Three minutes later a newer model Ford Mustang pulled up alongside. It was far enough out in front to where the license plate was exposed. I paused the tape but neither Harvey nor I could make out the number. The film quality was too poor. That was going to be something for the techs to sort out.

Shortly after I hit play again two men exited the Mustang and the driver sped away. They were hard looking, thick bodied Latinos. We got a great look at them as they passed directly under the security camera on their way over to the consulate car.

"The muscle has arrived," Harvey observed. I nodded in agreement.

After a very brief conversation the two men entered the apartment building presumably with bad intent. The consulate car then pulled away from the curb and was gone. The time was 12:18 p.m.

"We've got enough for a search warrant now," Harvey said. "That was some damned good detective work OT. Let's go."

Harvey handed the cassette over to one of his junior detectives with explicit instructions as to what he wanted done. Two minutes later we were in my truck heading back over to Otto's. We had a black and white in front of us and another directly behind, both with their cherry tops lit up. As I drove Harvey got Victoria on the phone and the two of them worked seamlessly in preparing the search warrant. Victoria typed as Harvey dictated. He then called a judge who also happened to be an old surfing buddy letting him know the request would land in his inbox very shortly. Harvey assured him it was rock solid and that's all the man needed to hear. They chit chatted for a moment about life and surf breaks until the judge said 'got it.' He electronically signed it and emailed it back to Victoria who in turn texted the document to Harvey. Victoria then emailed a copy to Otto so we could print it out for him upon our arrival. Wielding power isn't really my thing but boy it sure is fun to watch.

Otto was waiting outside the office when we came flying into the parking lot with the sirens blazing. Harvey said they prefer to roll in hot for effect. It's intimidating and that gives the police the psychological upper hand. Plus, he added, it's a lot more fun to do it this way. Poor Otto, you really had to feel for the guy. Just yesterday morning his biggest worry was whether or not to take the boat out on to the lake. Now, here he stood, waiting for the meteorite that was about to land directly on top of him and there wasn't a damn thing he could do about it. Before we got out of the truck I asked Harvey if I could reprise my award winning portrayal of Detective Hannah but he told me in no uncertain terms just to keep my mouth shut.

Sometimes artistic genius is under appreciated.

The units that were rented out to Frank Jr. were all on the fourth floor in the smaller of the two buildings. By the time we herded ourselves into the freight elevator we had gathered together quite an ensemble cast. There was Harvey and myself of course along with the four uniformed officers that blazed our trail across town. Then Harvey, out of professional courtesy, invited along a detective friend from the Sheriff's Department since Otto's physical address technically fell within their jurisdiction. It must have been a slow night at the station house because he showed up with three deputies in tow who were there for no other reason than to sate their own morbid curiosities. Even Otto tagged along for the ride. I guess some people prefer to be present when the hammer falls.

In regards to the storage units, Frank Jr. had chosen well. They were tucked away in a squared off alcove sandwiched between a large maintenance closet and a room that housed the steady drone of the building's power supply. One of the LAPD officers brought along a large bolt cutter and began snapping the locks off of the units. The doors themselves were roll tops and when we opened them in unison the sounds of sliding aluminum echoed off the cinder block walls in a very dramatic fashion.

Have you ever had one of those moments when you really wish you'd been wrong? Well this was one of mine. All the units had been set up as crude holding cells. Flush against the back walls sat metal framed beds that had been bolted to the concrete flooring. The unmade bedding consisted of wafer thin mattresses and frayed coarse blankets. Next to the beds sat oversized, white, paint buckets which I assumed had been used in lieu of the nonexistent toilets. There was no outside ventilation in any of the units which made the smell putrid enough to make Otto excuse himself and empty the contents of his stomach into a nearby 55 gallon trashcan. The chief source of the odor came from the unit adjacent to the maintenance closet where the lifeless body of a young, Latina woman lay handcuffed to the bed with a large swath of gray, duct tape covering her mouth.

With my role of detective stripped away I knew better than to cross into the unit and compromise what was now officially a crime scene. Harvey put on latex gloves and shoe covers then went in to examine the body. He looked back at me and shook his head. It wasn't Reina and I exhaled sharply in relief. He snapped a picture of the victim and immediately texted it to me. She was young, pretty and no longer alive. Staring at her photo took me back to that train platform at Colleville-sur-Mer where so long ago I looked out at the sea of white crosses and contemplated the tragedy of young lives cut short. I could feel my anger beginning to manifest itself into something tangible, something almost lifelike. I was going to track these people down if it was the last thing I ever did.

I snapped out of it and began taking a closer look at the crime scene. Scattered across the flooring of the units were discarded needles and syringes undoubtedly used to make the guests at the Hotel Otto sleepy and very compliant. Something had gone terribly wrong here. These holding cells had been designed to detain on a very temporary basis. I'd say no more than 24-48 hours before the victims needed to be moved again. This poor young lady's death was undoubtedly a horrific side effect of the unraveling of Mr. Nine Finger's operation. She had been a loose end that no one bothered to tie up and because of that she had paid the ultimate price.

Much like at Bump's apartment earlier this evening, Otto's was soon crawling with crime scene investigators. Word had spread amongst the team that this one was personal to Harvey and they were processing the scene like a pack of foxhounds trying to locate a scent. I'm sure their hard work would reveal some of the answers to the questions surrounding Reina's disappearance but they weren't the kind that would come quickly.

Even if the case received prioritized attention it would take days, if not weeks to get some results. They'd arrive through an IAFAS hit, a CODIS match or perhaps from the top of a coroner's table. This case was going to be solved one way or the other before the scientific process had time to worm its way through the system. Harvey knew this and told me it was time for us to take off. He again directed a few of his best and brightest to take over and we were on our way back to Eagle Rock so he could pick up his car.

"Well," Harvey said on the drive over, "all in all a pretty simple favor I asked of you huh?"

That was his way of apologizing for dragging me into this but it wasn't necessary. I glanced his way and he immediately recognized the look. That look.

"Uh oh," he said, "it's happened again hasn't it?"

I nodded. It's a problem I encounter with cases more than I'd like to admit. I seem to be missing that dispassionate gene that all great detectives possess. The one that allows them to work objectively without preconceived prejudices. Just follow the evidence and keep emotion out of the equation. The Reina Montes cased had crossed over for me. It was personal now and Harvey knew there wasn't a chance in hell I wasn't taking this one to the finish line.

"Ok then Detective Bob Hannah," he said, "what's next?"

I rattled off my plans for the next day and as I did I realized I'd have to clone myself once or twice to cover half of them.

Harvey chuckled. "Well I guess it's a good thing I've taken the rest of the week off. I'm all yours."

I told Harvey if that was indeed the case then we needed to reverse roles. I suggested he take the lead now and I'd do whatever he felt needed to be done.

"OT," he said, "whether you realize it or not, I have some news for you. You're twice the detective I've ever dreamed of being and I know I'm a pretty damn good one. What you've accomplished on your own over the last two days is nothing short of some of the best investigative work I've ever witnessed. If you hadn't been such an obstinate prick when you were on the force there is no doubt in my mind I'd not only be working for you right now but I'd be damn proud to be doing it."

I didn't know how to respond. He was wrong of course but to argue the point would only serve to cheapen the incredible compliment I just received from a man I could only aspire to be. So instead we simply kicked the emotional moment to the curb and agreed to meet at Jeremy's, a coffee shop up my way, when it opened tomorrow morning at 6:00 a.m.

It was approaching midnight when I dropped Harvey off at his car. On the way up the 2 Freeway I really hit the wall. Man was I tired. I'd been running all day on minimal sleep and one uninspired meal. My only concrete plan at the moment involved a cold beer and a grilled cheese sandwich before collapsing on to my bed. I was officially done with the Reina Montes case for the night but when I turned down Ocean View Boulevard it became painfully obvious that the Reina Montes case wasn't done with me.

CHAPTER 26

I counted a total of seven first responder vehicles as I parked across the street from my building. There were four Glendale PD squad cars, a ladder company, a paramedic's van and an ambulance that was speeding away as I got out of my truck. The night's marine layer had arrived settling in low and thick. I couldn't see any smoke but the aftermath of a fire filled my nostrils with dread. A group of curious onlookers had set up shop in my small parking lot and I headed over to join them. Brigid spotted me and ran out into the street meeting me halfway. She hugged me and then buried her head into my shoulder. It was completely out of character for her and it took me by surprise. The crowd diverted their focus momentarily to bear witness to the reunion taking place in the middle of a busy street.

"Brigid," I said, "how many times do I have to tell you, not in front of the kids."

She didn't laugh probably because it wasn't funny. Gallows humor rarely is.

"Where have you been?" she asked. "I've been trying to reach you for almost an hour." Her eyes were red and swollen. She had been crying.

I extricated myself from her embrace and pulled the phone out of my pocket. The battery was dead. I'd been so caught up in this case I'd forgotten it even existed. I showed her the blank screen and she gently slugged me in the chest. She put her arms back around me and I returned the favor. It felt good. It felt right.

"I heard all of the sirens and then I saw the ambulance pull up," she said. "I thought something terrible had happened to you."

Cars started to honk so we made our way over to the sidewalk. I then placed my hands on her shoulders, looked her square in the eyes and said, "Brigid, please tell me what's going on here."

Before she had time to answer a detective from the Glendale PD made his way over to us. His name was Jerry Lam. He and I'd crossed paths on several occasions over the years and none of the encounters had been pleasant. Awhile back I took on a case of his that had ultimately gone unsolved. A young woman had been murdered and her parents hired me on the fourth anniversary of her death. They were convinced the killer was the manager of a restaurant where their daughter had worked as a cocktail waitress. The guy's alibi was rock solid however and Jerry was never able to break it. It had been supported by a group of four friends who steadfastly maintained the suspect was with them the entire night including the time of the murder. There were no other viable suspects to pursue so the investigation eventually ran out of steam. It had been kicked down to the cold case squad just three weeks before the family retained my services.

Lam had a surreptitious reputation amongst his peers as a hack and it became clear to me early on that he had bungled the investigation. I was able to expand the suspect's circle of friends and family and I learned rather quickly that many of them, off the record, doubted not only the veracity of the alibi but also the character of the men involved. I continued to dig which eventually led me to an ex-wife of one of the four men. An acrimonious divorce had left her angry and bitter. She gladly served up a completely different version of that night's events giving proof once again to the old adage, 'Hell hath no fury like a woman scorned.' Her story shattered the alibi and I used it to drive a wedge in between the suspect and his protectors. After that the rest of the dominos fell quickly and I delivered a confessed murderer to the police eight days after I took on the case. The story went viral and ended up being covered by the national news services. The police department had been momentarily embarrassed but after the dust settled I received a warm letter of thanks from the chief of police himself. It's actually framed and hanging on the wall behind my desk. Lam, on the other hand, had been completely humiliated. I brought closure to a grieving family and he's never forgiven me for it.

He approached with a smirk on his face. I got the impression my misfortune was bringing him some form of sadistic pleasure.

"Kane," he demanded, "I'm going to need you to account for your whereabouts over the last four hours."

His tone was condescending and given the current situation, completely unacceptable. Apparently we weren't going to work through the normal pleasantries.

"Why do you ask Jerry? Do you need my help in solving one of your cases?"

His face reddened and he took a step closer to me cutting the gap between us in half. He leaned in and I could smell breath mints which were probably masking the gin and tonics he was well known for drinking. He then went full tough guy on me.

"Well we can have this conversation here or we can hoof it down to Isabel Street and make it official."

I laughed. I was so punch drunk at this point I didn't have much of a handle on my emotions. My response was inappropriate but I'm sorry; my world is possibly spiraling out of control here and the guy comes at me with a line that's been used in just about every cop movie ever made. It was utterly disingenuous, especially coming from a weasel like Jerry. I was still functioning enough however to realize he was just petty enough to carry out the threat so I relented and gave him the sordid details of my night making sure I dragged Harvey's name across the entire timeline. This seemed to appease him and the two of us smartly took a step back from the ledge.

"Now, Jerry, if I ask nicely, can you please tell me what in the hell is going on here?"

To his credit he did. He pulled out his notepad and gave me the precise facts. "At 11:13 this evening the Glendale PD responded to an active alarm originating from your building. The first squad car arrived at 11:17. The front door was locked so the officers went through that tunnel there."

He was pointing towards the breeze way but I didn't see any point in arguing semantics so I let him keep going. "When the officers reached the patio they discovered the large plate glass window had been shattered and a there was a fire inside the office gathering strength. One of the officers called it into the fire department then retrieved an extinguisher from the squad car. He was able to put out the fire but not before it caused extensive damage inside the building."

The nine fingered man was sending me a message to back off. I'd been poking the tiger in his cage and now he was out and he was hunting.

Jerry continued. "The other officer called in for medical assistance and then attended to the victim."

My tired, numb body jolted to attention. I instantly felt nauseous.

"Victim? Jerry what do you mean? Did someone get hurt?"

Brigid walked up from behind as Lam flipped through his notes. "Able, it's Nate. I saw them loading him into the ambulance."

"Yes, that's correct," Lam said, "a Mr. Nate Isaacson was found face down when the officers arrived on the scene. He had suffered multiple stab wounds. The attending officer stanched the bleeding to the best of his abilities and performed CPR when he realized the victim was no longer breathing under his own power. The paramedics arrived at 11:35 and the ambulance three minutes later."

That must have been the ambulance I saw driving away. "Please tell me he's alive." I was pleading to both Jerry and Brigid hoping one of them could give me the answer I so desperately wanted to hear.

Lam put away his notebook and spoke to me compassionately for the first time ever. "He still had a pulse when he was placed in the back of the ambulance but it was very weak. I'm sorry."

"Where'd they take him?"

Brigid spoke first. "Able, I heard the paramedics say they were taking him to Verdugo Hills."

This conversation was over. I ran back across the street towards my truck and Brigid matched me stride for stride. If Lam had any more questions they'd have to wait. The hospital was just five minutes away and I hoped the proximity would help save Nate's life.

The emergency room was deserted which was probably typical for the earliest hours of a Tuesday morning. The admitting nurse was sitting behind the glass partition playing with her phone. She looked up as the automatic doors opened with a whoosh. She waved to me. Her name was Carly or Kelly, something along those lines. I'm absolutely terrible when it comes to remembering people's names. If you find me calling you partner or buddy it probably means that I've forgotten yours.

I've been volunteering at the hospital for almost three years now. There is a dedicated group of volunteers here and I'm proud to be a small part of it. We do the simple things. Wheelchair assistance, prescription deliveries and the messengering of documents back and forth from the hospital to the surrounding medical offices. I made my approach to Carly, or maybe Kelly.

"What's wrong Able?" she asked. She must have noticed the worn out expression on my face.

I slyly glanced down at her nametag. Kylie. Well, I was close. I explained why I was here.

"Are you a relative of the patient?" she asked me.

"No I'm not Kylie. Just a very good friend and to be honest with you, I think I'm all he's got. Can you help me out here?"

She smiled. "Of course. Anything for our favorite volunteer."

I looked back at Brigid. Normally a comment like that would invoke an eye roll but this time she simply eliminated the space between us and wrapped her two arms around one of mine. I could definitely get used to this.

"I just got on shift," Kylie remarked as she began tapping away on her keyboard. "Let's see what's happening. Here he is. Mr. Isaacson was admitted just fifteen minutes ago and he's already in surgery. He must be in pretty bad shape Able. I'm sorry."

I appreciated the blunt assessment. "Who's doing the surgery Kylie?"

She looked at her monitor again. "Dr. Jenkins."

Finally some good news. I know Jenkins personally. We both belong to the same golf club. He's ex-Army, doesn't cheat at golf and has an excellent reputation as a knife man. Nate was in good hands. I told Kylie I was going to wait until they got out of surgery and asked her if she'd let Jenkins know I wanted to see him when it was over. I then told Brigid to take my truck and go home but she wouldn't hear of it. We sat down, she laid her head on my shoulder and we waited.

We both must have fallen asleep because the next thing I knew I was being awakened by Dr. Jenkins tapping me on the shoulder. I had been in such a deep sleep it literally felt like I was climbing out of a bottomless well as I made my way back to the land of the living.

"Wake up Sunshine," Dr. Jenkins said to me. He had a mischievous grin on his face and I prayed to God his expression was a harbinger of good news.

"He's going to make it," he succinctly informed me. The relief was so overwhelming I broke down in tears. As I cried he went on about a nicked artery and vital organs that had been miraculously missed. I'm sure it was all very important but at the moment I didn't care. Nate was going to survive and that was all that mattered.

Brigid was awake now and Dr. Jenkins diverted the conversation to her.

"Get this man to bed young lady. Mr. Isaacson will not be receiving visitors for at least forty eight hours. Tell this marine I'll call him tomorrow afternoon and give him a full debriefing. I can't have grown men crying in my ER. It's undignified."

He was of course being sarcastic but it was exactly what I needed to hear. I laughed through the tears and allowed Brigid to escort me back to my truck. She insisted on driving.

"You're coming home with me tonight," she announced. I didn't say a word. Who am I to argue such things?

She lived several blocks away from me on the alley side of my building. We pulled into her narrow driveway and without saying a word she leaned across the driver's seat and kissed me. It was the best kiss I've been on the receiving end of in a very long time. Actually, it's the only kiss I've been on the receiving end of in a very long time but trust me, it was a darn good one. Brigid got out of the truck and I watched her walk up the short flight of stairs to her front door. The porch light and the heavy fog combined to produce an ethereal image of her. It was transfixing. She looked back, smiled and then crossed over the threshold. She purposely left the door wide open and I hoped it was not only an invitation for the night but maybe to a life that no longer had to be lived alone. My next thought though was, dear lord, I smell like a week's worth of garbage.

She asked me what I wanted to eat and then strongly suggested I hop into the shower. I ran the water long and hot letting it scorch my tired, aching body. It was the perfect elixir for what was ailing me. I toweled off, plugged my phone into a charger and lied down on Brigid's bed waiting for it to power up. The digital clock on her nightstand read 3:16. I was asleep before it flipped over to 3:17. I dreamt of God and devils and of men and monsters. It was undoubtedly my subconscious reminding me that I would soon be waging war against an enemy who had already proven he would stop at nothing to achieve victory. It would be a war I probably had no chance of winning but one that must be fought all the same. I had crossed the Rubicon now and there was no turning back. The die had been cast. Eventually my dreams retired themselves and released me into the calm. The calm, that is, before the storm.

CHAPTER 27

(Back to the past)

October 6, 1985

I arrived in San Diego mid-morning on a Sunday. The temperature outside was a perfect seventy three degrees and the sun sparkled off Mission Bay while the sailboats bobbed up and down tethered to their moorings. This was obviously a special place and I hoped it was just the remedy to help lift my spirits. I had spent the last three days either up in the air being diverted away from severe weather or sitting in airports watching my connecting flights get delayed and cancelled. I was tired, jet lagged and to be honest, more than a little depressed. My funds were at an all-time low and I felt a growing trepidation about seeing my family again. I was angry at each and every one of them for a variety of reasons. First, there was my brother Jonah who wished death upon me the last time we had spoken. 'Able, I hope you catch a bullet' was precisely what he said. To this day when I think of those seven words it feels like someone has stabbed me in the heart. We're twins and we've always shared a special bond. How he could so easily sever it was both perplexing and hurtful to me. I wanted to know why. Then there was my father, the great prevaricator. I hated the constant lying, the terrible way he had treated my mother and the newly discovered realization that he never wanted me in the first place. That was probably the biggest wound of all. My grandparents wouldn't get a free pass either. I'm well versed in the Kane family dynamic and I know a decision as big as the excommunication of Able could only have been handed down by them. One of my grandmother's favorite sayings was 'you're either with us or you're against us.' Never in my wildest imagination did I think she'd carry out that threat against one of her own grandchildren. As for me, well I was no longer that shy, timid teenager who boarded the bus bound for Parris Island four years ago. I was going to tell them all exactly how I felt and let the chips fall where they may. Today was beginning to feel a lot more like a confrontation than it did a family reunion. Probably what I should have done was check into a cheap motel for the day and emotionally regroup. Instead I went straight to the rental car area. I asked the agent, an attractive, sun kissed blond by the name of Kim, to get me the most inexpensive car available. We did some quick paperwork and then she apologetically handed over the keys to a Mercury Lynx. I purchased a road map and something called a Thomas Guide then headed northeast on Highway 94 for the short drive to El Cajon and the Eureka Community Church.

It became apparent very quickly that in the rental car game you get what you pay for. The Lynx wasn't much more than an oversized beer can with a four cylinder internal combustion engine. It strained to make its way up even the slightest of hills and when I buried the accelerator to help it along the entire car would shudder like an Apollo space capsule reentering the earth's atmosphere.

It did however get me to El Cajon and between the two of us we found the church without issue. It was a modest structure, much smaller than the churches we'd been involved with in the past. The Kane men had grown used to preaching to large assemblies of people including two so called mega churches during our stops in Des Moines and St. Louis. I was surprised they'd settled in to such modest accommodations.

There was a service ongoing when I pulled into the parking lot. Through the closed doors of the church I could hear the congregation singing How Great Thou Art just slightly off key. I didn't wish to be disruptive so I decided to take a walk around the property. On the other side of the parking lot, past a well kempt lawn and a flourishing rose garden sat another building sharing space with some outdoor playground equipment. Through the windows I could see children's art taped to the classroom walls along with big block letters spelling out the alphabet. The door opened and an elderly janitor emerged pushing a gray trash can on caster wheels. He looked my way and I gave him a friendly wave. He stared at me momentarily than darted back inside without returning the greeting. Okay, be that way I thought to myself not thinking too much of it.

Beyond that building, partially hidden behind a row of eucalyptus trees was a large construction site. The footings were in and several of the concrete pads had been poured. There was a small billboard off to the left. It was an architect's rendering of a large church and school complete with miniature cars and tiny people wandering about. The design was as beautiful as it was ambitious with lots of white block, reflective glass and a huge steeple stretching towards Heaven. When completed, it would be an impressive monument to God. There was a proud declaration above the drawing which stated, 'The Future Home of the Eureka Community Church and Christian Learning Center.' The billboard had begun to yellow with age and I could see no construction equipment anywhere on the site. I decided to take a closer look at the project. The foundations were flawless but the rebar had begun to oxidize and the trenched lines were being overtaken by weeds. A familiar, sinking feeling began to envelope me. A church building fund managed by the Kane family spelled nothing but trouble.

Eventually I headed back towards the church. I took a seat on a stone bench that was generously shaded by an old oak tree. While I sat there waiting for the service to end I couldn't get my hands to stop shaking.

At exactly 12 o'clock the doors to the church opened and the parishioners started filing out. They began to congregate just below the steps that led to the foyer. High Noon, how perfectly ironic. The first time I ever saw the movie I was just a young, naïve boy. When the main character, Will Kane, first appeared on screen I asked my grandfather if the sheriff was his brother. Ezekiel Kane got a big kick out of that one. My family of course didn't present the same dangers as Frank Miller and his clan but I think I knew exactly how Gary Cooper must have been feeling. Alone, with no ally other than his own convictions, as he readied himself for the fight that would soon be arriving on the afternoon train.

Life, however, wouldn't get the chance to imitate art on this occasion. The showdown never occurred. As an unfamiliar reverend emerged from the vestibule a flotilla of police cars sped into the parking lot. They were being waved in by the same impolite janitor I had encountered just twenty five minutes earlier. I was handcuffed with my arms around my back, read my rights and aggressively tossed into the backseat of one of the cruisers. My head hit the armrest on the other side of the vehicle gashing my forehead.

On the trip back to downtown San Diego the patrolman on the front passenger side turned around and informed me I was bleeding. The blood at this point was trickling into my right eye, moving down my face and dripping on to my pant leg.

"Hey thanks for letting me know," I said. He thought that was funny.

"So, we're all wondering, how'd you pull it off?" he asked.

Pull what off? I had no idea what he was talking about. "Well," I said, "when you tossed me into the backseat I reached out with my head to break the fall. All in all, I think I did a pretty good job."

The two cops, one old and one very young, looked at each other and broke out in laughter. My humor was spanning generations now. They quickly lost interest in me though and their conversation turned to football, the Chargers and Don Coryell's high octane offense. The how'd you pull it off question was soon forgotten.

I was taken to San Diego's central jail for processing and man handled into the anteroom by the same cops who had tossed me into the back of their cruiser. The corrections officer working the front desk couldn't help but stare at my bloodied face.

"Hey Billy," he said to the older cop, "how come you always seem to get the clumsy ones?"

That made Billy chuckle. "I know right? Just lucky I guess. So Fred, who do you like in the game today?"

"Take the Raiders and the five Billy."

"Tell you what," I chimed in, "give me the Chargers and I'll lay the points." I thought Fred may want my action.

Billy laughed again but this time it was at Fred's expense. Fred glared at me then gave me the two finger back and forth move insinuating that he was going to keep a close eye on me during my stay here.

"Watch this guy Freddie," Billy said, "he's already escaped from Tehachapi so there's no telling what he might have up his sleeve. He's a real comedian too."

It was a busy day at the old jailhouse. The queue included drunks, vagrants and Raider fans who apparently weren't going to make it to the big game. I was told to behave and go to the end of the line. I hate lines. Add it to the list. I especially hate the ones that end up with me being incarcerated.

When I finally got to the head of the line I found myself standing in front of two muscle bound officers, one black and one white, who were sitting behind a metal desk processing the paperwork. They came across as angry men who hated their jobs. It made me think of the 1930's gangster movies starring guys like James Cagney and George Raft when some mad at the world prison bull ends up taking out his frustrations on the skull of some unsuspecting inmate. I gave them both my best compliant smile.

"Spell your last name please," the black officer said never taking his eyes off the paperwork he was shuffling.

"K-A-N-E," I replied still trying to process the fact I escaped from something or someone called Tehachapi.

The black guy looked over to his partner who scanned the list. He pointed to a spot on the clipboard.

"There he is, blue."

Manned with that information the black officer strapped a blue band on my wrist faster than I could blink. I had noticed the harmless drunk in front of me was issued an orange band.

"Can I choose my own color?" I asked. "Orange really makes my eyes pop."

"Orange is for misdemeanors, blue is for felonies," I was informed by the white officer rather matter of factly.

A felony? I just got into town two hours ago. What's the charge? Driving a motorized Budweiser can?

"Officers," I pleaded, "can you please tell me what charges have been brought against me? I really have no idea what's going on."

The white officer shrugged his shoulders and looked once again at his clipboard. "Class C felony Kane. First degree escape from a correctional facility. You're our guest until the U.S. Marshalls Service can come and grab you. FYI Kane, bail is not an option for you so you might as well make yourself comfortable."

"But I'm innocent," I blurted out. "I haven't done anything wrong." I regretted the words immediately. I can't imagine how mundane my short soliloquy must have sounded to them.

They looked at each other and I could see it. The two of them non-verbally asking each other is it your turn or mine.

Apparently that privilege belonged to the black officer. "Oh,

I apologize," he said, "I didn't know you were innocent. You should have said so before I strapped that bracelet on you. Louis, did you hear that? My goodness, the paperwork we're going to have to fill out now."

He then stood up and cleared his throat until he had the room's undivided attention. "Listen up everyone, we have some big news here today. This man has just informed us that he is innocent of all charges. There has obviously been a gross miscarriage of justice here and on behalf of the City of San Diego I'd like to offer him our humblest of apologies."

It was a good bit and it received a well deserved laugh especially from the guys wearing the silver and black. This obviously wasn't their first rodeo.

Sporting my newly acquired blue wristband I was then fingerprinted, photographed and placed into what the guards called the phone tank. It was named that for good reason. Affixed to the wall were four collect-call only phones and two payphones. Every inmate had up to three hours to contact a family member, attorney or bondsman to arrange bail. Since that wasn't in the cards for me I quickly grabbed an open seat and took in the scene.

I counted thirteen of us squeezed into an area the size of a modest living room. Next to the bank of phones stood a cold water only sink and an exposed toilet I hoped and prayed I wouldn't have to use. The combination of vomit, urine and feces hung heavy in the uncirculated air. The odor was horrific. There was a lot of pushing and shoving going on as people argued over phone usage, skin color and insults, both real and imagined. The place felt like a powder keg ready to explode.

Thankfully things began to settle down after everyone got to make their one phone call. The guards began calling out names and one by one inmates were escorted out of the cell. Then a new group would arrive and the cycle would begin anew.

When my three hours were up a group of us were led into an adjacent room to be strip searched. I was told to stand on the red line, keep my mouth shut and completely disrobe. Every pocket, sock, shoe and stitch of clothing were closely inspected for makeshift weapons and contraband. The few legitimate belongings I owned were placed in a plastic bag and sealed. A latex gloved guard then probed and examined every part of my body and I do mean every part. It was humiliating. When they were convinced we had nothing to hide we were handed back our clothing and allowed to dress. From there we were escorted to a large dormitory style room and individually assigned a cot complete with a blanket and a paper wrapped pillow. There was a mere two feet of space separating my bed from my neighbors and I was prepared to defend that twenty four inches if it became necessary.

Once we settled in the supervising officer spoke. "Listen up everybody, especially those of you who will be with us for a few days. Breakfast is at 6:00 sharp, lunch 11:30 and dinners at 5:30. If you wish to eat show up on time. This is not a Carl's Jr. Toilets and showers are to my right and they are closely monitored. Cigarettes can be purchased for $2.00 a pack and you can buy up to four a day. Are there any questions?"

No one spoke up. "Good," he said. He then pointed to a television set mounted high up on the wall and far out of reach. "I'm going to turn the game on now. It will stay on as long as you all can behave like human beings. Let's not make this anymore difficult than it already is." And with that the guards left the room leaving us to our own devices.

While the majority of the inmates headed over to the sitting area to watch the game I laid down on my cot hoping sleep would come so I could move this nightmare further down the road. It wasn't going to come easy though. I was in a dolorous mood and my brain was working feverishly to try and figure out why I was in jail resting my throbbing head on a paper covered pillow. I was afraid Mr. Occam's razor was in play here.

The most logical explanation was my brother was now a felon and I was caught in a case of mistaken identity. I had no idea what he'd gotten himself into but it certainly wouldn't be the first time we'd been confused for each other. Jonah and I are identical twins and we used to reverse roles on purpose. Sometimes for fun, sometimes for our own benefit and sometimes just to see if we could get away with it.

CHAPTER 28

On April 1st, 1981, during our senior year of high school my brother wanted to play an April Fool's Day joke on his girlfriend, Kathy. She was the prettiest girl at Clay High School and she was madly in love with my charismatic brother. He had planned a date with her that evening to grab a bite to eat and then go see Jack Nicholson in The Postman Always Rings Twice. His iniquitous plan was for me to pick her up and take her to the restaurant all the while pretending to be him. He'd then, at some point, walk into the Burger Chef and reveal the joke. No harm, no foul he assured me. To sweeten the pot he promised me fifty dollars if I successfully pulled it off. I told him no. I liked Kathy a lot, in fact I'd go as far as saying I had a secret crush on her. As far as April Fool's jokes go I felt this one was mean spirited and way over the top. Jonah disagreed. He thought she'd find it funny and he badgered me until I acquiesced. In the end I begrudgingly agreed to play along.

My hair was longer than his at the time so that afternoon we went to the barbershop together and got the stylist to match my cut to Jonah's. You would have been hard pressed to tell us apart. At 6:00 that evening I put on Jonah's favorite button down shirt and joylessly drove across town to pick her up.

There was one silver lining in this clouded charade. I got to switch cars with my brother. I had been working part time jobs since I was thirteen years old and finally saved up enough money to buy myself a car, a 1971 AMC Gremlin. It was birthday present to myself when I turned seventeen. It was world class ugly and a terrible automobile but it ran and it was all mine. Three months later, the day after my brother quarterbacked our high school football team to the league championship my grandparents surprised him with a 1969 Oldsmobile 442. It was a beautiful, muscled out car that accelerated like it was shot out of a cannon. I didn't speak to my grandparents for weeks afterwards. I'm not sure they even noticed.

As I pulled up in front of the Pierson home Kathy was sitting on her front porch dutifully waiting for me. As she bounded down the steps I got out and opened the passenger door for her. She was wearing a white sundress and her skin was bronzed from a recent family trip to Miami over spring break. She looked incredible.

She had an amused smile on her face as she approached. "Well this is different Jonah," she said, "I think I like it." She followed that up with an intimate kiss on my cheek and I hoped that would be enough to unravel our devious plan. It wasn't meant to be. Things would have been so different if I'd just followed my instincts and come clean right then and there but the need to please my brother was always present. He held that kind of influence over me.

The Olds had a front bench seat and Kathy slid all the way over until our bodies were touching. "How do I look?" she asked.

Fantastic, out of this world, I think I'm in love with you. "Very nice," I said instead, "we should get going."

She leaned into me and rubbed my upper thigh. It was meant only as an innocent, loving gesture but I got aroused immediately. What happened was involuntary and totally unwelcomed but that didn't make it any less obvious. My heart was beating a mile a minute but Kathy just looked down and giggled. No big deal.

"Okay," she said, "let's go, I'm starving." Jonah, in the land of bad ideas, this one is king. What in the world were you thinking?

We parked in the lot behind the restaurant and made our way around to the front entrance. I held the door opened and Kathy passed through. Before entering I looked across the street to the city park and spotted Jonah sitting on a swing sipping a beer. He gave me a thumbs up and I flipped him the bird.

Kathy chose a table in the busiest part of the restaurant. She sat down and I went to the counter and ordered our food. I brought it back to the table and set her tray down in front of her. That was when she opened up the bay doors.

"I have something to tell you." She sounded nervous, serious. "I need you to promise me you won't get angry."

I sat down and really looked at her closely for the first time that evening. Her eyes were slightly red around the edges. She had been crying fairly recently.

She grabbed both of my hands and locked her eyes onto mine. The target was now acquired and she armed the device. "I've missed my period Jonah. I'm a week late now and I'm never late. I think we're pregnant."

Bombs away.

It's so strange the things that can enter your mind at the most inappropriate of times. They're not invited but they come barging in all the same. As Kathy sat there crying I was reminded of a joke my father once told me. The Lone Ranger and his Indian sidekick Tonto were trapped in a box canyon as a group of Apache warriors were advancing on their position. The Lone Ranger, after firing his last bullet, turned to his partner and said, "Tonto, I think we are in a lot of trouble." Tonto looked at him and said, "What do you mean by we Kemosahbee?"

I now understood why Kathy had chosen the busiest area of the restaurant. Jonah was known for his quick temper and she was practicing mitigation. Smart girl. I just stared at her speechless. The earth had spun off its axis and was careening around the solar system about to do great damage.

"Well aren't you going to say something?" she implored. Her face was now pinched in and furrowed.

Yes I should say something, but what? I was way out of my depth here. If relationships were math I could barely add and subtract. Now I was being asked to solve an advanced calculus problem.

"Uhm, I'm sorry," was the best I could come up with. I think it fell a little short.

"You're sorry?" she asked incredulously. "That's all you have to say? You're the one that talked me into doing it without protection in the first place. You said everything was going to be alright. Jonah, what are we going to do?"

Kathy had her back to the street front window but I didn't. Jonah had finished his beer and was crossing the street heading our way. Boy was he in for a surprise. I told Kathy I had to use the bathroom. I left her alone with her tears and snuck out the back door to the parking lot. I caught Jonah's attention just as he was about to enter the restaurant.

"Hey little brother, how's it going in there?" Jonah had beat me into this world by the sum total of eighteen minutes and he loved to lord that over me.

"We have to change clothes right now," I said on the verge of hyperventilating.

"What are you talking about? What happened?" He was picking up on my vibe that something had gone very wrong.

I told him everything that had occurred as quickly as I could. He leaned against the Olds and then collapsed backwards on to its hood. Jonah began cussing, first to himself, then to me and finally loud enough to draw the attention of a group of men playing pickup basketball across the street. He remained there on the hood, motionless for a moment or two then stood back up again. I could tell the panic he initially felt was gone. Anger and resolve had taken its place. The transformation was as impressive as it was disconcerting. Jonah then shocked and grossly disappointed me.

"Give me my keys," he demanded.

I couldn't believe what I was hearing. "Why Jonah?" I asked. "Where do you think you're going?"

"I'm getting out of here. That bitch tricked me into having sex with her. I'm not going to let her ruin my life. You're gonna have to break up with her for me."

He wasn't thinking straight. His survival instincts were kicking in and he was tossing women and children out of the lifeboat. I've witnessed Jonah being cold and selfish before but this was way beyond that. This was cruel and a complete dereliction of basic human responsibilities. I would readily admit I was naïve when it came to the complexities of relationships but I did know that it takes two to tango.

I stood my ground. "Like hell I will Jonah. You need to get your ass in there and face the music. Kathy deserves at least that much and a heck of a lot more if you ask me."

I might as well have been arguing with the wind. He was hearing none of it. "Able, either you're going to give me my keys or I'm going to take them from you. You decide."

"Jonah you aren't going anywhere. It's time for you to do the right thing."

He lunged for my pants pocket but I took a step back and slapped his hand as hard as I could. That seemed to calm him down.

"Okay, okay. You're right Able," he said. "Sorry. This whole things just got me freaked out. Let's change clothes and you can get out of here. This isn't your problem."

Jonah was wearing just a t-shirt and he quickly stripped it off and handed it to me. I set it on the hood of his car and started undoing the buttons on my shirt. On the second button down he sucker punched me in the stomach. I dropped to my knees gasping for air that wouldn't come. He grabbed his keys from my pocket and fish tailed out of the parking lot without saying a word. It took a minute or two before I could breathe regularly again. When I finally stood up Kathy was coming out of the back door of the restaurant. She ran over and gave me a hug.

"My God, what happened Jonah?" she asked. "You're hurt. Did someone steal the car?"

It was reckoning time and I gave her the unvarnished truth. I exposed our misguided plan, my true identity and the hard fact Jonah would not be joining us. The look in her eyes would be forever burned into my soul. Her heart had been broken into a million pieces and I loathed myself for the role I had played in its breaking.

"I'm sorry," was once again all I could manage.

Her retort was both simple and devastating. "I hate you Able Kane and I never want to see you again." She slapped me hard across my face and walked away.

Ironically, three days later Kathy did get her period. The day after that she and my brother were a couple again. Jonah managed to rewrite history and this terrible idea of his had magically become mine. Not only would Kathy never talk to me again but our mutual group of so-called friends circled the wagons against me. I had been surgically ostracized. Jonah eventually offered me a lukewarm apology but it was too little and too late. The following Saturday I drove up to Chicago and acted upon something I had been considering for quite sometime. I enlisted in the United States Marine Corps effective immediately upon graduating from high school.

CHAPTER 29

'The mills of God grind slowly, yet they grind exceedingly small. Though with patience he stands waiting and with exactness he grinds all.'

Give or take that's from Sextus Empiricus, a second century philosopher. He was referring to the sometimes slow but inexorable pace at which justice marches along. The old thinker must have done a stint or two at the San Diego Central Jail. For two days I sat, slept and kept my head well below the foxhole line. During this time, not once did a prison guard or official update me regarding my purgatory like status. I ate on occasion and it was consistently terrible. The food was all starchy carbohydrates which I'm pretty sure had been doctored to keep the inmates' volatility at bay. After several meals I found myself in a mood that was equal parts ambivalence and indolence. I couldn't shake my gloomy disposition nor did I have the desire to do anything about it. I was just doing my time and not rocking the boat. That was a good thing because I witnessed what happened to those who did. If you fought, acted out or made amorous advances towards a fellow inmate the guards shipped you off to the fifth floor where the violent offenders were housed. This here wasn't living but it was certainly better than the alternative.

Finally, on Wednesday morning as I was headed to the dining room for another soporific meal, I heard my name called out.

"Abel Kane," the man said as he waived me over. He was Asian, short of stature and probably in his early forties. He was holding the plastic bag containing my personal items and he had a bemused smile on his face as I made my way over to him.

"Wow," he said, "identical twins. Who would have thunk? Able, my name is Kenny Takahashi and I'm a detective with the San Diego PD. Are you ready to get out of here?"

If there was ever a more rhetorical question I sure would like to shakes its hand. We walked out of the jail stride for stride. Me with a newfound bounce in my step and my liberator with a noticeable limp.

Twenty five minutes later I was sitting in a cracked, red naugahyde booth at a roadside diner that served the best Denver omelette I would ever eat. As I attacked it along with a short stack of pancakes Detective Takahashi sipped on black coffee and took an occasional bite out of a blueberry muffin. In between bites he puffed away on his Camel non-filtered cigarettes.

"Not bad huh?" he asked while watching me devour my breakfast. "Here's a tip Able. Whenever you want a good, hearty meal always look for a parking lot full of pickup trucks. It never fails. I take people here whenever I have to apologize on behalf of the city."

"So how'd you finally figure it out?" I asked him.

He picked up a fork and carved out a small section of my short stack before answering. "Damn, that's good," he said. "No great mystery. These things just take time. Your passport was the first red flag. Then on Sunday night I was notified your fingerprints didn't match. Unfortunately for you I was out on a date and by the time I got home it was too late to do anything about it. I contacted the warden's office at Tehachapi the first thing the next morning."

"What is a Tehachapi by the way?"

"Not a California kid huh? It's a state prison up in Kern County about two hours north of Los Angeles. It took all of yesterday for them to get back to us. Finally they confirmed Jonah was still tucked away in his prison cell. While I was waiting to hear back from them I pulled your military file. You had quite a short but impressive career didn't you? I'm an ex-Marine myself."

I didn't respond. Instead I kept ploughing away at my breakfast.

"Fine," he continued, "if you're going to keep badgering me I'll tell you all about it."

I did my best to suppress a smile but it didn't work.

"I was in 'Nam with the 5th and I fought at Rung Sat, Chu Lai and Phu Bai. That's where I got this lovely going away present," he said rubbing his right leg. "Shrapnel from a toe-popper. I was just five days away from rotating out. That same mine took out three of my closest friends. God I hated those rice paddies. For years my VA shrink kept telling me I needed to do a better job of counting my blessings. I got tired of hearing it and finally had to fire him. Since then I've learned to just get up every day, keep moving and try to be productive. So far so good."

"And date," I jabbed, "don't forget about the part where you go out on dates."

He smiled. "I think that falls into the being productive category."

He stayed in his own thoughts for a moment before coming back to planet Earth. "Anyways, after we heard back from the warden's office I filed the release order with our jailer. That was Tuesday morning. The paperwork sat on his desk until about two hours ago which brings us to now. How'd you manage in there by the way?"

"Well I still have my virginity if that's what you're wondering. It wasn't for a lack of potential suitors though."

"I'm glad to hear it. You look like you could have had a full dance card in there."

"Ok detective, now that we've established I'm the victim in this little passion play of yours, can you please tell me what in the hell happened with my brother?"

He made eye contact with our waitress and signaled for the check. He then took one last drag off his Camel before dropping it into his coffee mug. "I'll do you one better Abel. I'll take you on what I like to call the Kane Family's Path of Destruction Tour."

Our first stop was back to the Eureka Christian Church. On the drive back to El Cajon I told Detective Takahashi that in April of my senior year my father and grandparents informed Jonah and myself they were on to something big and took off to parts unknown. I think he believed me when I told him that was the last time I had any contact with them.

He then started telling me what my family had been up to since they disappeared from my life. Apparently Eureka Christian had offered both my father and grandfather pastoral positions based on the strong recommendation of its most influential member. His name was Rick McHugh and he had big plans that extended well beyond this small, non-denominational church. He was part real estate developer and part elite con man who spent his life dealing with people from the bottom of the deck. I had met McHugh briefly in the late 1970's when he was a parishioner at the mega church in Des Moines, Iowa where my father and grandfather were co-pastors. In 1976 he and my family concocted a scam to allegedly raise money for the earthquake victims in Guatemala. They would go on to raise over a quarter million dollars mainly due to the oratory eloquence of my father and grandfather who convinced the parishioners and local businessmen to open their wallets for a good cause. I'm not sure how much the Kane family pocketed from the scheme but I do remember very little ended up in the hands of the earthquake victims. The fraud was eventually exposed and my father and grandfather were forced to resign their positions. The congregation's wealthiest members covered the shortfall and quietly swept the incident under the carpet to save their church from any public humiliation. McHugh fled west and we moved on to the next thing. The Kane's and Rick McHugh were like the proverbial two peas in a pod so it shouldn't have been a surprise to anyone when he contacted my family to help him pull off his biggest con of all.

At this point in Takahashi's story we pulled into the church parking lot where the Mercury Lynx sat right where I had parked it. Unfortunately it had been burned to the ground from the inside out and there was nothing left to salvage. My duffel which contained all of my clothes, the pictures of my mother and the bulk of my meager life savings had been incinerated. My entire net worth had literally been reduced to the clothes on my back and the $93.00 I carried in my wallet.

Takahashi must have noticed my look of despair as we examined the shell of the car.

"Yours?" he asked.

"I'm afraid so."

"Well," he said, "I know none of this is on you but I can't say I'm surprised. This is all about taking a pound of the Kane's flesh. Your family destroyed a lot of lives around these parts. The suspect list of who might have done this is a mile long."

I simply nodded because there really wasn't anything to be said. I ran as far and as fast as I could from my family but it wasn't far and fast enough. The long arm of their legacy once again reached out and pulled me back in.

We then met with the pastor of the church and Takahashi explained the unfortunate case of mistaken identity. He was a brown skinned, middle aged Latino man and I watched his face turn ashen white with guilt. I'd bet dollars to donuts he either started the conflagration himself or he knew who did.

"It must have happened late last night," he argued. "The car was fine when I left for home yesterday evening. I'm sorry for your loss Mr. Kane. I've already called for a tow truck to haul it away."

Takahashi spoke up. "Not so fast reverend. That car is now evidence in a felony arson case. That is, if Mr. Kane wishes to press charges."

All eyes turned to me awaiting my decision. I shook my head. What would be the point? It wouldn't bring back what I'd lost and pressing charges would inevitably shine the bright light of public scrutiny upon me. That's the last thing I needed. And let's face it, one less Mercury Lynx in the world isn't such a terrible thing. The look on the reverend's face was one of pure relief.

Takahashi and I then walked up to the halted construction project.

"I'm sure you don't know this," he said, "but your family arrived in town using the last name of Smith. They certainly don't get any brownie points for creativity but the alias worked until the whole thing came crashing down."

I had a million questions bouncing around in my brain but I decided on the drive up here I was going to hear him out first. We walked past the eucalyptus trees and made our way to the center of the large, abandoned concrete pad.

"From the day your father and grandfather arrived here we were convinced the good Lord had sent us two dynamic men of God."

"Wait," I interjected, "you're a member of this church?"

"Yes I am. I live in El Cajon."

"So you knew my family?"

"I did and I can tell you I didn't suspect a thing until it was too late." Some detective you are I thought to myself as he continued on.

"As you have seen, our church is relatively small. Our membership was chiefly made up of hard working people in the lower and middle classes. That is until the Smiths showed up. Within a year you could find yourself sitting shoulder to shoulder with many of San Diego's elite. Politicians, business leaders and even professional athletes found their way to El Cajon every Sunday to listen to these two men who were at the very top of their game. The services quickly became standing room only affairs so we added more. When that didn't satisfy the demand we erected a circus size tent outside and held them there. That was the kind of charismatic personalities we were dealing with. Your father and grandfather connected with people from all walks of life. Rich or poor, black or white, none of that mattered. Money, and I mean real money, started finding its way into our coffers and we foolishly started dreaming big. Rick McHugh motioned the idea of establishing a building fund for a new church and grade school. Our board eagerly approved it with a unanimous vote. Things were falling precisely into place for him. He had already laid the groundwork for his master plan and he was now ready to spring 'Operation Amen' on an unsuspecting world."

Takahashi and I were back in his car again this time travelling southeast on Interstate 8. The topography was changing as we climbed into an area known as the Mountain Empire. We were over three thousand feet in elevation now and the arid flatlands had given way to boulder strewn hills dotted with scrub pine and live oaks. The towns we drove through were aptly named. Alpine, Pine Valley and Mount Laguna just to name a few. It was quite a juxtaposition from the white, sandy beaches that were only an hour's drive away. When I-8 made its turn due east towards Arizona we exited the interstate at a place called Buckman Springs. As we headed south towards Mexico Takahashi took the opportunity to give me an interesting, local history lesson.

Well before Pearl Harbor was attacked President Franklin

Roosevelt and his cabinet were taking serious notice of Japanese aggression in the Pacific theatre. Washington was greatly concerned with the vulnerability of our southern border and felt a Japanese invasion could very likely come through Mexico. The decision was made to strengthen our military presence at the border with several horse regiments including the

famed Buffalo Soldiers of the 11th cavalry. Power, buildings, roads, water supply and a sewage treatment plant were constructed by the Army Corps of Engineers and in late 1941 Camp Lockett was born. It would ultimately be the last horse cavalry base ever to be built by the United States Army. In its heyday Camp Lockett was home to over 5000 Army personnel transforming the sleepy border town of Campo into a bustling military post. By early 1944 however the antiquated cavalry brigades were transferred to North Africa where they were either mechanized or disbanded all together. The era of the horse soldier had come to an end.

Later in the war Camp Lockett transitioned into a POW camp and then was finally decommissioned in 1949. At that point ownership of the property was transferred over to the County of San Diego. There it sat, forgotten and frozen in time, until Rick McHugh came along.

We pulled into the center of Campo which was just one mile away from the Mexican border. There was a post office, hardware store and a scattering of apartment buildings and small houses that supported the town's meager population. Takahashi described it as an 'almost ghost town.

All the existing buildings were the original wood-framed structures built by the Corp of Engineers. There were barracks, officers' quarters, a mess hall, a gymnasium and even a movie theatre. All dilapidated but still standing. As we walked further away from the center Takahashi pointed out the corrals, stables and a weather beaten veterinary hospital. There were tack rooms, saddle storage and even concrete watering troughs that could still function if called upon today. All the infrastructure necessary to keep a horse regiment operating was still here as if it were refusing to allow us to forget such a romantic piece of our military past.

Finally we made our way up to the top of Buglers' Rock. This was the exact spot where the regiments' bugler would announce morning reveille and evening taps. It was a great vantage point and we enjoyed a commanding view of the entire valley. I drank from our shared water bottle while Takahashi took the opportunity to have himself a smoke. He then got down to the crux of the matter.

"What you're looking at is almost six hundred acres of land just an hour away from downtown San Diego." He then waved his hand across the horizon and said, "Welcome to the grand illusion Able. Welcome to Amen, California."

I would readily admit it was an impressive piece of land. The majority of the acreage sat in a saddle shaped valley enclosed on all four sides by rolling, craggy hills that afforded 360 degree views.

"In 1979," Takahashi continued, "the County of San Diego, like everyone else in the country, was suffering through soaring inflation rates and the budget shortfalls that inevitably followed. They began taking a hard look at their balance sheet and it was decided that Camp Lockett with its high maintenance costs and zero tax revenues needed to be sold off."

We climbed down off Bugler's Rock and started making our way back to the car. I noticed that his limp was more pronounced than ever.

"Are you alright detective?" I asked him.

He nodded. "It's that damn shrapnel. Over a decade later and pieces are still coming to the surface." He set his foot on a boulder and lifted his pant leg to show me. A small piece of shrapnel was just beginning to protrude through the skin on his lower calve.

"I'll to go to the ER tomorrow and get them to cut it out. Hurts like hell though."

We started walking again and he explained in detail what happened next. I didn't understand some of the financial complexities but I can certainly give you the broad strokes. McHugh caught wind of the city council's decision and with a few well placed bribes he was able to circumvent the auction process and acquire the camp for just under a million dollars. It was a substantial amount but he negotiated the deal with a minimal down payment and very favorable terms. He quickly hired the most powerful architectural firm in the city with the mandate to turn his vision into reality. Six months later the completed plans were filed with the county to approve the construction of a brand new town complete with 2,000 homes. The community would be faith-based and adhere to Christian values. It would be called Amen.

After submitting his plans for approval the lawsuits came fast and furious. Environmental groups led the way. They had grave concerns over the rare plant species in the area along with the declining numbers of something called a horned toad. The historical societies were next. They suddenly developed a strong interest in 'such an important part of our California history.' Various religious groups joined in on the fun voicing concern over Amen's exclusionary philosophy. Even Atheist's United filed a lawsuit apparently finding something they could finally believe in. McHugh hired an expensive law firm, put them on retainer and vowed to fight each and every 'scurrilous' legal action.

Water was the next big problem. The county reneged on their promise to turn on the spigots citing severe drought conditions for its change of heart. That was the first of many suits and countersuits filed by McHugh's attorneys. On and on it went. Two years of battling had cost him two million dollars of the bank's money and he still hadn't turned over a shovel's worth of dirt.

This was about the time he had his epiphany. Instead of building Amen he was simply going to sell people the dream. With the flip of a switch he ceased being Rick McHugh the real estate developer and reverted back to his true self, Rick McHugh the con man. He knew he couldn't pull it off himself. He'd need some brilliant partners so he picked up the phone and called the family Kane.

CHAPTER 30

We were once again heading back to El Cajon. Takahashi said he had one last place to show me. The final stop on the Kane Family Path of Destruction Tour. He drove and talked while I listened.

"So McHugh had 2,000 lots to sell and he knew the quicker he got rid of them the better chance he had of succeeding. The idea was to bank as much cash as possible and then when the heat started rising he'd disappear forever. So how did he plan on pulling off the biggest con of his life? That's the multi-million dollar question."

I assumed the question was rhetorical so I kept my mouth shut and let him continue.

"You sell the dream and you sell it on the cheap," he said answering his own question.

Apparently that's exactly what McHugh set about doing. The pricing on the lots ranged from $10,000 to $25,000 dependent upon size and desirability. I'd say that's dirt cheap if you'd pardon me for the pun. He also offered them up for as little as $5,000 down with the balance due when construction was set to begin. I did the quick math in my head. Even if he sold only 80% of the inventory that's a cool eight million dollars in deposits alone.

"What was missing," Takahashi said, "was the vehicle to bring Amen to the people's attention. Using real estate brokers would never work. They had an annoying habit of wanting to protect the best interests of their clients and they'd doubtlessly ask a lot of unanswerable questions. Print advertising was too impersonal and besides, publishers had their own brand of advertising ethics. McHugh instinctively knew he had to have complete control over the message and its delivery. So he came up with this."

We pulled into a five space parking lot directly in front of a small cinder block building. The gray exterior had been covered with spray painted graffiti and the windows had been boarded up with plywood sheets. The vandalism seemed incongruous alongside the radio tower that stood majestically untouched atop the building's roof reaching some fifty plus feet into the air. Painted across the tower's base were the station's call letters, WWJD. What Would Jesus Do.

"Here it is," Takahashi explained, "the final piece of the puzzle. A radio station. It's only 5,000 watts which covers about one hundred square miles. The previous owner played something called hard bop jazz twenty four hours a day. The world wasn't quite ready for the format and he had to file bankruptcy. McHugh swooped in and bought it for cents on the dollar. He changed the station's call letters and reformatted the programming to Christian talk radio."

We got out of the car and made our way to the front door. Takahashi pulled a key from his pocket and inserted it into the lock. I looked at him raising my eyebrows in curiosity.

"Crime scene," he said shrugging his shoulders.

The interior had also been heavily vandalized. The large plate glass window that would normally separate the talent from the engineer had been obliterated. Large chunks of glass were still scattered across the linoleum floor while the jagged shiv-like remains clung dangerously to the sills. There were a few pieces of cheap office furniture that remained intact but anything else of value had been stolen away and presumably sold for scrap. At some point the homeless must have taken up lodging here and neglected to pick up after themselves. They left behind a bevy of food packaging, empty liquor bottles and discarded clothing as their collective calling card. The place was a disaster.

Takahashi impulsively grabbed at a shard of glass wiggling it free from the window's edging before tossing it on the ground. He then continued. "McHugh immediately installed your father into the weekday morning talk show spot. I'm sure you won't be surprised to hear that he was a natural."

It didn't surprise me at all. Old feelings of anger and frustration welled up inside of me like spring water. My father is a brilliant man and he would have been highly successful at whatever career he had chosen. I've no doubt he would have been an amazing litigator or perhaps even an accomplished surgeon had he set his sights on a more righteous path. Instead he chose to follow in my grandfather's footsteps and headed down the road to perdition. Maybe it's just a part of the Kane's genetic coding. Does that mean it's inside of me also, lurking around my DNA like a thief in the night? That's a scary supposition. Hopefully the answer is no but if it ever decides it wants to come out and play I know I'll try to fight it off with everything I've got. We exited the building and Takahashi locked the door. We leaned against his car and the two of us looked up at the radio tower looming over us. He finished the story.

"He was such an engaging guy, your father. He'd take on any and all controversial subjects then invite his listeners to call in for a lively debate. One day it might be the veracity of the Bible, the next day abortion and perhaps the day after that euthanasia. Everything was fair game. There were no sacred cows. I listened to him on my way into work every day and without fail I always learned something new and thought provoking. Advertisers wanted in but this was never about putting a small radio station on the map nor Isaac Kane becoming a star. He was there to sell the Amen dream and he did it very well."

"Well detective," I said before he cut me off.

"Call me Kenny please," he said.

"OK, Kenny, so am I correct in assuming that we're at the point of the story where I ask you what went wrong?"

He chuckled. "Indeed we are Able. Indeed we are."

We got into the car and headed back towards the coast.

"In a way," Kenny said, "they were victims of their own success. A producer for one of the local television affiliates was a fan and he asked Isaac to participate in an upcoming television broadcast. The format called for a round table panel to debate both historical and current religious topics. Every major religion would be represented by one of their more prominent local leaders. McHugh like the idea. He felt the increased exposure might allow them to wrap things up more quickly. Half the lots had been sold at this point and they had banked close to three million dollars but greed is greed and much like the casino gambler who's riding a hot streak it's never easy to know when to walk away from the table. Your father agreed to go on the show."

A few years later I obtained a copy of the broadcast. I've watched and analyzed it so many times I kind of consider it my own personal Zapruder tape. It aired at 7:30 on a Sunday morning so I'm pretty sure hardly anyone was watching it live. If the debate had been a boxing match I'd say my father had been ahead on points. Everything was going well until the real fight broke out. From the onset it was quite obvious there was a lot of animosity between the imam from the local mosque and Rabbi Schultz. Their arguing was becoming heated and churlish making the other members of the panel feel rather uncomfortable. That is except for my father who didn't seem bothered in the least. The bemused look on his face suggested that he was actually enjoying it.

The subject concerning the rightful ownership of Jerusalem was the final straw. Back and forth they went at each other until Imam Amir called the rabbi a 'Jesus Killer.' Rabbi Schultz picked up the pitcher of water and tossed its contents across the table dousing both the imam and the Buddhist monk who had been quietly minding his own business. Imam Amir flew across the table with a grace that belied his advanced years and wrestled Rabbi Schultz to the ground. The old men grappled on the floor for a while screaming at each other in their native tongues. The rabbi's hairpiece somehow ended up in Imam Amir's right hand at just about the same time Rabbi Schultz's dentures found purchase in the imam's left arm. Eventually, thank goodness, they both ran out of steam and collapsed on the carpet trying to catch their collective breaths. It was all very entertaining and the young, ambitious producer knew he held television gold in his hands. He sent the feed to New York and the network ate it with a spoon. It took the lead on the six o'clock news that evening and all of America had a chance to watch.

"Well that did it," Kenny said as we neared San Diego. "Calls started coming in from places like Des Moines, St. Louis and Providence, Rhode Island. The callers identified your father not as Isaac Smith but as Isaac Kane and what they had to say wasn't very complimentary. There was a real story here and journalists from all over the country booked flights to San Diego. The principals however were unavailable for comment. At the first hint of a problem your father, grandfather and McHugh activated their escape plan and crossed over the border at Tijuana disappearing into the Mexican night."

CHAPTER 31

As we approached Interstate 5 Kenny told me he thought I could use a drink. He was correct. Instead of heading south towards downtown he veered north and exited at Solano Beach. Moments later we pulled up to a repurposed Quonset hut called the Belly Up Tavern. We sat at the bar and ordered some burgers and a round of draft beers.

"I am now," Kenny said after taking down half his beer in one gulp, "opening up the floor to questions."

Needless to say I had a few.

"Not once did you mention my brother," I said. "How did he figure into all of this?"

Kenny gave me the details. The majority of the facts came from Jonah himself. Shortly after I hopped on the bus bound for Parris Island my father had returned to South Bend to bring us both back to California. I can't imagine how angry he must have been when he learned of my treasonous enlistment into the Marine Corps. Jonah's original plan was to enroll into San Diego State in the fall but that never happened. McHugh needed a right hand man to be on site at Amen. He needed a closer and Jonah became that guy.

"Like the rest of your family," Kenny said as the burger plates were set in front of us, "your brother was a natural salesman."

No surprise there. Jonah lived his life selling the Jonah mystique and he was damn good at it. He sold it to our family, to girls, teachers, coaches and of course to me. Most of us bought what he was selling hook, line and sinker.

"I think McHugh set your brother up to be the fall guy," Kenny said. "Jonah's signature was on every sales document, escrow paper and deposit receipt that we confiscated during our searches. Rick McHugh's signature was never anywhere to be found. But don't delude yourself, your brother was anything but an innocent victim. He sold and resold several of the premium lots over and over again collecting a commission each and every time. He would also neglect to file the paperwork when a deposit was paid in cash. That money would find its way straight into his pocket. He was fully aware of the fraud he was committing. This isn't my opinion Able. These are all things he stipulated to in his written confession."

I found that part hard to believe and I expressed my doubts to my new drinking partner. It would have been completely out of character for Jonah to readily admit to anything that would land him in hot water.

Kenny had a mouthful of burger so he just nodded in agreement.

"You're right," he said after chasing it down with a swig of beer. "Your brother refused to cooperate with the investigation even when the DA put a fairly attractive plea bargain on the table. Jonah and his attorney knew this was going to be a complicated financial case so they invoked his right to a fair and speedy trial hoping to catch the prosecution ill-prepared. It was a solid strategy. The district attorney confided in me more than once about his doubts of bringing home a guilty verdict. Then the Martinez brothers happened."

What he told me next made my skin crawl. The trial date had been set for February first and Jonah's defense lawyer was growing increasingly confident about creating enough reasonable doubt to force an acquittal. By then everyone who had acquired lots in Amen had been notified their money was irretrievably gone. The majority of the buyers were poor, working class families who had now lost their entire life's savings. For them the Amen dream had become a nightmare and nobody took it more to heart than Felipe and Benny Martinez.

They had each purchased a lot and took advantage of the ten percent discount when the parcels were paid for in full. The brothers then convinced their extended family members to do the same. In total, the Martinez clan bought eight lots and now shared a dream of raising their families together, side by side. On many a weekend you could find the group camping overnight on the sites of their future homes. Benny's daughter was even married on lot number E-6 just two weeks before my father's infamous television appearance.

Three nights before the trial was scheduled to begin the two inconsolable brothers drove up to El Cajon and parked in front of the now abandoned radio station. It had been locked and boarded up but no one had bothered to unplug the Christmas tree lights that had been strung up and down the radio tower during the holidays. They were set on a timer and when the Martinez brothers pulled into the parking lot the red and green lights were fully illuminated. Felipe and Benny laddered up on to the roof and scaled the tower stopping about ten feet from the top. The brothers had written goodbye letters to their wives and families and by the time they had been opened and read Felipe and Benny were already dead. The media circus arrived shortly thereafter.

Kenny ordered us another round of beers backed up this time by shots of Jose Cuervo. I guess we were going to get drunk together.

"All of San Diego got to see the two men dangling from their homemade nooses on the late night news. The Christmas lights were set on blinking mode so the bodies appeared and disappeared every two seconds like ghostly apparitions. One of the more macabre television reporters went as far as describing them as 'hanging there like human Christmas tree ornaments.' It was a classless thing to say but it hadn't been far from the truth. When your brother saw the news report he was visibly shaken especially when he heard his name mentioned in the reading of the suicide notes. The next morning he requested a meeting with the district attorney waiving his rights to have his attorney present. It was a very short meeting. Jonah simply asked him what the maximum penalty was for the crimes he had committed. Sixteen years was the answer. There was no negotiation for a reduced sentence. He agreed to the full term and pled guilty on the spot. The case never went to trial and your brother hasn't uttered a word about it since. I've been told he spends his days at Tehachapi reading the Bible in quiet contemplation refusing to speak to anyone."

"I need to see him Kenny," I said.

"That's entirely between you and your brother. He's allowed visitors but just to warn you he hasn't accepted a request yet."

Rounds of beer kept magically appearing in front of me as the Belly Up started getting more crowded and convivial. A local rock band was now on the stage working their way through a set of covers. They were loud and it was getting hard to hear each other so we just sat back and listened to the music. That was fine by me. I had asked a lot of questions and each new revelation seemed worse than the last. I found out my grandmother had passed away. She suffered a severe stroke three years earlier and never recovered. If my grandfather was the regal face of the family and my father was the crown prince in waiting then I would describe Ruby Mae Kane as the power behind the throne. Her decisions were always final and no plan moved forward without her approval. She was born and raised in the hard scrabble coal mining towns of Appalachia and to say her childhood was traumatic would be a gross understatement. My grandmother had been traded for not once, but twice before she turned fifteen years of age. The second time was to my grandfather to settle a gambling debt. Before that, when she was all of eight years old, her own father handed her over to a neighboring family in exchange for a milking cow and an old plow mule. She ran away two weeks later. She wouldn't talk about why she'd run away or the subsequent years that followed only that they were 'character building times.'

"My life," she would tell us, "started that night in Morgantown when your grandfather won me in a game of Faro and that's all you boys need to know."

The experiences she suffered in her youth would go on to forge the tough, pragmatic woman I had come to know. She was an intractable atheist who thought religion was 'a whole lot of silliness but a sure fire way of getting into people's pocketbooks.'

"Abel," she once said to me, "anyone who has seen what I've seen and still believes in a benevolent God must have bumped their head in a serious way." I always thought she was invincible and would outlive us all. Now here she was, gone before her sixtieth birthday.

My worst fears regarding the abandoned construction site at the Eureka Christian Church were realized. My grandfather had cleared out the building fund account just prior to performing his Mexican disappearing act. No wonder my rental car was set fire to on church property. The Kanes' did leave some assets behind surprisingly enough. There was a home, a few thousand dollars tied up in an IRA and three cars including my brother's beloved 442 Olds. Unfortunately for me however they had been seized and liquidated by the County of San Diego with the proceeds going into something called the Amen Victim's Fund. I would have to make do with the $93.00 in my wallet.

At 10:30 Detective Takahashi waived the white flag and asked the bartender to close us out. He graciously picked up the entire tab. He then called for a taxi and offered me his spare bedroom for the night. I turned it down.

"Well then," he said slurring every word, "I guess this is it." He offered me his hand and I shook it. "What's next for you Able?"

I had no idea. Well I did have one but it was a longshot. I pulled out a scrap of paper I had been carrying around in my wallet since my rehabilitation days at Landstuhl. I asked him if he knew where it was and the best way to get there. Kenny laughed and then pointed to the train station about three football fields up the road.

"Looks like it's your lucky day Abel," he said as he poured himself into the back of the taxi.

As it disappeared around the corner I thought to myself that's right, that's me, just a lucky kind of guy.

I walked up to the train station which was really nothing more than a stop along the line. I missed the last run of the night and that's when it dawned on me I had nowhere to sleep. Had there been a motel right across the street it wouldn't have mattered. I couldn't afford it. Given the fact I was about to spend my first night as a homeless person Takahashi's offer of his spare room was looking pretty good right now. To make matters worse I was bone rattling cold. Thick slabs of fog had rolled in on the back of a cold onshore breeze and my t-shirt and cargo shorts were offering little protection. The town was eerily silent now and the only ambient sounds were coming from the beach where the breaking waves refused to be quieted. I ran towards them with the sole intention of trying to warm up but the wind there was even stronger and the marine layer was so thick it began to dampen my clothing. I needed a solution and I needed it quickly.

Half way down to the waterline stood a small, wooden life guard station with the number three stenciled on its side. The access ramp had been lifted and secured to discourage people from doing what I was about to do. I climbed up the side crossbeams and swung myself over the handrail. The door thankfully had no lock so I was able to go inside and partially shield myself from the elements. It was a small space so I had to arrange myself in the fetal position which seemed appropriate given my current state of mind. It wasn't Depression that came knocking that night. I know that guy fairly well. He's always hanging around looking for the chance to come inside for a visit. No this wasn't him. This was his older, steroid injected cousin Despair and I had left the door wide open for him.

The drunk I put myself on that night had begun its chrysalis into a full blown hangover but I was still cognizant enough to realize I was now all alone in the world. I had no family, no friends and I was a day, maybe two away from being flat broke. This had to be the nadir, my rock bottom, because if it wasn't I really didn't think I could survive going one more rung down the ladder. I was back in that foxhole again praying to my God and hoping he could tell one Kane from the next.

I woke up to the manic cries of seagulls as they fought and scrounged for their morning meal. I rose to meet the day achy, sore and feeling terrible. Sometime during the night the breeze had reversed direction and deposited the fog back out at sea. It was all blue skies now and I watched the dawn patrol surfers enjoying a head high swell while a pod of dolphins horsed around just outside the wave break. The idyllic scene was completely wasted on me. I made it as far as the handrail before I purged the toxic contents of my stomach into the sand below.

When I caught my breath I climbed down from Lifeguard Station Number Three and headed into town. While walking up the main drag I couldn't help but notice the dog walkers and coffee grabbers were giving me the kind of space normally afforded to a leper. I think I needed a makeover.

My first purchase was a train ticket. That was $19.00. I then went to the mini-mart and bought all the necessary toiletries. The surf shop was already open and I overpaid for a new t-shirt, a pair of flip flops and a beach towel. All in I spent another $52.00. I went back to the beach and cleaned up using the outdoor showers then went inside the public bathroom and shaved away three days worth of stubble. The journey back to respectability had begun. There was a diner near the station so I splurged on a breakfast of bacon and eggs, hash browns and coffee, lots of coffee. I now had less than ten dollars to my name but my sepulchral mood was slowly lifting.

The train ride was just forty minutes up the coast and it dropped me off adjacent to the hustle and bustle of the San Clemente pier. I kept asking for directions until I found a local who was not only familiar with the street but offered to give me a ride. It was one of those random acts of kindness I'd never forget.

You probably don't remember this but back when I was rehabilitating at the Landstuhl Medical Center I received a call from Harvey. He was calling from Camp Pendleton where he was recovering from his own set of wounds suffered on that fateful day in Beirut. Before we ended the conversation he extended an open ended invitation to come visit him in California. It was surely one of those pie crust promises that are easily made and easily broken yet here I was walking up a driveway lined with banana trees and canna lilies knowing full well that this knock on the door was going to determine my fate one way or the other. I prayed someone was home.

I walked up a short flight of stairs to an enclosed porch where two green Adirondack chairs sat unoccupied. There was a white faced golden retriever on guard duty but he couldn't quite summon the energy to question my intrusion. I gave the old boy a pat on the head and he let me pass on by. Before I had the chance to announce my presence the door opened from the inside. I was greeted by a tall elderly man with excellent posture wearing a white polo shirt and khaki slacks. His stomach was flat and his short, gray hair could still easily pass muster. The family resemblance was unmistakable.

"I see you met Basilone," he said shaking his head at the dog. "I'm going to have to write him up on an Article 32."

That was funny. "Sorry to bother you sir," I said starting in, "my name is….."

He cut me off. "Able Kane. I know who you are marine. I see your face every day when I take my morning constitutional. I'm Colonel Robert Dwyer, retired US Marine Corp." He extended his hand.

"Morning constitutional sir?" I asked shaking it.

"That's civilian jargon for taking a crap Private Kane. There's a picture of you hanging on the wall of our downstairs bathroom. I see you every time I drop the kids off at the pool. Come on in and take a load off."

I entered into the living room and he pointed towards the couch. "Sally Ann," he shouted, "we've got company and by the looks of him I'd say he's going to need some provisioning."

The colonel's wife emerged from the kitchen wearing an apron with the words Semper Fry emblazoned across the front. She was an elegant, ageless beauty who could undoubtedly still fit into her high school prom dress. I watched the colonel eyeing her mischievously as she glided towards us.

"Sally Ann," he said, "meet Able Kane."

"I know who he is you old coot," she said sternly to her husband and then gave me a hug like she'd known me her entire life. She looked up at me, grabbed my chin and said, "My son talks about you all the time. Welcome to the family."

She asked if I was hungry and I told her about the large breakfast I had eaten just a few hours earlier. She was having none of it. "Nonsense," she said, "sit yourself down next to Audie Murphy here and I'll whip something up."

So we sat. The colonel reached into a drawer and brought out a box of cigars. Cubans. "Watch this," he said conspiratorially, "that woman not only has eyes in the back of her head but they can see around corners too."

He offered me a cigar and sure enough before we could get them lit Sally Ann stormed back into the room.

"Special occasion Sally Ann," he said pointing to his new-found partner in crime. She had been outflanked which probably didn't happen very often.

"Okay Robert," she said, "but only one." There wasn't a hint of anger in that voice and she happily retreated to the chow hall knowing there were troops that needed feeding.

We lit up. It was my first cigar. I really didn't like the taste but I truly enjoyed the ceremonial aspect of the whole thing.

"So," the colonel said, "tell me what brings your raggedy ass to my door and don't sacrifice any of the details."

"I'll be happy to sir," I said, "but I'm a guest in your house and it's a rather drawn out story. I don't want to be that guy."

He drew deeply on his Romeo y Julieta then leaned in closer to me. "Listen," he said pointing to the folded newspaper resting on the arm of his recliner, "I start my days by reading the half-truths and lies in that damn thing. After that I either head to the golf course and play a game I'm absolutely terrible at or I stay home where my commanding officer hands me a honey do list that keeps me busy all the way up to cocktail hour. So if you wouldn't mind will you please do an old warrior a favor and start at the beginning. And that, Private Kane, is a direct order."

I was outranked here so I did as I was asked. I explained my background and the shameful way the Kane's made a living. That segued into my enlistment and the subsequent ex-communication from my family. The colonel asked me a lot of questions about Beirut and I went into length about the various missions we had undertaken. These were things that father and son had apparently never discussed and I could see him swell with pride as I gave example after example of what a fine CO Harvey had been. Sally Ann, who must have had a listening device set up in the kitchen, had joined us now and sat on the couch right next to me hanging on every word. I went into exacting detail about 'the day' and all of the troubles that followed. From there I moved on to my rehabilitation, my travels through Europe and finally my disastrous return to America via San Diego. By the time I had finished we had smoked our cigars down to the caps and Sally Ann's meal remained on the stove burned beyond recognition. There was a brief moment of silence which I've come to expect whenever I tell my story.

"Yeah," the colonel said breaking it, "I heard about that nonsense down in El Cajon. An honest to God tragedy."

That it was. I asked to use the bathroom and he pointed down the hallway. "Second door on the right," he said.

The picture hanging on the bathroom wall brought a smile to my face. It was a photograph of the three of us, Harvey, Hassam and myself. We were sitting on the front steps of the war weary National Museum of Beirut with its four massive, limestone pillars framing the background of the shot. We were surrounded by the foot high Byblos figurines that had recently been stolen from the museum's basement. The statuettes dated all the way back to the Bronze Age and were originally unearthed at the Temple of the Obelisks near the Phoenician town of Byblos, hence the name. I was holding one of these funny looking guys in my hand. He was skinny, had tanged feet and was wearing a gold colored, conical hat with a matching skirt. He had one arm casually extended like he was about to come in for a fist bump. I was informed by a docent he represented Reseph, the Phoenician god of war and plagues and had been a valued offering at religious festivals back in the days of yore. He was decidedly unattractive but I guess looks can be deceiving because he and his counterparts were one of Lebanon's most highly regarded national treasures directly linking the country to its ancient past. Once the figurines were reported stolen we were given the assignment of trying to track them down. Through Hassam's intelligence sources we were able to recover them just before they set sail on a Liberian freighter bound for Cairo and into the waiting arms of an illicit artifacts dealer. It ended up being an inside job. The lure of a big payday was enough to corrupt the museum's assistant curator who had been bribed by a PLO crew to aid and abet them in the pulling off of the heist. The recapture of the figurines had been big news in Beirut at the time. It was late in the afternoon when a BBC correspondent asked us to pose for the picture. The setting along with the angle of the sun had worked its magic. The three of us, the figurines and the museum in the background all appeared to have been painted in liquid gold. There was a natural, sepia like quality to the moment and the photographer captured it perfectly. Sally Ann would eventually send me a framed copy and it hangs in my bedroom to this very day.

I stayed with the colonel and Sally Ann for three wonderful days before Harvey could drive down from Los Angeles to pick me up. Sally Ann took pity on me and acted upon the colonel's reprovisioning order. She wouldn't take no for an answer so the two of us drove north to a mall called Fashion Island where we shopped until I had a duffel bag full of new, designer clothes. I played golf with the colonel and two of his friends. He wasn't lying when he said he was terrible at the game. He shot 112 but laughed away every bad shot. At the end of the round the four of us sat on the club's veranda drinking martinis as we watched the sun disappear into the Pacific. On our last night together we drove down to Pendleton and had dinner at the 'O' Club just inside the camp's gates. We were joined by a half dozen of the colonel's peers along with their spouses. The wine was flowing that night and I was once again cajoled into telling my story. The other men followed suit and I was privileged enough to listen to amazing stories of war and heroism that spanned across every conflict from WWII to Vietnam. Harvey and Jennifer drove down from LA the next day to retrieve me.

I moved into their spare bedroom just long enough to gain some financial traction. Harvey had just joined the LAPD and I applied and was accepted shortly thereafter. Jennifer was pregnant with their first and I moved out just in time for them to welcome the arrival of Robert Jackson Dwyer. I am proud to call him my godson.

Over the years I have often reflected on what would have become of me had the Dwyers not been home to answer the door on that fateful day. After all, I was alone in the world, practically penniless and in a very fragile state of mind. There have been many late night occasions when I've awoken from a deep sleep shaken and soaked in sweat as the 'what if' scenarios played themselves out in my dreams. In the years that followed I would make an annual trip back to San Clemente for the Dwyer's epic Fourth of July bash. The colonel would eventually contract a severe case of Alzheimers but Sally Ann resolutely refused to check him into a care facility. She was his one and only caregiver until he passed in 2009. The familiar adage 'old soldiers don't die, they simply fade away' sadly isn't true and the world's a lesser place because of it. Sally Ann would follow him less than a year later. The coroner would officially state her death was due to natural causes but I'm pretty sure she died from a broken heart.

The two of them taught me many valuable lessons but none more important than the fact that family isn't bound by the cosmic coincidence of shared DNA. It is wherever you can find and give love in equal measure. I'm talking about the unconditional kind which is dispensed without question or recourse. They also gave me the gift of home. I received it the day I walked up a driveway bordered by banana trees and canna lilies and then stepped on to a front porch where an old dog by the name of Basilone was there waiting for me. It was a gift I'd been missing my entire life and hadn't even realized it.

I never saw my father or grandfather again. Kenny, that is Detective Takahashi, would call me whenever there was an alleged sighting up until the day he retired from the San Diego Police Department. The last report was twelve years ago and it came from as far south as Santiago, Chile. By then I'd come to grips with the fact I no longer mattered to either of them and I didn't even bother to follow up on the lead. That was not the case with my brother Jonah however. Once a month for five years I would make the two hour trip to Tehachapi and dutifully put my name on the visitor's list. Once a month for five years he would fail to show. I wrote him letters that went unanswered and tried to arrange phone meetings that never happened. I eventually gave up and tossed in the towel. When I think of my family now I'm reminded of something a wise man once said to me. "Able," he said, "God takes people out of your life for a reason. Don't go chasing after them."

CHAPTER 32

BACK TO THE PRESENT

Monday, June 19th

What is it about the smell of bacon frying in a pan that can bring a dead man back to life? I glanced out the window and I could tell by the brightness of the day I had grossly overslept. The clock on the nightstand now read 9:45 am. I was supposed to be on the 8:00 o'clock flight to Las Vegas out of Burbank where I was going to be met by a detective from the LVPD. He was an acquaintance of Harvey's and the two of us were going to head over to the address listed as EZX's corporate headquarters to see what we could find out. From there I was going to fly to Phoenix and do the same thing at their second location. The best laid plans right? I got my tired, aching body out of bed and noticed a fresh set of clothes hanging on the door jamb. Brigid must have made a trip over to my apartment while I was down for the count. I dressed quickly and then followed the confluence of aromas into the kitchen.

"Good morning OT," Brigid said grinning. "I hope you're hungry."

She had gone all out. There was the bacon of course and she had made skillet eggs with artichoke hearts and sun-dried tomatoes all topped off with gruyere cheese. This was accompanied by sides of homemade hash browns and a fruit salad consisting of black and blue berries, papaya and mango. There was hot coffee already poured and a pitcher of orange juice standing by to wash the whole meal down.

Damn. What I really needed to do is grab a couple of donuts and hit the ground running but that would be something akin to relationship suicide. "What, no English muffins?" is what I came up with instead. At just that moment the toaster popped and four perfectly browned halves presented themselves.

"Buttered or non-buttered?" she asked.

What a stupid question woman. "Buttered please."

She must have sensed my growing anxiety regardless of how hard I was trying to mask it. "Sit down and eat Able. Harvey already landed in Las Vegas and Hassam, who I absolutely love by the way, should be touching down in Phoenix any minute. He already has a construction crew at your building and I've dropped Nate's laptop off at the hospital. He's alert, acting officious and was demanding to see his computer as if it was a member of his own family. I guess in Nate's case that probably isn't far from the truth. Dr. Jenkins told me to tell you that you should raise his rent on general principles alone."

Brigid went on to explain that Harvey had called my cell phone when I failed to show up for our breakfast meeting. He kept calling and she finally picked up on the fourth attempt. She told Harvey what had transpired after I dropped him off at his car and twenty minutes later he and Hassam were knocking on her front door. I never heard a thing. Harvey was aware of my plan for the day so the two of them drove to the airport together and off they went. They'd call me later.

We dug into the feast and engaged in small talk until Brigid couldn't take it any longer. She asked me what the hell was going on. I owed her the truth and probably a hell of a lot more. If we were going to embark upon a relationship, which I hoped she wanted as much as I did, there shouldn't be any secrets festering between us. So I told her exactly how I'd spent the last seventy two hours since Harvey walked into the Celtic Cross asking me for a favor. I then explained my theory about how I thought it was all connected to a terrorist by the name of Mubari and what occurred at a ski chalet in the mountains high above Beirut. By the look on Brigid's face I got the impression there wouldn't be any more jokes about my feet.

"I want to help," she pleaded.

"Absolutely not. These are dangerous people Brigid."

"But that's exactly why I want to do it. Last night scared the hell out of me."

I had to get her off this train of thought before I relented and did something stupid like letting her get involved. If I ever put her in harm's way I would never forgive myself. I needed to change the subject.

"Can we talk about that kiss last night?" I asked.

"What about it?" she retorted in a tone that came off as pure nonchalance. Aah, answering a question with another question. Well played Little Ms. Irish.

But my point exactly. What was it all about? Was it a thank God I thought something happened to you kiss, a sorry I had way too much to drink last night kiss or was it a hey, I'm a good looking woman so it's my inalienable right to mess with your head kind of kiss? When it comes to reading these kinds of tea leaves a gypsy traveler I am not. I decided to put the romance cards out on the table.

"You kind of caught me off guard last night Brigid. We went down this road awhile back and just when I thought we were going to drop the Love Bug into fifth gear you put up the detour sign. I respected that decision and down shifted back into neutral because the last thing in the world I want is not to be there when you're doing the daily crossword puzzle. It would break my heart to see you using a pencil again."

She didn't say a word and the lack of expression on her face could have advanced her to the final table at the World Series of Poker. She got up off of her chair and walked around to my side until she was standing directly over me. I was trembling like it was junior prom all over again.

"That orange juice over there," I said, "I don't suppose there's a chance that it's freshly squeezed?"

Finally she relented and smiled. "You're damn right it is Mr. Able Kane."

And with that she lifted one leg over the two of mine and we had ourselves a face to face sit down. She kissed me again in a way that made last night's kiss feel like amateur hour at the piker's ball. We retreated to the bedroom where she showed me all of her artwork. When the tour had ended it was well past 11:00 am and I really needed to get going. Brigid thought of a brilliant way to help without me putting her into any kind of danger. She commandeered my phone while I put my painting supplies back where they belonged. It was now 11:35 and I was out the door.

I stopped by my building to assess the fire damage. Hassam's five man crew was feverishly working away. Two of the men were cutting sheets of plywood to cover the open space where my large plate glass window used to be while the others were busy stripping away the ruined carpeting, dry wall and ceiling tiles. I checked my messages while I watched them work. I had been a very popular boy while my phone and I were recharging in the early hours of the morning. There were Brigid's three voicemails from last night with each new one sounding more frantic than the last. Harvey also left me three messages when I failed to show up for breakfast. They didn't have the same emotional edge of Brigid's but I certainly detected a growing concern as he left one after another. There were several more important calls I needed to return including one from Marta who sounded very upset. I'd handle those when I was on the move again.

As I was standing there I got a text from Nate telling me to check my email as soon as possible. I went up to my apartment and turned on the computer. His email was sitting atop my inbox with a blue colored link attached. It was footage from a security camera. The time and date stamps were telling me I was watching something from last night at 11:11 p.m. as the tenths of seconds continued to tumble away. The picture was pitch black until the scene suddenly illuminated. I realized I was looking down at my own courtyard as the motion lights triggered. Nate must have installed a security camera for me when he was recalibrating the sensors. I paused the footage and looked out my bedroom window. There it was. He had mounted the camera to the wall next to the stairwell that led up to his apartment. It was positioned perfectly of course. I returned my focus to the computer and hit play again. Two men now entered the camera's purview coming in from the alley side of the building. The taller of the two was carrying a cardboard box that he set down in the middle of the courtyard. Unlike Dorothy from Wichita's security system this was a brand new model and the video quality was excellent. It was the same two thugs who had followed Bump into his apartment complex yesterday. At 11:13 one of the men grabbed a cinder block out of the box. He lifted it over his head and heaved it two handed through my office window. The timing jived perfectly with last night's activation of my alarm system. They then both reached into the box pulling out two large bottles. Molotov cocktails. They lit the exposed rags then tossed them into my office producing two brilliant flashes of light. Job completed, they started to head back towards the alleyway. The time stamp now read 11:15 which was when Nate unfortunately bounded down the stairs and on to the scene. The next part was difficult to watch and I can't imagine how Nate must have felt viewing it from his hospital bed. He's not a fighter, in fact I'd say he's the antithesis of one. As soon as he realized what he had stumbled upon he tried retreating back up the stairwell towards the safety of his apartment. He made it about half way before he was tackled and dragged back down to the courtyard with his head bouncing off each and every concrete step. At that point the smaller of the two men pulled out a knife, knelt over Nate and stabbed him multiple times. He surely would have finished the job had something off camera not spooked him. The two men fled leaving my friend to die. Ten seconds later the first patrol officers arrived on the scene. Their actions, which were quick and decisive, saved Nate's life and more than likely prevented my building from being burned to the ground. I sent the video link to Jerry Lam and asked him to forward it on to whoever was doing the arson investigation for the fire department. As I headed back to my truck I prayed to God and this time I directed those prayers to the younger, more vengeful Old Testament version of him. I asked if he'd let me find these two lowlifes before the authorities did so the three of us could settle our differences on a neutral playing field.

I was now on the road again heading west on the 210 Freeway. Before I could start returning some calls my cell phone rang. The number wasn't on my contacts list.

"Hello," I said.

"Able, it's Joe Lewis."

"The boxer?"

A chuckle. "No, smartass, the detective. Are we still playing sharezeeys?" he asked.

"Absolutely. I love that game." To show my good faith I even went first again. I told Joe everything that had happened since he offered me that stick of Juicy Fruit gum yesterday. Bump's murder, the raid on Otto's and the attack on Nate and my building. I didn't tell him about Brigid's art collection however. That was strictly on a need to know basis. He let out a low whistle when I had finished.

Now it was his turn. "Talk to me Goose," I said.

I did some more digging," he said. "I called a few neighboring police departments and asked them to take another look at their missing person cases to see if there were any connections to Top 2 Bottom."

"And?"

"Jackpot. I haven't heard back from everybody yet but so far we have one in South Pasadena, two in West Covina and three in San Gabriel. All six victims were undocumented young women who had interviewed with Top 2 Bottom two to four weeks prior to being reported missing. I've got copies of the files being sent over to me later today. This thing's getting more interesting by the minute Able."

Indeed it is. "Joseph," I said, "I'm going to recommend you for Monterey Park's employee of the month award." I then had an idea. "Hey, what are you doing right now?"

"Not much, why?"

I told him my less than perfectly thought out plan.

He didn't have to think about it very long. "Sounds like fun. I can get down there in about thirty minutes. See you when I see you."

I then called back a Carl Leon but he didn't pick up. He was a sergeant with the LAPD's Gang Enforcement Detail and his message cryptically said he had some news regarding the two gang bangers that had been caught on the surveillance footage outside of Bump's apartment complex. The same two guys that tried to kill Nate. I left Leon a message asking him to call me back as soon as possible. I had better luck on my next callback to Victoria. She picked up immediately.

"Who's Brigid?" she asked right out of the gate, kicking the normal pleasantries to the curb.

I'm fine Victoria, thank you so much for asking. Oh and by the way, mind your own damn business. "A friend," is what I actually ended up saying.

"She called me this morning," Victoria informed me. "Harvey gave her my number and she told me about the plan. She's nice Able, I like her. I think we could be friends."

Oh merciful God in Heaven, please no. "Well thanks for your blessing," I said. "So what's going on?"

"Oh, not much. I've got some vacation time coming up soon so I'm looking forward to that."

She has to be doing this to me on purpose, right? "Victoria darling, you called me and now I'm calling you back. That's how these things work. Can I assume it's got something to do with the case?"

"Oh yes, you're right, sorry. I've got those credit card statements from Mr. Gamal's American Express card. The account was recently closed but prior to that there's a lot of activity. Looks like someone was living quite the life of Reilly. I've scanned them and I'm emailing them to you right...................now. Also, the techs were able to clean up that video footage from yesterday and positively identify the license plate."

"Stolen right?" I interjected.

"Yes," she said, "the registered owner reported it missing three weeks ago."

"Anything else?"

"Yes. I also just sent you the rap sheet on Frank Garcia Jr. that you requested."

"How's it look?"

"Pretty light really. Mostly troubled teenager stuff. A little B & E, a car theft and a couple of possession charges."

"Thanks Victoria. You've been a big help."

"I know."

The line went dead. Ok then, bye.

It was time to call Marta back. She picked up on the third ring.

"Hello Able," she said sounding tired and defeated.

"Marta, I'm sorry I didn't pick up when you called but

things have been a bit hectic."

"Yes," she said, "so I've heard. That's why I'm calling. Remember our conversation from yesterday? We agreed if this all became too much for me that you'd……how did you phrase it?"

"Call off the dogs."

"Yes, the dogs, that's it. Well that's exactly what I'm asking you to do. Terrible things are happening to good people and I feel personally responsible for all of it. I'm hanging on by a thread here and I don't think I can shoulder anymore blame. Enough is enough."

She must have talked to Harvey. I'm not at all surprised that's why she called but I was in way too deep of water now just to swim back to shore.

"Marta," I said then hesitated as I tried to conjure up the right words.

She took care of it for me. "You're going to tell me that it's become personal and you can't let it go aren't you Able?"

I sighed. "Yes I am. I'm sorry Marta but I'm going to see this through to the end."

She was trying not to cry but wasn't having much success.

"Marta, are you alright?" I felt terrible.

"No, but I will be eventually," she said trying to gather herself. "Able, I know you well enough to realize I'm not going to talk you out of this so I'm going to ask you for just one thing."

"Of course. Name it."

"Please be careful. I think these are very bad people."

She was certainly right about that.

I was now bumper to bumper on the 405 South as I headed over the Sepulveda Pass trying to make my way into West LA. Off to my right I noticed one of the Getty trams passing me by as it slowly ferried patrons up the hill to the museum. My phone rang. It was Sergeant Leon calling me back.

"Sergeant," I said, "this is Able Kane. Thanks for getting back to me."

"My pleasure," he replied, "any friend of Harvey's."

I took the lead and told him about last night's incident at my building and how I was able to identify the assailants as being the same thugs that were caught on the surveillance footage outside of Bump's place.

"Where did you say you lived?" he asked.

"Well, I didn't but up in North Glendale, Montrose really."

"Interesting," Leon said, "guys like this don't normally swim that far upriver. They prefer remaining inside shark infested waters if you know what I mean. Messing with civilians only means trouble for them. You must really have them running scared."

"So do you know who these pieces of trash are?"

"I do. Their names are Hector and Jacob Gonzalez."

"Brothers?"

"No senor. Ellos son primos, cousins. In the hood they're known as Heckle and Jeckle. I'm told the reference is to a couple of crows from some old cartoon."

"Magpies actually."

"I'm sorry, what?"

"Heckle and Jeckle. They aren't crows, they're magpies. Anthropomorphic yellow bellied magpies to be exact."

Laughter. "That's awesome. Yeah, Harvey told me you're a trippy dude. Anyways, they run with a pretty rough crowd that go by the name of Calle Reyes."

"Street Kings," I translated as the knot of traffic on the 405 began to loosen.

"Correct," he replied. "Calle Reyes wholesales heroin. They're loosely affiliated with the Tijuana Cartel but we haven't quite figured out the relationship yet. If those two birds are messing with you it means they consider you a threat to their business. That's the only thing they care about."

"What about human trafficking?"

"What about it?"

"Calle Reyes, do they dabble in that also?"

"No. They're strictly into sprinkling the fairy dust."

"So where can I find them?"

"Don't know yet but we're working on it as we speak. Over here we basically play a game of Whack-A-Mole every day. We hit them, they disappear and resurface and then we hit them again."

"I want a shot at these guys Sergeant."

"Whoa, let's hit the brakes there Dirty Harry," Leon said. "Let us do our job."

I expected that response but it opened the door to ask him for one big favor. He said he'd consider it and then we said our goodbyes.

CHAPTER 33

I exited the freeway at Wilshire just after passing the National Cemetery off to my left. The vast majority of the eighty five thousand interred here are veterans of our foreign wars including fourteen Medal of Honor recipients. The fallen from each and every conflict beginning with the Mexican-American War of 1846 to the current imbroglio we are suffering through in Afghanistan is represented here. The group that isn't are the 241 U.S. Marines that perished in Beirut in 1983. It's an omission I find both insulting and shameful.

I don't get over to West L.A. very often so I haven't driven the corridor in quite awhile. The area seemed grittier and more angry than the last time I was here. Things like hookah lounges, all night convenience stores and nameless massage parlors had been allowed to profligate at the boarded up expense of more traditional businesses such as restaurants and grocery stores. The scene reminded me of Bedford Falls, the town in Frank Capra's classic 'It's a Wonderful Life', when George Bailey's guardian angel Clarence is showing him how drastically different things would have been had he never been born. I think we could all use a little more George Bailey right about now.

I pulled into the nursery parking lot at the corner of Wilshire and Centinela and found Detective Joe Lewis leaning against the trunk of his car typing on the keyboard of his phone.

"Something important?" I asked.

"Extremely," he replied, "playing Words with Friends and I

just fired off a seventy eight pointer."

"Nice, what was the word?"

He turned his phone around to show me. Syzygy. The cosmic occurrence when three or more planets are perfectly aligned. Remember, I hang out with a woman who uses a pen to work the daily crossword puzzle.

"Well," I replied, "for our sakes, let's hope so."

He looked at me quizzically and I told him what it meant. "Are you using the cheater app Joe?"

He nodded. "Just sometimes but always when I'm playing my brother-in-law. I can't stand losing to the prick."

As a utility cart loaded down with twenty five pound bags of steer manure drove by us I told him about Heckle and Jeckle, Calle Reyes and my conversation with Sergeant Leon. It interested him enough to pause the game.

"Okay," he said, "let me think myself through this out loud. First we have Mr. Nine Fingers. He's a human trafficker who needs a constant supply of product so he sets up, rather ingeniously I may add, these seemingly legitimate businesses which give him unfettered access to young, undocumented women. In how many cities?"

"Three that we know of," I replied, "Las Vegas, Phoenix and Los Angeles."

"Right," Joe continued on, "all well known landing spots for illegal immigrants. He's a smart guy and he makes two solid decisions. First, he never abducts an employee and second, he waits anywhere from two weeks to a month before moving on those that he does. How am I doing so far?"

"Ten out of ten Joe. Plus remember he pays his people an above market wage while providing them with health benefits. If you're an undocumented worker it's a dream job and you want to hold on to it. That would make you far less interested in sniffing out whatever's rotten in Denmark."

"Agreed. Excellent point Able. Then we move on to the second piece of the puzzle. Calle Reyes and your cartoon character enforcers. According to Sergeant Leon the gang is strictly in the business of distributing heroin yet they find themselves repeatedly doing Nine Finger's dirty work. Then there's the final piece, the Saudi consulate car that shows up at Otto's and whisks your friend Bump away to his ultimate demise. Does that about sum it up?"

"Yes," I said, "at this point that is what we know."

"I'm missing something here Able. We have all the players assembled but I don't quite understand how the game is being played."

I told him exactly what I thought was happening.

He nodded in agreement and then asked me never to befriend him for a game of internet Scrabble.

"So," I said, "are you ready to go start an international incident?"

Now I was talking Joe's language. "Hell yes," he said, "let's go rattle some cages."

I left my truck at the nursery and rode shotgun in Joe's Crown Vic as we drove into the subterranean parking structure across the street. Underground parking lots. Add it to the list of things I hate. I find driving a car deeper and deeper into the bowels of the earth to be both disconcerting and against the natural order of things. This particular one had six levels which grew darker and more depressing with each and every right hand turn we made. It also provoked an uncomfortable memory from my childhood.

When I was very young we were living in St. Louis and there was a basement in our home. It was a narrow, gloomy space full of dark recesses where my grandmother would store mysterious items in unmarked cardboard boxes. The majority of the room was taken up by the house's antiquated heating system which strained and moaned with the rise and fall of the Kane's forced air demands. Being a timid, twitchy child I had convinced myself there were dark forces at work down there just waiting for the opportunity to move against me. I didn't understand the meaning of the word détente at the time but it was certainly my operational strategy. My plan of avoidance and acceptance was solid but it wasn't full proof. I'd be sent on random errands that would require a descent into this underworld. Abel, fetch me a jar of those bread and butter pickles. Able, go check on the mousetraps. Able, please bring me up that yellow box with the red duct tape across the top. Each trip down that creaky, splintery staircase filled me with an ever growing sense of dread. I tried my best to hide those fears, especially from my brother Jonah who, even way back then, would prey upon my weaknesses with skills akin to those of a jungle cat.

It was a Saturday morning just a few days away from Christmas. Jonah and I were eight years old at the time. My father and grandfather had left early that morning to help prepare our church for the upcoming Vigil. This left my brother and myself under the not so watchful eye of our grandmother who was suffering through one of her debilitating migraines. She instructed us to stay indoors and play quietly just before going upstairs to lie down. We gave her about fifteen minutes to fall asleep then headed for the mud room to put on our snow gear.

A storm had moved into the St. Louis area the night before depositing six inches of fresh snow. There was a hill at the end of our street and when conditions were right, like today, made for an excellent sled run. Earlier in the week my father presented the two of us with matching Flexible Flyers as an early Christmas present. He thoughtfully had our names individually etched into the frames just above the Yankee Clipper logo. I made a pilgrimage to the garage every evening where I'd run my hand up and down my sled's smooth, polished pine slats and then carefully trace the edges of the sharpened red runners. It immediately became my most prized possession and I yearned for the opportunity to take it out and run it through its paces.

Now I had my chance. It was a beautiful after the storm kind of day with the temperature in the high forty's, nothing but blue skies and the most gentle of breezes. The sounds of laughter and shouting were emanating from the hill as the neighborhood kids began to congregate. Jonah and I walked across our snow covered front lawn and opened the door to the garage. There was just one sled leaning against my father's work bench where last night there had been two. It was Jonah's.

"Where's my sled?" I asked as the trepidation snuck into my voice.

"I saw Dad take it down to the basement last night," Jonah said as he quickly grabbed his.

The basement of all places. "Why'd he do that?" I asked.

"I don't know," Jonah said shrugging his shoulders, "you'd have to ask him. Hurry up and go get it. I'll wait for you."

As I headed back inside my brother issued me a stern warning. "And don't wake up Grandma."

Our heating system was groaning and hissing at me as I made my way down the stairwell. The cacophony of noises sounded remarkably like the monsters that had come to roost in my nightmares. My sled was in plain sight at the bottom of the stairs. This was going to be a quick grab and go operation as I planned to be gone before anyone or anything knew I was ever there. I snatched up my sled and began my ascent to freedom only to find Jonah at the top of the stairs holding cut up pieces of the shoelaces in his hand.

"This is for the shoes Able," he said tossing them down the stairs. He then locked the basement door and turned off the lights.

Two weeks earlier I had played a cheap, vindictive prank on my brother that was born from a place of anger and jealousy. We had both tried out for the local YMCA basketball team a month earlier. It was a sport I absolutely loved. My grandfather had fastened a rim and backboard to the side of our garage and I would spend countless hours playing imaginary games while trying to better my skills. I was both play by play announcer and the star player who never failed to hit the game winning shot. Jonah's interest in the game was lukewarm at best so I was shocked when the coach taped the final roster to the window of his office. There was the name of Jonah Kane prominently displayed at the top of the list while mine was nowhere to be found. I was totally gutted and brooded about it for days on end.

My father then bought Jonah a brand new pair of All-Star Chuck Taylor's to celebrate his achievement. They were my dream shoes and the fact that Jonah now owned a pair and I didn't pushed me over the edge. On the morning of his first game I borrowed a steak knife from the kitchen and proceeded to slit the laces of both shoes rendering them useless. My actions would earn me a week's worth of grounding but at the time I foolishly felt it had been worth every minute. Jonah ended up being late for the tip-off and had to ride the bench for the entire first half. He went on to be the game's leading scorer anyways but that was beside the point.

I now stood motionless in a darkness so thick I couldn't see my hand as I pressed it against my face. I started yelling at the top of my lungs for Jonah to let me out but when I heard the familiar squeak of the mud room door opening and closing I knew the due bill for my pettiness had arrived. Revenge truly is a meal best served cold.

My sense of hearing began to overcompensate for the loss of sight and I was now hearing things I'd never noticed before.

In addition to the continued belching of the furnace, there was the cracking and popping of the house as it settled on its foundation and the mews of unidentified rodents could be heard as they moved freely about the crawl space. To me and my imaginative eight year old mind the sounds were all demonic in origin and I resigned myself to an upcoming, violent death.

I was locked in the basement for over three hours while my brother enjoyed his new sled and my grandmother slept off her headache. When my father finally found me at the top of the stairs I was unresponsive, my knuckles were bleeding and I was lying in a pool of my own urine. He rushed me to the hospital but I had already started coming around by the time we arrived. A doctor checked my vital signs and issued me a clean bill of health. He diagnosed my symptoms as a panic attack but I instinctively knew it was something more serious. It could have been a nervous breakdown perhaps or maybe even a psychotic break. Regardless, I felt broken and ashamed. My father was more than willing to accept the doctor's prognosis however which left me to my own devices to quietly and slowly put the pieces of my mental health back together. My grandparents questioned my brother about the incident on more than one occasion but he defiantly never deviated from his original story which was he thought I had gone out sledding and he simply closed and locked the basement door before going upstairs to watch television. I had neither the fight left in me nor the inclination to challenge his version of events. Our relationship would eventually repair itself but Jonah and I were unknowingly becoming a real life version of the frog and the scorpion where love, fear and dependency somehow find a way to symbiotically coexist. Along with that came the realization that sometimes identical twins are not identical at all.

CHAPTER 34

Joe and I found what we were looking for when we circled back up from the bottom of the parking structure. Tucked away in an alcove on level P2 were two black town cars parked under a sign that read 'Parking for the Royal Consulate of Saudi Arabia Only. Violators Will Be Beheaded.' Sorry, I meant to say towed, violators will be towed. The license I.D. on one of the cars read S-KV2378 which was the plate I hurriedly photographed leaving Otto's Warehouse last Sunday. This had to be the same car that picked up my friend Bump and delivered him home to meet his maker. Now it was time to find out why. Joe parked directly behind the two cars eliminating any chance of either one of them making a quick exit.

"Ready to do this?" I asked him.

He was grinning from ear to ear. "Are you kidding?" he replied, "I live for this kind of thing."

I headed for the bank of elevators as Joe popped his trunk and got to work. When I got off at the seventh floor I was greeted by the green and white flag of the Kingdom of Saudi Arabia. Hassam had explained the symbolism to me years ago. The color green represents Islam and the Arabic inscription across the body of the flag is the religion's declaration of faith, the shahada. It reads 'There is no god but Allah; Muhammed is the Messenger of Allah.' Under the shahada lies a sword. It is a pointed reminder of just how severe Islamic justice can be meted out whenever the situation arises. Sometimes you can learn an awful lot about a nation simply by the flag they fly.

I made my way into the consulate's small, empty lobby and

was met by a security guard named Randy. I fully expected I'd have to spar with some tough, ex-Mabahith officer but Randy was as American as a slice of apple pie on the Fourth of July. He warmly asked how he could be of assistance and I offered up a lie about the oil business and my need to obtain a visa for an upcoming business trip. That seemed like a reasonable enough request to Randy who asked me to have a seat before disappearing down the hallway. I obediently sat down and took the opportunity to take in my surroundings. I was underwhelmed. I've seen more ornate waiting rooms in a dental office. The carpet was heading towards threadbare and whoever chose the chairs had chosen poorly. They were stained, uncomfortable and the color choice of avocado green seemed tacky and unimaginative. There was no fanciful artwork on the walls and the magazine rack offerings were hopelessly outdated. I guess I just expected more from a country that boasts the world's largest oil reserves. I picked up an old, dog-eared pamphlet entitled 'The Business Man's Guide to Saudi Arabia' and started skimming through it.

The Kingdom of Saudi Arabia was founded in 1938 by King Abdulaziz who conquered and unified the region. The House of Saud has since provided the country with six additional kings and it continues, to this day, to be a true monarchy in every sense of the word. It is the largest sovereign nation in the Middle East and the second largest in the Arab world. The capital city is Riyadh and it is home to Mecca and Medina, the two holiest cities in all of Islam. Oil was discovered there in 1938 and now Saudi Arabia is the largest exporter of crude on the planet. They are also, perhaps not coincidentally, the largest arms importer in the world. If you don't protect what's in your pot they'll come and steal everything you've got.

My history lesson was interrupted by the return of Yankee Doodle Randy. He made a photocopy of my driver's license and then escorted me into an empty office. He asked for my phone and informed me I'd get it back when my business at the consulate had come to an end. He never said which one or how many so I handed over an old burner that had been collecting dust in the glovebox of my truck.

I first met with an attractive woman who introduced herself as Adele Daher. She was the epitome of the modern Arab female. There would certainly be no hijab in this pretty young lady's future. She was wearing a very stylish herringbone blazer with a matching skirt that hovered just above her knees. The outfit was nicely complimented by a white, silk blouse that may or may not have had one too many buttons unclasped. I thought she looked fantastic but I could easily picture her Bedouin great grandfather rolling over in his qabr right about now.

I knew to get to the right person I'd have to move my way up the consulate food chain and Randy and the lovely Ms. Daher were just links along that chain. I decided to engage her in a bit of small talk before lowering the boom. She was from Riyadh originally but her businessman father moved the family to the toney colony of Malibu when she was just seven years old. She recently graduated from UCLA in May with a degree in communications and began her position here as an associate consular officer just two weeks ago. She seemed very nice which made me feel terrible for what I was about to do. Just as she began explaining the visa process I rudely snatched the blank application form out of her hand, tore it in half twice then threw the scraps of paper into the air. It was all very melodramatic on my part but I achieved my goal of intimidating her while at the same time receiving her undivided attention.

"Miss Daher," I said in the sternest of voices, "I apologize for the false pretense but I'm not here to apply for a visa. My name is Able Kane and I'm a private detective in the middle of a murder investigation. I'm here today because I have reasons to believe that someone from this consulate is involved and I won't be leaving until I get to the bottom of it."

Adele, bless her heart, looked forlornly up at the security camera mounted on the ceiling silently pleading for help. She turned several shades of white which made me believe none of her college courses had prepared her for this moment. I suggested she call someone and with trembling fingers she did just that.

Four minutes later I was sitting in the office of the consulate's director of security (DOS). He and I were facetiming Joe who was still down in the parking structure. Joe first flashed his badge then went on to describe the series of events that had brought us here today. The DOS was another American by the name of Jack Kerrigan. After Joe had his say Mr. Kerrigan countered with the good old diplomatic immunity defense. I figured that would be his go to move so I had prepared a speech for that exact contingency.

"Well you're right of course Jack," I said, "and I'm sure when this is all over you'll be able to say I told you so. But way before the lawyers finally get together for the pissing contest Joe and I will have towed that car of yours to a forensics lab. We're going to find the evidence we're looking for and then I'm going to post it all over social media for the entire world to see."

That produced the first fidget out of the placid Mr. Kerrigan but he still wasn't budging.

"In that case," he replied, "I'll have you both fired and then I'll sue your asses for everything you've got."

Well the only person that can terminate Able Kane's employment is the guy I look at in the mirror every morning but he did get me thinking about the wisdom of dragging Joe into all of this.

"Joe," I said speaking into my phone, "did you get all that?"

"Every word Able and guess what?"

"What," I asked.

"Tell him I don't give a shit. How about you Able? Do you

give a shit?"

"Not one single ounce Joe," I said. "Is the tow truck here?"

"He's across the street just waiting for my call."

"Okay," I said, "screw this guy, let's do it."

There was no tow truck standing by but Kerrigan didn't know that. I got up out of my chair and headed for the door. I didn't make it very far.

"Mr. Kane," Kerrigan said, "you don't really think the Saudis are involved in this do you?" He was remaining defiant but I could hear the first trace of uncertainty creep into his voice.

"No I don't actually," I said turning towards him, "but someone at this consulate is and that makes your stance of non-cooperation all the more puzzling. I've given you the opportunity to help solve a murder, bring down a human trafficking ring and keep your client's reputation intact. You've chosen not to help and that's your prerogative. But I hope you realize when I blow this thing up the majority of the debris is going to end up in your lap."

Most diplomats are chess players by nature and all good chess players intrinsically know when it's time to tip over their king. Jack Kerrigan was no exception. I had him checkmated and he knew it.

"What exactly do you want from me?" he asked, sounding defeated. I told him what I needed to know and from that point on Jack Kerrigan was very forthcoming.

Kerrigan had an interesting backstory himself. He had thirty years in as a career officer in the U.S. Diplomatic Corps. before coming home and starting his own private security firm. During his time working for the government he had been stationed at U.S. embassies all over the world including stops in Riyadh, Cairo, Doha and Beirut. He had some interesting answers to several of my questions. He did not know Mubari or any other nine fingered man for that matter but over the years he crossed paths with Victor Ortiz on several occasions at embassy socials. Ortiz was known for being well connected and like a bad penny he always seemed to be showing up. Kerrigan had heard a rumor awhile back that Ortiz hadn't retired from the CIA but had been terminated for some type of gross misconduct. He didn't know the particulars. All of this information should have moved the DOS to the top of my list but there was something about his body language that cried out he wasn't my guy.

He explained due to a variety of legal reasons access to the consulate vehicles was very tightly controlled. This was definitely not a situation where the keys were hanging on a hook by the door and you simply grabbed them on your way out. Kerrigan himself had implemented strong security protocols that monitored and controlled their usage. The keys to the town cars were locked up in a safe the staff had nicknamed the mini-bar. To gain access you not only needed the eight digit keypad combination but you also had to own a six digit PIN number that was issued to authorized staff members only. The original keys and their spares rested on sensors that automatically recorded when they were taken and by whom. The process would then reverse itself when the keys were returned. As if that wasn't enough there was a security camera mounted directly above the mini-bar which monitored the comings and goings 24/7. The net result was it didn't take very much sleuthing on Kerrigan's part to identify the culprit and that was when his anxiety levels began shooting through the roof.

The original set of keys belonging to S-KV2378 were taken from the mini-bar at 8:41 on Sunday morning and never returned. They were taken by one Daniel Mansour, a Lebanese national who was a low level employee in Kerrigan's security company. He was here in the United States on a green card and held no diplomatic status with the Saudi Arabian consulate. Mansour somehow had obtained the combination to the safe then used Kerrigan's PIN number to get inside. To make matters worse, actually much worse, Mansour also happened to be the nephew of Kerrigan's wife, a Lebanese woman he had met twenty years ago while stationed in Beirut.

Over the years Kerrigan had sponsored many of her relatives for U.S. citizenship and even provided employment when it was needed. There were never any issues until now. I guess if you do enough good deeds they'll eventually find a way to punish you in the end. We both desperately wanted to talk to Daniel but he hadn't shown up for work since Friday and he wasn't returning phone calls from Kerrigan, his aunt or his roommate. He had gone full ghost. By the time we got into the elevator that magic seed of worry I had sown inside his Jack's mind had grown to the size of a giant beanstalk.

As we descended towards the parking structure I asked him if he thought it was possible Ortiz and his nephew had crossed paths sometime in the past. There had to be some kind of connection.

He thought about it for a moment then nodded. "My wife's family rubbed shoulders with the elite of Beirut society which was where you'd find Victor whenever he was in town so yeah, I'd say it's definitely a possibility."

Kerrigan further divulged Daniel Mansour owned a side business. It was a limousine service and he'd foolishly let Daniel borrow the consulate cars on occasion. It was an amateur, boneheaded move but one for which I could empathize. How did Jesus put it? 'It's easier for a camel to pass through the eye of a needle then it is to say no to family.' Okay, well maybe I'm paraphrasing just a bit. I know he was actually comparing dromedaries to rich men in heaven but I'd bet you a basket full of loaves and fishes Jesus would have rethought the quote if he hadn't been an only child.

We got off the elevator at P2 and made our way over to Joe who was just finishing up dusting the car door handles for fingerprints.

"Any luck?" I asked him.

He shook his head. "Nothing. Everything's been wiped clean. Someone did a very thorough job."

That's pretty much what I expected. I turned to Kerrigan and held out my hand. "Keys?"

He handed over the spare set and the three of us climbed into the car. Kerrigan and I got into the front and Joe hopped into the back.

Since Mansour was incommunicado we'd have to let the car's GPS do the talking for him. Unless you've been living in a cave somewhere up in the Hindu Kush for the last twenty years you're probably aware your vehicle's navigation system is watching and recording every move you make. It is a technological advancement unanimously endorsed by divorce attorneys everywhere. I powered up the car and went to the GPS app. Tab history, tab search filters, put in the date and voila. We were now looking at the town car's complete travel history for Sunday. Every road taken and every stop made between 8:50 in the morning when it left this parking structure until 7:32 in the evening when it returned was now available on the screen for our viewing pleasure. Kerrigan wasn't much help. He didn't recognize any of the addresses.

As we were finishing up Joe asked me a question. "Able, are you smelling what I'm smelling?"

I wasn't until I took a long, deep breath and caught the faintest whiff of a familiar odor.

"Esters?" I replied.

"Yep."

"Someone want to fill me in here," Kerrigan asked sounding a bit perturbed. "Who's Ester?"

Not who but what. I handed him back his keys. "You better pop the trunk."

You'll get a lot of different opinions from a lot of different people as to what a decomposing body smells like and to be fair the odors evolve as the cadaver continues its journey. During the early stages of the process the body emits a group of molecules called esters which is a trait it shares with, of all things, an over ripened piece of fruit. That's probably why I was thinking about three week old pineapples when Kerrigan pressed the key fob and the trunk slowly opened.

There wedged into the boot was the lifeless body of a handsome young man with two small caliber bullet holes in his forehead. He was smartly dressed in all black and his chauffer's cap was still resting atop his head. The original set of keys had been tossed into the trunk coming to rest on the deceased's chest.

I looked to Kerrigan. "Your nephew?"

He simply nodded without saying a word.

I had told him I'd do my best to remain discreet but all bets were off now with Daniel's dead body being added to the equation. To his credit, Kerrigan didn't have a hissy fit nor did he call me an Indian giver when Joe called 911. He instead excused himself and wandered off in stunned silence to break the news to his wife.

My phone rang. It was Frank Garcia Sr. who had returned to Anchorage from the wilds of Alaska. With everything that had transpired over the last few days I'd completely forgotten about him. There was no way I was going to let him escape to voicemail again.

I put him on speaker so Joe could listen in. "Mr. Garcia, thanks for calling me back. How was the fishing?"

"Great, but it always is up here." There was a nervous uneasiness to his voice this time around. "Have you heard from Reina or my son yet?"

I told him the truth and just enough information to raise his concern levels up to where they should be.

"I've been calling and texting the both of them for two hours now without a response," he informed me. "I even tried the landline at the house. Do you think I should come home?"

"That's probably a pretty good idea Frank," I said. "Hey, I've got a question for you. Is Frank Jr. living with you?"

"Yeah. He and Reina are both staying at my place. The plan was for them to house sit until I get back in late September then they were going to get a place of their own."

"Frank I need to get into your house now."

He didn't object. He gave me his address and told me where he hid the spare house key. There was something familiar about the street name but I couldn't quite put my finger on it.

"Call me when you get there Mr. Kane and I'll shut off the security system for you."

"You have a security system?"

"Absolutely. When you're gone as often as I am you need a state of the art system for some piece of mind. I've got armed response, motion sensors, the whole nine yards. The only problem is Junior keeps forgetting to turn it on when he leaves. I'm constantly having to manage it from my phone."

"Cameras?" I asked.

"Of course."

"Inside and out?"

"Yes but the inside cameras don't start recording until the alarm is triggered. I think my son's worried I'd be spying on him all the time."

I explained to him those cameras of his might have recorded some very important footage which was currently just drifting along on a cyber cloud somewhere.

"Mr. Kane," he explained, "I can pack you into the wilderness to a stream that's probably never been fished before then put you on a thirty pound rainbow trout or a sixty pound king but figuring out this computer stuff is a nothing but a bird's nest to me."

I appreciate a good analogy as much as the next guy so I fired one right back at him.

"Trust me," I said, "you're singing to the choir here. But I've got a guy who couldn't catch a fish even if it jumped into his creel but he sure can make those cyber clouds rain."

He chuckled at the image and asked me what I needed. I gave him Nate's email address and he promised he'd forward along the proper log-in information.

Joe spoke up as soon as I ended the call. "Able, that could be the break we've been waiting for."

"I sure hope so Joseph."

The original plan was for Joe and I to retrace the movements of the town car together but now we had two bonafide leads that needed to be chased down. We were going to have to split up which was far less than ideal considering all the bodies that were washing ashore.

"Joe," I said, "I'm afraid we're going to have to divide in order to conquer."

He agreed so we decided he'd double back on the town car while I headed over to Frank Garcia's house.

"You might as well take off," Joe told me, "no reason for both of us to wait around for the LAPD to arrive. We're burning daylight here."

Before I headed towards the bank of elevators there was something I needed to get off my chest.

"Joe." I said, "I feel like I kind of shanghaied you into this mess so if it's more than you bargained for just say the word and I'll completely understand. Let's face it, you have a wife and a daughter to consider, I don't."

He smiled. "Able, just so you know, I see my daughter

once every other year at Christmas and the minute she walks through our door she's looking for an excuse to end the visit early. As for my wife, well she just booked two first class tickets on a four month cruise to Asia and the South Pacific. I actually allowed myself to start getting excited about it until she informed me the second ticket was for a friend. I have zero hobbies to speak of and the one and only true friend I had in the world died three months ago. He was a German Shephard by the name of Duke. The point I'm trying to make here is that being a detective is the only reason I have for getting out of bed in the morning so you'll have to hit me with that fancy taser of yours if you want to go it alone."

I didn't have a reasonable rebuttal for that so we agreed to check in with each other at the first hint of trouble.

Before I made it to my truck I received a text from Nate letting me know he was in possession of Frank's log-in information. He followed that up with a row of question marks. Instead of texting him back I took a deep breath and dialed his number. He picked up immediately.

"How are you my friend?" I asked him.

"Getting better. I'm sore as hell Able but the drugs are a big help."

"Be careful with that stuff Nate. The ones that really work are the ones that are the hardest to walk away from."

I then went on to apologize as profusely as a human being possibly could. I fought back some tears to make it to the finish line.

Nate got emotional also and the two of us took a moment to have a good cry. We eventually recovered our manhood and started talking about the business at hand.

"Able, how far back on this footage do you want me to go?"

"I know it's a lot to ask, especially given the circumstances Nate, but I'd say at least three weeks."

"No problem but I figure you owe me three months free rent considering all the trouble you've put me through."

"It's settled then," I said, "four months free rent plus utilities."

He paused to check his emotions again. "Dammit Able, I absolutely hate when you do that. You must be the worst negotiator on the planet. I was ready to settle for a dinner at Brigid's place but now you went and ruined everything."

He made me laugh which was just what the doctor prescribed.

"Nate?" I said.

"Yeah Able?"

"I love you buddy and once again, I am so sorry."

I heard him choke up right before he disconnected the call.

CHAPTER 35

I got off the 10 Freeway at Hacienda Blvd. and started making my way south towards an area the locals simply call the 'Heights.' Hacienda Heights is part of the original Spanish land grant known as Rancho La Puente and for generations the population was chiefly comprised of hard working, blue collar Latinos and whites. But typical of neighborhoods everywhere within the Greater Los Angeles area, the 'Heights' has witnessed some transformative demographic changes since the new millennium. As disillusioned residents began cashing in their real estate chips and moving on to places like Reno, Boise and Scottsdale new faces flooded in to fill the void. I guess nature truly does abhor a vacuum.

Now as you make your way through the city's center you'll notice almost all the storefronts are signed in Asian. For years I was the typical 'gweilo' who couldn't tell the difference between Korean and Chinese lettering until an Asian golfing friend gave me a quick and easy tutorial. It's very simple. If the symbols contain rounded or oval shapes and there is spacing between groups of words it's Korean. He further explained Chinese symbols, known as hanzi, look more like run on sentences and have no rounded shapes, only intricate designs that never stray from their box like containers. There were plenty of both examples as I made my way up into the hills.

As I neared Frank's house it finally dawned on me why the street name had sounded so familiar. This was the street where Reina's Toyota Camry had been ticketed. It was a cul de sac and a quick lap around it confirmed the car was no longer there.

I pulled into Frank's driveway which earned me a glare from his neighbor, a white, octogenarian holdout whose rather impressive boiler had currently escaped the confines of its owner's tee shirt. He was spot watering the burned out areas of his front lawn while enjoying a mid-afternoon Coors Light. I texted Frank to let him know I'd arrived then exited my truck to introduce myself. His name was George and I think he might have been starving for some human contact. He was an ex-merchant marine as well as a retired lathe operator in the aerospace industry. The Mrs. died ten years ago, ovarian cancer, and he was just 'riding the train to the end of the line.' There was nothing to watch on television anymore except for football but the powers that be are trying to ruin that game too. Nothing surprised him anymore and his stance on life could be summed up by 'been there and done that.' He had several other key insights on life and I'd say he was doing a pretty good job of keeping his latent bigotry in check. I can't quite recall the frame of reference but he closed with one of my favorite quotes. 'A lie can travel half way around the world before the truth has a chance to put its shoes on.' He gave the credit to Winston Churchill who surely delivered some beauties in his day but I'm pretty sure Mark Twain gets the nod on this one. Regardless, George needed to blog.

He offered me a beer which I graciously accepted. As he handed it over I gave him a copy of Reina's picture. We then retreated to his front porch to get out of the summer heat.

"Do you recognize her George?"

"Sure," he said, "she and Frank Jr. are an item aren't they?" He polished off what was left of his Silver Bullet then grabbed another from the ice chest in a seamless, well practiced motion. "Nice girl," he continued, "pretty as a Georgia peach. Always took time out of her day to say hello whether she was coming or going. What happened to her?"

I went on to explain she'd gone missing several weeks ago

and there were a lot of good people very worried about her.

He nodded. "That's probably about the last time I saw her. She, Frank Jr. and some other gal were carrying grocery bags up the driveway arguing about something or other."

"Can you describe the other woman to me George?"

He shook his head. "I'm sorry, I can't. I was inside my house and by the time I took a peek to see what all the fuss was about they were already walking through the front door."

"Do you remember what day that was?"

"Sorry, I don't. It was quite awhile ago."

"Is there anything else you can tell me?" I asked him.

"Not that I can recall. Guess I shouldn't be surprised she went off and got herself in some kind of hot water though."

I took a sip of my beer. Ice cold, just the way I like it. "Why do you say that George?"

"Well what's the old saying?" he quipped, "if you lie down with the dog you'll wake up with its fleas."

"Frank Jr.?" I asked just to be clear.

"Yes sirree Mr. Kane. I've been around the block enough times to know that some kids just come out of their momma's womb the wrong way. In my opinion Frankie happens to be one of them. You can knock on any door on this street and people will bend your ear about the crap he's pulled."

"Can you give me a for instance?"

"Sure. Stupid stuff. Egging our cars, firing off M-80's, racing his dirt bike up and down our street all day long and when Frank Sr. is gone he'll throw parties that last until the cows come home. He's a royal pain in the ass."

I couldn't argue with any of that. I'd be super pissed if he was my neighbor. George offered me another beer but I demurred. Not that I'm against doing it but today wasn't the right day to go toe to toe with a true professional. I gave him my card and asked him to call me if Reina, Frank or anyone else for that matter happened to show up. He got up, shook my hand and told me he had to go see an Indian about a blanket which I think meant he had to relieve himself.

I found Frank's key right where he said it would be which was on the side of the house, behind the camellia bush and under a stone frog. He texted me back confirming he shut off the alarm system and I was good to go. That's when the excitement truly started.

I turned the key and cracked open the door. They say when your number is up Death will arrive at your doorstep and refuse to leave without you. But today I came knocking on his door and he let me in willingly. He was probably wondering what in the world had taken me so long to get here.

The stench kicked me in the stomach like a rented mule and followed me all the way back to my truck where I retrieved a pair of latex gloves and my jar of Vicks Vapor Rub. I applied a liberal dose directly under my nose then walked through the front door to one of the strangest crime scenes I would ever encounter. It was cool, almost downright cold in the house. I checked the thermostat. The temperature had been set at an aggressive sixty two degrees and I could hear the compressor outside humming along at a fevered pitch as it tried to comply with the orders handed down from central command. The living room to my right was tidy and deserted as was the den to my left with its seventy two inch plasma television mounted on the wall. I continued down the hallway into the kitchen where the smell continued to grow stronger and more menacing.

The kitchen was hopelessly outdated with aged tile counters and antiquated appliances but it was clean and utilitarian and I couldn't imagine Frank Sr. giving a damn about the aesthetics one way or the other. At the other end of the room separated by a floor to ceiling wall was the eating area. I could see just the edge of a table and two empty chairs through an open archway. The miasma was exponentially increasing now with each step that brought me closer to ground zero. I paused at the threshold to take a deep, protracted breath hoping the vapor rub would work its magic. Out of habit I made the sign of the cross and took that last fateful step forward.

The room was a windowless alcove with framed family pictures adorning the walls. There were photos of the two Franks catching fish, photos of then riding in boats drinking Corona beer and then more photos of them catching other fish. I counted eight chairs surrounding the oval shaped table but only three of them were currently occupied. A month ago all three of the occupants would have been considered attractive, young adults but the science of death and decay is a stern taskmaster and no one is spared its rod.

I made my way over to the one person whose identity I couldn't readily confirm. There was a purse slung over the side of her chair and I reached into it pulling out a wallet. The driver's license sadly confirmed my suspicions. It belonged to one Julie Herrera and I lifted her head off the table to make sure there was no mistake. I now understood why she hadn't returned any of my calls.

The man was much easier to identify. I'd never met him before but there was a framed photo of him holding a trophy size King salmon on the wall directly above his lifeless body. Here sitting in state was the fall guy, Frank Jr., who wouldn't have the chance to terrorize George or the neighborhood ever again.

The third and final victim died with her eyes wide open. Her stare wouldn't let me go and I instinctively knew she had already passed judgement against me. The same eyes I looked at every time I handed out one of her missing person posters had found me guilty of letting her down, for not being there when she needed someone the most. But in my defense I never really had a chance did I Reina? By the time Harvey walked into the Celtic Cross asking for my help you were already gone weren't you?

I walked over to her and closed those beautiful, brown eyes for the very last time. I had just tampered with a crime scene but I couldn't care less. It was a small price to pay in exchange for giving her back this small shred of dignity. I couldn't save Reina Montes' life but atoning for her death was still very much on the table. I would push all my chips into to the pot to make that happen.

My phone rang. It was Harvey.

"Hey," I said rather succinctly.

"I'm back at the airport OT. I'm looking at a departure board telling me my flight's been delayed for at least another hour. That's really the last thing I wanted to be staring at right now."

"I'll trade you Harvey, straight up, no questions asked."

"Uh oh. What's going on?"

I delivered the bad news including the who, the what and the where along with my best guesstimate as to when. As for the exact why, well that was still a work in progress. I followed this information up with the earlier events of the day including my conversation with Sergeant Leon and the international incident Joe and I may or may not have set in motion at the Saudi Arabian consulate.

There was a dramatic pause on Harvey's end of the call as he processed the new developments. His thirty plus years of experience had undoubtedly prepared him for this outcome, in fact he probably saw it coming.

"Jesus OT, next time I give you a job the least you can do is fully commit to it."

"Thanks Harv, I'll take that under consideration."

"Cause of death?" he asked hopping right back into detective mode.

"There's no blood so knives and gun play are out of the question. Could have been hotshots for everyone around the table but I don't want to compromise the crime scene any more than I already have. It's a bizarre one though Harvey. The chairs have all been pushed in tight against the table to make sure the victims remained upright. It looks like they just fell asleep waiting for a meal that was never served. I have no idea what to make of it."

"Yeah," Harvey agreed, "I'm not sure what that means either. What I do know is anyone you go looking for has a tendency of showing up dead. Try not to take it too personally."

"I just want people to like me."

He chuckled. "Do you have any more moves?"

"Just one but I was hoping it wouldn't come to this." I told him my plan and he decided maybe it wasn't such a bad thing his flight had been delayed.

"So what did you find in Vegas?" I asked.

He went on to explain EZX's corporate headquarters turned out to be nothing more than a lockbox at a UPS Store. The physical plant was located in an industrial park on the outskirts of Henderson operating under the name of Clark County Professional Cleaning Services. According to the landlord they cleared out in the middle of the night several months ago even though the rent had been prepaid through June.

"Sounds like a wasted trip Harvey," I said, "sorry about that."

"Hold on young grasshoppah, I'm not done yet. We canvassed the neighboring businesses and multiple sources confirmed the existence of the job fairs. We were told that once a month hundreds of Latina women would descend upon the industrial park seeking employment with the company. We also had multiple witnesses who remembered both Reina and your nine fingered friend. My LVPD buddy called in a sketch artist and they were able to reach a consensus on his likeness. It's a little rough around the edges but they all agreed this is the guy. I'm sending it to you right..............................now."

In a matter of seconds I was looking at an image of a handsome, middle aged man. This guy was beardless, owned a headful of curly hair and was a little rounder in the face but I just knew it was the same man that brutally tortured me over thirty years ago. It was the eyes, those black, serpentine eyes staring back at me that left no doubt in my mind. This was Mubari. I shivered as an onslaught of memories breached my defenses. I was just beginning to ponder the enormity of this cosmic size coincidence when a voice at the front door interrupted my thoughts.

"Mr. Kane, what the hell's going on? It smells like something died in there."

You'd have to get up pretty early in the morning to pull one over on ole Georgie boy.

"Who's that?" Harvey asked.

"I'm afraid that's curious George."

"The monkey?"

"No the neighbor. Hold on."

"George," I yelled out, "do not come in here. This is officially a crime scene. Sit tight, I'll be right out."

"Okay," he said, "but I think you should know I just called 911."

Dammit George. Why'd you go and do a thing like that? I thought we were friends.

"Harvey," I said, "I've gotta go."

"Yeah, I overheard. I'll call Marta. We haven't talked since Friday and I think I'm the one that should deliver the news. Call me when you can."

"You got it," I said before signing off.

I couldn't afford to still be here when the first responders started arriving. I'd be delayed for hours on end answering their questions and getting castigated for interfering with the crime scene. There was probably a fifty-fifty chance I'd even be escorted down to the cop shop for a formal interview. That had to be avoided at all costs.

I knew from experience the average response time to a 911 call is right around ten minutes but if a team is motivated and efficient they can cut that down almost in half. What I really needed was about an hour to do a thorough grid search of the house but instead this was going to be the investigative equivalent of speed dating. I set the timer on my phone to four minutes and thirty seconds then hit the start button.

First, I started rifling through Julie Herrera's handbag. It was an oversized Coach model and she had somehow managed to fill it to the brim with odds and ends including clothing changes, make up, snacks and apparently every receipt from every purchase she had ever made. There was no phone however. This was already taking way too long so I decided to just take the whole damn thing keenly aware of the legal hole I was digging for myself. Frank Jr. had a wallet in his back pocket containing a drivers license, two credit cards and what looked like about one hundred dollars in cash. He didn't have a phone on his person either. I took a picture of the two credit cards then moved on to Reina. She was wearing a snug fitting red and white polka dot sundress that had been designed to leave very little to the imagination. It was an easy search. No phone, no wallet, no nothing. Elapsed time now, one minute and forty seven seconds.

The kitchen counter was clear except for a bowl of rotting apples and bananas that was slowly being devoured by a colony of fruit flies and a portable phone with one of those old school answering machines plugged into it. Unfortunately the small cassette tape which recorded and played back messages had been removed rendering it useless to me. I did hit *69 on the phone and wrote down the number of the last incoming call before moving on. I was already half way through my allotted time and I still hadn't left the kitchen.

If there was any good news it lay in the fact that this was a smallish house and all the remaining rooms were connected by one short hallway. There were four closed doors staggered in a left, right, left, right configuration. The first room to my left was the guest bathroom. It was uncluttered, spotless and had nothing to tell me. The first door on the right led to a small bedroom that Frank Sr. had at some point converted into a home office. There was a brown, leather couch long enough to nap on and an Apple computer sitting atop a battleship gray, metal desk. It was powered down so I turned it on and made myself a mental note to check it before I left. The next room to the left was obviously Frank Jr.'s and I'd bet you a month's salary it hadn't changed since his adolescent days. Thumbtacked to the walls were posters of motocross legends including Ricky Carmichael and Jeff Ward, the Flying Freckle. There were stacks upon stacks of comic books that reached head high and a Play Station game console that sat prominently displayed on a small table between two E-Z Boy recliners. I did a quick check of his dresser drawers but they'd been emptied out and I then confirmed he wasn't stashing anything under the bed. The final room to my right was the much larger master bedroom with its own en suite bathroom. Frank Jr. had moved himself and Reina into these far swankier digs while dad was up north catching fish. I guess it's true what they say about the mice when the cat's away. They were both, how can I say this nicely, unneat. Neither one seemed at all interested in such trivial matters as hanging up clean clothing or tossing the soiled ones into a hamper. I maneuvered my way around the debris field as I rummaged through the closet space, the armoire and the nightstand but once again found nothing of importance. I then hurried back to the computer in the home office. It was now booted up and not password protected. I quickly scrolled down through two weeks worth of emails. The bulk of them were business in nature: Frank Sr. managing his bookings, arranging lodging and ordering supplies. What I didn't see was any communications with a nine-fingered man, an ex-CIA agent gone bad or any other nefarious characters for that matter. The elapsed time was now three minutes and fifty seven seconds. I had to get going. On my way out I noticed another door on the far side of the den. There were two sets of keys hanging from a row of wooden pegs just to the right of it. It was an access door to the attached garage.

As I opened it the timer on my phone sounded off. I silenced it. This was a risk worth taking. Parked next to a cherry red Harley Davidson Road King was the Toyota Camry Marta had gifted to Reina. It was an older model so there wouldn't be any GPS data to scroll through. Not that it mattered. I was already pushing the envelope time wise. I could now hear the faintest sounds of multiple sirens heading in my direction.

I unlocked the car and took a look inside. Rena's untidiness hadn't been contained to the master bedroom. The car was littered with fast food wrappers, dirty clothes and God only knows what else. I opened the glove box and it was crammed full with papers. I didn't know what if anything was important so I took it all. The sirens were growing in strength now and to me they sounded like war drums announcing the approach of an advancing army as they prepared to move against my inferior position.

I popped the trunk. Staring back at me was a leather briefcase embossed with Reina's initials. Enough was enough. I grabbed it and headed for the door. I must have been quite a sight to see walking away from a triple homicide with a briefcase in one hand, a sheaf of papers in the other and a very fashionable Coach bag slung over my left shoulder.

As I exited the house I was confronted by George and a half dozen other curious villagers who were in the early stages of coalescing themselves into an angry mob. This was a bud that needed to be nipped before any thoughts of vigilantism entered their minds.

I walked directly over to George who was vying for the role of ring leader. I got the feeling he was now eyeing me through a different lens and no longer considered me the happy go lucky, beer drinking private investigator he once knew. I needed to take him out of the equation and it had to happen quickly. I stepped into his personal space grossly violating it. This made him rather uncomfortable which was exactly my plan.

"George," I said in my most authoritative voice, "do you have Frank Sr.'s phone number?" Like a good litigator I already knew the answer to my question since it came up earlier while we were sharing a beer together.

"Yes I do," he said taking a step backwards to create a little breathing space. "I always keep an eye on things for him while he's gone."

Good answer George. I closed the gap between us again as the symphony of sirens grew louder and louder. I figured they were no more than a minute away.

"Well George," I said, "you really ran the ship on to the rocks then didn't you? There's three people dead in that house and it all happened on your watch."

I gave it just that small nautical twist figuring it would score well with an ex-merchant marine.

The crowd let out a collective gasp and turned their attention to George. Could this all really be his fault?

I think he felt the tectonic plates shifting beneath him and he wasn't very happy about it. He tried to defend himself. "Hey, wait a minute there mister it was you who................"

I cut him off. This was no time for logic and common sense to come waltzing along. I decided to come over the top and land a haymaker.

"No George," I said in my very irate voice, "you wait a minute. Your neighbor entrusted you with the well being of his home and family and you let him down in spades. Now get your ass into your house and make that phone call. Do the right thing George. You owe Frank Sr. at least that much."

That was my play. It was all I really had. My argument was ridiculous but I was selling the sizzle without owning the steak. George's eighty year old hardwired brain began to short circuit and I actually grew concerned he might stroke out. He began listing to one side but still stood his ground. He just needed that final push.

"Dammit George, don't just stand there," I was yelling at him now, "get in there and make that call."

It worked. He was shaking to the point I thought I might have triggered some dormant Parkinson symptoms but he begrudgingly went inside to make the call.

I could see the sirens now. They were two blocks away racing up the hill and closing fast. As soon as George was out of earshot I pulled out my badge and held it high above my head as I pushed through the confused crowd.

"My name," I proclaimed, "is detective Mike Rutherford of the LAPD." I then pointed to the house and said, "That is now officially a crime scene and do not, I repeat, do not enter it under any circumstances."

In other words, do as I say, not as I do.

With that I got in my truck. Although the villagers were confused they were far from satisfied. Just as I started backing out of the driveway one of the younger men in the crowd stepped forward demanding to see my badge again. My side mirror clipped him as I hit the accelerator and he did a complete 360 degree spin before falling on to Frank's lawn. He wasn't really hurt but the incident unnerved me and I momentarily lost my concentration. I entered the street at too shallow of an angle and hit the car parked across the street shattering my right brake light in the process. This was turning into a complete disaster. In less than thirty minutes I had compromised a crime scene, robbed a house, impersonated an officer of the law, engaged in a little aggravated assault and now I was driving away from a hit and run accident. As I lurched forward I noticed everyone in the crowd had their phones out videotaping the entire thing. Within an hour's time I would not only be a person of interest in a triple homicide but I'd also be a social media cause celebre who would be shared, liked and commented on for all the world to see.

CHAPTER 36

I drove away from the crime scene making sure I followed all the rules of the road. The last thing I needed was to be pulled over for some routine traffic violation. As I turned right on to Hacienda Boulevard my phone rang. It was a 310 area code and I didn't recognize the number.

"Hello," is all I decided to offer up. Given my current predicament I felt it was a good idea to remain as anonymous as possible.

"Able, it's Jack Kerrigan from the consulate."

Oh yeah, the guy who's life I ruined earlier today. "How can I help you Jack?"

"That's a nice gesture but I'm afraid there's nothing anybody can do for me now. I might be able to help you though."

Well that's a pleasant surprise. "So no hard feelings?"

I think I heard him groan. "I wouldn't go that far but what's done is done. Besides, I want Daniel's killer brought to justice and I figure at this point you're the best man for the job."

"Fair enough," I said, "so what do you have for me?"

He had been able to confirm through his wife's grieving sister that Victor Ortiz had indeed been a friend of the Mansour family thus establishing the link between Victor and Daniel. Kerrigan also had met with the building's chief of security who surreptitiously shared Sunday's video footage from the parking structure.

"I sent you a link via email just a few minutes ago," Kerrigan informed me. "I hope it helps. I've gotta run. There's a line of people here all waiting to extract a pound of flesh from me."

I pulled over to the curb and watched the footage. At 8:48am Daniel, and Daniel alone, made his way over to the town car with a set of keys in his hand. At 8:50 he backed the car out of its parking space and drove away. Later that evening, at 7:32pm, the town car reappears and is returned to the same exact spot. I fully expected I'd be watching the third episode of the Heckle and Jeckle series but I was wrong. Seconds later a man and a woman exited the town car and absentmindedly looked directly up at the security camera. They threw the keys into the trunk and headed for the elevators disappearing out of sight. Did I recognize them? I didn't think so. Well, maybe. To be honest I wasn't really sure. There was something vaguely familiar about them but I couldn't quite put my finger on it. One thing was for sure though, two new players had entered the game.

My phone rang again. It was Hassam.

"Hey pal," I said, "I want to thank you for doing what you did today. I can't tell you how much I appreciate it."

"Khosh aamadid," he replied, "ghorboonet beram."

He loves to do that to me.

"What a coincidence," I said, "lately my bowel movements have been a little bit chalky too."

He thought that was funny but he wasn't laughing after I told him what a mess I'd made of things.

Hassam then told me about his much more uneventful day. After landing at Sky Harbor he rented a car and drove out to the address listed on EZX's website. It turned out to be a small, industrial building on the south side of town which was now empty and advertised as available by a commercial real estate company. He called the listing agent but the young man was fresh out of college and knew nothing of the previous occupants nor the buildings leasing history. Hassam then drove over to the Phoenix Police Department where he was met by another detective acquaintance of Harvey's. Together they spent several hours poring over unsolved missing person cases looking for any kind of connection to EZX's Phoenix operation. They had zero luck but the detective told him about an attempted abduction case that might have some merit. It involved the kidnapping of a young, undocumented Latina woman who was forcibly taken from a bus stop by two masked men in a stolen white, cargo van. According to her statement she had been bound, blindfolded and gagged then placed on a mattress in the cargo area. Just outside of Tucson the van had been involved in a minor traffic accident and the two kidnappers fled on foot when the driver of the other car forced them to pull over with the intent of exchanging insurance information. The young woman was discovered and saved when the Tucson PD arrived on the scene. That was two months ago and the case remained open with no tangible leads. The detective said he'd circle back with the victim and see if she'd ever interviewed with EZX seeking employment. Hassam gave him my contact info and the detective said he'd get a hold of me if anything developed. I found this new revelation interesting because it dovetailed with a theory about Reina's case that was slowly metastasizing inside that small brain of mine. I thanked Hassam once again and told him I'd pick him up at the airport but he informed me his beautiful, strong American wife and five children had already volunteered for the job.

I was now heading west on the 60 Freeway and decided to check in on Joe. He answered on the first ring.

"Hello, this is detective Lewis."

"Joe, it's Able."

"Adam and Eve's son?"

Touche. "No, the dashing private detective. Although I

might be willing to trade places with the other guy right about now."

"I'm not a big Bible guy," Joe remarked, "but didn't the other guy get murdered by his brother?"

I told him all about the fun he had missed at Frank Sr.'s and he actually laughed at me.

"Well," he said, "sometimes you gotta crack a few eggs to make an omelette right Able?"

All of a sudden Joe was getting all the funny lines. That was unacceptable.

"True," I said, "but you kind of hope the chicken doesn't get incarcerated during the process."

I asked him how things were going at his end and he told me that by the time he left the parking structure there was a virtual alphabet soup of law enforcement agencies trying to wrestle control of the investigation away from each other. The LAPD, CIA, FBI, DHS, the County Sheriiffs and the State Department were all strutting around flexing their biceps. Even the commissioner of the Los Angeles County Department of Weights and Measures was sniffing around. Nobody could quite figure that one out. He ended up just being a crime buff who considered himself something of an amateur sleuth. He was asked to leave.

"So where are you now Joe?" I asked him as I transitioned on the 605 Freeway heading north.

"I just left the first stop on Daniel's ill fated trip," Joe informed me. "Looks like he picked someone up at the Tom Bradley terminal at LAX."

"That's the international terminal isn't it Joe?"

"Yes it is. He looped around the airport three times before pulling up curbside in front of the Aero Mexico gate."

"Interesting," I said, "that seems significant somehow."

"I thought so too," he said agreeing with me. "I'm heading up Sepulveda right now. My next stop is about two miles ahead. I'll let you know if anything significant happens. So what's next on your docket Able? Are you gonna go rob a bank or something?"

"Funny you should mention that. I plan on meeting up with you but first there's one more crime I have to commit."

I told him where I was headed and he laughed at me again. Joe sure does have a strange sense of humor. Before we ended the call I told him I'd text him a copy of Mubari's composite drawing and then we both reaffirmed our promise to stay in touch.

CHAPTER 37

The attorney that handled the purchase of Marta's business on behalf of EZX Enterprises had an office on Lake Street in Pasadena. His name was Benjamin Goldman and I was banking on him being complicit in the criminal activities of his clients. There was just too much malfeasance orbiting around Planet Benjamin for him not to be dirty.

The parking lot for the building was not, thank goodness, underground. It was your garden variety outside lot just off the alleyway behind the building. It was full of automobiles you'd immediately associate with life's upper crust. There BMW's, Tesla's, Range Rovers and Cadillac Escalades all parked side by side but none of them could hold a candle to the one sleek looking black, turbo Carrera Porsche resting in parking space number twelve. I agree with Joel Goodson when it comes to Porsches. There is no substitute. I parked then made my way into the lobby and called the number on the business card Marta had texted me.

"Good afternoon," a cheery female voice said on the other end of the line, "law offices of Benjamin Goldman, how can I be of assistance?"

"Is Ben there?" I tried to match her enthusiasm but I wasn't up to the task.

The familiarity seemed to throw her for a loop. "I'm sorry," she said with a slight stutter, "but Mr. Goldman's in a meeting at the moment and he can't come to the phone. May I ask who's calling?"

I looked up at the directory on the wall next to the elevators. "Tell him this is John at Capricorn Insurance on the third floor. Let him know someone's trying to break into his car right now."

I hung up before she could press me for further details and then went back to my truck and waited. I didn't have to wait long. Less than a minute later a Napoleon sized forty something year old man dressed in business casual came running out the front door of the building and headed straight for, you guessed it, the Porsche. Like I didn't hate this guy enough already. Goldman checked his car inside and out for damages then retreated back to the building satisfied he had dodged a bullet. I gave it a thirty count then casually made my way over to his car. I dropped my keys on the ground and as I picked them up I stuck the magnetic tracking device under the rear wheel well. The flashing green light was confirmation enough that it was up and running.

I called Brigid and she picked up on the first ring. I took that as a good relationship sign.

"Hi," she said, sounding like she was sincerely happy to hear from me. "Have you caught all the bad guys yet?"

Man she sounds cute on the phone "Not quite yet. Can you check your phone for me?"

"Why?"

"Because the eagle has landed. I repeat, the eagle has landed."

"God Able, you are such a dork. Hold on."

Dork? Maybe she meant it as an acronym. Could she possibly consider me her Dashing, Omnipotent, Regal King?

"Yes," she said, "it's working. You're at the corner of Lake and Cordova in Pasadena. This is so exciting."

"Let's pump the brakes there Nancy Drew. I first have to convince him to get into his car and drive away."

"And how are you going to do that?"

"I'm going to appeal to his most altruistic self," I said.

"You're lying to me right now aren't you?"

"Yes."

"Then please be careful Mr. Kane."

"Okay Ms. Mcglaughlin. Oh, and Brigid?"

"Yes?"

"The moss grows on the north side of the tree. I repeat the moss...."

She hung up.

Now for the hard part. I rode the elevator up to the sixth floor. There was a CPA's office to my right and the attorney's office to my left. I've had better ideas, lots of them, but unless Joe could come up with something big on his end this was our last shot at glory. All my other leads were either dead or hiding in places I couldn't find them which made this diminutive fellow my last legitimate connection to the case. I took three deep breaths and then entered the Law Offices of Benjamin Goldman.

Out of general courtesy I stopped off at the receptionist's desk and showed my badge to the pretty, young woman sitting behind it. "My name." I said, "is Detective Michael Utley. I'm with the Pasadena Police Department and I'm here to see Benjamin Goldman."

The badge made her anxious in the same way it always seems to make people feel who are free of guilt and have nothing to hide. She managed to remain professional enough however to tell me to have a seat and wait. Apparently Mr. Goldman was still in a meeting that couldn't be interrupted.

"Young lady," I said, "the Pasadena Police Department waits for no one. It's our official motto."

I stormed into Goldman's office unannounced. He was at

his desk berating a couple of young associates and he appeared to be thoroughly enjoying the process. The short man's complex strikes again.

I introduced myself then got right down to the business at hand. "You two, out, now," I said to his minions. "I need to speak to your boss alone regarding one of his clients."

They got up to leave.

"Whoa there," Goldman responded, "hold on just one minute. Jason, Alex, stay right where you are." He wanted to spar with me. I could feel it. It was in his DNA. "Is this how the Pasadena PD goes about their business these days detective? Barging in on law abiding citizens and using Gestapo like tactics to intimidate us?"

That was a little melodramatic but I decided to play along. "Well as a matter of fact it's all part of a new community outreach program we've instituted. The whole thing's currently in beta testing right now and we're still trying to work out some of the glitches if you know what I mean."

He didn't think that was very funny. "Detective, let's see that shield of yours again. I want to record your badge number."

Well that wasn't going to happen. "There's two things we don't do Mr. Goldman. We don't hand over our shield and we never give up our gun. Don't you watch any cop shows at all?"

He got out of his chair and made his way over to my side of the desk. I think he was showing off now for the minions whose heads had been swiveling back and forth as if they were watching the Wimbledon finals. I checked his empty chair for pillows. There weren't any. He had smartly purchased one of those pneumatic chairs that go up and down with the flick of a lever. Good choice. Much more dignified than pillows.

"And there's two things I don't do detective," he said. "I never, ever violate attorney client privilege and I don't cooperate with bully cops. Don't you ever watch lawyer shows?"

He was pleased with his rebuttal. It was a very nice come-back and in a weird way I admired his bravado. It also made me realize I played this scene completely the wrong way. This guy was never going to kowtow to a law enforcement officer much less a private detective no matter how handsome and dashing he might be. I needed to change the script and I decided to go back to my truck to do the rewrite. I thanked him for his time and on the way out I overheard him tell the minions what an asshole I was. They all enjoyed a healthy snigger at my expense.

Reina's briefcase was combination protected but it was cheaply made and I had it unlocked in less than a minute. I needed to go through its contents at some point but now wasn't the time. The clock in my truck told me it was 5:08 p.m. and one by one the office dwellers were exiting the building calling it a day. I couldn't let Goldman slip through my fingers. I dumped everything out of the briefcase and replaced it with three days worth of old newspapers. I returned to the building and rode the elevator back up to the sixth floor.

This time around I didn't extend the courtesy of stopping off to say hi to the receptionist which earned me her evil eye as I strode by. I entered Goldman's office and pointed my gun at the two minions ordering them to leave. I didn't have to say it twice.

"Okay," I said now that it was just the two of us, "let's begin anew. Where is he?"

"Where's who?" he asked. There's something about a gun that gets a man's full attention.

"Mubari, aka Rahid Gamal. You know, EZX Enterprises, human trafficking, murder, mayhem. Do I need to continue? I know he's your client so let's not waste time on the back and forth. I find that whole thing rather tiresome."

He shifted uneasily in his pneumatic chair and I thought he

might press the lever up and down a few times to alleviate his mounting anxiety.

"I don't know who you're talking about but if I did you know as well as I do all client inquiries are protected by privilege."

"Wrong answer," I said. This time I came to his side of the desk and slapped him hard across the face, drawing blood.

He screamed like someone who's never been hit before. "Jesus man," he said, "I think you just loosened a tooth. I can't believe you just did that."

"One more chance," I said, "where is he?"

"Go screw yourself. When I'm done with you I'm going to own the entire city of Pasadena."

Oh how funny. He still thought I was a cop. Well it was high time I purged those thoughts from his pint-sized head. I plucked him out of his chair with one hand on the back of his collar and the other hand firmly holding on to the back of his belt.

"So you want to play games?" I asked him. "I love games. This is one I like to call office shuffleboard."

I've actually never played it before. This was pure off the cuff improvisation. I dragged him across the desk on his stomach making sure it was his face that knocked everything off the surface. The computer, the printer, an antique clock, client files, they all went crashing to the floor. I gave him a little extra push when he reached the desk's edge and he caught some decent air before landing nose first on the expensive jute carpeting. Before he could come to his senses I turned him over, stuck the barrel of my gun in his mouth and pulled the trigger multiple times. Sadly, it wasn't loaded.

"Since you're so concerned about attorney client privilege," I said, "I'll let you deliver this to him yourself." I tossed the briefcase onto his chest. "Listen to me very carefully because your life depends on it. You need to hand this over to him personally and it needs to be done today. Do you understand what I'm telling you?"

He nodded. Finally a breakthrough.

I gave him one last warning. "If Mubari doesn't get this sometime tonight I'll be back and this time I won't forget to load my gun. Make sure you tell him his friends in Mexico are extremely unhappy right now and that's an emotion they've never been comfortable with."

As I got up to leave I couldn't help but notice the wet spot quickly spreading around his groin area. Benjamin Goldman, Mubari's Napoleon size attorney had just met his own private Waterloo and I felt blessed for the opportunity of playing the role of his Duke of Wellington.

CHAPTER 38

I was travelling north on Lake Avenue heading towards the 210 Freeway and home when Victoria called.

"Hey Victoria, what's happening?"

"Unfortunately you Able. You're what's happening."

She went on to tell me there was a BOLO (Be On The Lookout) report issued against me. It was now official. I was a person of interest in a triple homicide and should be considered armed and dangerous. There was also mention of me driving a blue, Toyota truck with a broken, right taillight.

"That's not good news Victoria. Have you called Harvey?"

"I did but he's not picking up. I think his plane finally boarded and he's incommunicado."

I assured her everything would ultimately work out but she didn't sound convinced. That made two of us.

"Thanks for the heads up," I said. "I know I'm putting you in a tough spot here but I have another favor to ask of you."

She sighed for effect into the phone. "What is it now?"

I told her what I needed which momentarily rendered her speechless.

I finally broke the silence. "Earth to Victoria, are you still transmitting?"

"Yes I'm here," she said. "Are you sure about this?"

"Am I sure? No, not at all. But the way this case is going I'm not sure about much of anything anymore. Let's just say it's one more thread to pull on."

"Okay, I'll do it," she said, "but you know I have to tell Harvey."

I was afraid she was going to go there. "Victoria you can't. Not yet. I need you to keep this between the two of us for at least the time being."

"I can't do that Able. I could never lie to Harvey."

I considered that. "Well it's not really lying if you just simply forget to mention it right?"

That at least got her thinking. "I don't know," she said, "that sounds like a bunch of Able Kane fancy double talk to me."

Smart girl. "I'll tell you what Victoria, give me twenty four hours with the information and then I'll tell him myself. As an added bonus I'll throw in a new garage door when I do the repaint."

Her reticence magically vanished into thin air. "I want the kind that automatically rolls up and has those cute little windows across the top that let in the sunlight."

One thing was for sure, this woman really knew how to trade horses.

"That's exactly the one I was thinking about," I said. "Do we have a deal?"

"Deal," she said, "but after twenty four hours we go to Harvey right or wrong. Agreed?"

"Agreed."

"I have to go now," she said then terminated the call.

I really think she has trouble with goodbyes.

I then called Brigid and fessed up to what a mess I had made of my day including the sobering fact that I was now a wanted man. This is the kind of thing you normally don't spring on a girl until after the third or fourth date so I fully expected her to tell me to go and find my own crossword puzzle to work on.

"Well," she said instead, "I sadly hate to admit this but you're not the first man I've ever dated that was on the lam. I sure know how to pick 'em don't I?"

"Brigid," I said, "I'm sorry about all of this. I know the timing for you and me is terrible but I promise you everything's going to be alright."

"I hope so Able, I really do. By the way, you better not head back to your place. You'll probably get arrested.

"Any suggestions?"

"Come here. Park in the garage. I'll move my car out onto the street."

"Thank you," I said simply enough.

"Your welcome," she said but then added the caveat, "but you need to fix this and you need to do it now."

Well that was certainly the plan.

Her garage was small, barely wide enough to fit my truck into the tight space. I shut off the engine and sat there for a moment listening to the pinging of the hood as it cooled down. I began to ponder my fate, our fate. Brigid and I had been dancing around a relationship for quite awhile and on the day she finally unlocked the gate to let me in, what did I do? In my wake I stacked up enough crimes and dead bodies to match a winter's worth of cordwood. Had I already blown my chance with her before we even got out of the starting gate? Was it all too much for her? I didn't have the answers to those questions and there was only one way to get them.

The garage was attached to the house and accessed through a kitchen door. When I entered Brigid was busy at the stove and the redolent smells of garlic bread, Italian sausage and homemade spaghetti sauce alluded to the fact she had cooked my favorite meal. That was a good sign, right?

But the fact she didn't come rushing into my arms much less even make eye contact with me said something else entirely. Aah, behold the beautiful woman and all of her complexities. Understanding them is like trying to navigate yourself through a minefield blindfolded.

"Honey, I'm home," I said hoping my wit would win the day.

Silence. She poured a glass of wine for herself without offering me one. It was a not so subtle reminder that my day wasn't quite finished. She pointed to a chair and set a large plate of pasta in front of it. I was starving so I dove right in. If I was going to spar with Brigid I'd need a full stomach in order to compete.

She sat down and still without looking at me asked the big question. "So is this the way it's always going to be with you?"

"No, not at all," I deadpanned, "it's usually a lot more exciting."

Strike two. Apparently humor wasn't going to get it done so I decided on a more serious, forthcoming approach. I explained how most of my days were filled with the mundane. Running background checks for corporations, photographing cheating spouses and chasing down bogus insurance claims. I then told her on the days when I had no work at all, which quite frankly were far too many, my normal routine consisted of a round of golf and a quick game of gin rummy before showing up for a late afternoon meal at my favorite restaurant where I'd check in on the progress of the daily crossword puzzle.

"I then head back to my apartment," I confessed, "and wait until the next time I can see you again."

There, finally, eye contact.

She reached over to me and grabbed my hand. "How can I help you end this?"

I went back to my truck and retrieved all the ill-gotten booty I had stolen from the crime scene. The contents of the briefcase, the glovebox and Julie's oversized Coach bag.

"There's gotta be something in all of this that will help fill in some of the blanks," I explained. "Each and every item needs to be examined and inventoried regardless of how innocuous they may appear. That would be a tremendous help. By the way, has my little attorney friend made a move yet?"

She checked her phone. "He left the office about fifteen minutes ago and headed to an address on Mentor about two miles away. I googled the address. It's a condominium complex. He's still there."

I nodded. "I'm guessing that's his place. He probably went home to change. There was a bit of a wardrobe malfunction at the end of our meeting."

Brigid refilled her glass, grabbed a pen and a pad of paper and started diving into the Coach bag. I excused myself and went out into the backyard to make a few phone calls.

My first call was to my tenant Mark, the CPA. In all of my running around I'd forgotten to tell him his office had almost burned to the ground last night.

"Hi Able, looks like I missed all the excitement."

"Is everything okay on your side of the wall?"

"A little smoky but nothing we can't manage."

I gave him the play by play and told him to keep his head on a swivel.

"Well," he said, "that explains your visitor and why he's still sitting in his car across the street."

It was Jerry Lam who undoubtedly was aware of the BOLO report issued against me. I'm sure he was licking his chops in anticipation of slapping the cuffs on me personally.

"Mark," I asked, "are you still at the office?"

"I was just getting ready to leave but yeah, I am."

"Do you still have that spare key to my garage?"

"I do. I'm looking at it right now. Why what's up?"

"I don't suppose you know how to drive a stick shift do you?"

"It's been awhile but I'm pretty sure I can fake it."

I asked a big favor of him and he didn't hesitate.

"Much more interesting than the credits and debits I've been balancing all day," he opined.

My next call was to Joe. His journey so far had produced nothing fruitful so he had made the command decision to fast forward to the end. He was on his way to the final location the consulate's town car had been driven to before it was returned to the parking structure with Daniel Mansour's dead body in the trunk. It was an address up in Kagel Canyon just north of Lakeview Terrace.

"Keep me posted Joseph," I said, "and remember any hint of trouble right?"

"You got it buddy boy," Joe said before signing off.

Before I could dial Nate's number I received a call from a Detective Ross with the Phoenix PD, the same man Hassam had met with earlier in the day. His instincts had been correct. He circled back and reinterviewed the victim who had been abducted at the deserted bus stop. She had indeed applied for a job at a company by the name of Camelback Commercial Cleaning Services which had been the fictitious name EZX operated under at their Phoenix location. Furthermore, he added, the victim had informed him she had two other friends, both undocumented, who had interviewed with the company on the same day and had since disappeared. Neither one of them were ever reported missing. I told him what was happening on my end and he let out a low whistle.

"Anything you need Mr. Kane," he said, "do not hesitate in

calling me."

I called Nate and it went direct to voicemail. This concerned me so I called the nurse's station but I was assured he was doing fine.

"What he needs Mr. Kane is sleep," the nurse on the other end of the line said, "and it's sleep that he's going to get."

I then checked in with Sergeant Leon from the gang squad but so far they'd rolled snake eyes in the search for Heckle and Jeckle. I asked him to keep me posted. Finally, I checked on the *69 phone number I had written down from Frank Sr.'s landline. It was nothing earth shattering. The number was Frank Sr.'s cell phone. He was probably just checking in with his son and reminding him to activate the alarm system before leaving.

I was about to head back inside when I heard the familiar muffled tapping sound of an old friend turning on to Brigid's street. I went through the side gate and greeted my tenant Mark as he pulled into the driveway in my 1972 VW Bus. I couldn't drive the truck at this point since every law enforcement officer on the road would be on the lookout for a blue Toyota with a broken right taillight. This was my best not to mention my only other alternative to meet up with Joe. Brigid exited her front door to see what all the commotion was about.

"What in the world is that thing?" she asked.

"This," I said stroking the side of the van, "is the Barely-Drive-Able."

"The what?" she asked again.

"The Barely-Drive-Able. It' a long story that I'd love to tell you about some day."

"Able Kane and his long stories," she said shaking her head in exasperation. She then promptly turned tail back into the house.

Mark watched our interaction with amusement as he

handed over the keys. "I didn't think this old dog was ever going to start. I was just about to give up and call you but I tried one last time and well, here we are."

I smiled. "He can play a little hard to get sometimes especially if he doesn't know you."

Mark laughed at what he thought was typical Able Kane humor but then furrowed his brow line with genuine concern for me when he realized I wasn't joking.

He lived about fifteen minutes away and I gave him a lift home. When I got back to Brigid's place she came running out the front door.

"Able," she said in an excited voice, "the attorney is on the move."

CHAPTER 39

Canyons. Like earthquakes, the Dodgers and the Chandler family, the canyons of Los Angeles are intricately woven into the fabric of this city's history. From the music that was created in Laurel Canyon to the pantheon of movie stars that still call Benedict Canyon home, their existence is a part of an angelino's DNA. Names like Coldwater, Topanga and Malibu are all part of our native tongue. These are the places where the Santa Ana winds howl their fiercest and where the brush fires rage out of control. They are quintessential to the Los Angeles story.

Kagel Canyon is really no different. It was settled in the 1800's by overly optimistic gold miners and has stubbornly resisted the temptations of modern society ever since. It's the kind of place where you dig for your own water, pick up your mail at the side of the road and ride a horse to the local watering hole.

Somewhere in the upper canyon was an address to a location where Detective Joe Lewis was set to cross paths with Benjamin Goldman, attorney-at-law. I figured I was twenty minutes behind them and driving as fast as a 1972 VW Bus could take me. It was dusk when I exited the 210 Freeway at Osborne which meant I had about fifteen minutes of serviceable daylight remaining. I had tried calling Joe several times but his phone at this point was going directly to voicemail. I passed a polo field, a shooting range and several equestrian centers before climbing a steep grade into the upper canyon. As I entered the Angeles National Forest three white cargo vans with the logo of Top 2 Bottom Cleaning Services emblazoned on the side panels rounded a bend and sped past me heading in the opposite direction.

As I came around that same turn I began to hear the sounds of gun shots emanating from further up in the canyon. This left me with a terrible Sophie's like choice to make. As the gun fire increased in intensity I realized Joe was in danger. Should I go to him or should I turn around and chase after the three vans I was certain were full of abducted, young women? Ultimately the decision was made for me. It was completely dark now and the road up into the canyon was very narrow with a mountainside on my left and a sheer cliff off to the right. There were no turnouts to be found and only sharp, blind turns lay ahead making a reversal of direction extremely dangerous if not outright impossible. I would be no good to anyone if I ended up at the bottom of some ravine. So I continued on praying I wouldn't be too late to help Joe. About another quarter mile up the road I came across an aged, wooden sign welcoming me to the Wildlife Sanctuary. I remembered hearing about this place and all the great work they had accomplished in the past. It had been an animal rescue facility that over the years had taken in tens of thousands of unwanted and injured animals including some exotics such as lions, tigers and chimpanzees. The operation was irreparably damaged during a savage wildfire a few years back and was forced to close its doors. All the animals were relocated to other habitats around the world and this 160 acre property was put up for sale with no takers.

The main entrance had been sealed off but another hundred yards up the road was a service area whose gate was wide open. I pulled in, turned on the VW's high beams and took in the scene. There was a parking area off to my left that was now filled with rusted out horse trailers and dilapidated shipping containers. To the right stood a corrugated, metal maintenance building with a private security vehicle parked out front. The driver side door was open and the dead body of a uniformed guard sat slumped in the front seat hanging half in and half out of the car. On the asphalt directly below his lifeless hand lay a gun that would be forever just out of reach. I pulled out my phone to call 911 but there was no cell phone service this far up the canyon.

At the other end of the parking lot there was a road that dipped severely down into the main area of the abandoned sanctuary. It was quiet now as I drove to the edge of the dip. Below me, maybe thirty yards ahead, was a large home surrounded by several outbuildings. Beyond that as far as the headlights could travel were the empty pens and cages that once housed the animals. Goldman's beautiful black Porsche was parked directly in front of the house and off to the right was Joe's Crown Victoria. Joe was in deep trouble. He was sitting on the ground behind the passenger side rear tire with his head resting against the bumper and his legs splayed out in front of him. He had a grip on his service revolver but it was resting lazily on his lap when it should have been pointed at Heckle and Jeckle who were cautiously advancing on his position.

The next part is a bit murky in my mind. I must have hit the gas pedal but I truly don't remember doing it. The Barely-Drive-Able suddenly lurched forward and sped down the slope like it was shot out of a cannon. I now had the full attention of Heckle and Jeckle who turned to me and opened fire with automatic weapons. A fusillade of bullets tore through the van's front end as we bore down on our assailants. I felt a searing pain rip through my right shoulder as the Barely-Drive-Able's windshield shattered into a thousand tiny pieces of safety glass. At ten feet away they decided to run in separate directions but for one of them it would all be for naught. I veered left and sent either Heckle or Jeckle flying against the wall of the house at over fifty miles per hour. I swerved and slammed on the brakes but it was too little and too late. We crashed into the Porsche and the Barely-Drive-Able was launched airborne before crashing on to its side. I was stunned, hurting and seriously concussed but I was alive. Another round of bullets tore through the roof of the van which reminded me this was far from over. I released my seatbelt and crawled out through the open space created by the shattered windshield. My right arm was useless but I managed to grab my Sig from its shoulder holster with my left hand. I triggered off a couple of rounds of cover fire and tried to make my way over to Joe. I didn't get very far. As I came around the back end of the Barely-Drive-Able my assailant was there waiting for me. My concussed brain had made a terrible error in judgement and I would now pay dearly for the mistake. I raised my Sig to shoot but I was incrementally slower with my left hand. He was now carrying a pistol and got off a round hitting me squarely in the chest. I was wearing my vest but the force of the impact lifted me off my feet before slamming me to the ground. As I laid there trying to get some air back into my lungs he made his way over to me and smiled. He was going to enjoy this. He pointed his Beretta at me and I closed my eyes resigning myself to the worst of all fates. I heard two shots ring out and I recall thinking how strange it was to remember hearing the gunshots that killed you. Like I said, I wasn't thinking very clearly. I opened my eyes just in time to roll out of the way before he could land on top of me in a dead heap. Detective Joe Lewis had saved my life. I laid there for a moment trying to collect myself while the pungent smell of cordite drifted along in the night sky. It was eerily quiet now except for the stridulations of the summertime crickets.

Joe spoke first but his voice had a scary death rattle to it. "Are you alive Able?"

"Yeah," I said, "are you?"

He coughed and winced. "Jesus Able, don't make me laugh. I'm not doing so well."

I finally managed to get up and make my way over to him.

Joe had been gut shot and he was bleeding badly through his stomach. He noticed the concerned look on my face.

"It's bad isn't it Able?"

"Let's get you to a hospital," I said ignoring the question. It wasn't easy but I got him into the backseat of the Crown Vic one handed and laid him down. I pulled the socks off of my feet and wadded them up inside his wound to help staunch the bleeding. I then placed the bubble gum machine on the hood of the car and we raced down the canyon with the siren blazing. Harvey called as we merged onto the 210. I steered with my knees just long enough to fumble around and connect the call one handed. I put him on speaker then regained control of the steering wheel.

"Hey Harvey," I said as I drifted over to the fast lane.

"You don't sound so good OT," he said. "What in the hell is going on? I just got off the phone with Brigid and Victoria and it sounds like this whole thing has turned into a complete shit show."

Before responding I looked back at Joe. He had been unresponsive on our way down the canyon and now his breathing was coming in short, labored gasps. He was fading fast. I then took a quick look at my own injury for the very first time. The bullet had passed clean through my shoulder but it must have severed an artery on its way out. I was losing blood at a pretty good clip which was making me dizzy and lightheaded. Using my foot I pressed down on the car's cigarette lighter.

"Harvey," I said, "listen closely. I'm losing Joe and to be honest I'm not doing all that well myself so I'm gonna make this quick. We're making a run for the hospital in Joe's Crown Vic. There's quite a crime scene at the top of Kagel Canyon you're going to want to check out but more importantly there are three Top 2 Bottom cargo vans somewhere out there full of abducted women. If I was a betting man I'd say they were setting a course for the Mexican border. You have to find some way to save them."

At least that's what I think I said. My speech had felt slurred and jumbled and I was having a heck of a time just driving the car much less trying to string coherent sentences together. I disconnected the call hoping it had been enough.

The cigarette lighter popped out letting me know it was ready. We were flying down the freeway now but I had no choice other than letting my legs take control of the steering wheel again. I grabbed the red hot lighter with my left hand and pressed it against my shoulder holding it there for several seconds. I screamed in pain as the heat seared my flesh but it partially cauterized the wound slowing down the rate of blood loss. I tossed the lighter to the floor, grabbed the steering wheel again and punched the accelerator. I don't remember much of anything after that.

CHAPTER 40

Tuesday, June 20th

I woke up the next day to a world full of heart monitors, IV drips and plasma bags. There was movement to my left and I looked in that direction. It was Hassam performing one of his five daily salats. He was currently prostrated on his prayer rug and I was familiar enough with the ritual to know this position was called the rakat. I watched in silent admiration until he stood up, turned his head to the right and then to the left signaling the end of the prayer.

"I hate to tell you this fella," I said, "but Mecca's in the opposite direction."

He smiled at me then folded his hands back into the prayer position as he looked up towards the heavens. He was either thanking Allah for answered prayers or maybe just trying to count the tiny holes in the acoustical ceiling tiles. I wasn't quite sure which.

"Salam dooet e man," he said. "Hal e shoma chetoor ast?"

"Sometimes," I said, "but just on Wednesdays after pickle ball and only if it's raining."

He laughed. "You are you again," he said putting his hand on my good shoulder, "and that is all that matters."

He started filling me in on what I had either missed or simply didn't remember. Apparently I had lost consciousness just as I drove the Crown Vic into the emergency room parking lot at Verdugo Hills. The only thing that saved me from crashing through the sliding glass doors were the yellow, cast iron bollards that the hospital had installed just two weeks earlier. Harvey, thank God, had indeed heard me loud and clear and wasted no time in organizing a massive multi-agency manhunt for the three cargo vans. My instincts had been correct. They were first spotted on Interstate 5 just north of Dana Point and finally brought to a complete halt just south of Carlsbad after a slow, drawn out chase that invoked memories of O.J. Simpson and the Ford Bronco.

"Victor Ortiz was driving one of the vans," Hassam informed me.

"And?" I asked.

"And," Hassam said, "he is dead. After about an hour's standoff he exited the van and pointed his weapon at more than a hundred armed law enforcement officers. He never actually fired his gun but I think that was his plan. They're probably still counting the number of bullet holes in his body. Apparently the prospects of a lifetime spent in prison was more than he could bear. Harvey say there's a name for it. It's called…"

"Suicide by cop," I said finishing his sentence. "And the other two vans?"

"They were driven by a man and a woman who surrendered immediately after Victor was gunned down. Harvey said they've already lawyered up and are refusing to cooperate."

Hassam pulled out his phone and showed me a picture he'd taken from a television news feed. It was the same couple who had killed Daniel Mansour and then stuffed his corpse into the trunk of the town car.

"What about Mubari?" I asked him.

Hassam shook his head. "He's in the wind Able. It looks like he got away. Harvey thinks he's probably already out of the country by now."

I asked Hassam about Joe but he had not heard anything yet and the medical staff hadn't been very forthcoming.

"There's something else you need to prepare yourself for Able. You're not going to like it."

Uh-oh. "What is it Hassam?"

"You're now a bonafide celebrity hero. There was a total of seventeen young women in those vans who are all going home today because of you. Somehow the press caught wind of your name and now it seems like every news agency on the planet wants a piece of Able Kane, private detective. I know how much you love the spotlight."

That was terrible news indeed but I know how these things work. Today's bright, shiny toy can usually be found in tomorrow's goodwill bag. Or at least I hoped so.

"If I'm such a hero Hassam, why is my wrist handcuffed to the hospital bed?"

"I can answer that," Harvey announced as he entered the room. He pulled out a key and unlocked the restraints. "Last night you were a wanted man but obviously things have changed quite a bit since then. I've never seen more law enforcement agencies involved in just one case. Half of them wanted to lock you in jail and throw away the key while the other half still wants to throw you a ticker tape parade."

"What about the County Commissioner of Weights and Measures?" I asked. "Which way was he leaning?"

"Who?" Harvey asked, confused.

"Never mind. Inside joke."

"Anyways," Harvey continued, "they all reached a consensus that the best course of action when it comes to you is no action at all."

"So no ticker tape parade?" I asked trying to sound disappointed.

"Nope, sorry OT. But you're also not going to have to introduce yourself to a new bunk mate either."

Fair enough. We were then joined by Sergeant Leon from the gang unit who had just returned from the Kagel Canyon crime scene. Hector and Jacob Gonzales, aka Heckle and Jeckle were yellow bellied magpies no longer. The dead security guard also ended up being a member of Calle Reyes. He had a full time job with the security company which gave him complete control over who was allowed into and out of the abandoned sanctuary. That explained a lot.

"So Joe must have taken him out," I said.

"That appears to be the case," Leon said. "We also found a huge cache of heroin stored in one of the outbuildings. The DEA's up there nosing around and they say the stuff is super pure Afghanistan dragon dust. They are estimating the street value to be around twelve million dollars. It was a righteous bust Able, thank you."

"What about Goldman, the attorney?" I asked.

"Dead," Leon informed me. "We found him in the main house with his throat slashed. It wasn't a pretty sight."

Another loose end that Mubari needed to tie up. Maybe I should have felt guilty about that one but I didn't.

We were then interrupted by the arrival of Dr. Jenkins. I immediately asked him about Joe.

"We had to induce a medical coma to get his vitals in check," he said. "They aren't where we want them to be but he's holding steady which is a really good sign. I've got my A-team on this one so keep your fingers crossed." Jenkins then picked up my chart and took a look.

"Is he going to live Doc?" Harvey asked.

"It certainly appears that way. I'm going to have to find a new partner for our member-member tournament next month but with some determined rehab he should be out there three putting greens in no time at all." He set my chart back on its hook. "I've got to ask you Able, those socks tucked into Detective Lewis' abdomen, were those yours?"

I nodded.

"That was some really quick thinking," he said. "I'm fairly certain you saved his life. And your shoulder, what was that, a cigarette lighter?"

I nodded again.

"Incredible," is all he said before walking out of the room.

Harvey's wife Jennifer and their three sons dropped by with get well cards and a bottle of vintage Middleton Irish Whisky. Mark the CPA showed up to offer his support as did a host of my fellow volunteers from the hospital. Several of them asked for my autograph which I prayed wasn't a harbinger of things to come. Marta called in tears and I ended up consoling her more than she did me which was fine. Victoria also phoned to see if I was okay and told me to check my email for the records I asked her to get for me. She also wanted to know if this setback was going to delay the painting of her garage. I no longer harbored any doubts that she was anything other than deadly serious about it. The one person that didn't come by was the one person I desperately wanted to see. Brigid was a no-show. She did send a quick email informing me that she needed to step back and think about things. I wasn't angry. I threw way too much at her in way too short a period of time. Sometimes the timing on these things just sucks. She did include a pdf file inventorying all of the items I had liberated from the crime scene at Frank's house. I'd take a look at that later when I felt up to the task. I tried calling her twice but she decided not to pick up either time. I decided to just leave it be and give her the space she asked for. Besides, I still had some work to do.

CHAPTER 41

Wednesday, June 21st

By 3:30 p.m. I was pulling out of Frank Sr.'s driveway behind the wheel of Marta's Toyota Camry. I called him earlier in the day to see if it was okay if I swung by and picked it up. In all of yesterday's madness I'd forgotten I still had the keys in my possession. The Sheriff's Department finished with the crime scene late last night and I think Frank was happy to rid himself of anything and everything that would remind him of the terrible events that occurred in his home.

It took a lot of begging and pleading on my part to get Dr. Jenkins to release me from the hospital. In addition to the shoulder injury which was going to leave me one handed for the next few months, I had three cracked ribs, multiple contusions and a monstrous headache stemming from the concussion I had sustained. There were a myriad of legitimate medical reasons for him to keep me there but when I told him exactly why I needed to be released he went ahead and signed the paperwork.

I borrowed Frank's phone to call Marta letting her know I was on my way over to drop off the car. She was still very distraught and quite frankly who could blame her. The events of the last five days had taken a huge physical and emotional toll on me also.

I was heading south on the 605 Freeway when Victoria returned my call.

"Able Kane, hero private detective, how can I help you?"

"Okay," she said, "that needs to stop immediately."

"Sorry," I said. "I couldn't resist."

"Able, you remember our deal right?"

"Yes. Alpine white, Kelly green trim and a new garage door. The kind with the cute little windows."

"Well that too but I wanted to warn you I'm going to tell Harvey about those records I procured for you."

Yes I remembered. "No worries Vic, I already told him myself."

"Truth?"

"Truth."

"Okay," she said, "good luck."

"Wait, wait, wait," I said, "are you still there?"

"Yes I'm still here."

I explained my plan and asked for her help. She actually said yes without making any new home improvement demands then of course hung up without saying goodbye.

Fifteen minutes later I arrived at Marta's house. She was waiting for me on the front porch as I pulled into the driveway. I think she was coming in for a hug until she saw my right arm in a sling and how badly my body had been bruised and battered.

"Able" she said, "I can't believe they let you out of the hospital so quickly."

"Bad insurance," I said shrugging my one good shoulder.

"There aren't any words to describe how sorry I am for getting you involved in all of this," she continued. "It just breaks my heart every time I think about what you've been through."

It was a nice thing to say even if it did come across a tad bit rehearsed. "I'm sorry it ended the way it did," I told her.

She leaned in and gently kissed me on the cheek. "This feels like a nightmare I'm never going to wake up from," she added.

I know how she felt. We stood there for a moment in silence until it started getting awkward. "Marta," I asked, "can I use your bathroom?"

I passed the photo gallery in the hallway again. There was the picture of Marta and her employees standing in front of the Top 2 Bottom van but for the most part the framed photographs were of Reina. There were action shots of her playing youth sports and some of her posing with boys at high school dances. The one picture that was no longer hanging on the wall was the photograph of Reina and her parents. That was the moment everything crystallized for me and the last tumbler clicked into place.

"Red Rover, Red Rover," I said hopefully just loud enough for only my accomplice to hear.

When I returned Marta was in the kitchen pouring herself a cup of coffee. "Able, would you like a cup?"

I held out a handful of newly prescribed meds and asked for a glass of water instead. I swallowed the pills in one big gulp and then pointed to the suitcase in the living room. "Are you heading somewhere?" I asked.

"Oh, the suitcase. Yes I am. I'm going to Merida for a few weeks. I need to get away for awhile and clear my head."

That was certainly understandable. I could use a little R & R myself. "Merida?" I asked, "I'm not familiar with it."

"It's on the Yucatan Peninsula. It's where I grew up."

I nodded. "Hey Marta, do you mind if I use your phone? I somehow managed to lose my cellphone last night and I need to call for a taxi."

"Of course Able, help yourself." She pointed to the wall phone directly behind me.

I picked up the receiver, paused and then returned it to its cradle. "Marta, I need to ask you about something that's really been bothering me."

"Of course Able. Anything. What is it?"

"Well what I can't figure out for the life of me is why."

Her face had changed. It quickly became guarded and more serious. "Why what Able, I'm not quite sure I understand?"

"It's simple. I'm asking you why did you do it?"

She grabbed her coffee mug with two hands pulling it close to her chest. A classic defense mechanism. "You're scaring me now Able. I have no idea what you're talking about."

I sighed. I guess we were going to have to do this the hard way. I sat down at the kitchen table and told her to go ahead and pour me that cup of coffee.

I first started considering the unthinkable yesterday when I stumbled upon the crime scene at the Garcia's house. Wandering around the master bedroom and bath it was readily apparent that cleaning and tidying up were low priority items for both Reina and Frank Jr. To put it more succinctly, they were slobs. Their untidiness was completely incongruous to the rest of the house which was immaculate. Of course any calculating killer would try to wipe away their presence from a crime scene but this felt different. This was the result of either obsessive compulsive behavior or maybe someone that professionally cleaned for a living. The only other house I've ever seen that spotless happened to be the one I was sitting in right now, Marta's.

"Do you remember when you called me yesterday," I asked her. "When you wanted me to stop the investigation?"

Marta was now sitting at the table directly across from me. She chose to defend herself. "Of course I wanted you to stop the investigation Able. People were dying and it was all because of me. I couldn't live with myself if it happened again and I'd done nothing to prevent it. Especially you Able. I was mostly worried about you."

I had set my trap and she'd walked right into its snare. "But Marta," I said, "when I talked to Harvey later in the day he told me the two of you hadn't talked since Friday. So that begs the question if Harvey wasn't updating you on the case than who was?"

She didn't respond but not because she thought the question was rhetorical. She didn't respond because there wasn't a logical answer out there to be found. I then told her once my suspicions were aroused I had Victoria pull her phone records.

"You never called Julie Herrera like you said you would," I said. "I guess why call someone if you know they're already dead. You also never tried to contact any of your old employees like you promised me you would. Victoria went back and called every number you dialed over the past few days and not one person on the receiving end had ever worked for Top 2 Bottom."

Marta sat there stoically but the anger was flashing in her eyes. "Able, I'm curious, what exactly are you accusing me of?"

It was time to get down to brass tacks. "The whole nine yards Marta. Human trafficking, heroin distribution and conspiracy to commit murder."

Her voice went up several decibels now. "How dare you come into my house and accuse me of such things when you have no real evidence to support it. You do realize that right?"

She was right. It was all supposition on my part. Maybe Frank Jr. and Reina kept every room in the house clean except for the master bedroom and bath. Maybe Marta found someone else on the police force who offered her updates on the case and maybe she had simply been too depressed to make any of those phone calls. Maybe. But I wasn't quite done yet.

"Where's the picture Marta?"

"What picture?" she asked doing her very best to remain composed.

"The picture of Reina and her parents that was hanging in the hallway on Saturday. It magically disappeared."

"Oh that. I bumped into it yesterday and the glass broke. I took it in to get reframed."

Her answer was simplistic and pathetic but I let it slide.

"Your brother and sister-in-law didn't die in a car crash did they? Because if they did it would be awfully hard to explain why they're currently sitting in jail now on seventeen counts of human trafficking as well as for the murder of Daniel Mansour. I'm sure you'll be happy to know they're refusing to cooperate."

Marta glared at me and there it was. She finally took off the mask and I saw the evil lurking behind those brown eyes of hers. She flashed a malevolent smile knowing she didn't have to hide her true self any longer.

She changed tactics. "You have no idea how deep of a grave you're digging for yourself Able. These people are capable of things far beyond your wildest imagination."

I'm not sure if she meant that as a threat or a warning. Perhaps it was a whole lot of both.

"I think I do," I said. "In fact I've been living it for the past five days. Now Marta if you don't mind I am going to use your phone. I think it's time we call Harvey."

Before I could stand up I felt the barrel of a gun press against the back of my head.

"I'm afraid that isn't going to be possible Able," a man said. I then recognized the familiar sound of a bullet sliding into a chamber.

It had been thirty plus years since I'd heard that voice but it was exactly how I remembered it. My hubris had assured me that I had this whole thing figured out which is why I came to Marta's house alone and unarmed. That arrogance had now landed me in the deepest of trouble. If there was to be any chance of getting out of here alive I'd need to buy myself as much time as possible.

Mubari came around the table and handed Marta the gun. She immediately pointed it directly at my chest and I had no doubt she'd pull the trigger if provoked. There was body language between the two of them which inferred some level of intimacy and I now realized there were layers to this case I'd never considered. Mubari pulled two zip-ties out of his pocket and quickly fastened my wrists to the chair. I winced in pain as he manhandled my bad arm into position.

"Sahid, he doesn't have his cellphone," Marta said. "He lost it last night."

"Well it never hurts to double check does it Marta?" He patted me down until he was satisfied I hadn't lied and I wasn't carrying. He then stepped back and we both took a long look at each other. The composite drawing created by the Las Vegas PD sketch artist hadn't done Mubari justice. His appearance belied his sixty plus years of age. He was taller than I remembered and he had kept himself in excellent shape. He had a head full of curly hair that was just a little more salt than it was pepper and he draped himself in designer clothing stylishly rounded off by a Patek Phillipe secured to his left wrist.

"Well you look great," I said, "been staying out of trouble?"

He slapped me hard across the face. Apparently this wasn't going to be that kind of reunion.

"You seem to always find a way to make my life more difficult Able," he said, "and it's time to put an end to that once and for all."

"I'll tell you what Mubari," I said, "you let me walk out of here and I promise you I won't tell a soul about this. Except for maybe a few close friends .....and family of course."

He squeezed my bad shoulder right at the stitch line. The pain was excruciating.

"I was there last night you know, at the animal sanctuary," he said. "I watched the whole thing from the upstairs window. Life would have been so much simpler if you and your friend had just been killed but here we are, together again with me needing to know what you know and you needing to convince me you're telling the truth. Seems like old times doesn't it Able?"

"So you killed Goldman I presume?"

"I did. Killing that little prick was very satisfying. He was always trying to find a new way to extort money out of us. His greed was insatiable. I actually followed you down the canyon in his Porsche. It's a nice car, I think I'll keep it."

He then asked me what I knew and I decided to tell him everything, drawing it out as long as possible.

I started with the low lying fruit. "Well I know that you and Victor were smuggling undocumented women into Mexico and I know that Reina, Frank Jr. and Julie were making the runs. I'm assuming it was as simple as bribing a few border guards to look the other way. I also know you were trading the women for heroin being flown in from the Middle East then turning around and selling it to the Tijuana Cartel for cold, hard cash. How am I doing so far?"

Mubari smiled. "Spot on."

Some of that was educated guessing on my part. When Brigid had gone through the briefcase and the Coach bag she found Sentri I.D.'s for Reina, Frank Jr. and Julie. You don't go through the laborious process of obtaining a Sentri pass unless you're making frequent border crossings. I also knew that Victor Ortiz was running an import-export business out of the Middle East which would logically explain how the heroin-human trafficking arrangement began.

"I do have a few questions though, if you don't mind."

"Be my guest Mr. Kane."

"You and Victor make some pretty strange bedfellows. How'd that happen?"

He told me quite a tale. Ortiz continued to pursue him long after Hassam had given up the chase. About the same time Victor was cutting off all avenues of escape Mubari found himself growing disillusioned with living the life of an internationally known terrorist. It was a young man's game he said and he'd lost the passion and zealotry that once fueled him. What he wanted now was money and lots of it. Enough to buy beach houses, mountain chalets and put beautiful women on his arm. He wanted it all and he had a plan to make it happen. Through intermediaries he arranged a clandestine meeting with Victor and three hours later the two of them walked out of a coffee house in Damascus as newly minted business partners. There was one rather significant hurdle that needed to be overcome however. Mubari was still wanted by almost every westernized nation on the planet. They had to find a way to officially kill him. That opportunity presented itself when President Bill Clinton authorized Operation Infinite Reach. Over fifty high level terrorists were killed in the mountains of Afghanistan that day and Victor Ortiz simply added one more name to the list.

"So now you have access to some world class heroin and lots of it," I continued on. "But your suppliers don't want to be paid in cash because they have plenty of that already. Like anyone else they desire what they don't have and in this case it's women, lots of exotic women. At some point their predilections shift and Latina women become the new flavor of the month. I'm guessing this is about the time you started doing business with the Tijuana cartel and Raul and Valeria Ramirez."

While America was watching the Ramirez's surrender to authorities on Interstate 5 last night the DEA was already busy declaring the event a major victory in the war against drugs. According to agency officials Raul and Valeria Ramirez were the cartel's top enforcers who went about their business in a ruthless and psychotic way. The fact that they were also Marta's brother and sister-in-law still seemed unfathomable to me.

"What I don't understand is why you didn't just abduct women already living in Mexico. Better yet, why not just have the cartel do it for you?"

"That," Mubari said, "was one of the cartel's non-negotiable demands. They have the federales bought and paid for but the one thing Mexican law enforcement officials do not tolerate is the kidnapping of its own citizens on sovereign soil."

Okay I thought to myself, that made some kind of twisted sense. "So you start a commercial cleaning company in Las Vegas because one, it's a city that attracts illegal aliens by the thousands and two, it's the type of menial, anonymous work that appeals to young, undocumented women. Things are probably going along well but it's human nature never to be satisfied. Your suppliers want more women and the cartel wants more heroin so you start a second company in Phoenix, another hot spot for illegal aliens. Business doubles but so does the risk factor. You're abducting a lot of women now and there's always going to be a few mistakes made along the way. Maybe the cops are beginning to connect the dots or perhaps some employees are beginning to ask too many questions. And that's the thing isn't it? It's simply impossible to control all the moving parts. So you're beginning to feel the heat now and you decide it's time to start winding down the operation. The problem is your partners aren't very keen on the idea. They're very happy with the way things are going and they're not the kind of people who like to be disappointed. So when Raul Ramirez tells you he has a sister in Los Angeles who has a cleaning company for sale you're smart enough to realize he's telling you that you're the new buyer."

Mubari smiled and shook his head. "Very impressive Abel.

You really are too damn smart for your own good."

When it was all said and done it didn't really matter how much I knew. Mubari was never going to let me live and the only question remaining was how he was going to kill me. He must have been reading my mind because he made his way over to the stove and turned on the front burner. He then pulled a packet of white powder out of his shirt pocket and dumped the contents into a small, metal measuring cup. My question had been answered.

"What's on the menu today?" I asked him.

He poured a small amount of water into the cup and starting mixing up the concoction.

"This is a special recipe I came up with myself," he said. "It's three parts pure, uncut Afghanistan heroin, two parts fentanyl and one part arsenic. I call it the Widow Maker."

Clever name I thought to myself. I had to keep the dialogue going so I steered the conversation to Marta.

"So you must have changed Reina's last name to protect her?"

"Yes. When the cartels went to war with each other it was no longer safe for her to be in Mexico. Raul sent her north to me and we changed her last name"

"But why kill her, why kill your own niece?"

"Because my brother told us to and I would do anything for Raul."

It was her turn to tell me a story. When Marta was eight and Raul was ten they were both abandoned by their parents and forced to live on the streets of Merida. Everyday Raul would somehow beg, steal and borrow enough money to keep them clothed and fed. By the time he turned twelve Raul was muling for the cartel and by fifteen he was running his own crew selling marijuana and cocaine to the tourist trade. On Marta's sixteenth birthday Raul had saved up enough money to hire a coyote to smuggle her across the border and escort her to Los Angeles where there were distant cousins who had agreed to take her in. The journey itself was uneventful but when they reached L.A. the man demanded an additional five thousand dollars before he'd release her. The relatives did not have that kind of money so they contacted Raul who somehow scraped it together and wired the funds the very next day. When the coyote returned to Merida the following week Raul paid a visit to his home as the man and his family were sitting down to Sunday dinner.

He demanded the man not only pay back the ransom amount but to also return the original smuggling fee as a penalty for violating their agreement. When the man laughed at what he thought was an absurd request Raul went to his wife and calmly slit her throat. When the man still refused Raul moved on to the youngest son and slit his throat too. Five minutes later he walked out of the man's house with fifteen thousand dollars and an understanding that whenever Raul needed someone or something smuggled across the border the man would do it for him free of charge. That was Raul Ramirez.

The story shocked me to my core but I needed to keep engaging her. "But what did Reina and her friends do to deserve such a thing?"

They got greedy," she said.

According to Marta, Frank Jr. exerted a lot of influence over Reina and Julie and he convinced them since they were taking the lion's share of the risk they should be reaping a bigger share of the profits.

"They confronted us and demanded a seat at the table," Marta said, "so that's exactly what we gave them."

"A seat at the table," I whispered to myself and all of a sudden the bizarre crime scene at Frank Sr.'s house made perfect sense.

"That little bitch and her boyfriend ruined everything,"

Marta continued. "They threatened to go to the police if we didn't meet their demands and of course the cartel was never going to let that happen. We were going to return the next day to dispose of the bodies but Frank's father must have activated the alarm system remotely and we couldn't get inside without generating an armed response. We had no choice but to leave them there."

Mubari's cocktail was ready now and I looked on as he filled the syringe. As he moved towards me Marta gave me this final consideration.

"We knew we had to file a missing persons report and everything still would have been okay if Harvey hadn't asked you to look into Reina's disappearance. I thought I gave you just enough information not to arouse your suspicions but obviously I was wrong. I tried to warn you off Able, but you just wouldn't let it go."

I played the last card in my deck. Before I turned on to Marta's street I had called Victoria and then fastened my cell phone under my bad arm using double sided tape. It was hidden by the sling and neither Marta nor Mubari thought of checking there. Victoria muted her end of the call but she had been listening this entire time. When I had quietly said Red Rover, Red Rover that was Victoria's cue to contact Harvey and let him know I was right.

"Did you get all of that Victoria?" I asked her.

Victoria unmuted her phone and she was crying hysterically. She then started screaming into the phone. "The police are on their way Marta! You're never going to get away with this! Oh God, please, please, please don't kill him!"

Mubari ripped off my sling, tore the phone off my arm and hurled it across the room.

"Enough of this!" he said, "goodbye Able."

As he buried the needle into my arm I distinctly remember

the front door flying off its hinges and then hearing gunshots, lots of gunshots. The heavy weight of nothingness suffocated me until I no longer existed. I was out of my body now hovering above the room and taking in the scene below. Mubari and Marta were clearly dead, their bodies sprawled across the kitchen floor. Harvey was screaming something unintelligible into his phone while Hassam sat straddled across my chest attempting CPR. He was crying like a lost child. I remember thinking how nice it had been to have people in my life that truly cared for me and with that came the realization I should have been a better friend. After that, everything Hassam told me about dying was absolutely true. I felt a gentle force guide me away from this worldly place and lead me into a tunnel of light. It was beautiful and I was now very much at peace with the events that had delivered me here. My mother and grandparents were there waiting for me as I reached the end of the tunnel. The amount of love we shared at that moment was incalculable but they weren't there to help me cross over. They were there to block my path. It wasn't my time. I begrudgingly agreed to return to the world and that same gentle force guided me back to Marta's kitchen. The paramedics were on the job now and they had the paddles out. One of them shouted 'clear' and he then zapped my body with enough voltage to lift it off the ground. I didn't feel a thing of course because I was still on the outside looking in. They recharged the AED unit and shocked me again. This time it hurt like hell and I gasped for air as I opened my eyes. I had reentered life and I felt like I was seeing it again for the very first time.

EPILOGUE

(Three months later)

Life is good. I'm the same person now but different if that makes any sense. I think near death experiences will have that kind of effect on you. It made me realize everyday is truly a gift and should be treated with the utmost respect. I hope people will tell you that Able Kane is a better friend now and perhaps maybe even a better person. Lord knows I wake up every morning trying. The clinical reason I'm still here is because Mubari was only able to inject a fraction of the Widow Maker into my vein before Hassam put two bullets into his chest. One for him and one for me just as we talked about so many years ago in that hospital room in Germany. Like I said, that's the clinical reason. I know for a fact there were greater powers at work that day but these are things I only talk about with Hassam.

Marta was able to fire off two rounds before Harvey was forced to put her down. She wasn't proficient with a gun and her shots ended up being wildly inaccurate. I empathize with Harvey. He's still struggling mightily with the fact he had to kill the woman who played such a key role in the raising of his children and was still considered family right up to the very end. Marta's duplicity remains the last great mystery of this case. There is no one left to shed any light on why she traveled down the road she did. All of the Top 2 Bottom employees have scattered into the wind and Raul and Valeria Ramirez were both found hanging in their jail cells on the same day in separate facilities one week after being arrested. The Department of Corrections conveniently ruled both deaths a suicide but I think they underestimated just how far the cartel's arm can reach. I have my own theory about Marta and it's very simple. I think she fell in love. She allowed herself to fall in love with an evil man who took her by the hand and led her step by step through the gates of Hell.

Enough of that. As we speak, I'm currently crossing over the Oregon border back into California after visiting my brother Jonah. Yes he is once again a part of my life. In February of 2002 I received a letter from him asking me if I'd pick him up from the Tehachapi Correctional Institute. After seventeen long years his sentence was finally drawing to an end. When I pulled into the visitor's parking lot I was greeted by the warden himself who asked me if I'd join him in his office for a quick chat. He told me in all of his forty plus years of working in the prison system he'd never met a man more fully rehabilitated than my brother. Jonah, he said, is genuinely a man of God and the ministries he delivered here would be sorely missed. He was keenly aware of the Kane family history and he assured me he'd seen jailhouse charlatans come and go over the years and Jonah definitely was not one of them.

As I watched Jonah make his walk through the prison gates I counted no less than seven guards either shake his hand or give him a heartfelt embrace. He stayed with me for a month and without going into a lot of detail I'll just say we became brothers again who care very deeply for each other. Jonah had accepted an invitation to live with an order of Benedictine monks in a small monastery in southern Oregon. I drove him there myself and we spent seven days making the two day trip. I showed many of the wonderful places in California that I had fallen in love with over the years. San Luis Obispo, Cambria, Monterey and San Francisco just to name a few. When we said our goodbyes he handed me a gift and made me promise not to open it until I got home. I honored the request and when I walked through my apartment door I tore off the wrapping.

There was a short note from Jonah scotch taped to the box.

'Dear Able, I can't put into words the regret I continue to carry for the way I treated you over the years. You never realized you were always the stronger brother as well as the beacon that prevented the Kane family ship from crashing upon the rocks. When you left it was like our lighthouse had ceased operations and nothing but dangerous, unchartered waters lay ahead. Inside this box is our family Bible. You know its history. It originally belonged to our great grandfather Jacob and it now has four generations of handwritten notes in its margins. For better or worse, this book is a living piece of our family history and you are its rightful steward. Take good care of it brother. I love you.'

I keep both the note and the Bible tucked away in my safety deposit box at the bank. Jonah would go on to publish several best selling novels under a pen name I have vowed never to disclose. The profits, of which there are many, are channeled to the monastery and prison ministries all over the country since Jonah himself has pledged a chaste life of poverty. He truly is a man of God.

As we neared Eureka my phone rang. "Able," the voice said, "it's Joe."

"Broadway Joe the quarterback?"

"Good one. No Joe Lewis the most recent hire of the Able Kane Detective Agency. I want you to know I'll be in Monday morning bright eyed and bushy tailed."

That's right. Joe is working for me now or at least he will be as soon as he and his wife and daughter return from their South Pacific cruise. He's okay but his wound was severe enough to get mandatorily retired from the Monterey Park Police Department. Their loss is my gain. The demand for my services has dramatically increased since my one day of fame and I can really use Joe's help.

"Sounds good Joe but when you get in you and I need to talk about all of these vacation days you've been taking."

He laughed. "I've got to go buddy, we've got karaoke on the sky deck in five. See you soon."

Seconds later my phone rang again. It was Victoria.

"Hi Victoria," I said.

"Hi Vic," Brigid said chiming in.

Yes Brigid and I are officially seeing each other and she graciously agreed to copilot this road trip with me. As you'd expect it became impossible for her to resist my charm although I've been informed we'll be moving forward at a very slow pace. So far so good though.

"Able," Victoria said, "I just got home from my trip and I love it, love it, love it."

Sigh. Guilty as charged. I painted Victoria's garage Alpine white with a Kelly green trim and I threw in one of those garage doors with the cute little windows that let in the sunlight. How could I not? I wouldn't be here today without her. I did however sign my initials in chartreuse on the bottom slat in the back as my mild form of protest.

"You are welcome my dear. It was my pleasure."

"Brigid," Victoria asked, "are you coming to book club on Thursday? I'm so excited to host."

Brigid looked over at me as I rolled my eyes. "Yes Vic, I wouldn't miss it."

"Isn't it great?"

"What's that Victoria?" I asked.

"The three of us being friends. Okay bye, gotta go."

Yes Vicky, it is fantastic and I mean that.

"So Able," Brigid asked me with a mischievous grin on her face, "when are you going to paint my garage?"

I looked at her and winked. "I thought that's what I've been doing over the last few months."

She turned red and told me I was a naughty boy. The Barely-Drive-Able must have thought it was funny though because he accelerated and moved into the fast lane. While I was recovering Harvey and Hassam quietly had it towed to a body shop that specialized in repairing bullet ridden cars. The fact that this is a thing doesn't speak very highly about us as a society but when they were done the Barely-Drive-Able had never looked better. Unbeknownst to me 1972 VW buses are now collector's items and the owner of the body shop offered me $100,000 to take it off my hands. I demurred. The Barely-Drive-Able is not for sale nor will it ever be.

Finally, you'll be happy to know I have fully mended my fences with God. As it turns out it was never his fault. I had grown so jaded over the years by men distorting his message that I guess you could say I couldn't see the forest through the trees. On Sundays I'll usually join Brigid at her Catholic Church but on occasion I'll stop in at an ashram, mosque, synagogue or even the local Buddhist temple. Wherever I go I'm always warmly welcomed and it's become clear to me that there's never been one singular path to get to where we all trying to go. Oh, I almost forgot. Nate's fully recovered and doing great. I thought I was all he had in the world so you can imagine how surprised I was when all eight of his siblings flew down from Sacramento to be with him. I let them all stay in the empty apartment next to Nate's. Just when you think you've got someone figured out right?

I looked over to Brigid and patted her affectionately on the leg. She leaned over and kissed me on the cheek then pulled out the daily crossword puzzle with a pen in her hand.

"Okay," she said, "what's a twelve letter word for a complete and thorough search? The first letter is a P and the fourth is a Q."

I considered it.

The author, copyright info,
acknowledgements and a
'very short' dedication.

I'm certainly not a writer by trade. My wife and I have run a small business for thirty three years and as we near retirement I knew I'd need something to fill the void. Writing a novel has been a dream of mine for as long as I can remember. I've started and stopped dozens of times until Abel Kane sat me down and told me his story. I'm leaving my email below and I'd love to hear your thoughts about The Search. I have told myself that if one person I do not know reads this book and likes it then this whole journey was a tremendous success.

I'd like to thank my wife for coming up with the title. It's perfect. Anytime you can encapsulate one hundred thousand words into two I think it's safe to say she got it right. I'd also like to thank my sister for being my pro bono editor-in-chief. She has been with me every step of the way and has handled the sensitivities of a writer like a seasoned professional. Lynn, thank you, this wouldn't have happened without you.

Finally, I'm dedicating this book to the five people I know won't be reading it anytime soon. This is for Owen, Elle, Rory, Evie and Eli. I hope someday you'll give it a read and think of me kindly. I love you all to the moon and back.

Contact me at skeehanbill@yahoo.com